THE HEART OF JUNE

THE HEART OF JUNE

A NOVEL

MASON RADKOFF

BRADDOCK AVENUE BOOKS
UNCOMMON BOOKS · UNCOMMON READERS

Printed in the United States of America
10 9 8 7 6 5 4 3 2 1

First edition, November 2013

ISBN 978-0-615-86970-4

This book is set in Gotham and Plantin.
Cover photo and book design by Katherine W. Radkoff.
Author photo by Kristina Deckert.

Braddock Avenue Books
PO Box 502
Braddock, PA 15204

www.braddockavenuebooks.com

THE HEART OF JUNE

For Scott + Peg,
this tale of
Reconstruction.

Autumn

Walking back from the gravesite, the prim woman directed the now parentless boy toward the waiting car.

"Well," she said. "That would be that."

Chapter 1

LIVING ABOVE HIS EX-WIFE'S GARAGE had its advantages. Granted, it seemed like he'd been kept only for nostalgia—a one-speed bicycle that had earned lingering affection—but he liked it there, and it was free. Plus, he figured he'd probably already pissed her off as much as he was ever going to. Standing in the drive, his back against his truck, Walt took in the house that he and Sam had bought together a decade before. Though Sam was now married to someone else, Walt remained in her life in a lesser capacity, not let go completely. When the end had come, his parting gift was an assortment of unfinished projects around the house, and while Sam had long before given up that he might complete them during their marriage, she did retain hope that he might finish them during her subsequent marriage to Arthur. Though this living arrangement wouldn't sit well with other men, it was good enough for Walt. His history of peculiar relationships with women had for the most part been spared the scrutiny of his ego.

"Hey there, big fella. You look lost," she said from the kitchen window, pulling him from his reverie.

"I'm always lost, lady." He slammed the rusty tailgate. "Any idea where a guy can get a hot meal around here?"

"Sorry, mister. My husband told me not to talk to strange men. Try the 'Y' downtown," she said, and shut the door. After a beat, she reappeared suggestively.

"On second thought, he's not due home 'til late. But we'd better be quick."

Not acknowledged by either of them was the truth of her joke — that maybe it would be better if Walt wasn't in the house when Arthur got home. Arthur had been a good sport about him not moving all the way out, but, increasingly, Walt felt conspicuous in the main house if he didn't have his tools in his hands. While Arthur wasn't concerned that Walt's renovation efforts might extend beyond the house and to Sam's old feelings for him, he knew that Walt's romance with Sam had included a passion that his would never know. And while they were all friends, Walt sometimes wondered if Arthur, generous though he was, would have preferred that he did not live there.

"I would prefer that you did not live here, Walter," he sometimes said.

Arthur Steedle was one of two people who called him Walter. He'd always been a Walt, through and through. Walt, in turn, called Arthur, "Dr. Art," a moniker that Arthur, who leaned toward the formal, didn't like. Dr. Art was Chair of the university's dental school — fit, reliable, competent, earnest, well-regarded, well-groomed, and well-paid. "He's nothing like you," Sam had said. Walt liked Dr. Art, and though he couldn't resist taking advantage of the man's earnestness by occasionally messing with him, he was happy for them both.

"Well, thank you, little lady," Walt replied to Sam's playful offer, and started toward the door.

"Wait!" she said suddenly, startling him for real. "You aren't one of those traveling salesmen I've heard about, are you?"

"No, they tend to pass right through," he sighed. "I entrench."

He settled in hard at the kitchen table.

"How are you, Sam?"

The chair was uncomfortable and expensive—too small for his big frame—another strange object in the house he'd once owned. It was one of the larger homes in the Pittsburgh neighborhood of Friendship, and when Sam and Walt had found it, it was a wreck. A foreclosure, they had bought it from the bank while still in graduate school, using down-payment money from Sam's parents, although the gloomy house was a far cry from the suburban bliss that Phillip Rothman had envisioned for his eldest daughter. Buying an oversized, dilapidated house was just the kind of mess he'd expected Walt to get Sam into. Walt was a disappointment to the Rothmans, and they blamed him for pretty much everything they could, including their lack of grandchildren, although it was Sam who had been adamant about that—she had been on the pill for as long as Walt had known her. On the afternoon of the closing, alone in the house and inspired by glasses of post-signing champagne, Walt had attempted to make the moment grander than it was, persuading Sam to make love on the bare oak floor of the entry hall. In doing so, she'd gotten a terrible splinter in her left buttock, an injury he then made worse by mistaking her sounds of pain for sounds of pleasure, not slowing down until the wooden shard was seated firmly within her body, a privilege he himself would not again be allowed for weeks to come. Now, Walt watched Sam as she moved about the kitchen. She was wearing, of all things, an old-fashioned frilly apron, and she handed him a bottle of Iron City, beer she kept on hand just for him. At the counter, she chopped a large onion that didn't make her cry but stung his eyes like hell.

Sam was tough and plain, fetching to Walt, though her beauty was of a decidedly utilitarian sort. She looked every bit her age, forty-six, but she'd looked forty-six for as long as he could remember, and so eventually, to him, she'd begun to look young. Sam's formidability was daunting to most, but Walt found it sexy, a challenge that had long ago dared him to rise to her occasion. She wore a giant men's wristwatch with a Twist-O-Flex band; he'd tried it on once and its bite was vicious. She was sturdy, and her pearl-rimmed reading glasses rested squarely upon her breasts, suspended from her neck by a thick black shoelace. Ever practical, she had picked them up from her grandmother's bureau the morning of the old woman's funeral, and began to wear them that same day. Oddly, they suited her well, and the prescription was apparently close enough. Sam's sweaters were too big and her hair was always almost brushed, mussed a little at the back, like that of a baby who'd been asleep in her stroller. Walt had once fit in nicely among her oddball accessories—too big or clumsy for most women to keep, but serviceable enough for Sam. And he'd remained in service for twelve years—through two apartments, one house, one trip to Portugal, two Plymouth Valiants, one orange Saab, two orange cats, one successful dissertation (hers, not his), and many unfulfilled promises (his, not hers).

"The question is," she asked, "how are you? You look like shit. And why haven't you seen Arthur about your tooth? He's concerned."

One of Walt's lower left molars had been singing for some time, and Arthur had been after Walt to visit his office. The tooth's throb had briefly been keen, but eventually had settled into merely a warm pulse, a steady reminder that things could be worse.

"It's not so bad," he lied. "It'll get better on its own."

"Like my dining room ceiling?" She was referring to the labyrinth of cracks he was to have re-plastered months before.

"Not quite. The damage isn't visible on my tooth."

"It will be when I get through with you."

She dropped the playfulness. "Seriously, honey, take care of it soon."

"I will," he promised, not sure whether he was promising to fix her ceiling or his tooth.

"Your tooth, you moron," she said in answer to his thought.

Walt was transparent to Sam. She put down her knife and regarded him closely, eyeing him up and down as if buying a horse. That his disrepair exceeded that of the house escaped neither of them.

"I know, dear," he lied again. "I'll get to the ceiling soon, though. And the back door too." He looked through the doorway at the dining room bay window. "And the window seat."

He stopped the list there. Walt's particular brand of procrastination was a thick fog—equal parts good intention, inertia, and near-guilt. It had prevented him from finishing the Friendship house during his tenure there as husband, and was managing to do so during his stay as tenant as well.

Sam slid the onions into a skillet and the aroma was immediate and, for Walt, arousing. Smells had that effect on him. He'd happened upon Sam ironing Arthur's shirts the week before, and the crisp smell had caused him sudden desire for her. But like the house, she no longer belonged to him, and this, he knew, for Sam, was a good thing. She removed the lid from a pot and steam surrounded her face in a soft veil, painting her in the moment. If he hadn't loved Sam as he did, it would have fully broken his heart. She was happy.

"Hey, listen," she said. "Before I forget, we're having people over for dinner Friday to celebrate. Arthur's textbook proposal was accepted."

"And you want my truck out of the driveway."

"Actually, we'd like you to join us."

"*We* would, would we?" His tone contended that they both knew better.

"Come on, you know Arthur is fond of you."

Although this was in a peculiar way true, Sam was up to something. Walt had little in common with Art's colleagues, and the presence of Sam and Walt's old friends just made things strange.

"Besides," she continued, "Muriel Weber will be there. You haven't seen her in a while."

Sam, bless her heart, had been trying to marry off Walt since they'd split.

"And that should be of interest to me?"

"I would think so. You were hot as hell for her when we were married."

"That's because I couldn't have her then. Besides, she's rail thin."

"Jesus Christ, Walter. She's beautiful, and you know it. She's also smart and interesting and, at the moment, available. And, I happen to know she has a little thing for you."

Walt rolled his head in a circle, stretching the muscles in his neck. His toolboxes had become heavier of late and he'd begun to concede that carpentry might be a younger man's game. Sam lowered the burner, came around the counter, and began to knead his shoulders. Her hands were strong, able to break through the knots. It hurt a little, but her familiarity with his landscape told her when the pressure was too much, although for him it rarely was—he was dog-like in wanting to be rubbed. Massage was an intimacy that survived the divorce, though it was something they didn't discuss. Occasionally, when Arthur wasn't home, Sam would have Walt take off his shirt and lie on the floor, and she'd rub his back until he'd snore. Arthur, by comparison, was scrawny and ticklish, unable to be touched without jerking away. She'd sometimes tell Walt that she was just keeping him in shape to finish her house, but he knew her too well to believe that. Sam had always liked the feel of a strong man.

"I'm telling you, you should strike while the iron's hot," she said, taking a sip from his beer. "And get a haircut."

But Walt couldn't picture himself pursuing Muriel Weber, smart and attractive though she was. Anymore, he was most comfortable when left unchallenged by sophisticated company.

"You would do that to her? Fix her up with me?"

"Hey, stop that. There are a lot of women who would feel lucky to have you."

He didn't point out that she was no longer among them. "I was joking, Sam. You worry about me too much."

"It's true," she replied softly, moving back to the stove. "I do worry." She paused. "About what will become of you."

"Hey, why don't you and the doc adopt me, then? Art would never have to worry about us having an affair, you being my mother and all."

She ignored his nonsense and considered, with some sadness, her ex-husband's life.

"You still don't think about the future, do you?"

Walt began to answer, to crack wise, but hesitated. What did he think about? For the most part, the present, but increasingly, it seemed, the past as well. What might things be like had he stayed on the tenure track? He thought about his many unfinished carpentry projects, about what he owed people. About his need to duck people around town. Those things combined, he decided, were his version of thinking about the future, an understanding that once he somehow took care of his ever shifting list of what he owed, he could finally move forward. Then real life would begin. If he could stop living day to day, if he were *legitimate*, then he might feel comfortable with a woman like Muriel Weber. Though Walt had not uttered any of this out loud, it was in the air. Neither of them spoke for a few moments, and Walt was grateful to Sam for it.

"There's something I need to talk to you about," she said finally. "Something big."

Those were the sort of words he didn't like. He had finished very little on the house in the past year, though he had started more projects than ever. Much of the place was under construction, and while this was not an unusual atmosphere for Sam, it ran against Arthur's tidy nature. An ultimatum would not be unreasonable. Of course, there was a worse possibility. Living in the carriage house had become comfortable for Walt, and it was possible that Arthur, as kind as he was, really might want him gone. Through the wavy old window glass, the March sky had darkened. They watched the glow of Dr. Art's headlights looming against the old wooden garage doors as he pulled forward.

"But it will keep. So, we'll see you Friday night?"

Walt moved toward the side door, an exit that was just out of sight from where Arthur was parking. Sam cleared his beer bottle from the table and tossed it into the trash. There was no reason to hide their visit, but both did so, without mention.

"Friday night," he replied.

"Okay then, honey." In an old habit that Sam had not broken, she still sometimes referred to Walt in terms of endearment.

As he was leaving, she called to him, "Walt, I want you to remember ... "

He stopped in the doorway.

"... the dining room ceiling."

Chapter 2

THE NEXT MORNING FOUND HIM in his work boots and tool belt, once again lobbing verbal exchanges with Miss June Bonwell Creighton, an octogenarian, who, with bird-like wrists and teeny shoulders, was a force less deniable than any he'd known. Miss June ruled Shadyside from her stone mansion on Fifth Avenue, a street once known as "Millionaires' Row." A century before, both sides of Fifth had been lined with elaborate houses commissioned by the titans of Pittsburgh's steel and glass industries, though most of those great structures were demolished after the Depression, making way for brick apartment buildings that offered tiny windows and security door buzzers—safe nests for worried spinsters. Fifth Avenue was no longer cobblestone, and its streetcar tracks were no longer there to carry well-coifed women downtown to shop at Gimbel's and Horne's. Miss June's house was one of the few great mansions to have survived. It had been built by her paternal grandfather, Clarence Creighton, who made his money fabricating industrial machinery parts for Pittsburgh's then booming mills and factories. His machine shop had created mysterious items of various shapes and sizes—curious looking cogs and gears, perplexing cams and widgets. The house, Hardwick, was a cavernous, Vincent Price hall of coffered ceilings, velvet curtains, and repressed passion. On rainy days, it smelled of haunted library. From the street, Hardwick was unwelcoming, and its fenced perimeter had a disguised gate that required uninitiated visitors to stop and ponder how to gain entrance. Stranded on the sidewalk, they'd stand there, confused, exposed to the house's judgment as though it considered them complicit in the death of its demolished sisters. When Walt was a boy, his father worked for Miss June on weekends, caring for the estate, performing light maintenance and cutting the grass. During the week, his dad was a low-level manager for the Gilbert Chemical Company. But their Saturdays were spent at Hardwick, where his father performed chores for modest amounts of money with no complaints, cumulatively spending a good month of his life, Walt figured, fruitlessly pulling the rope on Miss June's ancient gas lawnmower. He never understood his father's allegiance to the woman, and, judging by the size of her house, he figured that she could have afforded to hire a professional landscaping crew had she been so inclined. Her frugality wouldn't allow it, he supposed, and so his father showed up week in and week out. As a small child, Walt stayed close to his father during those long Saturdays, as Miss June was not a woman around whom young children felt comfortable. She wasn't warm like the ladies who fawned over him at Rosenblum's bakery where he and his dad would stop on the way. Young Walt's fear of Miss June made it easy to fight the temptation to touch the exotic objects that adorned her coffee tables and sideboards, lest she serve him one of her disapproving looks. Each week, after eating their pastries in the big kitchen, Walt was dispatched to a corner of the sitting room to leaf through a stack of aging travel magazines while his father worked outside. After the first half dozen Saturdays had gone by, the boy was deemed not likely to break anything, and was allowed to venture into other parts of the house. He cautiously began to explore, each week finding new rooms and unexpected staircases.

Walt's father was reserved by nature, and seldom engaged his son as he worked, so the boy watched in silence, filing away all he saw for future reference. The amount of maintenance required for such a large house was considerable, yet Walt noticed that the tasks Miss June insisted on having done often made little sense, such as the yearly moving of the upholstered furniture to the back yard for an hour after being cooped up for the winter. *The davenport must breathe.* Walt's own first encounter with such a senseless chore occurred at age eight, when he was given the weekly task of emptying the silverware drawers in the kitchen and wiping down the wooden drawer boxes before putting the silverware back in its place. Perhaps the most unusual task that Miss June insisted on having performed, the pointlessness of which was matched only by its difficulty, was the removal each spring and the re-hanging each fall, of the massive wooden shutters that hung on all sides of the great house. For years, his father undertook this task dutifully, never questioning the logic, wrestling with the painted monsters from atop a rickety ladder, bringing them down and hosing them off each spring and then putting them back up each autumn. The shutters hung from cast-iron hinges and were meant to be swung open and closed, not taken down. But as with all endeavors performed at the command of Miss June, this one wasn't negotiable—it would be done because she had deemed that it must. And decades later, entrenched in middle age, and having inherited the litany of Hardwick chores from his father, Walt found himself once again atop the same shitty ladder, perpetuating the ritual act for no reason other than having been told to.

"I've never understood the purpose of this, you know," the adult Walt called down to her. He weighed a hell of a lot more now than he had as a kid, and the ladder hadn't become any stronger.

"Yes, I know. Mental acuity was never your strong suit," she replied from the grass below. "Your father understood."

"I beg to differ, Miss June. I sincerely doubt that my father understood. He was just more polite than me."

"Poppycock. Your father was a good man. Moving those shutters about was just the sort of task that built his character. Although, given that you've performed the very same task for as many years, and upon considering how you've turned out, perhaps I should conclude that your father's strong character was, instead, constitutional."

Jesus, he thought.

The shutter he was wrestling with was ridiculously heavy, and it was nearly impossible to get the hinge pins to line up. But at least this part of the job, the autumnal hanging, was easier than the spring removal. The damned things were supposed to lift straight up, and a hundred years ago they probably did. In the current century, though, an unbelievable amount of upward force was required to get them to pop, and when they did, it was never when Walt expected, with each solid-pine killer attempting to throw him to the ground. In anticipation of next spring, he now greased the hinge pins before dropping the shutters into place, knowing full well that, come April, they'd be welded tight once again. But as awful as the chore was, it was ritual, and Walt doubted that he could fully register the passage of time without it. Here they were as always, the shutters, Miss June, and him.

"You'll catch me if I fall, right?"

Walt loved Hardwick as much as he had ever loved anything or anyone, save maybe Sam. He felt a terrific kinship with its thick stone foundation, its formal widow's walk, and its patinated copper turret that regarded the city darkly from its perch. He had tended to the house for years, keeping its exterior wood trim a step ahead of the always threatening rot, ensuring that the pocket doors that separated the music room from the parlor slid smoothly, and re-skimming the miles of old horse-hair plaster as it sagged. It was a labor of love for them both, although Miss June's contributions mostly comprised making grand announcements of the work that Walt was to do, telling him to be careful near her antiques, and succinctly noting his lack of progress. Her chief duty, though, was to lecture him about how he conducted his life.

"When a man of your age has yet to find a legitimate path on which to embark, it is not attractive to act as if it doesn't matter. Would you like more tea?"

The upstairs hall of Hardwick was adorned with sepia photographs from long ago, images that told of riding lessons and private schools, of formal dances and hopeful suitors. Walt found the photos to be sad, with Miss June's prim youth bringing a glumness to the space. The majority of the photographs were of her long-dead fiancé, Dwight, a legendary figure in the mythology of Miss June, and from all accounts a splendid man who had died a hero just months before they were to be married in the garden at Hardwick. The upstairs hallway felt to Walt like a somber museum, one meant to preserve the history of a young girl who he, despite the photographic evidence, had trouble believing had really existed. After Dwight's death, Miss June never entertained the thought of anyone else. She'd found and lost the love of her life early, the only man of sufficient character to be her match, and there would be no other. Walt had never been able to reconcile her life of voluntary solitude, being appreciative, on one hand, of her devotion to Dwight, but equally frustrated with her choice. How might her life have been different had she allowed herself other love?

"Did you leave that broken-down truck of yours in the drive again?" she asked now.

"I'm sorry, are you talking to me?" Walt replied, the arches of his feet aching from the ladder. "I can't imagine so, because the only truck I see in the drive is mine, and a fine specimen it is."

"It's a horrid contraption. It should be melted down for scrap."

He saw his pickup in the drive below. A '74 Ford, its color was an improbable mixture of metallic gold, olive green, and shit brown, and it leaned forward and to the left like a tired porch dog. When he parked it in Miss June's drive, Walt took care to slide a piece of cardboard underneath to protect the cobblestones from the various fluids the sad vehicle could no longer retain. Covering its tailgate was a patchwork of bumper stickers, placed there not only by previous owners, but by the occasional passer-by as well. "Kiss me I'm Irish" was overlapped by "South of the Border" which was to the left of "Support Mental Health Or I'll Kill You." When Walt bought the truck for eight hundred bucks and a broken jack-hammer, its glove box was for some reason filled to the brim with little sample boxes of peppermint Chiclets, each tiny cellophane-wrapped package offering two of the small white squares with the caveat that they were not marked for individual sale. The Chiclets, present for decades, seemed capable of reproduction, as they appeared everywhere in the truck—on the floor, wedged in the seat cushions, and, oddly enough and more than once, in the engine compartment. Long ago, some wiseacre had rearranged the metal letters on the truck's faded hood, turning the poor thing into a "DORF."

"You're just afraid the neighbors will think you're having an affair with the handyman," he said.

"Hmmph. That truck is not the vehicle of a respectable businessman."

"Respectable? I don't consider myself to be a businessman at all."

He spoke the truth. Walt was indifferent to commerce, a carpenter who paid little attention to the relationship between effort exerted and money collected in return. Although usually broke, he tended to think of jobs not as tasks to be done in exchange for cash, but rather as items on some cosmic list of things he was supposed to do, one that would never be complete. Items would always be added no matter how much progress he made. And given that, why bother trying to get ahead? He seldom referred to himself as a contractor, as that term seemed to imply a level of ambition and acumen he did not possess. Walt floated from project to project when he wasn't at Hardwick, with work managing to find him by word of mouth. He had never been easy to track down, and recently, after years of hearing complaints that he didn't have an answering machine, he'd gotten rid of his phone altogether. If someone needed him badly enough, they'd find him. Those in the know would call him at Gene's Bull's-Eye Bar, and when Miss June wanted him, which she usually did, she'd call Sam with instructions to find and send him over directly. Aside from the ongoing saga at Hardwick, most of Walt's other work was done for academic types around the East End, smart, successful people who couldn't drive a hot nail into a snowbank. But what his customers lacked in ability they made up for with patience, as it took a special breed to have Walt Farnham as their carpenter. The work he managed to produce was excellent, and he had true affection for the older houses of Pittsburgh, but finishing things was not his claim to fame.

The markings of a Farnham job could be found throughout the finer homes of Squirrel Hill and Shadyside—odd bits of missing trim, the occasional absent cabinet door or pane of glass adding a Mister Potato Head quality to an otherwise fine job. The mild guilt Walt felt about this was offset by his being equally bad about asking for money. Plus, he often left tools in their garages as unwanted collateral. The way he saw it, his customers usually came out ahead.

From high upon the ladder at Miss June's, Walt looked beyond her garage toward Howe Street, where a few years back he had rebuilt an old wooden porch for an associate dean who had since tried to get him back to install a new back door, although Walt proved elusive. Walt could now see that the man had found someone else to do it instead. How long had it been? To his left was Negley Avenue, where he owed a doctor's wife a few cabinet door pulls and one last section of crown moulding, the errant piece of trim gathering dust in Sam's garage. Further west lay Amberson Avenue, and a house he had measured for new windows, having had a grand old time chatting up the owners who were very excited about the job, with the promise of much more work to come. Walt had figured out a price, but never sent the quote. His leaving things unfinished was a product of his composition, and along with having long ago accepted it, he took pride in knowing that his unreliability had no deceit or trickery behind it—he was just fucked up. He never took money for work left incomplete, and further, many of his clients had paid Walt only half of what the project was worth, with the balance due waiting for him to collect. And those people wanted to pay up. "Please, Walt, just send me the bill," they would say. "We've wanted to write you a check, but we don't know how much we owe you. How do you live without a phone?" "Just drive those last few nails, Walt, and we'll settle up."

And he wanted to. Install the door knob. Drive the last few nails. Send the bill. *Finish*. But as infuriating as he was to his customers, Walt remained in demand. People liked him. His clients would tell him things while he worked that they wouldn't normally share, seeing him, for one reason or another, as a kindred spirit, a confidant. Walt figured it was the temporary nature of their relationship that caused them, with no prompting, to open up to him. The rhythmic sound of his tools probably helped — he preferred, when possible, to work with hand planes and chisels rather than power tools. Old houses deserved old tools. As he moved his hands across his work, he would hear of insecurity and sadness, of affairs and past loves, of disappointment and hope. Beyond being a doctor for their houses, he became an unintended therapist of sorts for them, and they seemed to know that he would care for their secrets. And about that, they were right. Walt could be trusted. First, do no harm.

"Are we enjoying our nap?" Miss June said directly to his face from through the second-story window, nearly startling him off the ladder.

"Jesus Christ, you scared the hell out of me."

"Had you fallen, it would have been the fastest thing you've done all day, although I suppose you would have found a way to do that slowly, too."

"What's eating you?" he asked, not because of her caustic banter, which was normal, but because she had been flitting about the house all morning, fidgeting and fussing with this and that. Plus, it was after eleven, and she had not yet presented him with his morning snack.

"Nothing that concerns you, young man. But as your productivity seems to have ceased anyway, you might as well come in and have some tea."

Miss June's kitchen — Walt's favorite room — was a

marvelous affair, nearly unchanged from its days as an area for servants. Family meals had not been intended to be eaten there, and eaten there they were not. This was a space meant for cooking. The cupboards were tall and wide, though curiously shallow, and were painted a wonderful robin's-egg blue. An immense cast-iron sink with built-in drainboards spanned an entire wall, with a beautiful network of threaded chrome pipes serving the well-worn faucets. There was a big cook-top, a black masterpiece of Herculean mass. While there was no table, there was, instead, a very long butcher block, its worn surface a testament to the many cuts of meat and game that in grander times had been prepared by a full-time cook. This was where he sat as Miss June brought him his morning tea, a ritual that had become the foundation of his every day.

"Here you are, Walter," she said, her tone softer now that she was a hostess. "This should hold you until lunch."

She had presented him with, as usual, a sterling silver tray that held a porcelain cup and saucer that felt absurdly small in his big hands, a matching sugar bowl and creamer (although she knew he took it black), and a small plate arranged with crustless cucumber sandwiches, a carefully peeled and sectioned tangerine, and a small pastry from Prantl's on Walnut Street. Miss June's purse sat at her end of the butcher block, and her sharp eyes checked her tiny wristwatch once again.

"So, where are you off to today, Miss June?"

"I have an appointment at the bank, but first, a luncheon to attend."

Walt had been eating lunch all his life, but had never, as far as he knew, attended a luncheon.

"Would you like to borrow my truck?"

"Could you imagine me arriving in that contraption?"

They both smiled at that as Reverend Nate Cornsweet appeared at the back door, a man of Miss June's occasional employ who kept the citizens of Pittsburgh safe by driving her to her various functions rather than allowing her to pilot her massive car herself. Tales of Miss June behind the wheel were legend, with her many mishaps and collisions stemming not from poor eyesight or inability to control "the machine," but rather from her belief that because she had places to go, others on the road should move out of her way. Most did. Because he was between vehicles himself, Reverend Nate took the bus from the Hill District to Oakland, and walked to Hardwick from there.

"Mornin', Miss June. Hello, Dummy."

"'Dummy'? What did I do?" Walt asked.

"You drove right past me at my bus stop, you knucklehead. What, you don't like black people now?"

"Don't be absurd, Reverend—I love black people. I just don't like you." He pointed with his ladyfinger to emphasize his bullshit—he liked Nate a lot, although Nate was a Reverend like Walt was a contractor. There were rumors galore of his seamy past, and he had a deserved reputation as a womanizer, but he gave a near-convincing appearance of doing good for the people in the Hill, taking credit for the food bank his Aunt Lucy ran from his ministry on Wylie Avenue.

"I'll get the car, Miss June. Don't let this big dummy eat all your food here."

"I'm glad you mentioned that, Nathaniel. I was hoping you could stop at the market for me while I'm tending to the day's agenda."

"Of course, Miss June. I'll pick up more bananas for your gorilla while I'm there."

"See you in church, *Reverend*," Walt said through a mouthful of pastry as Nate headed for the garage. Then, after swallowing, "I'm running errands myself today, Miss June. I can stop at the bank for you, if you'd like."

"Thank you, Walter, but I'm meeting with my banker. We need to get my affairs in order. I can't leave a mess behind, you know."

This again. Miss June had been getting her affairs in order for so long that the affairs themselves must have changed numerous times, necessitating, Walt assumed, repeated rounds of crossing of t's and dotting of i's. He understood that responsible people thought of such things, and Miss June was nothing if not responsible, but he suspected that she thought of her eventual demise in historical terms, that her passing would mark the end of an era, like the passing of a president or a queen, but with no successor in line. Conversely, she had also, for years, deemed herself invincible, in direct conflict with her occasional talk of leaving her affairs in order. Miss June was whip-like in pointing out inconsistencies in others, but she herself was rife with contradiction. And pointing out these contradictions, as only Walt dared to do, always resulted in her spinning the point around, deftly shifting the focus back onto him, using his very argument against him, only much more effectively. Still, occasionally, he tried.

"So you're concerned about your health. And your last visit to the doctor was when?"

"None of your business, young man."

"You should go, you know. It's been a while."

"There has not been a worthy physician in this town since Doctor Townsend retired in 1978. And he used to come to me, not me to him."

Miss June was a believer in home delivery.

"And the medical school that's a mile from here?"

"Children with stethoscopes," she dismissed. "And anyway, I'm fit as a fiddle."

"And ready for love?"

"That's none of your business, either."

Walt sighed. It was true, Miss June seemed as healthy as ever, but still, he worried. And so, once again, they had visited an old, circular line of conversation, that of Miss June needing to get her affairs in order, which was at odds with her reluctance to see a doctor, the need of which Walt had to concede seemed unnecessary as the woman was apparently impervious to any ailment whatsoever, which she noted by drawing comparisons to old friends who were dead or dying, which led back to her worrying about "getting her affairs in order." Despite years of this, Walt still went through the motions of prodding Miss June about her annual checkup, but privately had decided that she, like the giant maples in her front yard, would live to be hundreds of years old. Through the window, Walt saw the nose of Miss June's 1956 Chrysler Imperial ("America's Most Carefully Built Car") nudging forward out of the garage. The car had belonged to Miss June's father, Julius, who'd always preferred Chryslers, and who'd died just one year after buying this one. The poor thing seldom left Shadyside and would never have seen the other side of twenty-five miles per hour had Walt not stolen it occasionally out of mercy, taking it out on the turnpike and letting the huge motor roar in what his friend Jimmy called an "Italian tune-up." Walt was largely uninterested in possessions, but did have unapologetic lust for that car.

"Come on, Miss June. Aren't you due for a little romance?"

"Please. I've no need for tomfoolery. And I'm too old, besides."

"Don't give me that baloney. You're going to outlive us all, and you know it."

She gathered her purse, her expression distant. "No one lives forever, dear boy." She paused, looking at the car. "Not even me."

As he heard the Imperial's rumble, the peculiar look on her face made him wonder for the first time if perhaps this could be true.

Chapter 3

GENE'S BULL'S EYE BAR sat a mile from Sam's house, con-
veniently waiting for Walt each day. He took most of his meals
there, running a tab that was unclear in its workings, with
Gene never writing anything down and Walt's queries regarding where they stood never producing a specific number in
response. From time to time, Gene would acknowledge that
Walt should give him some money, but the amount requested
seemed arbitrary and not based on what had actually been
consumed.

"Gimme thirty bucks, why don't ya?"

Gene wasn't much for small talk. His thinning duck-tail
and indifferent posture suggested an aged street-corner hood-
lum—arms crossed, shoulder against the cooler, Viceroy in
place. While so many denizens of the 'Eye sat and watched
the TV that hung from dusty chains in the corner, Walt preferred to watch Gene scrape the grill and ignore his customers.
Gene opened the 'Eye every morning at 8:00 so that the local

rummies could look on as he made the starchy soup he would serve to the lunch crowd, his apathy as both host and chef having been forged during his stint as an army mess cook. The place was pleasantly boring through dinner and *Wheel of Fortune*, but lately, to Gene's chagrin, it had become a nighttime hangout of the college crowd. Gene had little use for university people, and among the rules in the 'Eye were no books, no writing, no computers, and, had it been enforceable, no big words either. At the same time, it was hard to support the place off of the daytime cheapskates alone, guys who would nurse a beer for so long that Gene might finally give them one for free out of disgust. But the evening crowd spent money freely. The 'Eye had a jukebox, but the regulars knew to check for a disapproving look from Gene before inserting their money, at least until the early evening game shows were over, which marked the end of Walt's favorite time of day at the 'Eye, the transition period when daytime stragglers overlapped with the after-work crowd that arrived to get lubricated before heading home to face their families. It was the mix of these worlds that Walt enjoyed. After dinner, as the students and occasional faculty arrived, Gene would proclaim himself sick of the place, shut down the grill, and head upstairs, leaving the bar to his nighttime bartender, Milt, who didn't care much about anything. Gene lived above the bar with his mother, who had not yet given up hope that he would get married someday. Walt knew that poor Mrs. Greb would die disappointed. It was 5:30 when Walt entered with a rare two hundred dollars in his pocket, payment from Miss June and, after scanning the place for people he might want to avoid, sat down at the bar. His eye, as usual, was drawn to Gene's hair, obedient from BrylCreem and improbably black. Gene gave Walt a blank stare. He is an odd bird, Walt thought, one who will chat with you one day and then act as if you've never met, the next.

"What's good tonight, Gene?"

"Nothing. Same as always."

"Good. I'll have a steak sandwich."

"Look at you," Gene brightened. "Mister aristocat."

The steak sandwich, at $5.25, was by far the most expensive thing on the menu. It came with what Gene considered to be a salad—a wedge of iceberg lettuce sharp enough to put your eye out, graced by a couple of tired bar olives. It always pleased Gene when someone ordered the steak sandwich, not because he stood to make much money on the deal, but because steak was the mark of class.

Gene was right. The food at the Bull's-Eye was awful. It killed Sam that Walt ate so much of it, and she lectured him about it occasionally, describing how Gene's gravy was coursing through his veins. Given the gravy's incandescence, this was a disturbing thought. Walt occasionally wondered what the visual effect would be if one were to shine a black light on the stuff. Gene spat on the grill, scraped it off, and tossed the steak on to sizzle and pop. On the television, Vanna turned another letter of an obvious phrase that had the bar-side viewers stumped.

Gene put a beer in front of Walt.

"Here you go, college boy." Gene's worst insult, delivered good-naturedly.

The comment referred to the dozen years Walt spent listlessly pursuing a doctorate in history, which had been meant to supplement his master's in Egyptology, an academic path that led to his career in carpentry. Walt's remaining in school for so many years stemmed less from a quest for knowledge than from habit, one that he couldn't garner the energy to break, even long after his lack of interest in studying was apparent to all involved, including himself. He'd simply continued to show up. He had spent so many years at the university that even the janitorial crews knew him well, which made sense, given that they were there year after year, while the students, and indeed some of the faculty, came and went. Being an unreliable middle-aged carpenter caused him no shame. Talk of his college career sometimes did.

Walt ordered an uncustomary shot of bourbon to brace his aching tooth for Gene's steak. From the end of the bar, he heard the familiar voice of 63-year-old Jimmy DeLuca, offering wisdom to a couple of twenty-somethings who were listening raptly.

"So, goddammit, boys, you gotta date a nurse! You listen to me, now."

After years of private deliberation, Walt had decided that Jimmy's stories were not bullshit. No one could make this stuff up. Although a new listener to Jimmy's tales might suspect that they should know better than to believe him, his delivery was so heartfelt and his style so vibrant that he made it possible to believe the fantastic. A small man with a great head of white hair, Jimmy had talked himself into and out of outrageous situations that would have ended with anyone else dying, if only from embarrassment. But he always survived to tell the tale, and to do so with panache. He sometimes showed up to help Walt with his jobs, although he'd never been asked to do so. Jimmy was no carpenter—and not much of a laborer either—but his enthusiasm was unmatched. He'd appear at Walt's clients' houses, uninvited, wearing street clothes and shiny shoes, leaving Walt to wonder how he'd figured out where he was working. Jimmy at a job-site could be danger-ous. "Fuck that sledge hammer. Tie a chain to Walt's bumper and give me the keys. I'll pull that bastard down," was among the ill-advised decisions he'd made while out of earshot of his unwitting boss. Had anyone else given that directive, the result would have been disastrous, but not for Jimmy, who always landed on his feet. And when things didn't work out so well, he'd scold the witnesses—"You people worry too much." Jimmy's work history described a random path cut by inappropriate confidence, with his vigor trumping whatever thought he might have given as to whether or not he could actually perform the role in question. He had had many jobs, though none for more than a couple of months. He'd been a warehouse manager for an appliance wholesaler—a job that ended when he was caught in the back office with the owner's wife—and had tended bar at numerous establishments. He'd delivered potato chips, ushered at ballgames, serviced beer tap equipment, and managed an apartment building, the latter being another job he'd lost by not being able to keep it in his pants. He had also held numerous sales positions, confidently hawking items he knew nothing about—vinyl siding, bowling alley equipment, tuxedos, boats, gyro-rotisseries, prosthetic limbs, corrective footwear, and, for about twenty minutes, department store mattresses. Jimmy was one of those guys who always had, simultaneously, a wife, a girlfriend, and a fiancée, all the while chatting up every woman he met regardless of age or marital status, theirs or his. Somehow, though, he wasn't exactly a cad. His appreciation of women of all shapes and sizes was immediate, vast, and sincere, and in addition to his not paying heed to accepted rules of fidelity, his peculiar charm often led others to ignore those rules as well. The women he met knew better than to get involved, but he just sort of wore them down. Walt could attest that Jimmy was both persuasive and hard to stay pissed at. He had four ex-wives, five, if you counted Irma twice, and although they'd all left him, none held feelings harder than nostalgic exasperation, writing off their time with Jimmy as an exuberant mistake, one that had been made by others as well. Walt figured what saved Jimmy from getting shot by one of his wives was that he had genuinely fallen in love every time, that the very quality that consistently got him into trouble was also the one that got him back out. Walt watched Jimmy's reflection in the back bar mirror, the little man throwing his hands in the air as he talked, displaying those great white teeth, a brilliant set of chompers that, despite being his own, looked like dentures. The two had met some years before, after Jimmy had stopped his car in front of one of Walt's jobs, having noticed from the street that scaffolding was going up in front of a house. He asked Walt what he was doing, how much he was charging, didn't he know that there was a better way to do it, and whether or not the owner was a woman. When the answer was yes to the last question, Jimmy'd shot back, *"Is she home?"*

"I still don't get it," said the not-so-bright Louis, who was seated on Jimmy's left. Apparently, some aspect of the nurse story had been unclear.

Louis's combination of youth, strength, and stupidity made people uneasy, and he often boasted of prowess in things at which no one else would care to excel. Among his claims was being able to eat more than anyone in town, and he had issued a standing challenge to anyone, anywhere to a "food-eating contest." Walt's money would have gone with Louis in an eating contest of any sort—he'd seen him in action.

"Hey, moneybags," Jimmy called from down the bar. He somehow always knew when Walt got paid.

"How's your gray-haired girlfriend? You two married yet?"

"No, Grandpa," Walt replied. "She's yours."

"You get them shutters moved yet? Fall's a-comin'."

"Yes, wiseass, and if you want the money I owe you, shut up."

Walt moved down the bar, peeled off three twenties, and gave them to Jimmy who waved for Gene to bring more drinks. Gene ignored the gesture, and then, a few minutes later, brought the drinks over as if it had been his own idea.

"So when's our next job, chief?"

For Walt, it was always a tough decision whether or not to take on jobs that required helpers, as his occasional crew — Jimmy, Louis, and whomever else he could dredge up — required so much babysitting that it was not often worth the trouble.

"I don't know, Jimmy. Our ship is rudderless. I might keep doing smaller stuff for a while."

Louis was trying to get Gene to put free pretzels on the bar, which Gene did only occasionally, which made the dim young man crazy. The plastic "wicker" baskets of off-brand pretzels and stale chips would appear at those odd times when no one was drinking with any real steam, Gene's hope being that priming the pump with salty snacks might help. For Louis, the random presence of the free snacks served to show the winds of fate for what they are, with the plastic baskets being yet another example of life being alternately generous and unfair.

"Today ain't a pretzel day," Gene said, he being one of the few people not afraid to fuck with Louis.

"Why?" Louis responded, bewildered by the workings of the universe. "Why ain't it a pretzel day?"

"It just ain't. I don't know what to tell ya, kid. I don't control these things."

Jimmy ran a comb through his hair as Walt smiled.

"What about Sammy, she don't need no work?" Jimmy asked.

"Not at the moment," Walt lied. "Not much."

"Not much? There's all kinds of work up there."

"Yeah, and the last time I had you two help, Arthur came home to find Louis pissing in his laundry tub and you teaching Sam the tango."

"She was getting it, too."

"I'm sure you would have seen to it that she did." Walt cracked his neck. "Maybe it's best if I work alone for a while."

"I'll go talk to Sam. I know just how to talk to broads like her," Jimmy assured.

"She'd be thrilled to hear you say that."

"I'd like to ball her, too," Jimmy elaborated.

"How nice of you to say."

"I'm serious," he continued, in case there was doubt. "I'd do it in a second. I would."

"You're quick—I've heard."

Jimmy exhaled through pursed lips, as if to let off pent-up sexual pressure.

"Your ex has one classy chassis," he said. "No disrespect, of course."

None was taken. Walt would have been more offended had Jimmy not wanted to "ball" his ex-wife. This was classic Jimmy. Though Sam was a handsome woman, she was certainly not a head-turner. In women, Jimmy saw only good.

"All right. I'll see if we can't get some work up there next week. Just you and me," Walt said, lowering his voice and nodding toward Louis, although the big kid was still preoccupied with the pretzels. "I'll come up with something."

Jimmy was good for Walt in this way, moving him off of top dead center. Lately, work had taken a gloomy turn. Leaving tasks undone and bills uncollected was nothing new, but historically Walt felt that the next job might be the one that would somehow go better, at least offering a clean slate. That basic optimism, misguided as it was, had always kept him chugging along. Recently, though, he had begun to consider that the next job to come down the pike might not be any different, that maybe his rut had become deep enough that he could not get out.

"Uh-oh," Jimmy reported. "Trouble at two o'clock."

Walt looked toward the door in time to see Deena Waskowski stride in.

"Better run, boy," Jimmy laughed.

Walt slouched as best he could behind Jimmy, who, on a good day, was all of five foot six. Jimmy leaned forward, and then back, repeating it quickly a few times, laughing and exposing Walt, making him attempt the same maneuvers in an effort to stay hidden.

"Look out! She's gonna get you!"

Although his breakup with Sam had long been permanent, Walt had since been in no relationship of significance. He had avoided doing so, partly out of laziness, but partly too because it didn't seem fair to subject another woman to the frustration that accompanied his existence. The thrill of new romance was lessened by knowing that he would eventually be discovered for what he was, that his idiosyncrasies would at some point no longer be seen as interesting quirks, but as deficiencies that were frustratingly real. Which is not to say he didn't still occasionally like to get laid, which led him to his current mess. Deena Waskowski was a tough and mysterious woman, maybe in her mid-thirties, whose features suggested equal parts Polish and Native American bloodlines. Her long black hair and lean body always drew the attention of the room, though her fierce presence kept anyone from looking for too long lest they get caught staring. Deena could kick your ass. The prospect of sex with her had long been an ongoing discussion at the bar, although privately, the men—except for Jimmy—knew that they were no match for her. Walt had been amused by the macho chatter regarding the striking woman, figuring the point to be moot, as it was rather unlikely that she was interested in men of any sort. That assumption would prove not to be the case however, as one night, after Gene had gone upstairs, Deena, who'd never before even acknowledged Walt's existence, simply walked over and informed him that he was coming home with her, her tone no different than if she'd said, "Get out of my way" or "Your fly is open."

Walt did as he was told, following her rumbling El Camino and its mag-wheels to her bungalow. The tiny house, he was surprised to discover, was adorned with frilly curtains and other feminine touches, leading him to wonder if Deena hadn't broken in, killed its occupants, and taken up residence. The ensuing months found him summoned to her house with some regularity, although, not unlike the riddle of the pretzels for Louis, it could not be predicted when Walt's services would be required. On the nights she would appear at the bar, he never knew which way things would go, whether she would tell him to follow her back to her place, or give no indication that she had ever seen him before, the latter being an occurrence that made him feel simultaneously slighted and off the hook. And while the sex was technically successful, it was, for Walt, pretty damned strange, as when Deena would climb on top of him, it was definitely she who did the work, with Walt's role reduced to no more than that of required accessory. They spoke few words during their trysts, and when Deena was done, she said things like, "You can go now."

Now, she gathered her long hair back into a ponytail, lit a cigarette, and walked over to the bar's lone pool table, where she shot alone and well. Her break clapped like a gunshot, making even Gene look up.

"Jesus, she hits those things hard," Jimmy said.

"Tell me about it," said Walt.

While screwing Deena had given Walt exalted status among the regulars at the 'Eye, he'd wanted out of the situation for some time. But because he wasn't sure how to end something he'd had no part in starting, the odd relationship had been going on for nearly a year. And tonight, he was tired and definitely did not want to go home with her. He finished his sandwich and pondered his options, which were decidedly few. He could sit at the bar and hope that she had only stopped in for a quick beer. Or, he could gather his nerve, act like a man, and walk right past her on his way to the door, maybe even add a jaunty little wink and "Hello." His last option, the one that he always took, was to go ahead and do whatever Deena wanted, which did, he had to admit as he watched her bend over the pool table, have its occasional benefits.

"Look at that ass," Jimmy said as she sank the five ball. "What the hell is she doing with you?"

"Whatever she wants. And I don't know how to stop her."

"You don't know what you're doing, son. A girl like that needs flowers, candy. That'd straighten her right out. Buy her a dozen roses and she won't know whether to crap or wind her watch."

For someone who'd had so many women, Jimmy's knack for getting things exactly wrong with them was amazing. For a hard woman like Deena, he'd buy flowers, whereas for a sweet woman, he would do nothing. But at least he took action, not letting the tides pull him as they pleased. Bolstered by a third drink, Walt decided that tonight he would not go home with Deena, regardless of what she wanted.

"Sayonara, losers, I'm outta here," Gene said, wiping down the bar one last time before, literally, throwing in the towel.

Jimmy had launched into a story about one of his ill-fated sales jobs, and a number of guys at their end of the bar were cracking up. The rest of the place had begun to fill with academics, with Walt stationed pretty much in between, not fitting in fully with either crowd. Near the front window was a table of former colleagues with whom he'd taught, people he liked and who could be counted on for spirited conversation.

"Walter!" one of them called, raising his glass. "Come drink with us!"

Through the smoke, Walt saw it was Phil Harris, one of the heavier drinkers in the history department, which is saying something. Walt had lost many hours with him.

"Hey, Phil," Walt said through the din, gesturing that he was occupied with someone else, although Jimmy had moved down a couple of stools and Walt was obviously alone. He didn't feel like getting sucked into the vortex of conversation that would take place at that table, not tonight. He was still feeling a bit off over Sam's oddness of the day before, over her mention of "something big" that she needed to discuss with him. Whatever it was, she didn't want to talk about it in the presence of Arthur. Walt's guess was that Dr. Art—and possibly now even Sam—had run out of patience with his slow progress on their house, and that perhaps an ultimatum was in the works. And if that was the case, Walt would understand. Dr. Art had been a trouper for a couple of years now, having married Sam, but gotten Walt as well, a large and unexpected stepchild who couldn't be made to clean his room. But the thought of another contractor working on the Friendship house bothered Walt more than the idea of Samantha now sharing their bed with another man. Walt knew he should bring up his lack of progress first, should save her the displeasure. Acknowledge that he was failing them, and then draw up a plan to get the house done. He'd hire legitimate sub-contractors if that's what they wanted, and he would oversee them. Number one on the list would be Dr. Art's den. In the back of the house was a sun room that Arthur had long envisioned as being a space where he could build his model ships, a painstaking hobby whose appeal eluded Walt, but about which Art was passionate. He would do it. Talk to Sam and Arthur about the house, draw up a plan. He'd had such ideas before, plans to take charge, to reinvent himself, but it never took long for reality to dissolve the momentary fantasy of effectiveness. This time, though, would be different. Assisted by the bourbon, a new focus took hold, and he foresaw the arrival of an era of self-command that would no longer allow the wind to decide his next move. He was middle-aged, for God's sake. It was time to grab the wheel. He raised his glass to himself and toasted his newfound independence, only to have his self-congratulation interrupted by a tap on the shoulder.

"Let's go," Deena said, gesturing toward the door like an impatient hitchhiker. Her eyes were shark-like. Over her shoulder Walt saw his former colleagues arguing some arcane point, drunkenly confident within their tenure. Jimmy and the boys were sharing a dirty joke. Gene was upstairs with his mother.

Walt sighed. Grabbing his keys, he said, "What the hell."

Chapter 4

WALT WAS BACK AT HARDWICK the next morning, taking a scraper to the wooden filigree on the side porch, feeling for soft spots that would betray the presence of rot. Miss June sat nearby, smart in her pressed khaki working slacks and safari hat.

"Dwight loved this porch," Miss June said.

"I know he did," Walt replied.

"I can see him clear as day, sitting in the chair right next to me." Her head was turned as if she were doing just that. "He was a marvelous looking man. Did I ever tell you that?"

"You have," he said, because it was true. She had been telling him stories about her dead fiancé since he was a boy, and Dwight Keating had taken on near-mythical status.

"The day he died…" she started.

"The galaxy lost a star," Walt completed in his mind.

"The galaxy lost a star. I lost him three months to the day before we were to be married, you know. It was during the

St. Patrick's Day flood of 1936."

Although Miss June did not have the old person's tendency to repeat stories due to forgetfulness, she had told Walt this particular story often, and always as if for the first time. They honored a tacit agreement to pretend that she had never before recounted her stories about Dwight, as to acknowledge that they were being re-hashed would reduce them to something less than her years of pining deserved. These moments brought a softer side of Miss June, oiling the leathery quality of her affect, introducing a suppleness that was not usually present. Although her reluctance to move beyond Dwight and open her heart to others both saddened and frustrated Walt, he was touched by the tenderness that filled her voice when she spoke of the man she had loved.

"We'd been sitting right here on this porch," she said. "That morning. He'd come calling, you know. There was no newspaper that day, but the radio was working. For days the waters had been rising. It just wouldn't stop. The Allegheny had met the Monongahela way back on Smithfield Street, filling the stores downtown. Thousands of hats from the haberdasheries on Liberty Avenue were floating down the street. Can you imagine such a thing? We had no locks and dams back then, you know. And that day. Oh, that day. Dwight had no reason to go down there. His office was on the upper floors, well above the water's rise. He just wanted to see if he could somehow help. And about civic duty, there was no reasoning with that man. He was always the first to volunteer, even for work that should have been done by someone else. He was not beyond moving below his station."

Ignoring the snobbery, Walt allowed her to continue.

"He hadn't needed to leave this porch that day, is my point. And yet he did." Her eyes scanned the side yard. "I looked him right in the eye and said, 'Don't you leave me, you impossible man. I can't afford to lose you,' but he called me a silly goose and said that he'd be back before I knew it." She pointed with her slender finger to demonstrate Dwight's resolve. "The man's name was Murphy. A vagrant. They say he was drunk, riding along the waters atop a metal drum when it slipped away from him, and he had just managed to reach the big bronze clock at Fifth Avenue and Smithfield Street, the one that hangs from Kaufmann's department store. Do you know of that clock, Walter?"

"Yes, I do, Miss June," he said, not pointing out that every-one in Pittsburgh knew that clock although Kaufmann's was no more and, further, that Miss June asked him that very question each time she told the story.

"The man had managed to pull himself out of the water and seat himself up there, right on top of the clock. He just sat there laughing, crazy as a loon, as the waters rushed by. Can you imagine that? Who would perch themselves in such a place?" She waited for Walt's usual response.

"I don't know, Miss June. It's hard to imagine."

"And so, from farther up Fifth Avenue, my Dwight saw this simple man sitting up there, and because the waters were still rising, he set off to help him. Oh, what a swimmer he was, my Dwight. Strength like you have just never seen. He used to swim for exercise alongside our sailboat when our families would summer together in Nantucket, you know."

She looked across the grass as if Dwight were there now, traversing the yard with his gallant strokes.

"He made his way to the clock and was trying to coax the poor soul down into his arms, when this Murphy, intoxicated as he was, slipped backward, causing his trousers to become entangled in the hands of the clock! Dwight worked desper-ately to free him, struggling with the thrashing man, working hard to keep both of their heads above water before finally managing to free the vagrant from his trousers entirely! He saved that man's life."

"And what about the trousers? What happened to them?" Walt asked, pretending not to know.

"Why, they hung on the face of that clock for two whole weeks after the waters receded, until the Kaufmann's maintenance staff finally cut them down. There was a photograph of them in the newspaper. But my Dwight. Oh, my Dwight. After struggling to get that Murphy to an open window, after using every last ounce of his strength to save that man's life, he submerged one last time, never to reappear."

There wasn't much to say after that.

As with the other times he had heard the tale, Walt was struck by how fresh it remained for Miss June. After more than sixty years, it was still, for her, as if a recent tragedy. And so she had been careful not to let Hardwick change much over the years—she wanted it to be as it was when Dwight had sat at its long dining room table, had played the grand piano in its music room. For her, Hardwick was evidence that she had once been a girl, that she had been loved. Walt considered how Hardwick had become, for him too, a place where time stood still, a place where it was easy to ignore the outside world. As frustrating as Miss June could be, with her caustic remarks and pointless chores, the house provided sanctuary, a place where he could busy himself while escaping modern life. It was a false reality, he knew, and while he was sometimes critical of Miss June for being stuck there in her past, he had to admit that he was stuck there in his present. He resumed his scraping as the autumn sun became low, casting an orange glow across Shadyside, tinting the stone walls of Hardwick with warmth and yearning. He remembered how, as a boy, the evening sky above Pittsburgh was orange, an effect from the steel mills by the river. He had thought that the sky everywhere turned orange at times, and it was unsettling to later learn that it wasn't true, that one of the accepted properties of his world wasn't what it had seemed.

"He loved taffy, you know."

"I'm sorry?" Walt said.

"He had a terrible sweet tooth, my Dwight."

And those were the last words they spoke that day, both left with images of years long past, with Walt thinking of Miss June graced with a young girl's heart, and her watching Dwight swim gracefully through the garden.

* * *

Walt's poking and prodding of the side porch revealed that it was in good enough shape for another coat of paint, thus buying a few more years. And thank God for that—replacing the elaborate railings and filigree would cost a lot if done right, and he doubted that Miss June could afford the repairs. She was tight-lipped about money, and whenever Walt had to break the news to her that cash was needed for the house, she made him assure her that the work he suggested wasn't meant to change or improve the house, but just to maintain it appropriately. Once convinced, she would meet with her banker and, soon after, the required amount—and not a penny more—would appear. Speculating about Miss June's financial status was common around the East End, and while most people accepted that the vast Creighton fortune was long gone, there were still holdouts—dreamers, Walt thought—who were certain that she had millions stashed away someplace. It was understandable. At its peak, before the Depression, Clarence Creighton's shop had employed nearly two hundred men along the Monongahela River, and the faded image of the family name could still be seen on decrepit factory buildings along the river in Hazelwood. Rumor had it that Andrew Carnegie himself had once made an offer to buy him out, but Miss June's grandfather was a proud entrepreneur who couldn't fathom his operation disappearing into the massive Carnegie holdings.

When in a rare talkative mood, Walt's father would tell his son stories about the fall of Creighton Industries, folkloric tales that changed with each telling, as if Walt, being a child, wouldn't remember that the last version had been different. The stories included, at various times, mention of the crash of twenty-nine, extortion, union problems, collusion among larger shops, and, once, a tale about Miss June's brother, Thomas, and a gambling problem. Walt was never sure if his father's tales of heartbreak, treachery, and deceit were true or if he was just pulling his son's leg. His father was not the joking kind, but the story changed enough in each telling that he couldn't possibly have believed them all to be true. Eventually, Walt figured that his father had merely fallen into the popular local habit of speculating about the fate of the great family's wealth. While still at the university, Walt did some research on the matter, and from what he could ascertain, the services that the shop provided to the giant mills nearby were increasingly performed in-house during the Depression, and the business suffered as a result. Small shops were crushed. Miss June's father, Julius, then sole owner following Clarence's death, understood the dire straits of the company and reluctantly struck a deal with U. S. Steel for Creighton Machinery, dissolving the company and its name. The Creighton building was emptied of its contents, and the operation was moved to the massive Edgar Thomson Works a couple miles upriver. Julius Creighton had sold his father's company for what amounted to pennies on the dollar. From what Walt could gather about the steel industry during that awful time, this scenario was not uncommon, and it seemed that Julius had made an understandable, albeit heartbreaking, move—sell or be driven to ruin. The question that remained was, how much money had been salvaged from the company's fall? Whatever the amount, the family, though its name may have been sullied a bit, continued its privileged lifestyle, not as wealthy as before, but comfortable enough. They maintained contact with the other great families—the Mellons, the Olivers, the Benedums—whose names are synonymous with the building of Pittsburgh. Miss June's mother remained active in numerous charities, if only, as was common with wealthy women of the day, in appearance, and Julius was a fixture at the country club. June and Thomas attended the same private schools they always had, and were set up with trust funds, which while significantly more modest than they once would have been, were hoped to be enough to see them through their lives.

Regardless of the particulars, the point Walt's father made was that, while Miss June lived in the grandest of houses and traveled in circles of society that would never include people like them, she didn't have as much money as it appeared. While Walt had had difficulty believing this as a teenager, he had come to accept it as an adult. Miss June gave great thought to each sum of money that she spent, and while most of her belongings had been very expensive, Walt suspected they were evidence of her belief in the value of quality rather than of splurging on luxuries. The old woman, like Walt, believed that the most sensible things were built to last and should be kept in service for a very long time, and her disdain for newfangled objects was one of the traits that they shared. Her clothes, made of heavy fabrics with fine thread counts, had been purchased long ago from the specialty shops of Shadyside, stores that catered to wealthy women who required personal attention. Her outfits were expensive, the styles plain and timeless, the quality high enough to ensure that they would last her for life.

Everything she purchased shared these characteristics. The juicer bolted to her kitchen counter was a simple and heavy device made of cast aluminum, doubtless the most expensive one available at the time, costing more than any of the Creighton workers would have earned in a week. And yet there it stood, still in use fifty years later, shedding no light on the mysteries of Miss June's financial status, having been more expensive than a working-class person could afford, but having been kept far longer than most people would hang on to such a thing. Miss June's twice-yearly meetings with her "banker," who Walt suspected was actually a lawyer, lasted for hours, which would seem to indicate that there was a significant portfolio to be handled, but again, Walt thought it very possible that, much like the juicer, Miss June would pay a premium for the best advisers available to manage a rather ordinary sum of money. Her one indisputable asset was Hardwick, but while the house was terrifically valuable, it was also a constant financial drain from which she would see no return, as it was out of the question that she would ever sell. It took money to keep the place intact, with Walt doing his best to ward off the elements and Father Time, and while he received little payment for his efforts, the materials were not inexpensive. Relining the copper box gutters a few years back was too large and specialized a job for him to tackle, and the bill from the roofing contractor was more than Walt himself had earned during the previous two years combined.

While the maintenance of Hardwick was normal business that all homeowners had to face, Walt knew that much more was at stake there for Miss June, that the memory of Dwight was forever entwined with the house. As brittle as she had become, she had once walked its floors as a young woman in love, and if work was needed to protect the building from decay, then the work would be done, no matter the cost.

Chapter 5

WALT ARRIVED AT ART'S PARTY with the best bottle of wine
that twelve dollars could buy. He was surprised to find that
he was looking forward to the night, welcoming conversation
of a broader scope than that available at the Bull's-Eye. Sam's
university cronies would be there, drinking and complaining
about the positions they'd fought so fiercely to obtain. They
were a funny and jaded bunch who didn't suffer their fools
gladly, with one exception being Walt, a fool they all liked.
Walt had met Dr. Art's friends a few times before, and they
seemed to get a kick out of him as well—a real live carpenter—observing him with interest as though a specimen to be
examined, one who might suddenly scratch himself or spit
in the sink. These professional men claimed to be jealous of
Walt's life, but he didn't buy it. He'd long heard the line, "Oh,
it must be nice to work with your hands," and while the comment sounded sincere, Walt suspected that it was often just a
statement of kindness, offered because it was such a shame

that someone like him, articulate and bright and seemingly not all that far from being someone like them, had ended up achieving so little.

Slipping in the back door, he saw that the kitchen table was already covered with gift bottles of wine, each far better than his. One had been decorated with absurd fussiness, pastel ribbons curling from its neck, a taped card bearing the signatures of a couple named Susan and Charles. Through the porthole window of the pantry door, Walt saw Dr. Art's smiling head talking to someone who, given his adoring expression, had to be Sam. Pushing through the pivoting door with too much force, Walt found that it was indeed Sam, and that she was holding a platter of homemade cheese puffs that she had pulled back in the nick of time. Walt could tell he had intruded upon an affectionate moment.

"Where's your apron?" he asked.

"I don't wear it in public," Sam replied.

"I was talking to him," he said, pointing to Arthur.

"Walter, how good of you to come," Arthur began before Sam could respond.

"Congratulations on getting published, Artie," Walt said, handing him the bottle. "We were all shocked when we heard. I mean it. Everyone. Utterly shocked." Arthur, still smiling, began to look mildly distressed. "Shocked, I tell you!"

"Oh, I see. Well, yes indeed, there are many proposals submitted each year for consideration, and while I do suppose there must have been some element of luck involved in this fortunate turn of events, I do feel compelled to point out that a great deal of research was done by my staff and that, subsequently, the selection committee must have found that … "

"He's joking, Arthur," Sam interrupted with familiar exasperation.

Dr. Art looked momentarily confused and then relieved.

"Oh! Ha! Yes! Of course. Well, Walter, you are the funny one, indeed. Ha-ha-ha."

Arthur laughed like that: *"Ha-ha-ha."*

"Oh, and you brought us wine, how thoughtful," he continued, accepting the bottle from Walt. Parting the fussy ribbons, he read its label. "My God! A '59 Lafite-Rothschild!" He looked up with disbelief. "How *supremely* generous of you, Walter."

Sam leveled a look at her ex.

"Yes, Walter, how supremely generous of *you*."

Walt took a cheese puff from her tray and popped it into his mouth victoriously. Sam rolled her eyes and tried not to smile. As Arthur headed through the second pivoting door, the one that led to the dining room, Sam grabbed Walt's big arm.

"Hey, before you go in, can we have a moment?"

She was too late, as Dr. Art, having decided to show Walt off to a group of his friends, had come back and grabbed his other arm, leading him across the dining room like a head of prized livestock.

"Fellows," he said, "I'd like you to meet a very dear friend of mine, Mr. Walter Farnham—craftsman extraordinaire, expert in matters both philosophical and material, and devoted friend to my wonderful wife. In general, a good egg."

My God, he's been drinking, Walt thought. He had never seen Arthur like this, so happy, so effusive. When they'd first met, Art was uncomfortable around him, perhaps fearful of his size, wondering if some innate, Neanderthal construction-worker quality would have Walt wanting to punch him for stealing his woman. Never mind that Walt and Sam had been divorced for a year, that Walt's construction career had mostly been spent performing light maintenance for a cantankerous old lady who cut the crusts off of his sandwiches, or that the only fight Walt had ever been in was in the fourth grade, and he'd lost quickly.

To a girl. Dr. Art's cohorts were harmless enough, going on about the deck that one of them was planning to have built, and about how handy the other's grandfather had been. Walt had little in common with these men, accomplished as they were, but they were nice enough, and he was happy to shoot the shit with them. The house was crowded and split down the middle, with Sam's friends on one side and Art's on the other, with the dental crowd chatting about the events of the day, and Sam's cronies hitting the booze and complaining and laughing.

Sam appeared and put a drink in Walt's hand for the second time in three days. Though he felt good, she seemed tense.

"Walt, help in the kitchen, please?"

She pulled him by the elbow, and he tried to guess what he'd done wrong, but the sound of a spoon clanging against the side of a glass stopped them in their tracks.

"Um, your attention, everyone? Attention?" Arthur was speaking from the squeaky stair landing that was also on Walt's list of things to repair. "Please pardon my interruption, but I must offer my most sincere thanks to all of you for coming tonight. I am so fortunate to have such friends, though I have to assume that many of you are really here for Sam's cooking. Ha!" He paused a beat too long after his joke, and the crowd tried to let their smiles linger for him.

"But all joking aside. I do thank you for celebrating with us this evening, and for your many kind words about my recent good fortune. Because many of you heard my small speech this afternoon at the luncheon, I won't bore you with it again here.

A collective breath was released—now they were really smiling.

"Today has been quite extraordinary for me, and as evening has come and I've had time to reflect, I know that the greatest reward I've been given is you, my friends.

Dr. Art was nothing if not sincere. He was clearly happy, and Walt felt good for him. This was Art's moment, and he was basking in it.

"And, I'm feeling, frankly, an exuberance that seems to be inviting an uncharacteristic spontaneity."

No shit, Walt thought. He'd already chatted up half the women in the crowd, told his coworkers that his wife's ex-husband was one of his closest friends, and, for one short moment while passing the stereo, made as if he were going to dance. He scanned the crowd until he caught her eye.

"Sam, where are you, darling?"

"Uh-oh," Sam said, nearly pulling Walt's arm out of its socket. "Walt. The kitchen. Now." Arthur spotted her, and they were trapped.

"Everyone," Arthur beamed, "Sam and I are expecting a baby."

* * *

When Walt was twelve, not long after his father died, Miss June had traveled to Philadelphia to visit a family friend whose health had faltered. A young woman named Julia came to stay at Hardwick while she was gone, recommended by a member of the bridge club. Julia was dark-haired and had driven to Pittsburgh from Baltimore in her Karman Ghia. For six days it was just the two of them, a crushingly beautiful woman and a thoroughly smitten boy—two peas, as Walt saw it, in a pod. They darted around town in her sporty little car, and she listened to Walt when he told her things. Walt pushed their half-sized shopping cart through the corner market with pride, and Julia bought anything they wanted. There was a whimsy about her that made him, too, feel free. She sang as they walked along Wightman Street, and picked flowers from people's yards as if they were her own. Walt had overheard Julia on the phone, and he had put together enough of the story to gather that she was finally leaving her boyfriend Ray, with Pittsburgh being a stop on her escape. No matter, after just one day together, Walt had never been happier. The unlikely pair played chess and she cheated, and they walked through Mellon Park and she laughed at Walt's kid jokes. They ordered pizza from Mineo's and ate in the television room where Julia removed the dust cover from the seldom-used set, and they watched a movie called *Trilogy of Terror* that scared the hell out of them both. Earlier that day, they'd gone to the Buhl Planetarium and walked through a dark room that lit up with pin lights and waves of color like the solar system. The floor was rubbery with craters, and a recorded nineteen-fifties voice told them of the wonders of science. *This is what God sounds like,* Walt had thought. The backs of their hands brushed together, a jolt that Walt would never forget. During their last full day alone, he was sullen and grumpy as they drove through the countryside north of Pittsburgh looking for a pumpkin farm, something Walt had never heard of. As far as he knew, pumpkins came from the grocery store, but Julia knew a lot of things that he didn't, and regardless, he would have gone anywhere with her, grumpy or not. They drove for miles on secondary roads, but there were no pumpkins at all. Picnicking by the river at McConnell's Mill, Walt climbed the rocks, showing off for her as best he could. Back on the road, the distant smell of burning leaves filled the car, and Walt asked Julia if she might move to Pittsburgh.

"I hadn't planned on it, kiddo, but anything's possible." She took a drag from her cigarette. "There's nothing for me back home. That much I know."

Heading back to town, Walt said little. Rounding a bend near Evans City, the two finally saw a pyramid of pumpkins on the porch of a pseudo general store, and Julia said "Ha! I told you so!" Inside, the strange woman at the register said unapologetically that "They's only for show, not for sale." Julia made a face when the woman wasn't looking, and Walt couldn't help but smile. They bought stale taffy apples as consolation, and then, after starting the car, Julia turned to Walt. Pressing her finger to her lips, she got out of the car and, with exaggerated pantomime sneakiness, tiptoed across the gravel lot and stole the pumpkin that crowned the pyramid. Driving their little getaway car as fast as it would go, they laughed at their larceny until they were in pain, their prize heavy on Walt's young lap.

Very late that night, Walt awoke to drunken laughter from the kitchen and knew that it was Ray. The next morning, he left the house early and spent the day alone in the thick woods of Frick Park, not returning until after dinner, dirty and tired. Miss June was home, the little blue car was gone, and he never saw Julia again.

* * *

Arthur stood on the stair landing, smiling across the room at Sam. Walt's smile was plastered hard, and he could feel Sam looking at him over the shoulders of those who were hugging and congratulating her—knew that she was trying to make contact, and knew also that if he had dared to look, her sweetness toward him would be too much. Exposed was the saddest of truths—that Sam hadn't simply not wanted to have children as she'd always claimed. She just hadn't wanted to have them with him.

Chapter 6

THE FOLLOWING MORNING, Walt dreamed that he was on Miss June's side porch, watching his father and Dwight, both of whom were swimming through the grass. Dwight was telling Walt that it was okay for him to swim too, that all he had to do was let go and try. Walt was afraid, fearful of the grass and its strange liquid state. The two men turned onto their backs and swam the backstroke, their movements like those of synchronized swimmers. Walt then felt an invisible hand tugging at his ankle, trying to pull him in. He grabbed the rail tighter, but the hand was strong. A soundtrack was then added to the dream, that of Jimmy DeLuca singing "Let Me Call You Sweetheart" as the grip on his ankle grew tighter. The singing got louder and Walt pulled back, but he was losing the battle and began to go under. As panic set in, Jimmy's voice broke through: "Come on, pal, it's time to join the living."

Walt started awake, but could still smell the grass. He was naked and in his garage apartment, on the sofa where he had passed out the night before, the real Jimmy DeLuca perched on the sofa's arm, shaking Walt's ankle and eating a banana.

Walt's head dropped back. "Don't you knock?"

"What for? It was open."

"My dog could've bitten you, you know."

"That'd be the day. Wouldn't it, boy?"

Dewey butted his big head against Jimmy's thigh, a slobbery tennis ball in his mouth. It was true, Walt thought. Anyone could rob the place and his dog wouldn't object, providing his belly was rubbed in the process. Walt tried to sit up, but his hangover met him halfway, hitting him on the forehead like a cast-iron skillet. He fell back down.

"Do you mind telling me what you're doing here?"

"We've got work, remember?"

He tried, but no, he didn't remember. It was possible that he had told Jimmy that there was work, but he couldn't think clearly enough to know what it was. At the same time, it was very possible that Jimmy was fucking with him.

"Oh, right. The work."

Walt sat up now, pulling a cover across his lap. Jimmy walked over to the fridge, poured two glasses of orange juice, and handed one to Walt, who gulped it down while Jimmy talked.

"Do you know that I still wake up every morning with a hard-on? Did I ever tell you that? Every goddamned morning." He slammed his hand on the table for emphasis, the report making Walt wince. "Bam! It just happens."

"Jesus, Jimmy."

"Like a baseball bat. Sixty-three years old. I never miss a day. Never."

Walt lay back down, pulled the cover over his head, and grabbed hold of his own, flaccid, penis. The sofa began to move through space like a raft, and Jimmy puttered about the garage apartment singing to himself. Walt saw flashes of the previous night, remembered drinking—not at Gene's, where Sam might have come looking for him—but at the Squirrel Cage, where he'd drunk enough imported beer to require a passport. He'd then found his way on foot to Chief's on Craig Street, where he drank alone, trying to fend off the drunken conversations and absurdly loud juke box on which someone repeatedly played "You Dropped a Bomb On Me" by The Gapp Band. He saw himself stumbling out onto the sidewalk at closing time, the red neon fireman's hat on the sign above him causing the wet sidewalk to glow like a beer-soaked funhouse. He recalled being lured to the nearby Elks Club by a new-found friend who introduced Walt proudly to his fellow Elk. The conversation there was as inane as at Chief's, but there was no jukebox to bury it, and by now Walt was participating in the pointless discussions with vigor. He then remembered a minor scuffle, as Walt's host had caused an uproar among his brethren by teaching him the secret Elk call, complete with thumbs to temples gesture and nasal honking sound, a breach of confidentiality serious enough to get them both tossed out. But, earlier in the evening, before the self-pity and foolishness, Walt had been at Sam's. Sam. That part came back to him all too clearly—Arthur's tearful speech, the rush of goodwill from the guests, Sam's blushing and looking more beautiful than he'd ever seen, and finally, himself, stunned and leaving, smiling and waving as he backed out the side door, his hand moving back and forth like that of a half-witted airline stewardess, repeating the words "Bye-bye, bye-bye!" again and again.

"Come on, pal, breakfast is ready."

Achieving focus through one open eye, Walt saw that Jimmy had made eggs. He must have brought the groceries with him. Eating seemed risky, but while there were few areas in which

Jimmy's expertise could be trusted, the treatment of hangovers was known to be one. Despite the amount of time Walt spent at Gene's, he was not a serious drinker. It had been a long time since he had been drunk, and it was the first time that he'd become so with such purpose. Sitting up, he took the plate, finding himself ravenous. Jimmy handed him a glass of thick brown liquid.

"Drink this," he commanded, which Walt did without argument. Jimmy hummed and read the paper.

"Do we really have work?" Walt asked.

"Nah, I was just fucking with you."

Walt looked around the apartment, assessing the situation. "Why are you here?"

"I come to borrow a ladder. Irma's gutters need cleaned."

"Working for your ex again?"

"You're one to talk."

"Good point. And I don't even get to sleep with mine."

"Divorce does wonders for a relationship," Jimmy said. "Irma and me screw better when we're divorced than we do when we're married.

"It's a fact," he added as if it had been documented somewhere. "We tried it both ways, and there's no doubt."

Walt looked at the mess Jimmy'd made in the kitchen, watched him as he studied the classifieds through his dime store glasses. "Cheaters," he called them.

"How'd you know I'd be hungover this morning, Jimmy?"

Jimmy dipped his toast in his yolk.

"Sammy came looking for you last night. Said you might be a little upset about something."

So he knew.

"I'm okay."

"Yeah, I was just thinking how great you look."

"No, really. I'm fine."

This was not completely untrue. Despite his night of barroom self-pity, he'd had a moment of clarity during his stumble home. Despite the initial shock of Sam's pregnancy, the truth was that he was happy for her. And wanting happiness for Sam was never a question. He had long before acknowledged that Dr. Art was a better husband than he, was better equipped to give Sam what she needed at this stage of her life. For the first half of their marriage, she had been okay with Walt's messes, with his inability to keep life's plates spinning. But when he lost interest in setting new plates a-spin, she retreated. Arthur lacked Walt's wry personality, but he accomplished things. For Sam, that had become enough.

After breakfast, Jimmy gave Walt a ride to retrieve his truck in a maroon LTD that Walt had never seen before. Jimmy changed cars often, for reasons that seemed ordinary to him—debts owed and bets won, women met and women divorced. He once obtained a Pontiac after crashing a borrowed Chevy into a Buick that was being driven by a newly divorced and still bitter woman, who, with the type of coincidence that only Jimmy could attract, had been looking to dump her ex-husband's car that still sat in her garage. Regardless of this car's origin, Walt noticed that it could not have carried the ladder that Jimmy had ostensibly come to borrow, a ladder that went unmentioned as they got in and drove off. Jimmy dropped him near the Squirrel Cage, where his truck was waiting with a parking ticket on its windshield. Under "Make of Vehicle," the cop had written "DORF." He threw it in the glove box with the Chiclets and the others, and headed to Miss June's with no specific plans for what to do once he got there. Despite its associated aggravation, Walt was always drawn to the house. Although its owner had social contacts that most contractors would kill for—the wealthiest old-money families in southwestern Pennsylvania—he wasn't interested in business opportunities. He preferred to while away his time at Hardwick, and, despite her continuous complaints about him, Miss June believed that only he possessed the concern required to work on her estate. She was also reluctant to share him with anyone else and became impatient when he took on other work. Walt's friends, familiar with his lack of ambition, figured that his situation amounted to relatively easy money, and that no one else would pay him to work at such a snail's pace. Others attributed his allegiance to his love for the house itself, its stateliness, its bond to more elegant times. There was truth in each scenario, but regardless, today, Miss June and her disdain for self-pity might be just what he needed to keep from thinking too much.

The sky was a blank slate of Pittsburgh silver above Hardwick, and the branches from Miss June's giant maples were black and finger-like in contrast. Walt leaned against his truck and looked straight up through the spooky web, pleasantly dizzy as he did so. The trees seemed to turn, and the truck turned too, moving slowly in a very large circle that would continue forever so long as he didn't look down. He shuffled his feet, lest they get sucked into the drive as if under a receding wave at the beach. Slipping in the side door, he found the house quiet—apparently the old woman was out. He breathed deeply, absorbing the smell of where old money had once been, a certain mix of furniture polish and Persian rugs, dried oranges and oil paintings, with a slight hint of dust at the edges. He liked being alone in the echoey manse, and walked slowly through the downstairs, reading the edges of linen-bound books, tracing the pads of his fingers lightly across rough, gilt-framed canvases. In the living room, Clarence Creighton's eyes followed Walt from above the mantle, regarding him silently as they had since he was a child. Looking at it now, Walt remembered how he had come to think of Miss June's grandfather as being God, serious in his portrait, firm and all-knowing.

Ascending the main stairs, Walt took in the stained glass window at the landing, the colors lit evenly by the cool sky beyond. As a child sitting on these steps, quiet and alone, in the presence of his oil-and-canvas God, Walt would sometimes pray toward the window, directing his pleading force at the somber glass where he was certain it was magnified and transported into the ether. He thought of his prayers as being almost tangible when they left him, that once they were out beyond the world, they would travel forever, weighty secrets he would never tell.

In the second-floor hall by the photographs of Miss June's early life, Walt's boots stopped as they always did. He remembered standing there decades before. In his mind's eye, his younger self became a part of the exhibit, the hall a faded diorama featuring a small boy pondering the grainy images, unable to fathom the passage of time. Heading down the hall toward her bedroom where he seldom ventured, Walt stopped outside the door. Miss June's "chamber" felt off-limits, a remnant from decades before when he had been admonished not to play in there. As an adult, he had been in the room while tending to the house, but always treaded lightly in that personal place, taking extra care not to leave footprints or to disturb the thick duvet that graced the bed. From within the room, he heard a soft humming—she was home after all. Walt moved quietly to the doorway, and through the crack saw her sitting at the small dressing table, her hair freed from its prison of clips and pins, a softer, more girl-like version of Miss June, one whom Walt had caught glimpses of only a handful of times. Her hair, usually gray in its tightly wound bun, had a slightly yellow hue, and it draped her slight shoulders with surprising length. In the mirror, she ran an antique brush through it slowly, humming her song as she completed the strokes, a moment of self-nurturing to which the usually hard woman would never admit. Her shoulder blades moved visibly through her thin nightgown as she worked the brush, the fabric betraying her frailty. In the mirror, Walt saw the flat plate of her chest, the thin lines of her ribs, wafer-like bones that comprised her armor. How was it that this dominant woman could be so slight? Had she always been so, or had she withered with her fortune? Walt moved back slightly so as not to be seen and drank in the moment, no more certain than the young boy in the hall of the mysteries of time.

* * *

"It's customary to perform some work before taking a break," Miss June said from above. "In fact, some measurable amount of work must be completed to allow for a break, by definition, to be possible. Leave it to you to pioneer new methods of shirking one's duties."

He had fallen asleep on the wicker sofa on the side porch while Miss June finished her private routine. Her hair was once again stern in its bun.

"Yes, it's that very Lewis and Clark quality of mine that people admire." He stretched. "Don't worry, though. I wasn't planning on laying here long."

"I should hope not. Hens lay—lazy men do not. Regardless, this isn't a day for laying *or* lying about. We've company due, and needn't have the place resembling a flophouse."

Walt stretched again and groaned, emitting a sound not unlike that of a walrus wooing a mate. Miss June often entertained in the afternoons—dainty affairs that included her reading group or the local chapter of the Victorian Society —and she often fussed about Walt's appearance before her guests arrived. His truck was not to be visible from the house, no tools or drop cloths were to be left about, *"And for goodness sakes, tuck in your shirt."* She couldn't risk the appearance of slovenliness by association. And while Walt usually complied, he did like to spice things up occasionally, to cause a mild ruckus among Miss June's blue-haired gaggle, his most recent performance being to walk through her Tuesday afternoon bridge club meeting sans shirt, his impressive belly leading the way from the kitchen as he drank directly from a carton of milk.

As Walt struggled to rise from the sofa, Miss June inspected his attire. His hair was unruly, but he had on a decent blue work shirt and clean painter's pants.

"Don't worry about me," he said. "I just stopped by to pick up a few tools." A lie.

She consulted her timepiece.

"Well, you might as well stay for tea. We'll have it out here."

He eased back onto the sofa, assisted by the hangover that was regaining ground. He closed his eyes and drifted off again, was beginning to dream when the slam of the screen door caused him to jolt awake for the second time that morning. She wheeled the tea cart onto the porch.

As she poured, he was out of sync and unsure. Miss June made up for his silence, chattering on about her latest project, a book that would chronicle her family's history. It was to map her grandfather's rise through industry, the devastation of the Great Depression—as if it needed to be described from within the context of *her* family's trials to be truly understood—and the ways that common folk of Pittsburgh have been helped by Creighton generosity. The project was a surprise to Walt. He had once suggested a similar endeavor to Miss June, that she should record some sort of history of her family, either written or spoken, and then donate it with her family photographs to the Western Pennsylvania Historic Conservancy or the university's history department. The suggestion had been met with dismissal, that the idea was pointless, because she wasn't going anywhere. Apparently though, she'd had a change of heart and had interested a historian from Boston in completing the task, a woman who was due to arrive that very afternoon. As if with scripted timing, the doorbell rang, and Miss June went to answer its call. From where he sat, Walt heard the murmur of greetings being exchanged. The voices got closer and the screen door opened.

"Walter, might you remember Gwenneth Thompson?"

He sure as hell did.

"Oh my God! Walt!"

Stunned, he rose to greet her. "Gwen —"

She threw her arms around him.

"I can't believe this. It must be, what, a dozen years?"

"At least," he said, wishing he'd showered before leaving with Jimmy.

Actually, he remembered precisely when he'd seen Gwen last, remembered that her hair smelled just as it did now, remembered what she'd been wearing. It had been on this very porch, during a department party celebrating the end of the semester when Gwen had finished her master's degree at twenty-two, a party after which she would be leaving town for good, off to the Ivy League to pursue her doctorate, a goal she would achieve in record time. She had pressed her face against his chest that night as she bade her unlikely mentor a tearful farewell, him closing his eyes and capturing her in memory. Gwen had been Walt's only big crush other than Sam, the perfect young woman who worked part-time at the university library, shelving books and distracting boys with her ponytail and sleeveless tops. Walt had taught her in an undergrad class, and the two became fast friends in the way that opposites can, although he hadn't fooled himself into thinking that, were he single, she would have thought of him romantically. Walt figured that, to her, he was a lovable buffoon with an affable way, one who reminded her to breathe and relax, that nothing out there was really so important. Sam, with her ample self-confidence, referred to Gwen as the true object of her husband's desire, despite his protests to the contrary. And now she was here, the years having added not the weariness of age, but substance to her beauty.

"This is incredible. Walt Farnham. And here, of all places! Miss June told me there would be someone else working on the book, but I never imagined it would be you!"

"Oh, no, I'm not working on the book. I was just here today, um…visiting."

"He visits quite often," Miss June deadpanned. "Please," she said, motioning for Gwen to sit down. "You're just in time for tea."

Gwen sat, and Walt, the last twenty-four hours having just become even more surreal, wasn't certain of what to say. Miss June tended to her new guest, pouring and offering cookies, and then held court.

"Enough pleasantries. Now let's talk business."

Gwen sneaked a smile toward Walt. He had introduced her to Miss June in college, and she could now see that his old foil hadn't changed a whit.

"Listen, dear, your assistant on the book will be my friend Donald Nettleman. He's president of the Western Pennsylvania Historical Guild, and sits on the boards of a number of other organizations. He'll provide you with any reference materials you need. Also, I've alerted the directors of both the Heinz History Center and the Carnegie of your upcoming work. I'm sure you'll find them to be accommodating."

"Oh, this sounds perfect. And how do I get hold of Donald?" Gwen asked.

"You needn't bother. He will simply appear."

This was true. Donald Nettleman, a bespectacled and fastidious little man who wore bow ties to the grocery store, was smitten with Miss June, and had been for years. His sedan was in the drive at Hardwick nearly as often as Walt's truck, his visits lasting until Miss June shooed him away.

"And might there be a space at the History Center for me to work?"

"Oh, heavens no. You will do your work here. In fact, I've decided you'll stay here as well. I know you've arranged for an apartment, but really, how better to prepare your mind for the task than to sleep within the walls of Hardwick? You'll find it quite restful. Walter can attest to the fact that this house is conducive to sleep. Isn't that correct, Walter?"

"Hmm?" He'd been lost, looking at Gwen.

"Speak of the devil," Walt said.

Donald Nettleman tooted his car's horn as he pulled into the drive, or, more accurately, Donald had pulled into the drive, brought his Buick to a complete stop, tooted its horn, and then proceeded to pull slowly forward. He was an absurdly cautious driver and, for him, attempting something so cavalier as tooting his horn in greeting while the car was still moving was needlessly reckless. Time crept as Donald inched up the long drive, approaching Walt's truck, which sat halfway between the street and the house. The drive was plenty wide enough for Donald to pull around and continue forward, which seemed to be what he wanted to do, but he appeared uncertain as to whether such a maneuver should be attempted. He pulled forward a bit and began to turn the wheel, but then decided that maybe he hadn't turned the wheel early enough, and that he'd better back up and try again. Donald had long ago devised a curious safety technique, one where, prior to backing up, even in an empty parking lot, he would check his mirrors three times and then sound his horn twice before setting the car into motion. And if indeed someone did happen to walk or drive behind his car during this procedure, he would count to ten and then repeat the operation until he had successfully maneuvered into place. This annoying habit often caused passers-by to turn and look his way during the tooting phase, assuming that it was someone they knew, honking to say hello. The trio on the porch watched as Donald checked his mirrors, tooted, and then moved back ten feet, a trip that took quite some time. Walt fought the urge to yell *"Look out!"* Gwen sipped her tea as Donald made his second attempt, this time allowing too much room between his car and Walt's truck, causing his opposite fender to brush against the hedges. This warranted another backup procedure, but not before wiping his brow with his handkerchief and waving at them through the window, letting them know that, while he was momentarily detained, he'd join the party just as soon as he could get there.

"Oh, for heaven's sake," Miss June said, rising to head into the house. "You'd think he was piloting an ocean liner. Please excuse me for a moment."

"Is that the gardener's truck?" Gwen asked. "Perhaps he could move it."

"Oh, I think he'll leave it right there," Walt said. "Donald will figure this out." Walt recalled once when Donald had given him a ride in his Buick when the DORF wouldn't start, and opened the glove box to show Walt that there were airline-style sickness bags in there, should Walt become nauseated. Because Donald suffered from motion sickness, he assumed the same was true for everyone.

"It really is good to see you," Gwen said. "Of course, I'd planned on looking you up when I got here. What a surprise to find you here at Miss June's."

"I'm here a lot, Gwen," Walt said, brushing against the

truth that his life had taken a path that she might not expect. "I'm sure we'll be seeing each other quite a bit."

"I'd love to have dinner one night. With Sam, too, of course."

"Actually, Sam and I are divorced."

"Oh, no! I'm so sorry. When did this happen?"

"A few years back, I think. I'm not so good with time."

"I can't believe this. I always envied your marriage. One of the great ones, like my parents'."

"Your parents? I'm not that old."

"I didn't mean that. But, still. You two were such a pair. A much better match than my husband and me."

"You're married? But you're so young…"

"I'm thirty-four. And separated."

Was this possible? It was hard to imagine Gwen being old enough to be married, let alone separated. Walt felt an immediate dislike for her husband, despite having learned of his existence only seconds ago. The idea of her being married was unsettling.

"That's part of why I agreed to write this book. Take a sabbatical, get some distance, you know? Take time to sort things out."

"I'm sorry to hear this. I hope things work out."

"Oh, I don't. And they're not going to. I spent a month crying, but when I came up for air, I realized my friends were right. He's an ass."

Walt was glad Gwen's husband was an ass.

"All right, Gwenneth," Miss June said, reappearing through the screen door. "I'll show you your room now. I think we'll have time before Donald arrives."

"You could write half the book by then," Walt offered.

Gwen rose. Turning to Walt, she said, "I'd like to call about dinner. Can I get your number? Oh, wait, I haven't a pen."

"That's okay," Walt said, because he hadn't a number.

"I'll call you."

"I could try you at the university."

"That's not a good bet."

"Okay, you call me, then. Here, I guess."

"Will do."

As Walt headed toward his truck, Donald appeared from beneath the porte-cochere, where he'd finally managed to dock his car. He straightened his bow tie as he approached, recovering from the ordeal.

"Hello there, Walter, how nice to see you on this fine day. That was a pretty tight squeeze you left me there in the drive, I must say. They certainly don't make automobiles as small as they used to, do they?"

"Geez, Donald, I'm sorry about my truck. And wouldn't you know, I'm leaving anyway."

"Hmm, I see," Donald replied with mild consternation, one of his two varieties of affect, the other being a tally-ho sort of cheeriness. "Well, no harm done," he said, shifting to the latter. "And how might Miss June be today?"

This was an important question for Donald, as Miss June's mood dictated a lot for him. On a more ordinary day, Walt would have messed with him a bit, but today he just didn't have it in him.

"She's fine, Donald. A little worked up over this whole book thing, but otherwise just fine."

"Oh, that's great to hear. I'm quite excited about it myself and, I confess, rather eager to begin. But of course I don't want my anticipation to start things off on a tense note, you know. Conversely, I'm hesitant to seem less interested than I really am." He screwed up his face, unsure of what tack to take with the grand dame. "It's quite a quandary, actually. You see, sometimes when I pay a visit to Miss June, she finds my exuberance to be …"

"Just be yourself, Donald. Try that, okay?" Walt's headache was returning.

"Yes, of course, myself. That does make the most sense." He paused a beat. "Really?"

"Really. Maybe just a little less so than usual, okay?"

"Right-o!" he said, recharged. " 'Less so,' it is. Cheerio!"

"Right," Walt said. "Cheerio."

His truck caught on the first try, a plume of blue smoke filling the rearview mirror that he, unlike Donald, seldom checked. He backed out onto Fifth Avenue and looked toward the house, seeing two things before pulling away—Gwen watching from the living room window, and the oily piece of cardboard he'd forgotten to retrieve from the cobblestone drive.

Chapter 7

INDIAN SUMMER HAD COME sudden and strong. Sam could see Walt through her kitchen window, digging fence posts at the back of the property. The backyard had been rocky and overrun with weeds and junk trees for years, but the previous summer she and Walt had cleared the lot, renting a Rototiller and creating garden beds with truckloads of topsoil. Gardening was a new interest for Sam, one of the many domestic pursuits she'd discovered since marrying Arthur. At the university library, she'd had no time for such things. But thanks to Arthur, financial considerations were no longer as important, and so she had renegotiated her job, first reducing her responsibilities, and then, in a move that surprised many, had quit altogether. Because the backyard had been overgrown for so long, clearing it showed that Sam owned more property than they'd thought, which, given that gardening was among the ways she'd planned on spending her new-found free time, was a pleasant surprise. Additionally, with the thick nest of vines and tall sumacs gone, they gained a nice amount of morning sun. The downside was that the backs of the neighbors' houses were now more visible, and the privacy they'd taken for granted for so long was gone. Sam hadn't bugged Walt about building the fence for some time, and was surprised to find him working on it now. In the week since the party, he had managed to avoid contact with her despite her knocking on his door and leaving notes on his windshield. She knew that working outside, in full view of the house, was his way of coming out of hiding.

"Hey, handsome," she said, stepping down the stone path, a plastic jug of water in hand. Dewey bounded up to see her. As far as the dog knew, there had been no divorce—he and Walt just slept in the garage now.

"Hi, there," Walt replied, pausing between swings of the pick axe he was using to pry loose the rocks that were buried where the fence posts would go. Sam was still amazed at Walt's power, and when he swung the axe hard, she could feel the impact from where she stood.

"So, we're building fences today?"

"It's too nice a day to be inside."

"Should we be mending them, too?" she asked.

Walt, ready to swing the axe again, stopped and let it drop to his side. "No, there's no need for that," he said. "Listen, Sam. I'm sorry."

"*You're* sorry?! For what? I'm the one who owes you an apology. It was shitty, the way things happened at the party. I had no idea that was coming. I was really mad at Arthur for doing that."

"No, no. It's fine. I would have been as excited as he was." These last words, although true, came out wrong. He tried again. "I'm sorry I've been ducking you. Sorry about everything."

"Sweetheart, I tried to tell you about the baby—I tried

more than once—but forces conspired to keep it from happening. Granted, I chickened out a couple of times, but I did try. It killed me to have you find out like that."

"You're talking like this is a bad thing. You're allowed to have a baby. I'm happy for you, I really am."

"I just hope you're not thinking…" She didn't know how to finish her sentence kindly.

"That you figured I was too screwed up to be a father?"

"Yes. No! You're not screwed up. I'm just hoping you're not thinking that I think you are. Christ, this is all so fucked up."

"No, Sam, it's not. Listen, look at what's happening here. You're going to have a baby. A *baby*."

"I am, aren't I." She clutched her shirt. "Can you believe it? Can I really do this?"

Seeing Sam, whom he once saw open a beer bottle with her teeth, awash in self-doubt was rare.

"I think you've already done it."

"No, I mean, seriously. Can I do this? I don't know the first thing about children."

"Well, you had me for twelve years." He saw that she had begun to cry a little. He dropped his pick and put his hands on her shoulders. "Hey, hey. What's the matter?"

"I don't know. Nothing, really. I'm just so emotional anymore. This isn't like me." This was true. Sam was nothing if not self-assured, and had never been prone to mood swings.

"Listen, you're going to be a great mommy." His choice of words surprised them both, that he'd said "mommy" rather than "mother" or "mom." It sounded silly, and they laughed.

"Do you really think so? Because I can, Walt, I really think I can," she said, words hopeful, tone bespeaking doubt.

He pulled her close. "You're going to be a wonderful mother. I'm as certain of that as I've ever been about anything."

She wiped her nose on his shirt and then sat down on a stack of used brick they planned to use for the garden path. Walt sat opposite her on an oak stump. She breathed deeply and regained her composure. Dewey waddled over and placed his slobbery ball in her lap, his usual offering, suitable for all occasions. She scratched under his chin like she'd always done.

"I'll be okay. My hormones are just flying all over the place. That's what the doctor says anyway. Another couple of years, I wouldn't have been able to get pregnant." Sweat appeared through her tee-shirt and she drank a slug of water straight from the jug, giving her the look of a tearful construction worker. "At least it happened before I had to start all of that fertilization business." With those words, Walt lost the shameful hope that the pregnancy had been unexpected. That Sam would have undergone fertility treatments was hard to take. "But, hey, back when we were married, when I'd said I never wanted to have children, I was telling the truth, you know. Back then, things were just so. ..."

She didn't finish the sentence because she didn't have to. Walt understood. He knew how things were back then, how *he* was back then—the same as he was now, steady in his unreliability, not quite a disaster, but without ambition. And it hadn't been from lack of support. Sam had always encouraged Walt, as had his advisors and colleagues. But he was surrounded by an odd bubble, one that kept him from moving beyond a certain point. And even when Sam had decided she'd had enough, that she couldn't take it anymore, Walt didn't have a big reaction, was neither angry with her nor with himself. His friends were disappointed about the divorce, mostly that he didn't fight it. That he saw it as one more thing that was inevitable and beyond his control.

"Arthur's a good man," she said. "He really is. And he's not as rigid as he seems, not all of the time anyway. But sometimes," she softened her voice, "sometimes, I wish you could have been a bit like him. Just a little."

Walt nodded in quiet agreement. Arthur was a good man. And while Walt's initial reaction upon first meeting him was to think that he was simply the opposite of himself, time had shown Arthur to be not only anchored and organized, but of greater personal depth than might first be assumed. Though he enjoyed spending his time with his model ships and dental journals—both easy targets for ribbing from Walt—he was also committed to charitable efforts, working twice monthly at a neighborhood dental clinic in the Hill, providing free dental care for the poorest of Pittsburghers. Walt understood why Sam loved Arthur, from his sincerity to his enthusiasm, and even his love of old-time banjo music, although that did get him banished to the lower part of the garage when he practiced on occasion, at which point it became Walt's problem, not hers. Arthur may not have always been exciting, but excitement was not Sam's greatest need.

She continued. "Oh, fuck, listen to me. What am I doing? I came out here to make sure you're all right, and I'm saying everything I can to make you feel worse. I'm making a mess of everything." She wiped her tears with the heel of her hand.

"Can I say something now?" Walt said. "I won't lie and say I wasn't upset at the party. I'm not dumb enough to think you'd believe that."

Dewey moved over to Walt, resting his big head on his master's lap and letting out an exaggerated sigh.

"You're incapable of lying—I know that. That's why you've been ducking me."

"I know I'm nothing like Arthur," he went on, although he was quickly interrupted.

"No, listen, I didn't mean that…"

"Shh, it's okay. Let me finish. I know how I am. I'm a pain

in the ass. No one could stay married to me. With Arthur, you have a normal life. Dinner with other couples. Regular vacations. Cars that always start. Those things didn't happen with me. I don't blame you for leaving. I don't. But I am sorry you wasted so many years."

"I didn't say that!"

"Let me finish." She did, because it was so unusual for him to speak like this, to not joke when conversation turned serious. "My underachieving, my self-sabotage—whatever the hell it is—I've always just accepted it. It is what it is, you know? Life just sort of happens with me. I never figured I had much say in its outcome. But lately, I'm thinking about it. Sam, as much as I will always love you, I'm glad you got out when you did."

She became tearful again.

"I wasted no time with you," she said. "I wouldn't be who I am without you. I only wish we could've lasted forever. And in some way, we will. You'll never be out of my life. And I wouldn't give back one minute with you."

At that, Walt raised his eyebrows with mock skepticism, and Sam laughed. "Okay, there are some moments I'd give back." And gesturing toward the garage where he lived, she said, "But it really does seem like you'll never be out of my life."

Now it was Walt's turn again. "Okay, but listen, and this is important. I really am okay, and I really want you to have this baby and live happily ever after. I need you to know that. And this life," he said, looking toward her garden and house beyond, "this is right for you. I know I make fun of Arthur—who wouldn't?—but really, things have worked out right. I'm glad for you both."

"I know you are, and that makes me love you even more, you big goof."

They stood, and she wiped her face on his shirt, all tears

and snot, and pretended to become stern Sam once again. "Now get busy and build my goddamned fence."

He looked at the partial row of holes he had dug and frowned. "Actually, I'm losing interest in this project. Maybe I'll start something different tomorrow."

And as he had done so many times before, he made her laugh.

* * *

"So who's the babe?"

Jimmy's question from the next barstool caught Walt daydreaming.

"I'm sorry?"

"You should be sorry. A pretty girl like that staying at the old lady's house, and you don't tell me?"

"Oh, that. She's just an old friend. Teaches history at Harvard."

"She don't look like no bookworm, that's for sure. If they all looked like that, I'd get me a library card."

"You ain't goin' to no li-bary," Gene chimed in. "They'd bounce your Italian ass right out the door."

Such was the literary discourse at Gene's. Walt had abandoned the fence project, and had headed there for lunch.

"Oh, and you're a big book reader?" Jimmy shot back. "You ain't read nothin' since high school, I bet."

Gene was in one of his talkative moods. "I read Shakespeare in high school. *Julius Caesar*. What a bunch of horseshit that was. '*You thou doth bequeath that to me*,' and '*Thou done stabbed me in the back, Bruno*.' I read half that book and doth shat my pants."

"Brando," Jimmy said.

"What?" Gene asked.

"Marlon Brando. He played 'im in the movie. Julius Caesar."

"No, that was James Mason," offered someone from down the bar.

"No," Jimmy went on, "James Mason was Brutus. Deborah Kerr was the broad. It was Marlon Brando that was Caesar." He sipped his weak bar coffee. "There'll never be another Brando, I'll tell you that. *Mutiny on the Bounty*. Now that was a movie."

"Shakespeare didn't write no *Mutiny on the Bounty*," said Gene. He looked at Walt. "Did he?"

"He wrote '*Mutiny Up Your Ass*,'" Jimmy corrected.

"Speaking of Marlon Brando," Walt said, exasperated, "can I get something to eat around here?"

"Thou taketh their life into their own hands," Jimmy noted.

"Screw-ith you-ith," replied Gene, who threw a burger on the grill for Walt. He did that sometimes, deciding what his customers were hungry for without consulting them.

"How did you know Miss June had a house guest, Jimmy?" Walt inquired.

"I stopped by there. I was hungry."

"You were hungry?"

"I figured it was time for your morning snack from the old lady, and maybe I'd get something too."

"She's not running a restaurant, for God's sake."

"Tell me about it—she didn't have nothin'. Just crackers and cheese. Old lady food."

"Anyway," Walt continued, attempting to reel the conversation in. "What's your schedule like? I've got work for us."

Jimmy consulted his watch. "I need to take a haircut, and then I'm heading to Irma's for a little afternoon you-know-what. After that, I'm yours."

"I didn't mean today, but good, I'm glad you're available. I was thinking we'd start Monday morning. We've got to make a baby's room."

"That-a-boy." Jimmy patted Walt on the back. "You're a good man. I don't care what anybody says about you."

"Well, I can't have Arthur attempt it. He can build a schooner in a bottle but can't plug in a toaster without consulting an electrical engineer."

"He's a scientist, that one."

"But listen, Jimmy, this project, this one's different. We need to get this one done, soup to nuts."

"You're tellin' me that? I'll get the fucker done. Let me at it."

It was this very energy that Walt was hoping to tap. He would just need to keep it under control, so that the rest of the Friendship house didn't get dismantled in the process.

"Just show up at Sam's Monday morning. We need to demo the plaster, *carefully* I mean, and then I'll get started on the re-wiring and insulation. With any luck, we'll be hanging drywall within in a week." And at that point, he'd need Jimmy to move onto something else, as his efforts were best when limited to the destruction and rough carpentry phases. But if history proved correct, Jimmy'd be off by then on some wild goose chase anyway, pursuing yet another strange car or unsuspecting woman. "I'll call and order a dumpster."

"A dumpster? Now what would you go and do that for?"

Jimmy was a firm believer in the redistribution of construction debris, and he took somewhat of a world view of the matter. He considered the globe to be large, and the amount of plaster and old lumber that Walt generated to be comparatively small. Why spend a few hundred bucks on a dumpster, when there were perfectly good half-empty boxes all over town just waiting to be filled? That Jimmy's contributions occurred at night when no one was likely to happen by was beside the point. To his credit, he didn't add to the dumpsters of other small contractors, but instead targeted those at big construction sites or that sat unattended behind hospitals or, worse, behind the university where Walt once taught. Walt was absolutely opposed to stealing dumpster space, no matter who it belonged to, but Jimmy, always up for adventure, was hard to contain, and he often made night deposits without Walt's knowledge, usually in Walt's truck, seeing as it didn't require a key to start. Jimmy borrowed the DORF fairly often without asking.

"We need to be legitimate about this," Walt said. "I can't have Art's name turning up in illegally disposed of trash. He gets upset if…" He was going to say "if his library books are late," but he didn't want to risk getting the library conversation started again. Instead, he said, "…if he gets a parking ticket."

"What, you think they put the FBI on something like that? I'm just trying to save you a few bucks, pal."

"I know you are. But this job, I want to do this one right."

Jimmy sighed. "Okay. By the book."

Gene set Walt's burger in front of him along with a bowl of soup, which, apparently, he was hungry for too. "Hey, your lady friend's been looking for you," he said.

Deena.

"It's been a couple of weeks, hasn't it?" He thought about her, tried to figure out how, despite having had sex with her so many times, he still knew so little about the silent woman. He could only picture her doing things he'd already seen her do—drinking beer from the bottle, shooting pool, peeling out in her El Camino. Where did she work? Did she have friends? Watch television? Sing happy birthday? Were there other guys like him out there, sexual utensils she beckoned when needed? It was hard to picture her at a grocery store or a doctor's office. Sometimes he thought he should knock on her door early some evening—just show up unannounced—and see if she'd like to go to a movie or something similarly civilized. He had no notion that she'd accept, but given that he'd seen her naked, the gentlemanly side of him felt that it might be the appropriate thing to do. Of course, his rational side was half scared of her, and suggested he'd do better to leave well enough alone. Still, he thought about her tiny house sometimes. About the frilly curtains above her kitchen sink.

* * *

The next morning he lay in bed snoring like he meant it, when Dewey woke him up with a resounding woof and a heavy paw to the belly. This meant that it was exactly 6:00 AM, and that it was a Thursday.

"Can't I just sleep, buddy? Just this once?"

Dewey groaned his best denial in reply, so Walt rolled out of bed and looked out his window, seeing, as expected, Edward Heinzleman sitting in his pickup, waiting to drive Walt to their weekly breakfast at the Apache Diner. They used to just meet there, but as Walt proved unpunctual, Edward now came to pick him up. Walt suspected that Edward actually arrived well before six, waiting at the curb until it was time to pull into the drive. Walt made his way down the stairs and let Dewey out to do his business in Arthur's yard while he went back upstairs to put some pants on.

"Good morning, sir," Edward said when Walt joined him in the truck. Edward had been combing his hair as he so often did, maintaining his perfect side part. His hair was black and oily, making the paleness of his skin that much more unfortunate. He wore creased khaki work pants and a matching shirt, both made of some synthetic fiber that was impervious to everything. On his belt was a custodian-style keychain that held ten thousand keys, along with a small tape measure. In his shirt pocket was a #2 pencil, a pen light, a small screw driver, and a tire pressure gauge.

"Would it be okay if we turned that thing off?" Walt yelled, wincing. Edward was a ham-radio enthusiast who kept his receiver on what had to be full volume. The noise coming from the oval speaker mounted on the transmission hump sounded like a static-charged room of caffeinated truck drivers talking excitedly about absolutely nothing. That some of the contributions were in foreign languages was a fact about which Edward was inordinately proud, given that he spoke only English. Mercifully, he shut it off.

"Thank God," Walt said. "How can you stand that thing?"

Edward looked mildly scolded. Walt closed his eyes. The odor from the cleaning products Edward used on the truck was piercing. Although his was not a luxurious model, Edward was particularly proud of his truck, and over the years, he had adorned it with various running boards, seat covers, bug protectors, and a shiny black tonneau cover. No flashy decals or boisterous stickers, just after-market add-ons meant to embellish a very pedestrian vehicle.

They rode in silence until Edward asked, "Can I at least put the oldies on?"

"Sure."

The Apache was clean enough—unremarkable, consistent, and cheap. It was run by a grumpy Greek named Gus and his affable, gap-toothed wife, Lynda, who set sticky menus in front of the two men. Lynda smiled at Walt each week with an enthusiasm that suggested, incorrectly, that they had some sort of history together. Walt figured it was a habit she'd picked up decades before, waitressing in America before she really knew the language. Judging from the photos behind the cash register, Gus and Lynda had had the place since the seventies, and he wasn't sure why it was called the Apache, which sounded neither Greek nor welcoming. Had there been a giant fiberglass Indian out front—which there wasn't—he might have understood. Regardless, the restaurant was, as with most things in Walt's life, a habit, and its smell of ashtrays, eggs, and gyro meat just felt right.

"So, Edward. Tell me what's up." For Walt, that's why they were there, what the weekly breakfasts were really about—an outlet for Edward, whose awkwardness left him few people to talk to.

"Oh, you know. I'm keeping busy. I got my eye on a new rifle some guy I know is selling. Two more weeks 'til deer season."

"Ah yes, the great hunt."

"You don't know what you're missing."

"That's all right, Edward. I feel safer in the city." Actually, Walt loved the outdoors, but had no interest in killing.

"Venison tastes good."

"So I've heard. You hunters say that all the time."

"You just got to know how to cook it right, that's all."

"You hunters say that all the time, too.

They placed their orders, Edward with his usual pancakes, and Walt going for the Greek omelette. Lynda gave Walt the creepy and possibly horny smile again, and he did his best to be cordial but not encouraging.

"What's Dickhead got you working on these days?" Walt asked.

"I got some apartments I'm supposed to paint this week. Tenant's movin' out. They ain't got much electrical or plumbing work right now. But work's work, you know?"

"Yes, it is."

Edward was a handyman for Creighton Properties, a development company owned by Miss June's nephew, Reggie. It seemed like an awful job to Walt, low paying and thankless, and he felt bad for Edward, who took great pride in his work.

But in some ways, it was perfect for him, as he wasn't the type who got on well as part of a large crew. Edward drove between apartment buildings, fixing leaky faucets and sticky dead bolts. He collected the quarters from the coin-operated washers and dryers, and kept the sidewalks clear in the winter. In addition to his scheduled duties, he answered service calls, day and night. His specialty was heating and cooling, for which he had gone to technical school, but because there was only so much of that kind of work to do, Edward handled whatever problems arose. Although Edward wasn't aware of it, Walt had been instrumental in getting him his job. Reggie's company retained its own construction crew for the re-working of old buildings into apartments and condominiums, and it was on this crew that Edward and Walt first met. Having just quit the university, and because he was broke, Walt had reluctantly accepted a few weeks of employment from his nemesis. By lunchtime the first day, it was clear to Walt that Edward was out of place. While the other guys on the crew weren't quite cruel, they weren't kind either, and Edward was obvious prey. His clothes were different, and he could never name the ubiquitous rock songs that blared from their radios. He never knew what to say when the other guys carried on with their juvenile comments about women, and they'd picked up on it right away. Blushing and conspicuous, he smiled along, offering little in return. When he did try to fit in—to go along with the guys as they talked about a good-looking tenant in one of the apartments—his comments about women didn't ring true, causing Walt to wonder if Edward was shy, gentlemanly, or navigating the quandary of sexual confusion. Walt was pretty certain that, despite being in his mid-thirties, Edward was a virgin. And though he'd felt immediately protective of Edward, coming to his defense too adamantly would have only made things worse. Instead, he privately convinced Reggie to give him a job where he could work alone, thus making him Creighton Properties' first "maintenance specialist," and none the wiser as to Walt's involvement. And Reggie couldn't have hoped to find a more pathetically loyal and dedicated employee than Edward, who kept notebooks of when each building's furnace filters were due for a change, and who would jump out of bed in the middle of the night like a volunteer fireman if his pager went off. About a year after Edward started the job, Walt ran into him one morning in the street and their weekly breakfasts began.

Between bites Walt asked, "So, have you seen this Donna lately?" Donna was a nurse's aide whom Edward had mentioned a few times recently. Walt was trying to monitor the situation.

"Yeah, I give her a ride to a collector's show last weekend. She don't like to drive so much, so she calls me all the time. And besides, you know how she is," he said, despite Walt having never met the woman. "She does love her precious moments."

Edward fiddled with the napkin dispenser as Walt watched taillights disappear down Centre Avenue.

"I'm sorry?" Walt asked after a moment. "She loves what?"

"You know, her 'Precious Moments.' They're like these ceramic figurine things. That's what they're called. Precious Moments. She collects 'em."

"Oh."

"It was out at the Sheraton near the airport. The show. I bought her two things she's been wanting for her collection. Some ceramic kid that was prayin', and a little girl in a wedding dress near a dog. You shoulda seen this place. It was kind of like a gun show, but instead of guys it was girls, and there wasn't no guns."

"I see. Well, that was rather nice of you. Spending your

money and all. Are you sure you could afford it?"

"Yeah, I'm doing okay. Her hours got cut back at work last month, and she was a little short, that's all. I helped her out with the Precious Moments. And the snow tires." He slid his plate toward Walt. "You want some pancakes? I can't eat 'em all."

"No, thanks, I'm good." Walt's head was spinning a bit from Gus's cigarette smoke. His forearm was stuck to the table from old syrup, but he chose to let it stay. Lynda poured more coffee. Walt frowned.

"Wait a minute. Did you just say you bought this woman snow tires?"

"Yeah, you know. Two of them. For her car."

"Jesus, Edward. Snow tires? Are you two … dating?"

"Oh, heck, no," he scrambled. "Not really." His face reddened and he rearranged his silverware. "I don't know. I'm not sweet on her, if that's what you're askin'."

"Well, you know, that's a really big gesture. To buy someone snow tires, I mean. It's sort of, unusual, you know?"

"I don't know. She just needed them. Winter's comin' and the roads'll be slippy."

Walt wasn't sure what to say next.

"We haven't been kissing or nothin'."

"But you like her?"

"Well, she's kind of mean sometimes, but she's all right when she's in a good mood. Her job makes her feet hurt."

Jesus Christ. Who the hell was this woman?

"She tried the grapefruit diet for a while, and that didn't go so well. She did it for a whole weekend and it got her pretty agitated, so I picked her up and we went to the Olde Country Buffet and that seemed to help. She's kind of heavy, you know?"

Walt rubbed his temples. "Can I ask you a question? It might seem kind of odd."

"Sure."

"Do you think this, this Donna—do you think she likes you back?"

"Yeah, she likes me just fine."

"Okay, that's good. Because, you know, I'm just hoping that if the tables were turned, she'd buy you snow tires, too."

"But I don't need no snow tires, Walt. My tires are in good shape."

"Yeah, I know that. I doubt there's a better maintained truck in North America, but do you see what I'm asking you here? I mean, I'm glad you found someone to spend a little time with, but I hope she likes you for you. The way that I do. You're a hell of a nice guy, Edward. But, there are some people out there who might try to take advantage of your good nature."

"Yeah, I see what you mean. I've known girls like that before." Walt winced at that thought. "But so far, this one's okay. She can be mean, though."

"Well, will you do me a favor? Don't buy her anything else? At least not for a while. Do you promise? If you want to buy something, buy me breakfast," he said as he took the check himself and got up to pay Lynda who was waiting for him at the register by the bad photos of Greece and the bowl of dusty breath mints. Edward reached for his overly-thick wallet, but then saw that his friend had played a little trick on him, asking him to pay for breakfast, but then taking the check himself.

"You sure you don't want to come huntin' sometime?" Edward asked on the way back to Friendship. "You wouldn't have to shoot nothin'. We could just walk through the woods. It's so beautiful out there." He pronounced it *beeyooteeful*. "When I'm out there, I don't know. I just feel … different. You know? Like when you look around for miles and no matter how hard you look, you can't hear no one."

"I do know that feeling. I feel like that sometimes when I'm working, especially outside. When no one else is around, and it's just me and my tools, and everything is just all right."

"I never asked anyone else huntin' before."

"I appreciate that, Edward, I really do. And one of these days, maybe I'll just take you up on it."

"Honest injun?"

"Yep. Honest injun."

Winter

The heavy mower started on the seventh try, frightening the gangly teen as it came to life. Moving away from the garage and toward the center of the yard was akin to heading for deep waters, an inexperienced captain piloting a difficult boat. He worked hard to make the machine track straight, but the beast pulled stubbornly to the left. The woman watched grimly as the boy struggled to fill his father's shoes.

Chapter 8

THE DORF'S TIRES CRUNCHED THROUGH new snow on Amberson Avenue, Walt's view framed by a canopy of pregnant white branches, the oaks on either side of the street reaching out high above the road, meeting in the middle. The wet snow had come overnight, blanketing the city, almost masking the disparity between the rich and the poor. He was headed toward Fifth Avenue when he saw Reggie Creighton's Lexus SUV approaching. Walt had a fleeting hope that Reggie wouldn't recognize him, but the SUV flashed its lights and stopped in the middle of the street, and Reggie motioned for Walt to roll down his window. Walt's truck was not often mistaken for somebody else's.

"Hey, putz, where've you been?" Reggie asked.

"No place that you frequent."

"That's good for me—I've seen the shit-holes where you hang out." Reggie looked at Walt, at his messy hair, at the crumbs on his chest. He gave his truck the once-over and said, "You know, you amaze me. When are you going to get rid of this piece of shit?"

"Not everyone has your money, Reggie. Besides, I like my truck. It's easy to find in a parking lot."

Reggie Creighton had been Walt's least favorite person since childhood. Mean-spirited as a kid, his nature now served his career as a real estate developer whose specialty was converting old buildings into soulless apartments and condominiums. While this was not necessarily an evil endeavor, Reggie approached it with no regard for aesthetics or history, gutting structures of architectural significance to squeeze in as much leasable space as possible. At the negotiating table, Reggie allowed the weight of his surname to imply, not incorrectly, that he was as ruthless as any of the previous century's businessmen. Basically, he was a prick.

"How come you're not at my aunt's house having tea and crumpets?"

"I'm not there all the time. I do have other work," Walt said, not mentioning that he had been heading to Miss June's when Reggie flagged him down. The DORF's engine struggled in the damp air, and so he put it in neutral and the idle smoothed out.

"Oh, right. You also work for your ex-wife. You and your crack crew of retarded helpers. Sorry. When are you going to come and make some real money? My offer still stands."

Reggie often made a point of offering Walt a steady job, knowing he wouldn't accept. Walt's reluctance irked him, as it defied his belief that anyone could be bought. He did manage to get Walt to do odds and ends on occasion, however, at times when his money was especially low. Reggie liked hiring Walt to perform menial and, in Reggie's eyes, humiliating tasks, enough so that he was willing to pay him skilled wages to do them. But Reggie never got the enjoyment he was looking for, as Walt foiled him by enjoying hauling debris or clearing out the occasional vacant lot, taking both Reggie's satisfaction and his money at the same time. Plus, he often got to salvage some of the old woodwork and plumbing fixtures from the buildings before they were trashed, although, admittedly, most of these recovered gems ended up in Sam's garage.

"No thanks, Reggie. Even I respect myself too much to work full-time for a bastard like you."

Reggie laughed. "Whoa. How can you talk to me like that? After all I've done for you?"

A car had pulled up behind the Lexus, not able to get past, and now others were approaching as well. A horn was sounded gently, but if Reggie noticed, he gave no indication.

"Hey, listen. You still owe me my rugs. Drop them by my office tomorrow."

In one of his typically unfair deals, Reggie had acquired a number of oriental rugs from an old woman's estate for a fraction of their value. They'd been sent out for cleaning, and Walt was supposed to pick them up and deliver them to Reggie's office, a task he'd blown off for some time. Walt would have pointed out that the cleaners would probably deliver them free, but he could use the thirty dollars he intended to charge.

"I'll get to it."

"Do it sooner, not later. I need them. And get a telephone, for God's sake."

"I had one, but you called it once."

"You probably didn't pay your bill and they shut it off, is my guess."

Reggie liked jousting with Walt.

"I'll stop by tomorrow with the rugs. And I'll expect a check, too. You still owe me for cleaning out those garages on Aiken."

"Excuse me? I owe you nothing. You never sent me an

invoice, you moron."

Touché. Reggie insisted that Walt submit written invoices for any work that he did, no matter how small the amount, knowing it to be just the sort of task Walt had trouble getting together. And although Creighton Properties was a sizable entity, with numerous big money projects under construction at any given time, Reggie always knew where he and Walt stood, right down to the penny. It was part of the game.

"I'll piss you one in the snow. You can read it from your office window," Walt said.

Multiple horns were sounding now, so Walt put his own truck back in gear and pulled away, but not before hearing Reggie's farewell of "Later, loser." Reggie cleaned and adjusted his sunglasses before setting the SUV in motion, while Walt fielded glares from the drivers being held up.

As a child, during Saturdays at Hardwick with his father, Walt dreaded the times when Eliza Creighton would visit her cousin June, her son Reggie in tow. Two years older than Walt, Reggie was fairly cruel to the younger boy, subtly so when in the presence of adults, but brutally when the two were alone. The torture was emotional. *"I could have your dad fired, you know. What would you do then?" "Look at that car your father drives. Our car is much better."* Walt was pretty sure that there was no connection between the Creightons and Gilbert Chemical where his father worked, and that Reggie couldn't really have his father fired, but still, he'd made his point. Although Reggie's own father was dead, his family *did* seem powerful. Their cars *were* nicer. Reggie always got the latest toys, even if he did tire of them quickly, breaking them intentionally after offering to give them to Walt. But Walt also knew that despite having nearly any thing a boy could want, Reggie wanted his company as well, and with the skilled instincts of an emotionally needy bully, knew just how far to go before pulling back. He was kind to Walt just often enough to keep him around — paying his admission to the movies or letting him try one of his toys while it was still intact — and Walt sensed that Reggie had few real friends. He dreaded their time together, but accepted its inevitability — because Reggie was a Creighton, Walt figured he was a problem he would have to endure. This acceptance of fate proved sadly prescient, as the sudden death of his own father would soon make permanent Reggie's place in Walt's life.

* * *

There had been a trip to the courthouse downtown, a large castle-like building where the woman and a robed man spoke in muted tones, just out of earshot. *"Heart attack,"* were among the few words young Walt did hear her say. He sat quietly on a hard, wood bench, stretching his leg so that his foot could press against the nearby radiator, its heat working its way through the flat rubber sole of his sneaker until it hurt just the right amount. The robed man looked his way once or twice as Miss June spoke, nodding his head in agreement. This was what authority looked like.

There was a trip to Horne's department store, where he was attended to by a brusque man with pins in his mouth. The service was modest and not well attended, mostly adults Walt didn't know. After the casket was lowered, the two began the walk back to the car, a uniformed driver leading the way.

"Well," she said. "That would be that."

He would stay with her now. There was no one else. They would fix a room for him — wherever he liked, she said, doing her best to seem kind. He chose one facing the back yard,

across from the greenhouse, high enough to see East Liberty
in the distance, from the big Sears store where his father bought
him his school clothes, to the brick Nabisco factory that smelled
of graham crackers on winter mornings. In the social strata of
elementary school, Walt resided among those whose common
trait was vagueness—silent observers seeking to avoid contro-
versy. The rented house he and his father shared was clean but
sparse, and his dad's reserve lent an awkward quality to the
air—there were few after-school visits from friends. The move
to Hardwick during the winter of sixth grade cemented his
status as an outsider. He didn't belong to any clubs or teams,
and though he was not disliked, he was also not thought about
in general, which was not bad given his strange new home life
and the teasing it could have provoked. Days at Hardwick were
quiet. Miss June went about her dry activities—club meetings,
letter writing, formal sounding phone calls. Walt was a shadowy
presence—a silent explorer. She treated him not as a child,
but as a small adult, with expectation replacing nurture in
her role as guardian, and with no softness to her being. The
surfaces of the house were equally hard—oak, plaster, china,
brass. While the place was usually still, sounds, when made,
were harsh and sharp in timbre. Beyond his selecting a room,
the two never discussed his living there. It simply would be.

Until, he thought, *my mother comes back.*

* * *

"Well, it's about time you showed up, young man. I was
foolishly beginning to think you'd found gainful employment
elsewhere." She was in the sitting room, as was Gwen.

Walt had been avoiding Hardwick, and each day he didn't
show up meant that his eventual arrival would be cause for
that much more grief. He didn't often go for more than a

day or two without checking in, if only to make sure that the old woman was doing all right, but since Gwen was staying there, he figured he didn't have to be so diligent. Although, of course, there the irony lay—Gwen was the reason he'd been avoiding the house in the first place.

"I apologize, dear lady. I've been quite busy with other things of late," Walt said, offering the exaggerated tip of an imaginary hat.

"Do tell. So I am now to believe that you have more than one string on your bow?"

Gwen enjoyed their volley.

"If that means that I have things to do other than spend all of my days in your pleasant company, then yes, you are correct, madam—my bow is well-strung."

"Hmmpf," Miss June replied with what was, despite the usual precise nature of her speech, one of her more effective responses. "Well, there is quite a list waiting for you on the piano nonetheless."

Miss June's lists were legendary. Written in her flawless hand since the beginning of time, they were a constant in Walt's life. The paper they were written on was peculiar and aged, having come, he imagined, from some stuffy stationer downtown, one of those narrow but deceptively long keyhole shops like Ness' Lamp Repair or Acme Button. As well as Walt knew every nook and cranny of Hardwick, he'd never seen her supply of tablets, and would have to admit to more than one afternoon of futile snooping trying to find them. And although any one of the lists would appear to the casual observer to be just that, an individual, finite list, they were, in fact, part of one continuous list, one that spanned decades, morphing from one sheet of mystery paper to the next. On the rare occasions when Walt had worked his way to the last remaining item, a new list would magically appear in its place, with the previously final item residing at the top and at least a half-dozen equally unappealing tasks spelled out below. If compiled into one epic tome, Walt's list would rival in length, he was sure, the lifetime production of Tolstoy, without even accounting for the repeats—perennial favorites such as the seasonal moving of the shutters, or the annual breathing of the upholstered furniture.

"A list? For me?" He took off his coat.

"Organization is not a virtue to be scoffed at, young man."

"I scoff not, I assure you. Your list will be addressed with my usual attentiveness." Why hide the nature of his relationship with Miss June from Gwen, he decided. The truth would become evident soon enough.

"If your usual attentiveness is what I should expect, then please excuse me while I go prepare myself a cocktail. Have we any arsenic?" To Gwen, she said, "Dear, I'll be upstairs. Please call if you need me."

"Will do, Miss June."

Neither Gwen nor Walt spoke as Miss June made the long ascent up the front stairs. The house had a small elevator that she'd never admit to using, but Walt suspected that in recent months she'd been sneaking rides when no one was around to know.

"So," he said, finally, plopping down across from Gwen. "How's history?"

Gwen was surrounded on the sofa by notebooks and photographs. She sat sideways, her legs tucked up under her like a schoolgirl, a posture Miss June would disapprove of, but one that for Walt was not without allure.

"The same as always. Just interesting enough to keep me involved. It's funny how that works. I'm still in search of that one small fact that will turn things on their ear."

"And you think you'll find such a fact here?" Walt asked,

nodding toward the boxes of papers and photographs Gwen had been given to pick through.

"Well," she said, lowering her voice and glancing toward the stairs. "I can't say that I've found much, but there are things to be uncovered. They just haven't surfaced yet."

"I can assure you that there's nothing in those boxes that she isn't completely familiar with. If it's skeletons you're looking for, you'll need to look elsewhere."

"This is sanitized material, isn't it."

"The Creighton men are saints. Don't you know that by now? Regardless, she couldn't have chosen a better historian than you to write this book. No matter what you have to work with, it'll be great."

Gwen went through the motions of straightening her scattered papers, embarrassed by praise from her former teacher. She absentmindedly placed a thick strand of hair in her mouth, a habit Walt remembered from her college days.

"I got the books you sent," he said. "They were brilliant." A few years before, he had received a beautifully bound and illustrated two-volume set, written by Gwen and published by Harvard's press. Walt had been remodeling Sam's powder room when the books arrived, the same day an old commode had cracked as he lifted it, causing a gash on the heel of his hand that required seven stitches to close. Walt had fixed the wound with duct tape, but Arthur had insisted he go to the emergency room to have it properly repaired. When Walt refused, Arthur did it himself.

"The department forwarded them to me at home. I was awestruck." Gwen glowed, and he saw that, incredibly, his opinion still mattered to her. "I'm sorry I didn't call to congratulate you. I'm pretty bad about such things."

"I know you are," she said with a laugh. "But it's you who should be writing this book, Walt." She then said gently, "Miss

June told me you've left the field."

And like that, it was out.

"Yes, well, there was no future in history for me."

"But why? You were so … inspired. So smart."

"Oh, please. I liked to teach, but that was it. I couldn't even finish my dissertation. It should have been done by the time I met you. I picked at it, but I had problems with …"

"Discipline?"

"I was going to say 'motivation,' but, yeah, I wasn't so hot on discipline either."

"But you were a fixture there." She looked at his work boots. "What happened?

Walt smiled at the question, and Gwen tensed, worried she'd been rude.

"Oh, no!" she said. "I didn't mean 'What happened?' as in 'What the hell happened?,' I meant it like, what happened to prompt your change in direction?' "

He smiled. "Actually, 'What the hell happened?' is the right question to ask." He considered the snow outside the window, as if the answer were out there to be found, his smile fading as the big flakes made their descent, falling lazily like in a somber old movie. "Not long after you left for Boston, I got …" He paused, not sure what he had "got." "Complacent, I suppose. School just became something I did. Time passed." He thought for a moment, wondering how to describe the inertia that eventually got so bad that not even his mentors objected when he decided to drop out. "I just couldn't get over the hump. I liked teaching, but lost the fire for the rest, you know? Anymore, I'm not sure I ever really had it. Not like you do — you're the real thing. I hung in there for another couple of years and then gave up. Even the janitors were relieved when I finally left."

She nodded, kindly.

"You're not surprised," he said.

"Well, not exactly. I mean…" She looked for words.

"I'm sorry. I'm putting you on the spot."

"No, it's okay." The two sat quietly for a moment, the only sound being one that Hardwick sometimes made, an occasional creak meant to confirm its presence in every scene. "I used to look up to you, do you know that? You were everything that was right about academia."

"I was a disaster! I couldn't grade papers on time, I took my students outside to play Frisbee—"

"But you cared! You really cared, and that's what mattered. Your classes were different. You're why I chose history, you know. I started out as an English major."

Gwen's poems appeared twice in the student quarterly, dreamy pieces that, had Walt been able to read objectively, he would have seen for the mediocre works that they were. At the time, though, he liked to believe they were better than the rest.

"My father was pushing for law school, which I began to entertain for all the wrong reasons, but after your classes, there was no question about what I would do."

"You didn't mention me to your father by name, I hope."

"You were a wonderful teacher."

He couldn't quite disagree with her about that. He may have been a lousy Ph.D. candidate, but he was spirited in the classroom, and his students responded. While he was no academic match for the brightest of them and their ability to connect dates with facts and learn arcane particulars by rote, he tried to help them grow in other ways, sharing his wry, subversive approach to life. And in a field as dry as history, his was a subversive message indeed, his classes being equal part philosophy, with every suggestion or slant inferred in the classic texts being subject to scrutiny. It was suggested to him more than once that he was doing his students a disservice by teaching this way—exactly who was he to dispute the approach of his more accomplished predecessors?—and he understood the argument. But what harm could he do by urging his students to question everything, when he included his own teachings among those that should be questioned? He loved when his students argued that he was wrong to question what had been long accepted by the venerable establishment, as the posing of that very argument proved his personal success right on the spot.

Gwen had begun her first class among the over-achievers, a group conditioned to fret about exams. These were the kids Walt had to work on the most, eventually easing the problem preemptively by holding a vote on the first day of class as to whether or not the class should even have tests. The under-achievers were a reliable no-vote, and played nicely into Walt's hands. Fair enough—no tests. But be prepared to explain, clearly and with originality, what you have learned. He wanted them to understand and be able to critique American culture, using its history to figure it out. To not merely study the past, but to judge it, to have opinions, and it was this stating of opinion that the brightest in the room often had trouble with as a measure of achievement—it's hard to quantify an opinion. Every once in a while, a complaint would be made to the department chair; twice, directly to the chancellor. "Are they unhappy with their grades?" Walt would ask. "Because I'll give them an 'A' if that's what they're worried about. It's just a letter from the alphabet—I've got plenty of them. Just so long as they leave my class having learned one thing—that while facts may be gospel, interpretation of them is their own." Gwen, at first, was not vocal in class. He privately pegged her as being one who would have trouble with the milieu, one who would find leaving the familiarity of clear-cut assignments and tests discomforting, a nervous-making trip into uncharted waters with no obvious path for success. But he had guessed wrong. Her initial silence was simply her style. For the first few weeks, she absorbed what was said in class. When she finally spoke, she provided insight into not only the topic at hand, but used Walt's own philosophy in an argument against his position, leaving him duly impressed. She'd cleaned his clock, and their mutual admiration grew. And now, years later, she was the professor and he the aimless one.

"I'm sorry if I disappointed you," he said now. "I really am. But I think I'm just supposed to be a carpenter."

"A carpenter's a fine thing to be. You've found your world."

"I suppose I have," he said, his answer flirting with both truth and lie. Since the news of Sam's baby, he wasn't sure where he belonged anymore.

"I bet you're the best at what you do," Gwen said. "Miss June speaks highly of you."

"Oh, come on," he replied. "She doesn't speak highly of anyone who's still alive."

Gwen laughed. "You're right. Actually, she complains about you endlessly. But she wouldn't bother if she didn't care. She cares about you a great deal, you know."

"Well, she's an odd duck, that one."

"I know she is. But I find your devotion to her to be... sweet."

"My 'devotion'? Jesus. Just how much do you two talk about me?"

She pretended to be coy. "Oh, not that much. Not directly, anyhow. But I'm learning how to read her, you know? I think I'm figuring her out."

"Well, be careful. That little woman lets nothing slip out that isn't intended for you to hear. She's sharper than you know. Anything you unearth in all of those papers and photographs is exactly what she wants you to find."

"Donald and me, you mean. My diligent helper."

"Yes, Donald. He'll lead the charge. Or at least lead you in the Creighton family cheer."

"He fancies Miss June something awful, doesn't he?"

"Awful it is. I hate to see him put himself through the wringer like he does. He hopes to win her heart but doesn't have a chance."

"Well, I think he's cute. I like his tidy suits, his funny way of talking. It's like he's from another decade."

"If not another planet."

As if on cue, the front door opened and Donald's little head popped in. "Yoo-hoo," he trilled in near falsetto. "Don't be alarmed, it's only me."

It was hard to imagine who could be alarmed by Donald Nettleman. The answer though, apparently, was Donald Nettleman himself, who, as he looked across the foyer, saw his reflection in the mahogany-framed mirror and, startled, exclaimed, "Oh! There I am! Ha-ha." Like Arthur, Donald also laughed by saying *"Ha-ha."*

Walt rose to face the music of Miss June's list when Gwen said, "You know, I've been getting a little claustrophobic here lately. Can we go for coffee some night? Maybe a drink?"

"That would be great. I owe you dinner, if I'm not mistaken."

"Hey, do you remember that dive bar you used to take us students to back when? The crappy place with the pool table? Not far from the library?"

"Gene's Bull's-Eye?"

"Yes! That's the place. Is it still there?"

"You know, I think it is."

"Wouldn't it be crazy to go there sometime? Just for a laugh, I mean?"

"Sure," he said. "Just for a laugh."

Chapter 9

ON THE BRIGHT SIDE, the contents of Sam's refrigerator had improved dramatically after her first marriage failed. She had been an indifferent cook at best, and Walt, happy enough with mere quantity, ate pretty much whatever she sat before him. But with her second marriage came a husband who was used to well-prepared meals, and because Arthur himself was quite the chef, Sam was determined to improve her own skills. For much of her first year with Arthur, Walt was her daytime guinea pig, trying out in secret the dishes she attempted while Arthur was at work, a fair number of which ended up down the garbage disposer. Walt enjoyed those weekdays in their old kitchen, with Sam uncharacteristically flustered, crusts burning, milk scalding, smoke detectors shrieking. One of his favorite moments was watching her attempt to assemble the latticework atop a rhubarb pie, struggling with the thing until it became a hopeless mess. "Fuck this shit," she'd decided, pitching it into the garbage, pan and all. He was fond of both

Sams—the new one, with her unexpected and quaint domestic aspirations, and of course the old one as well, she who reacted to ruining yet another dish not with tears or frustration, but with the declaration that the task she'd been attempting was stupid in the first place, and that it was time for a midday beer. And although Arthur continued to do much of the cooking, Sam's contributions had improved quite a bit. Now, this morning, alone and rummaging through their fridge, Walt landed on a pork loin and some sort of sweet potato casserole. He'd made the chilly trek from the garage to the main house wearing boxer shorts, over which his belly figured prominently, and a flannel shirt that draped tent-like, having first slipped into a pair of unlaced work boots that weren't quite as high as the snow was deep. He had also donned a Russian-style fur-lined hat with flaps that hung past his ears. He was bent over the fridge in this ensemble, loading his arms with food, when Dr. Art happened by.

"Hello, Walter."

Because Walt's mouth was holding a rolled Zip-Loc baggie of what he thought might be asparagus, he could only hum "hello" in reply, and he backed out, busted but unconcerned. With his full mouth and fur hat, he looked like a bear who'd been mildly surprised while pulling a salmon from a stream.

"Finding everything okay?"

"Pretty much so," Walt mumbled. "Care to join me?" His words would have been indecipherable were it not for Arthur's profession.

Arthur consulted his watch. "It's only ten o'clock. I don't eat lunch until 11:50. Oh, goodness gracious, perhaps I will. What the heck." He said this in a cavalier fashion, as if disrupting his usual dining schedule revealed a devil-may-care attitude. He took plates and silverware from the island cabinets and set them on the counter. A nice touch, Walt thought.

"How come you're not at work?" Walt asked.

Arthur sighed. "Actually, that's something I need to talk to you about." He sat down and fussed with the plates and napkins, readjusting the utensils so that they were parallel and equally spaced. "You know, it's not always easy to discuss difficult things with close friends."

"Just say it."

"I'm meeting a contractor here this morning. For the baby's room."

The words hit hard. Despite being used to being given up on, this was different. Someone else's hands on this house were nearly as bad as someone else's hands on Sam.

"Surely you understand. We simply need to get it done, sooner rather than later. I mean, as busy as you are, we're not sure how you'll find the time. But listen, Sam and I…"

"You don't have to say it, Art. I know. The kid'll be in college before I get my shit together."

"What I was going to say was that Sam and I know that whomever we hire won't do as good a job as you would have. I mean that. But we do have a fixed timeline here. I'm sorry, Walter."

As sometimes happened, Walt began to feel almost as if he were falling down a hole, slowly and backward, but with no fear of hitting bottom. It was a mildly sad sensation, but not completely unpleasant either. And while he couldn't recall exactly when he'd felt it before, he assumed the circumstances were similar to these—he was a disappointment once again. Although Art's decision wasn't a complete surprise, the timing was somewhat ironic, as Walt had been making unusual progress on the Friendship house, fueled by the last few weeks of avoiding Hardwick. The dining room ceiling was still cracked, but he'd finished installing the living room quarter-round, fixed the lock in the powder room, and pulled the carpet in what had once been his own study, the small room that would soon belong to a baby. Still, he knew that despite his progress, with this very different kind of deadline not six months away, Arthur was wise to doubt him.

"Walter, might I ask you a personal question?"

"Is it about what I'm wearing?"

"No, although there are questions I could ask about that. No, this is of a different nature. I'm not sure, though, precisely what it is I want to ask." He sat back and squinted at Walt. "Perhaps my question is, how is it that you're always so… comfortable?"

"Comfortable?"

"Perhaps 'unflappable' is the better term."

Walt considered. "Well, I don't set my sights too high, Doc. That's part of it. It doesn't mean I never worry, though."

"No, of course you do. But look at us, Walter. In some ways we're not such different fellows. We're both bright, both educated. But I rise each morning before the sun and do my calisthenics without fail—my routine is from the Canadian Royal Mounted Police Manual, you know. I then shower, read the papers over breakfast, and am in my office to see my first patient by 7:15. It's all precisely planned. Not a thing is left to chance. That's the best way to conduct one's life, I've always said—with consistency."

"And?"

"Well, if it's not too forward of me to say, I think you would benefit from a routine like mine."

"You want me to drill people's teeth?"

"You know what I mean. A bit of self-discipline might be good for you. That's all."

"I see. And might you have been talking to Sam about this?"

"No, no. Not lately, anyway. I mean, we talk, of course,

like married people do"—Arthur immediately regretted that particular choice of words and continued quickly—"but this comes directly from me. And I offer it as a friend. You do know that."

"I do know, Art, and thank you. For your concern. I mean it. But now let me give you a little advice." He paused. "Don't count on me changing too much. I don't come through."

Upstairs, Sam ran a vacuum cleaner while the two men ate in silence. Dewey lay below, hoping for fallen scraps, his guess being that, should they come, they would do so from Walt's side of the table.

* * *

That night, Walt lay in bed looking across at the main house, watching the glow of the television flicker through the curtains. He watched until the set was turned off, followed by other lights throughout the house, all but one in the bedroom. He watched until that window, too, became dark, leaving only the garage floodlight to cast shadows of tree branches across his own bedroom wall, a photoplay backdrop that moved flatly with the wind.

* * *

The car careened as his mother laughed. She was telling a story—one that he didn't understand. She was excited, like there was another grown-up in the car, one who would appreciate the hysterical nature of the tale. His side of the car scraped against parked cars as she went on.

He was four years old. He cried for her to stop.

"Don't you see how this is funny, sweetie?" she said. "It's like a ride!"

But the ride was going too fast and he wanted to get off, wished once again that she wasn't so happy.

The next day, Walt was still in his pajamas. Cartoons were over and Daddy was at work. He ventured into his parents' room, went to the bed.

"It's lunchtime, Mommy."

"Get it yourself," she mumbled, eyes closed, voice thick.

* * *

Winter in Pittsburgh is a long affair. After the first big storm, the snow turns slush gray with rust-colored streaks in the gutters, and the sky remains dull silver until spring, a test of endurance for those who flirt with melancholy. Having been excused from the work at Sam's, and with nothing else lined up, Walt headed to Miss June's, where his list would be waiting for him on the piano. He pulled into the cobblestone drive to find two men in the front yard, one of whom was rewinding a long tape measure while the other focused his eye through a transit that sat atop a surveyor's tripod. His dander rose immediately.

"What's going on here?"

"We're measuring," came the reply.

"Yeah, I can see that," he said, his anger increasing. "Measuring for what? Who told you to do this?"

"The office, like always. If you got questions, you'll have to call them."

Walt headed inside the house to get to the bottom of things.

"Miss June?" he called. "Hello?"

"Hi, there," Gwen said, entering from the hall.

"When did those men get here?"

"An hour ago? It looks like they're measuring or something."

"Did Miss June see them?"

"No, she's out with Donald. Another doctor's appointment, I think."

Another appointment? He hadn't been aware of a previous one.

"Did she say anything about this to you?"

"No. Is something wrong?"

Walt looked out the window as Reggie's Lexus pulled into the drive, further darkening his mood.

"Yes. No. Shit." He tossed his keys on the table. "I don't know."

"You're not making sense. Who are they?"

"Well, the asshole in the SUV is Reggie Creighton. He's the…"

"Son of James and Eliza Creighton," she interrupted, "born August 10, 1955, at Shadyside Hospital."

Walt look perplexed.

"I'm a historian," Gwen said. "Remember? It's my job."

"Oh. Right. Well, you can go ahead and mark down that he died on January 18th."

"He died two days ago?"

"No, today."

"Today's the 20th."

"Whatever. I'll do the killing, you write the history."

Walt stormed to the SUV where Reggie ignored his rap on the window, holding up his index finger and continuing his phone call without looking. Walt banged harder. Again, the raised finger. Finally, Walt opened the door, and, from the living room window, it looked to Gwen as if he were going to drag Reggie out. Instead, he reached in and laid on the horn for a solid ten seconds, interrupting Reggie's call.

"Hang up, Reggie, or I swear I'll rip this door off its fucking hinges."

There was no question he could do it.

"Okay, okay." Reggie got out of the SUV and adjusted his coat, establishing his composure. "Jesus."

"What the hell is going on?" Walt demanded.

"What are you talking about?"

"Don't give me that shit. What are these guys measuring for, huh? Have you got some plans I don't know about?"

"They're just surveying. It's for an appraisal, that's all. Sheesh, settle down."

"An *appraisal*? Don't tell me to settle down, you goddamned vulture. Get those guys out of here, now."

"It's not hurting anyone if they take some measurements. What's the difference?"

Walt started toward the yard. "Okay, fellas, that's a wrap. Go on, get out of here." The men exchanged looks, unsure of what to do. "Go on. Now!" Walt yelled, towering over them. When they didn't move, he grabbed the tripod in his massive paw and slammed it to the ground, sending expensive pieces flying.

"Hey, hey, calm down, you win. We're going!"

Walt took a breath. "Look, I know you're following orders. But you're done here, okay? And if Dickless over there tells you to come back, you'll deal with me. Got it?"

"Hey, we won't even drive down this street anymore. Just stop throwing our stuff."

Walt turned back to Reggie. "Just what the hell do you think you're doing? Did you know Miss June was going to be out this morning, or were you going to pull this little charade right in front of her?"

"If you must know, yes, I was aware that she'd be out. I'm not insensitive. But I don't understand what you're so upset about. It's not like I'm here to steal anything. I'm getting dimensions of the lot, taking some photographs, that's all."

"Hardwick belongs to her, Reggie. A Creighton or not, you have no business here." His pulse was high. "I swear to God, if you pull this shit again, I'll..."

"You'll what? Huh? What exactly will you do, Walt? What have you ever done? Are you going to hit me? Call the police? Just what is it you'll do?"

Walt's anger brought the taste of copper to his mouth, which was precisely the reaction he used to have when Reggie's childhood torment pushed him close to the edge of losing control. But he never did. Even after Walt had grown much bigger than the older boy, when he could have knocked him out with one blow, he still was held in check, paralyzed by a peculiar force he couldn't have described. And for Reggie, it was his ace in the hole. *"Pussy,"* he used to say. That one word said so much.

"She's an old lady, Reggie," Walt said. "This house is everything to her. Just leave her alone. Is that too much to ask?"

"Fine," he said, getting back behind the wheel and turning the key. "I can get this information from the city anyway. You know, you need to relax. You're going to have a heart attack getting worked up like that. Wasn't it your father who used to talk about stress? He was always full of sound advice." Reggie knew he was hitting a sore spot by bringing up Walt's father, an honorable man he used to mock. "What was it he used to say? Oh yeah, I remember: *'Don't fight the inevitable.'* I like that. He was a smart guy, your old man. Quiet, but when he spoke, he had something to say." Reggie began to back out of the drive. He looked dreamily at Hardwick. "*'Don't fight the inevitable...'*"

Back inside, Gwen looked at Walt like she'd never laid eyes on him before. "What was that all about? I would have called the police, but it would have been you they'd have carted away."

He rubbed his temples. "It was nothing. Reggie and I do battle from time to time. You want to know the strange part? He likes me. He thinks we're friends."

* * *

"So tell me about your husband. What was he like?"

The waitress cleared their lunch dishes and brought another round of Coke, which had arrived with slices of lemon speared with miniature plastic swords. Following the excitement on the lawn, Gwen and Walt had headed for the Squirrel Cage for an early lunch. On the television behind the bar, a soap opera occupied the bartender and his only customer.

"Well, he's not dead, for one thing," Gwen pointed out. "I just wish he were."

"Sorry. What *is* he like. He's a shrink, right?"

"Richard is a psychiatrist. A strict Freudian. They're not exactly in fashion these days."

"The shrinks I've done work for seem to have the most problems. At least their families do, anyway."

"I'm not surprised. He comes from a long line of psychiatrists, all of whom are either divorced or should be. The men in his family are very clinical. It's eerie." She sipped her Coke. "It's terrible to be lonely when you're with someone."

"I'm sorry."

"It was odd, like I was just there to play a role or something. Nothing about me mattered. Toward the end, I threw a drink in his face at a party. Not my best moment, I admit. It just flew out of my hand, I was so furious at him. But when it happened, right in a room full of people, he just dried himself with a napkin, and asked calmly, *'Now, what exactly caused you to do that? Can you tell me what you're feeling right now? While it's still fresh?'* "

"Jesus."

"To be fair, he is kind, that I can say. Generous, too. And that's what I saw in him at first. You know how people fall in love. They see only the good parts. At first I thought it was funny how he was so serious all of the time, so analytical. I thought he just needed someone to loosen him up a bit. And I did, you know? I brought him out of his shell for a while."

"But it wasn't enough."

"No. I tried, I really did. To have things be spontaneous, to not have everything be so … controlled. But what I realized, what I finally realized, was that that was our basic problem—it was always me who tried to make things work. He didn't try to change for me. We just shouldn't have gotten married in the first place." She played with the little plastic sword that had been impaling her lemon, bending it back and forth, back and forth. Walt watched it being bent, mesmerized. A white line appeared at the point where it was being folded, and he wondered if it would break, or if the soft plastic had enough elasticity to just keep being worked back and forth, over and over. He could have watched it forever. "It's my fault," she said. "I wanted him to be somebody else."

"It wasn't your fault."

"How do you know?"

"I just do."

She would always have men wanting her, he thought, would have to sift through many to find the one who was right.

"Do you think any of us meet exactly the right person?" he asked her. On the soap opera, two people thought they were doing just that.

"Our perfect mate, you mean?"

"Yeah. Is it possible? For two people to be perfect for each other?" He thought about Sam, about how perfect they'd almost been.

"I have to think so," she said. "It's too sad to imagine otherwise. Yes. I think it can happen at any time. It could happen right now."

Walt snapped his own plastic sword in half.

"You could look over at that door and the perfect woman could just walk right in," she finished.

"Oh." He put his broken cutlass in the ashtray. "I suppose that's true."

"What about you, Walt? Do you think you'll get married again?"

"Me? I'm not even dating anyone. Not really."

"I find that hard to believe." She traced her finger around the top of her glass. "You must have plenty of opportunities."

"Hardly. I've just not been in that frame of mind or something. Since Sam, things have been different." He thought about the housewives he'd spent so much time with as he worked, a number of whom had left no doubt that if he'd tried to kiss them, they would have kissed back. And then there was Deena, the sexual mercenary—he was pretty sure she didn't count.

"Do you miss Sam?"

"It's not like I don't see her often."

"I know. Miss June told me where you live."

"She tells you a lot, I bet."

"We chat, it's true."

"Are you surprised that I still live there? Disappointed, maybe?"

"No! I think it's sweet that you two get along. But are you sorry you got divorced?"

He told her the truth. "Yes, I am. I'm very sorry. It wasn't my idea and I hate that it happened. But I'm glad for her. She did the right thing."

"You know, I had a crush on you, back when. In school, I

mean. You were the handsome instructor, and I was the dreamy young girl. I feel silly telling you now. I was dazzled by how smart you were. And look at us now. Old friends, having lunch."

"Yes, the brilliant professor and the dreamy old man."

She smiled. "But, we *are* friends." The strand of hair found its way to her mouth again, a gesture he might have taken as flirtatious had Walt not known it to be a lifelong habit.

"I'm glad you're in town, Gwen. I can use a friend."

"Me too, Walt. Me too."

Chapter 10

BOTH THE BEAUTY AND DANGER of Gene's Bull's-Eye Bar and Grill is its refusal to acknowledge the passage of time. Minutes there turn into hours, weeks become years. Wars and natural disasters parade across its television but can't penetrate the screen. Anchormen and game show hosts grow old and retire, replaced by younger versions of themselves. A faded, hand-written sign reading *Pickles – 10¢, Eggs – 25¢, Sardines – Cheap!* had been taped to the back bar mirror for as long as Walt could remember, but that could have been a week or twenty years. He knew that this distortion of time occurred to some degree in dark taverns all across America, but it seemed especially strong at Gene's. He sometimes wondered about the daytime regulars, mostly men who were older than himself, wondered if they regretted how their lives had been spent, watching soap operas and waiting for the daily number. Walt had lost the last month to the place. It hadn't bothered him until the previous day, when he'd found himself invested in the outcome of *The Price is Right*. Twice, his day there had segued into evening and he'd ended up fucking Deena, grateful for the company, indifferent though it was. He knew he should feel guilty about wasting so much damned time, but the shock of Sam's pregnancy had rendered him useless. He left the garage early each day, so as to avoid the strange construction vans that would soon arrive to do his work. But once he left the house, he had no place to go. And though it had taken years, he'd finally frustrated his usual customers to the point where they were no longer tracking him down, and he was, for the first time, without much to do. He knew he could make a phone call and line something up, or even just show up at one of his unfinished jobs, but he didn't have it in him. Worse than directionless, he felt unnecessary. For the first couple of weeks after the work on the baby's room got started, he busied himself doing odds and ends for Reggie and then hanging a few cabinets for Jimmy's ex-wife Irma, a task that required more skill than Jimmy possessed, not that that was saying so much. And, Irma paid cash.

Of course, it being winter, he did have to tend to the heat at Miss June's. In the basement of Hardwick there resided a huge steam boiler, an ornate coal furnace of elephantine proportions, converted decades before by some mad genius to burn natural gas. The boiler had myriad pipes and valves protruding from its belly, and an array of glass-faced dials featuring wonderful old typefaces that denoted various pressures and temperatures, the exact meaning of which flummoxed even the most experienced of boiler-men. Over time, Walt had learned to conduct its symphony of pressures and temperatures perfectly by adjusting its many valves just so, discovering along the way the exact mixture of gas and air required to keep the temperamental pilot flame alive through even the windiest of nights. Hardwick's grand chimneys were prone to backdrafts, and getting the pilot re-lit was no easy feat. Replacing the boiler would have cut Miss June's heating bills in half, but at her age, spending the money made no sense. Besides, she refused to introduce anything modern to the house, and, truth be told, Walt would have been sad to see the old thing go. They shared a complicated relationship, that boiler and he, one based on hard-earned mutual respect, though it had taken years for them to become fully accustomed to one another. Early on, he'd been unable to get the thing to cooperate, with the pilot light in particular being especially recalcitrant, and with the radiators in different parts of the house choosing to be arbitrarily hot or cold with no apparent logic involved. The contraption seemed to enjoy fucking with him. But, having shown great patience with the beast, even tinkering with it straight through one very cold night until morning, Walt eventually earned its respect and it began to behave. The two had reached détente.

Other than tending to the furnace, however, Walt had spent little time at Hardwick since winter set in. He was uncomfortable being there near Gwen. He had tried for a couple of days, puttering about while she worked, but felt conspicuous and clumsy. As it so happened, the chores on Walt's list were very light, more suited for a butler than a carpenter. He'd picked through a few of the tasks, starting with those that required at least some skill, but after re-painting the pantry door, fixing a loose handrail, and re-wiring a lamp, he made himself scarce. He'd become a handyman, and it was embarrassing. Citing work elsewhere that he didn't really have, he stopped showing up. And so he'd become a daytime regular at Gene's, something he never imagined he'd do. And as he sat there getting sucked into an old movie one afternoon—something called *The Eddie Duchin Story* with Tyrone Power—it was Sam who entered the bar to rescue him before he sank completely.

"Hey, Sammi," Gene called, glad to see her. "Looky that,

fellas, we got a real lady in here."

"Hi, Gene. It's good to see you." Sam settled into Walt's booth. She had the healthy ruddiness that sometimes comes with pregnancy, and had begun to move with a subtle deliberation that was detectable only to someone who knew her as well as Walt.

Gene brought her an unrequested glass of ginger ale. "Good to see you, too, honey. We don't see you no more since you married that expensive guy."

"My new husband's not much of a barfly, Gene. That's why I keep the old one in reserve."

Walt felt like a kid whose parents show up unannounced at his grade school, which is not often a good scenario. He felt guilty, too, over having spent a portion of last night at Deena's, not that Sam would have known.

"What are you doing here, Sam? Is everything all right?"

"I'm not sure. Miss June called twice this morning looking for you. Twice in one morning is no big deal, but the second time, she asked if I would try to find you."

"Is her heat off?"

"She didn't say. With her, it could be anything." Sam had a certain appreciation for Miss June, the reluctant respect one tough woman has for another, but the octogenarian had a history of getting under Sam's skin. For years, the two had competed for Walt's time, and while Sam didn't mind sharing, she didn't like how the old woman treated him. Sam looked at the television and then at him. "Is everything okay?"

"I'm great. Why do you ask?"

"No reason."

They sat and watched for a few minutes as the movie unfolded, with someone—Eddie Duchin, Walt supposed—playing a piano in a swanky setting. The characters in those old movies moved through their lives with such exaggerated drama. No one had such determination, he thought.

"You know," she said, "when I came looking for you, I was hoping you wouldn't be this easy to find."

*   *   *

"He's here," Gwen called upstairs.

"Thank you," replied Donald, peering over the railing. "Miss June will be down presently."

The house was warm, Walt noted—nothing wrong with the boiler.

"Can you tell me what's going on?" he asked Gwen.

"No, I really can't. Nothing's happened that I know of, but she announced that she needed to see the two of us today." She lowered her voice. "She's been different lately. I mean, I don't know her like you do, of course, but for the last week or so she's been telling a lot of stories about things around the house, paintings and furniture and the like. She seems reflective. Maybe it's just a side of her I don't know. But she cancelled her bridge games and book circle the last few weeks. I'm not sure what to make of it."

Walt wasn't either, but he felt uneasy. Miss June's affect was one of life's constants, her personality fixed like stone. The only exceptions he'd ever seen were during her occasional remembrances of Dwight, and that one soft, private moment the previous autumn when he'd surreptitiously watched her brushing her hair. Her social schedule never varied, unless she chose to preempt one of her regular engagements with an emergency meeting of the local historical review board or to host a visiting scholar for afternoon tea.

"Yoo-hoo," Donald announced as the pair descended the main stairs. Miss June, looking perfectly normal, slapped away Donald's hand.

"If you fear you might fall, Donald, grasp the railing, not me."

"Oh, ha-ha. Yes. I mean, no! I'm not falling. I was just being gentlemanly, you know. Which was not meant to imply that you can't walk! You've been walking for many years, and with never an incident! Ahem. Ha!"

Miss June looked to the heavens. "I should have made him take the elevator." She turned toward Gwen and Walt. "Let's move to the front parlor. Donald, you may pour the tea. I believe Gwenneth has prepared the tray."

Walt perched himself on the edge of an uncomfortable chaise. None of the furniture in the parlor was right for a man of his size, always making him feel vast and impostorish, a large actor taxing a delicate prop.

Miss June, not one for small talk, looked squarely at Walt. "It seems I'll not be with you much longer."

For Walt, a shot had rung out. "What?!"

"Pay attention, young man. Try to keep up. I've lived quite the remarkable life, but it seems that now, with greater urgency than before, I must put my affairs in order."

The doctor's appointments, the book Gwen was writing.

"Wait a second, are you saying that you're …"

"Please, Walter. Let me finish. Hardwick will soon be without me, and there are things that must be completed before I depart. Things that need to be done before I can rest, knowing fully that I have done right by my family. And by Dwight."

Gwen clutched her sweater.

"Gwenneth, Donald. You seem to be making progress on the book. I'm confident you will capture my family's history in the correct light, and for that I am indeed grateful. Gwen, I know you've been curious about who exactly is going to publish this work, and I want you to be assured that I have received a commitment from the University Press. The book will be printed, bound, and put forth for the world to consider."

"It's a labor of love, Miss June. I hope you know that. I care about it a great deal."

"Thank you, dear. You were not selected to be its author by chance. And Donald, your help, as Gwenneth has told me, has been invaluable. Along with being an ardent agent in preserving our local history, you've behaved as would a true friend."

Beaming, Donald removed a handkerchief from his pocket.

"As for you, Walter, I'll be frank—I've not asked much of you during our years together."

Because he was having the falling-down-the-hole sensation again, he had no response to that incredible statement.

"Yes, I've kept you occupied with small tasks over the years, and while, admittedly, showing appreciation for every minor thing is not my wont, I have valued your work here at Hardwick." She put down her cup, the slightest tremor in her hand. "And it's of you that I will ask a great favor. This is some-thing—and God help me—that only you can do correctly. I want you all to look around. This is quite a room, isn't it?" Indeed, it was. The arched-top windows ran from the floor to well overhead, and the ceilings were twelve feet high. "But, as Walter knows, it's not what it once was. These walls were originally adorned with wainscoting that reached the ceiling. And the ceiling … oh, the ceiling. It was coffered, with beams and panels that were the talk of the East End. The carpenters who built Henry Clay Frick's house built this room. Dukes and duchesses have sat for high tea where we now sit. It was exquisite. But, in 1958, there was a fire here at Hardwick, a fire that destroyed our beautiful woodwork. The blaze was confined, thank goodness, to this room." She paused. "But, in some ways, the terrible events of that evening did damage that extended well beyond these walls, desecration from which I've never recovered. Walter, perhaps at some point you've heard the tale of which I speak."

So it was true. Walt was stunned. For the first time, Miss June was acknowledging that the fire had not originated from the unattended hearth, but that darker circumstances had been in play. The story, one of the many about the Creightons that his father had told, one that Walt had thought too far-fetched to believe, surrounded Miss June's younger brother, Thomas, the only known ne'er-do-well in the Creighton clan. If, as his father believed, every great family has one trouble-some member, then Thomas was it. Despite his private schooling and ample privilege, young Thomas was an endless source of embarrassment to the family. Never productive, he had cele-brated his way through prep school and then college, earning poor marks and getting by on the family name. Following graduation, he'd slipped even further, carrying on, as Miss June said once to Walt in a rare comment on the matter, with *"low company."* A dandy, he was boisterous and charismatic, and was seldom seen without a drink in his hand or a girl at his side, though not the sort of girl that his family would favor. He never worked a job of significance, despite his father lining up opportunities for him that other young men of the time would have wrestled over. Thomas was popular with the row-dier contingents at the Pittsburgh Athletic Club, and was quick to lead the others in nights of debauchery after rounds of golf. Reliably, his father, Julius, would bail him out of trouble, hop-ing his son would mature, only to be disappointed again. His older sister had little use for his carrying on, and had no problem turning her back when he phoned home drunk, hav-ing misplaced his car or needing money to settle a tab. But of Thomas's vices, gambling was by far the worst. He was reckless with bets, possessing the classic mindset of a compulsive gam-bler who believes he is just one bet from changing his luck, and with family money available to cover his losses, the descent was steep. Because of Thomas's wildness, upon Julius's death, the family assets were left to the two siblings, with the stipulation that the accounts were to be controlled by June. She was to write the checks and mind the investments, and Thomas, despite being an adult, was to receive an allowance, with the amount contingent upon his behavior. Though it broke Julius Creighton's heart to have to make such arrangements, he knew he could never allow his son access to the family money, and because his daughter had inherited the firmness of her grandfather, she would be a particularly fierce custodian of what assets remained. And in the years following Julius's death, June Creighton did tend to her brother's allowance, never wavering as he tried to coerce her into giving him more until his next amount was due. As Thomas's addiction advanced, he became desperate, selling heirlooms to pay off debts. The more honorable bookmakers in town, those who took gentlemanly bets on sporting events from the wealthy, were no longer willing to do business with him, as he not only had difficulty paying what he owed, he was no longer able to conduct himself with any degree of decorum—he simply called too much attention to himself. And so he placed bets with a rougher crowd, bookmakers from the underworld, tough men who enjoyed taking money from a once fancy young man in the throes of a downfall. Men who had little patience when it was time to pay up.

During a particularly bad string of drinking and betting, Thomas had run his debts to astronomical proportions, borrowing money from loan sharks to pay off the bookies, and then placing bets with the money he borrowed, certain that he could get ahead. He demanded money from his sister, becoming bolder by the day. Upon discovering that Thomas had sold their father's prized antique shotguns, June doubled her resolve. Thomas's demands became desperate pleas, but she would not give way, granting him only the designated amount on the first and the fifteenth of each month. Late night phone calls came to the house, with no one on the other end when June would answer. Thomas would disappear for days, hiding over his debt. Concerned, June hired a police detective to guard the house at night, not certain just how deep the trouble was her brother had fallen into. Then, on a brutal February night, a firebomb was thrown through the parlor window, setting the room ablaze in reprisal. The thick plaster helped contain the fire until the trucks could arrive, for if the flames had spread to its well-seasoned fir framing, all of Hardwick might have been lost. Thomas, who wasn't home at the time, showed up two days later, badly beaten and with both of his forearms broken. "They're going to kill me, June," was all he could manage through his bloodied teeth. And so, as the story began to match what Walt's father had relayed long ago, Miss June arranged, through her father's attorneys, for payment to be made to all whom Thomas owed. It was a staggering amount, the lawyers warned her, one that would change her financial standing. But clearly, there was nothing else she could do. Not only did she need to save her brother's life, but, being a Creighton, she would honor the debt because it was the proper thing to do. The attorneys gathered the money, and two off-duty policemen made the deliveries, along with the threat that they were to have no contact with Thomas lest they face the wrath of the police department, the FBI, or, worse, Miss June Creighton. Thomas had been shaken enough that he spent his remaining days drinking but had been, surprisingly, scared sufficiently to swear off gambling. The parlor was repaired, although not to anything approaching its original grandeur. The ceiling was plastered and crown moulding applied, but gone were the beams and wood panels. The walls were not the same either, as the wainscoting, the massive door and window casing, and the built-in bookcases were no more. The quality of the new work, while top-flight, was comparatively modest. Miss June, before today, had never said one word to Walt about the true cause of the fire.

She continued. "Dwight, my beau, the only man I've loved, proposed to me in this room. It was long before the fire. And, of course, before the St. Patrick's Day flood of '36. That's when I lost him, you know. He was a hero, that man. On that day, the day he drowned, the galaxy lost a star."

The rhythmic tick of the radiators sounded like clocks.

"And so, Walter. My request."

It was as if his life had been led in waiting for this moment.

"I want you to reconstruct the parlor to exactly as it was before the fire. And it needs to be done soon—there's no time to waste. Before I am gone, I want this room to look as it did on the day that Dwight kneeled to make his proposal—the one I so willingly accepted."

Gwen was in tears. Donald was in tears as well. Walt, however, was still incapable of anything.

"Now, I know that this won't be an inexpensive undertaking. I've instructed my banker to have the money you'll need at your disposal."

"Miss June … I don't know where to begin. I …"

"I'm not through speaking, Walter." She gestured toward the long side table against the far wall. "The blueprints for Hardwick are over there. You've never seen them. They were meant to go to you in accordance with my will, but it seems that you'll be receiving them sooner than I had planned. I've asked Donald here to make copies, so that the originals aren't damaged during your work. I've reviewed the drawings myself, and it appears that they show the woodwork in the greatest of detail." She clasped her hands on her lap, then rubbed them together, working her fragile joints. "Gwenneth, Donald, would you be dears and give Walter and me a moment alone?" The others cleared out, and Miss June spoke to Walt, more softly than before.

"I know this isn't easy for you."

"Why didn't you tell me about this before?"

"Don't be silly. I'm telling you now."

"What exactly have the doctors been telling you? When did this start?"

"I've mentioned no particulars of my health, nor should you ask. You know I've always believed that a woman—even one of my age—has a right to privacy."

"Don't toy with me. How serious is this?"

"What matters is my request. It's important to me that you do this work. It is paramount."

The tick of the radiators increased in concert with the conversation.

"And just think—you'll be doing work of the highest caliber. The sort of work to which, I suspect, you've long aspired. Let's be truthful with one another. We've become comfortable here together. You've been quite the companion, and together we've tackled many a small chore. But this is the type of work you should be doing. If you're not to pursue academics, if that's not where your heart lies, then please, allow your passions to find their way past your … curious habits. Allow yourself to accomplish bigger things."

"Miss June, this is a lot for me to absorb. I don't think I can tackle such a big …"

"Listen to me. I'm asking this of you personally. Do this for me, Walter." She leaned forward. "Do this for Dwight."

* * *

Movies were reliable escape. It was light outside when he'd arrived and dark when he left, an effect that was nicely disconcerting. With imagery from the film still in place, he drove away from the East End, away from both Friendship and Shadyside, toward parts of Pittsburgh that held no immediate claim. He drove by the river, down Second Avenue, where steel mills once belched fire into the night, then drove through downtown itself, where early theater crowds fought to ward off the cold. Walt liked downtown, though he seldom had reason to venture there, seeing it mostly during drives such as this, quiet excursions that found him crossing bridges and addressing inclines, traversing the angular streets that described the city. He thought of Miss June. Childish though his thinking may have been, her mortality seemed unreal. And the work she was asking of him was staggering. It was a serious project, larger than anything he'd ever attempted—a complicated restoration that would require considerable effort. If he could just magically give it to her as a gift, he would be thrilled to do so. But he felt incapable of tackling something so complex. The panels and trim would have to be fabricated by an architectural millwork shop, one able to reproduce the old moulding profiles, and it would have to be hand finished to match the wood in the adjacent rooms. The cost would be astronomical. He doubted her savings would be enough. But his reservations had little to do with procurement or expense. He was afraid. This project would have to be finished, absolutely. And his progress would be watched. He wouldn't be able to hide behind charm and eccentricity. This work meant everything to Miss June, and he knew that if he attempted it, he would disappoint her. Yet it would disappoint her more if he didn't try. Goddamn her for putting him in this position. *"I've not asked much of you during our years together,"* she'd had the nerve to say. Where did she get off? But it was hard to hold onto that anger. It was uncharacteristic of Miss

June to humanize herself as she had. He was caught between his upbringing under her gaze and his constitutional fear of action. As his truck crested Polish Hill—past the small houses with their mint green siding and aluminum awnings, past the corner bars with their unpronounceable names—and headed toward home, he knew he couldn't satisfy her request. And telling her would be the hardest thing he'd ever done.

* * *

Dewey wasn't there when he got home, Walt's guess being that he'd had dinner at Sam's and decided to stay.

On the kitchen table was a casserole dish and a note:

> *Eat this.*
> *Love, Sam*

* * *

Thrown by the kindness of Sam's food and not wanting to sit and listen to his own heartbeat, he headed to the 'Eye, its facade dark under tired streetlights. He scanned the lot for Deena's El Camino, but the only familiar car belonged to Gene. It was late, and the place was quiet, with just a few students playing a cryptic fantasy game with oddly shaped dice, and a couple of die-hard rummies securing the end of the bar. Walt had expected Milt, the nighttime bartender, but instead, Gene himself was at the helm.

"What're you doing up so late?" Walt asked.

"Knucklehead called off. I tell you, people these days don't wanna work."

Walt avoided comment.

"It's quiet in here."

"Yeah, I can't predict this place no more. Anyway, I'm gonna kick these guys out. They ain't spendin' any money no how." And with that, he did. "Hey. You guys. Hit the road."

The youngsters, scared of Gene, packed up their game instantly. The old guys pretended not to have heard their instructions.

"Hey, you two. Yeah, you—Seven and Seven—I'm closin' up." The old guys grumbled a bit, offering the lame protest of bar drunks who possess little power. "Go on, scram," Gene added, as he poured them each a free shot for the road, a contradiction, as always. He emptied the cash register, not counting the money so much as feeling its meager weight. Beside him stood the baseball bat that waited for trouble.

"Get the door, will ya, Walt? Stick around. Have a nightcap."

Walt threw the deadbolt after the rummies left and settled back down on his stool. He inhaled deeply, appreciating the bar smell—the stickiness of the soda gun, the dull lemon wedges in their stainless steel bin. Even the distant cherry chemical odor of the men's room had its own comfort to offer. The grill had been shut down for a couple of hours, but Gene asked Walt if he was hungry. He said that he wasn't, and Gene made him a cheese sandwich anyway. On the television, Jim Rockford drove his Firebird. Gene smoked a cigarette as they watched.

"That guy has it made, you know?" Gene said toward the television set.

"Why's that?"

"Sits around in his trailer, don't need to look for work, it just comes to him. Names his price, right up front. Two hundred dollars a day. And he gets it, too. Drives around, figures things out. I like him. He's not too slick right off the bat, like he don't always know the answers at first, but he gets it right in the end. The cream always rises to the crop."

Walt thought about that. "Would you like that job? Private eye?"

"Shit, I don't know. I know it ain't like in the pictures. But still, to get to do something different each day, have people come to you to solve their problems. That'd be something. What do I do? I come down here, I unlock the door and keep the ice cubes cold."

"Oh, I think people come to you to solve their problems plenty, Gene. Some of them, every day."

"Pfff. The young ones, they don't even know they got problems yet. The old guys, most of them live alone. They come here 'cause they got no place else to go." He pulled on his Viceroy and exhaled hard. "The middle-aged guys. The family men. They're the ones with the problems. They got everything goin' for them—good jobs, nice families—and they still come here looking for answers. 'You want an answer? Go home to your wife,' I wanna tell 'em. 'There's your fuckin' answer.'" He stubbed out his cigarette. "But I never say shit. What do I care?"

They watched the show in silence for a minute, the volume low.

"You ever wish you could go back in time?" Gene asked. "To the past, I mean?"

"I don't know. Maybe." It was a surprisingly complicated question. "What about you?"

"I know what I'd-a wanted to do if I could. I always wished I could've made a real classy bar, you know? Like a restaurant. With red booths and waitresses. Someplace dark. And the cigarette machine would be back by the restrooms, where you couldn't even see it. Hell, the people would already have enough smokes with 'em. That'd be the kind of people that ate there."

"Sounds nice."

"I'd have that wallpaper on the walls, and curtains, and maybe even a fountain when you walked in. Like a place you'd want to take a date. And I'd have those big pepper mills, the ones that come up to here." He gazed over Walt's shoulder, seeing the place. "And if people wanted pepper on their food, the waitresses would put it on for them. And those guys who hang out at the bar now, they'd have to go somewhere else, 'cause they wouldn't feel right in a place like mine. It would be outta their league."

"I can see it, Gene. It would really be something."

"And halfway through the meal, I'd come around to the tables and ask how everything was going, was the service okay?"

"You'd add the personality that makes the difference. That's what makes a place classy," Walt said, using Gene's word gently, without condescension.

"Yeah, well, pipe-dreams is all that is."

"You ever think of giving it a go? You're not too old," Walt offered, realizing as he did that Gene probably was.

"Who are you trying to kid? I'm sixty-three, Walt. I ain't young like you. My time's come and gone. I couldn't pull off no joint like that now." He leaned back against the cooler and surveyed his bar. "Besides, I know my place."

"Well, I think you're a success as it is. Everyone sees you that way."

"Eugene?" came the call from upstairs.

"Coming, Ma," he hollered. "Listen, Walt, I gotta go. Stick around if you like. You know how to lock up. Just turn off the idiot box before you go."

Gene hit a couple switches, leaving Walt mostly in the dark. The room felt different when empty—and while it always seemed nonjudgmental, the place now also seemed wise, and he knew he shouldn't underestimate the moment. He took his time with his drink. The beer clock glowed and the cooler motor hummed, and by the time the door latched behind him in the alley, he knew he would try to fulfill Miss June's wish.

Chapter 11

HE DECIDED TO TIE UP A FEW LOOSE ENDS before getting serious about the parlor, and delivering Reggie's rugs was one of them. He didn't give two shits about Reggie or his rugs, but he'd already picked them up some months before and stuck them in Sam's garage where they were in the way of his tools. Creighton Properties' office was sleek, modern, and devoid of clutter, all curved plywood and glass. The receptionist, an automaton with breasts, held up her index finger as Walt approached, finishing her call without looking up, a habit she apparently shared with her boss.

"May I help you?" she asked after hanging up, her tone indicating that she would prefer to do anything but.

"I'd like to see Reggie, please."

"And you would be …"

"I would be Walt Farnham. Same as the last three times you asked me that."

"I'll see if he's in."

"Well, his truck's outside," Walt offered helpfully, "and I can see his feet on his desk through that door over there, so I think it's safe to assume that he's in."

"I'll see if he's in," she said again. She pressed a button and spoke quietly into her phone and then hung up. "I'm sorry. This isn't a good time. He said for you to drop the rugs off at the dock out back, if that's why you're here."

"Not a good time? Actually, there's no time like the present. That's my motto these days. You see, I've decided to become more effective. But thank you."

He strode past her and into Reggie's office. Reggie was on the phone, balancing a golf club on the palm of his hand, going on about re-purposing square footage or something. Acknowledging Walt, he made a face meant to indicate that the person on the other end was an asshole. On the walls were a number of photographs of past Creighton projects. After a minute, Walt pointed toward Reggie's big private bathroom, and Reggie gestured as if to say, "Sure, help yourself." Taking a leak, Walt looked at the photos above the toilet, images of Reggie on golf outings with other Type-A types. On the long wall to his left were six poster-sized black and white photographs of Reggie in his early thirties, back when he had dabbled as a model for a local department store. Reggie's shallow soap opera handsomeness was well-suited for the ads, and his smarmy image had appeared in full-paged glory in the Sunday *Press*. In three of the photos, his hair was permed, and he wore garish sport-shirts and slacks. The other three were horrifying shots of him modeling jockey shorts, the posters apparently being blow-ups of early proofs, as they were in serious need of air-brushing. In each image, Reggie's abundant pubic hair burst free of the confines of the advertised briefs, a veritable forest for all to see. In one shot he was, inexplicably, holding a football. Walt flushed and got the hell out of there.

"Walt, my man. What's up?" Reggie said, finally off the phone.

"What's up? You owe me money, that's what's up."

"Is that right? Let's see, how much was that. Seventy bucks?"

"One-twenty-five, you crook."

"You're more honest than me, so I'll believe you. You want coffee?"

"Are you going to deduct it from what you owe me?"

"Please. I treat you too well. You know where it is. Get me some, too. Cream and sugar."

Once he figured out how it worked, Walt poured two cups from a space-age coffee maker down the hall and returned.

"How'd you get past Vanessa?" Reggie asked.

"I short-circuited her battery. I swear, I can't tell if that woman is alive or not."

"Oh, she's alive," Reggie leered. "Ask me if I'm fucking her." He waited—apparently the question was not rhetorical. "Go on, ask me."

"I don't want to know. Christ, you never change."

Reggie laughed. "And neither do you, so here we are."

"So here we are. Same old shit."

"Same old shit," Reggie agreed, "except I hear you've got a big project now. For the old lady. More handyman work."

"It's a lot more than handyman work." Walt sat on the sofa, put his muddy boots on the coffee table, and closed his eyes. "I should have my head examined."

"For once, I agree with you. Why are you doing this? It makes no sense. She's not even going to be around to appreciate it."

"It's hard to explain. I just have to."

"Well, I respect you for it."

"Really?"

"Yeah, I really do. Isn't that crazy?" Walt waited for the

punch line, but none came. "You know," Reggie continued, "I offered to do that work for her once. Send a crew over and put all the old-style mouldings back and everything. A first-class job, I was offering her. She wouldn't go for it. Of course, I had my own interests in mind, too, but still, she would've had it the way she wanted it. She's a tough nut to crack, my aunt."

His own interests in mind. That's what made doing this work so insane, but with irony being perfectly cruel, it made absolute sense as well: Reggie would inherit Hardwick. That was the hard truth. Miss June had told Walt long before that it was family protocol for the house to remain under the Creighton name. Walt campaigned hard for it to be left to the local historic conservancy or, at least, to the university with the stipulation that it be kept mostly intact, but Miss June dismissed those ideas as impossibilities not worthy of discussion. In keeping with her grandfather's wishes, Hardwick would be passed down through the family. One day—apparently not too far into the future—Miss June would die, and the house would be Reggie's.

"You know, I've tried to get her to move into one of my apartments," Reggie continued. "One of the nice ones, so she wouldn't have to knock around in that giant house by herself. Or heat the damn thing—I can't imagine what that costs. She wouldn't do it."

"What was in it for you?"

"Hey, not everything I do is motivated by money. I do have a heart, you know."

"Well, I just hope to put the parlor back to how it was," Walt said, "so she can be happy before she dies."

"Do you really think that's going to make her happy? Has she ever been happy?"

He had a point.

"She'll know that under her watch, things were put back

in order. And that, for her, means everything."

The two were quiet then. Walt knew that they were both recalling the childhood days they'd spent together at Hardwick, and he wondered if Reggie's memories matched his. Did he remember being so caustic, so cruel? Did he regret any of it? Or did he fondly recall their inequality and still feel cheaply superior because of it? Walt sometimes liked to think that Reggie felt at least a bit ashamed.

Reggie looked at Walt, considering, and then deciding. "Come here. I want to show you something."

Down the hall was a conference room, where on an easel sat a large promotional board of the sort typical of the real estate development business. On the board was a beautiful illustration of Hardwick. At the top was a title: *"Hardwicke Estates—The Finest in Luxury Condominium Living."* This was followed in smaller type by *"Coming Soon…"* The rendering, computer-generated but meant to have the look of a pencil and pastel hand-sketch, showed the great front lawn intact, but with the side yard and garden sacrificed for parking. The side porch was gone as well. From what Walt could tell, the floor-to-ceiling windows on the first floor were to be converted to entry doors. In the illustration, a couple stood next to an SUV, the stick-thin woman holding a shopping bag. Absorbing the image, Walt felt himself dissipate, as if his composition, too, was turning to pastel.

"Condos," he managed.

"*Nice* condos," Reggie corrected. "There's nothing like them anywhere. And the location is killer. We'll put the parking on the side, as you can see, allowing for a tennis court and pool in the back. Of course, we'll get rid of the greenhouse. I'm thinking maybe a putting green as well. The carriage house will be a separate unit, maybe a condo, maybe apartments—I'm still crunching the numbers on that." He looked proud. "So you see, and I knew you'd be happy about this, you don't have to fear I'll tear down your beloved building after all. It'll be standing when you and I die, let alone Miss June."

When Walt finally spoke, it was hushed, beyond disbelief.

"Jesus," he said. "It hadn't occurred to me you might tear it down. I figured you'd do some landscaping, maybe restore the carriage house, but then *sell* the place. I thought some rich family would end up living there."

Reggie waved his hand dismissively. "That doesn't make sense. What family would want to live there? The place is a monster. You just can't fill that many rooms, not these days. No one has that many kids. No, the real money would be in tearing it down and building new buildings, mixed-use struc- tures — either condos or apartments — maybe with first-floor retail. But, parking is troublesome with the retail, so the next best plan is to cut the thing up into separate units and sell them as condos." He saw that Walt was dumbstruck. "Don't worry, the shell will still look the same when you drive down the street. For the most part, anyway." Then, with a pat on the shoulder, he added, "I'll do my best not to upset your architectural sensitivities."

Reggie continued describing the plan, slipping into sales mode, as though Walt were an investor. "The plan is for it to be cut into quadrants, four units per floor, although it's possible that the third floor could be two larger units. Either way, I've got enough off-street parking, so zoning shouldn't be a problem. I've got the zoning board in my pocket anyway. This is a done deal."

Walt inspected the proposed floor plans. Almost all of the existing interior walls were gone, replaced by new, thinner ver- sions that would divide the building for maximum efficiency. Miss June's kitchen, the scene of their mid-morning snacks, would be gone. Also gone would be the grand front staircase, as would be the back stairs, under which Walt hid as a child.

"Coming Soon," the board said.

"When did you start working on this?" Walt asked, incredulous.

"It's been cooking in my brain for a couple of years. I mean, I always knew I'd do something big with the place. This current plan was drawn up last summer. I like to have my ducks in a row. That's how you make money. Timing is everything."

"Well, let's hope the market's hot when she dies," Walt replied. "To maximize profit."

"I've thought about that, but I'm safe either way. The type of people who can afford these places aren't concerned by fluctuations in the market."

"I was being sarcastic, you bastard."

"Hey, look. She *knows* I'm inheriting the place. She's the one who made sure of it. I'm not stealing anything here."

"No, you're not. But, shit. Did you have to go this far already? Couldn't you have waited until she's gone?"

"It's not like I showed this to her. We haven't even talked about it. I'm not as insensitive as you think. And if she brings it up, asks me my plans, I'll be evasive, that's all. I'm not going to rub her face in it. The weird thing is, she hasn't brought it up."

This was not at all weird to Walt. Unless Miss June was leaving the house to Reggie with stipulations regarding its future, she'd remain silent with the stoicism of a true Creighton. If there were to be stipulations, they would be clearly spelled out, with meetings held, attorneys consulted, and documents signed, both in ink and in blood. But given that no such arrangements had been made, Walt knew that Miss June was choosing not to exercise control beyond her death, nor to argue with the passage of time, but was instead simply fulfilling her obligation to her grandfather to keep the house in the family name, with the destiny of the property to be determined as its future Creighton-owner saw fit. In fact, she might take perverse pleasure in acknowledging life's brutality, how cold and ironic it can be even when one does just as one should. And yet, she was also managing to be true to herself, by making the place right, returning it to its original state. Making it right for her grandfather, making it right for her and for Dwight. She would see the front parlor as it once was, and that would be reward enough for a life lived in proper sacrifice.

Walt looked again at the floor plan, at what walls would be moved, at where the entrances would be. And naturally, chief among the changes, set to be sacrificed in the name of profit, was the parlor he would soon be restoring.

Chapter 12

DEENA'S HEAD LAY AGAINST WALT'S CHEST. Her mattress
was too soft, and his big body sank into the middle, his weight
taking her with him. After they had finished, Deena rolled off
him so that he could leave as usual, but this time he didn't
move, and so she lay back down and he pulled her close, her
ear to his heart. They stayed that way for a while, not quite
cuddling, but absorbed in warm quiet nonetheless. He wasn't
sure what to say. He couldn't claim to have another woman,
and he wasn't sure she'd care if he did. Were he to be honest,
he'd admit that as of late, she seemed less scary. She was as
tough as ever, silent and muscular, but she seemed closer to
human. Despite having had sex in the little house for over a
year, Walt still hadn't been offered so much as a sandwich
there, and his observation of Deena's things, his attempts to
learn more about her, took place upon his coming and going,
or during trips to the small bathroom. On the refrigerator were
photos of a few children—nieces and nephews, he supposed.

None looked to be all that bright, with one girl's school picture suggestive of fetal alcohol syndrome. The photos were held in place with Hershey's Kisses magnets, and Walt felt affection for Deena for caring about the motley kids. Also on the fridge was a flyer for an auto parts swap meet and a photo of Prince Charles and Lady Di on their wedding day. Taking up much of the living room was her disassembled Harley and its odor of gasoline, waiting patiently for spring. Deena's own scent was a combination of gasoline and fake lavender, and tonight, when Walt caught a whiff of it at Gene's, he'd suddenly wanted very much to come to this house. What an odd circumstance they shared. In some ways, she was the perfect woman for him, having no expectations about his performance outside of bed, and even there, she did all the work. She didn't give a shit about what he ate or when, whether he was getting things done or not, if he'd gained ten pounds or was under-utilizing his potential. That said, it had begun to bother him that while she would share her bed with him, if only for minutes, she barely spoke to him, not even offering post-sex small talk. He still didn't know where she worked, if she was alive when Kennedy was shot, or if she'd had something to do with it. But tonight, her presence felt good, and he put his arm around her, placing his hand on her hip. She began to shrug him off, refusing the tenderness, but he was firm, pressing his hand until she relented and allowed him this touch. After a beat, she placed her own hand over his. For once, they weren't so different.

* * *

Nearly a week had gone by since he'd last been at Hardwick, since the day when Sam had pulled him from the quicksand at Gene's so that Miss June could announce her impending demise. Now he was back, walking the parlor, tape measure in hand. A copy of the original interior drawings had appeared in his door a few days earlier, courtesy of Donald, he supposed. They were beautiful. Each moulding profile was hand-drawn in full scale, with sections of the wainscot, the built-up cornices, and the coffered ceiling assemblies shown in perfect detail. The draftsmanship was impeccable — precise, yet possessing an organic quality not present in the computer-generated drawings of today. Walt contemplated the order in which the work would proceed, what tools he would need, and when he would require help. His best work was done alone, and this project would need him to be at his best. At the same time, much of it would require an extra pair of hands, if only to hold the other end of the longer pieces of trim. The trick would be for Walt to have help there when he needed it, but unless the helper were as skilled as he, to also have them be absent when he needed to focus on his own. He already knew where he would have the millwork fabricated, a specialty shop on the North Side that could grind knives for their antique machines to match the trim exactly. An argument could have been made for putting the work out to bid, but he wasn't interested in dealing with a shop he didn't know. He considered the magnitude of the room, felt the weight of the drawings in his hand. Once again, the task threatened to become overwhelming, a mountainous ordeal he wouldn't be able to complete. There were too many facets to contemplate, no way to think through a plan.

"Organization is a virtue not to be scoffed at, young man."

He searched the house until he found Miss June in her favorite reading chair, and asked her a question that was better than any gift.

"Miss June, might you have a tablet I could borrow? It seems I have a list to make."

Chapter 13

"ARE YOU GONNA MAKE LOVE to that board, or are you gonna nail the fucking thing?" Jimmy asked. He couldn't understand why Walt kept adjusting the piece ever so slightly when it looked the same either way.

"'Make love' versus 'nail'? Haven't I heard you use both terms to refer to the same thing?" Walt asked.

"Har-dee-har-har. This is gonna take ten years at the pace you move."

"Well," Walt answered, "using your parlance, yes, I am going to make love to this board."

"Christ, I've made love for real that didn't take this long."

"Jimmy, you've had marriages that didn't take this long." Walt felt good, enjoying the back and forth. "But, seriously, this isn't some half-assed remodeling job, okay? I know it's just blocking, but it needs to be installed as accurately as the finished trim. Each piece needs to be cut just so."

"'Just so' my ass. Cut it, nail it, move on to the next one.

Where you get the patience for this, I'll never know."

Walt's hope had been that between the two of them—Walt with his precise, methodical approach, and Jimmy with his desire just to get done—they would be able to move at a steady pace while still achieving the level of quality the house deserved. Jimmy was burning out, however, and Walt knew that he would soon be without help. Still, in the two months that had passed since he'd made his list, things had progressed well. All of the furniture, rugs, and books were now in the rear of the garage, which had once been a stable. The old trim had been removed, the plaster touched up in preparation for the woodwork. Walt had written a fairly concise plan, and, judging by his list, it seemed that the project might just move along smoothly. But that didn't take into account the variable of Walt himself—while he had felt mostly confident about the project so far, he knew he would have to work hard to keep it from turning into another debacle. And with the millwork being delivered tomorrow, retaining focus was key. Ultimately, he was alone in the endeavor. Jimmy was far from the perfect helper, being both unskilled and impulsive. Fortunately, he was easily distracted, and didn't mind just hanging around until Walt needed an extra set of hands. He spent his time in the kitchen cooking soup, teaching Gwen how to tell dirty jokes in Italian, and teasing Miss June. *"How come you won't go on a date with me, June?"* he would ask. *"Ten years I been asking you out, and so far,* senza via d'uscita—*nothing. I might have to move on to Miss July or Miss August."*

Now, as he often did, Jimmy began to sing. This time, it was "Volare."

"Nel Blu Dipinto Di Blu…"

He had a surprisingly good voice, and would sing in unexpected places and moments, catching those around him off guard. He switched to English. *"No wonder, my happy heart sings ... Hey, Walt, won't you nail the damned thing ...*"

"Huh?" Walt had been daydreaming, and Jimmy was telling him to snap out of it.

From the next room, Gwen listened to the exchange and smiled. She enjoyed hearing them go on, these two very different men. In fact, the progress on her own work had slowed since Walt had enlisted Jimmy to help, as the entertainment was hard to ignore. And she loved this view into Walt's life. He was so much in his element with tools in his hands, so in command. During her first few months in town, he'd seemed vague, not quite there. She had begun to wonder if she'd remembered him wrong, that her expectations had been romanticized and unfairly high. Certainly, she had been young when they'd known each other back in school—but still, she couldn't have been that wrong, could she? Back then, he was passionate and certain. Upon her arrival last fall, he seemed to have dissolved somehow. Missing was the spark she had not forgotten. But now, since he'd embarked on Miss June's quest, she saw signs of that spark, and was pleased to think that maybe she had remembered him correctly after all. She listened to him and Jimmy working now, amused by the bickering that carried in from the next room.

"Jimmy, you cut that piece too short," she heard Walt say.

"Too short?" Jimmy protested. "You said cut off a hair, and I did. Bam! There you go."

"You cut off a quarter inch, at least."

"I'm tellin' you, I cut off a hair."

"No one's hair is that thick—what are you, a gorilla? I wanted you to cut off less than a sixteenth, for God's sake."

"A sixteenth? You mean of an inch? You gotta be kidding me—I can't see that small! Not even with my cheaters on, which I still can't find in that mess of a truck of yours. Every time I borrow that jalopy it's worse than before. Screw this anyway—I gotta go stir the soup. The old lady'll have a bird if I leave it go."

"Go ahead, you crazy Italian, make your damned soup. Don't worry about me, I'll just work here by myself."

"You want some soup?" Jimmy asked, suddenly earnest. "It's gonna be good."

"Why not. I am getting hungry."

"Yeah, well, people in hell want ice water. You ain't gettin' any!" He bounced out of the room. "Sixteenth of an inch, my ass…"

Gwen heard Jimmy approaching from the hallway, whistling as he walked, again with the "Volare."

"Hey, toots, how 'bout some soup?" he said leaning his head in the doorway. "I made it just for you."

"Ooh, soup with a handsome man, how perfect. I can't concentrate anyway."

"The hammering getting to you? That Walt, he's makin' a mess in there. That guy doesn't know what he's doin'. He's lucky he has me," he said with a wink that spoke volumes. Jimmy had terrific respect for Walt's skills and was fully aware that his own were, comparatively, for shit.

"Should we feed him, too?" she asked, her tone playfully suggesting she'd prefer it just be her and Jimmy.

"Nah," he said. "Let's go ahead and leave him be." Offering his arm, which she accepted, he asked, "Tell me sweetheart, do you know how to tango?"

The following week, Walt lost Jimmy to a wild goose chase that had him first borrow Walt's step ladder, a length of rope, a garden hose, a propane torch, a bumper jack, twenty bucks, and a hard hat. Walt didn't ask.

* * *

She had disappeared before, but had always come back. She could be colt-like—quick to move, quick to flash a smile. But other times she was sluggish—in her bathrobe at the kitchen table when he got home from school, sitting as she'd been when he left, the only evidence of activity the fullness of her ashtray. Of his mother's two states, Walt wasn't sure which he preferred. When she was happy—"sharp," as his young mind had named it—she was funny and impulsive. Trips out, to the park or the market, could take unexpected turns. "A live wire," he'd once heard her called. When she was sleepy, he did his best to leave her alone. "Your mother's not feeling well," his father would say unnecessarily, as there was no better barometer of his mother's state than the boy himself. Her absences—sometimes hours, sometimes days—were seldom acknowledged afterward, although when they were, it was with an affectionate, dismissive muss of his hair. "Don't look so glum, silly goose." She loved him, he knew. She just wasn't good at being there.

* * *

The room quiet, he surveyed the parlor, assessing his progress. Things had gone black. The new wainscoting leaned against the wall, waiting for his touch. The veneer flitches had been hand selected and numbered according to the plans, assuring that their grain was book-matched within the sections, which would follow a specific sequence around the room. Everything was ready for him to do what he loved—to work the material by hand, to give life to the parts and pieces. He considered the wall before him, pondered the chalk lines he'd made the day before, back when the work flowed freely, and possibility filled the air. So quickly things change. Now his tools were heavy, and the air was just thick. This was the familiar territory he'd hoped he could avoid, the deadening, muted state where progress simply can not be made. The mechanics of what he needed to do were clear. He could have explained it to anyone, shown them what pieces to install first and why, how to scribe the stiles of the wainscot before cutting them, ensuring proper fit against the plaster. Installing trim in old houses requires a fitting of pieces beyond straight and true. One must shape the material just so, allowing the new wood-work to rest correctly against the out-of-plumb walls, to make peace with the well-earned settling that took decades to occur. The straightest new work, the most square and level new cab-inet, while perhaps technically correct, can look terribly out of place in a crooked old room, an assault on the senses for those who care. Walt always made his work follow the contours of the existing walls, respecting the years they had seen. Each house, each room, had its own personality, and a quiet dialogue occurred between him and the structure as he worked. When things went well—when his demons were at bay—the process flowed as if by magic, his hands working the new wood until it was accepted. He didn't think too much about it as he went, aware that conscious thought can hinder the process. But that's where he was now, trapped by thought, awkward and obtuse. The harder he tried to overcome his inertia, the more elusive the magic proved to be. He considered the trim that lay stacked on his horses, waiting to be cut and then nailed. Just pick up a piece and do it. Stop thinking so damned much. Just move. This was when he usually gave into his state, moving on to greener pastures until the moment struck him as right to return, if that ever should occur. But this was different. Miss June had raised the stakes. And though he wouldn't have admitted it, so had Gwen. He wanted to perform for her, as well. He clenched his fists in self-loathing. The work before him was a path that led to where he so desperately wanted to be—the answer presented within the problem. There was no mystery as to what to do. But at that moment he could no sooner pick up one piece of trim than lift a thousand pounds. He closed his eyes and pressed his forehead to the cool plaster, uncertain of what he was, certain of what he wasn't.

* * *

Escape. The two sat in the Friendship living room drinking cider and watching Pitt play basketball on television. Walt had no interest in sports, never understood the rules or knew the names of the players. He knew the basic premise of basketball, but what was there to get so excited about? Sam loved sports, and in years past, the two of them had watched plenty of games together, her talking to the screen, him drifting off, his head eventually finding its way to her lap. Now, Walt had his own chair. Dewey got the lap.

"You shoot like a girl!" Sam complained. On her now-prominent belly rested a bowl of salsa, into which she would occasionally dip.

Sleepy, Walt closed his eyes and tried to ignore the television announcers. What the hell did "traveling" have to do with basketball? Art was in the kitchen, cooking dinner and listening to NPR. Walt hadn't spent a lazy Sunday at the Friendship house in a while, but now that the baby's room was done, he felt at home again.

"Okay, you two, I'll let you eat out there for once," Arthur called.

"I'd offer to help, but I can't get out of this chair," Walt replied. It was a modern affair of chrome tubing and leather slings that'd rendered him immobile.

Dinner was chili, biscuits, and a spinach salad with goat cheese. Pitt won and another game was starting, and Sam didn't ask her husbands if they wanted to watch anything else. Arthur offered periodic apologies for Sam's swearing during the game, as if Walt were a new acquaintance. After they ate, Arthur did the dishes, while Walt closed his eyes again and let his mind drift. He wondered about the baby, tried to decide who it would look like, what traits it might inherit. If she were a girl, he decided she should be just like Sam. Maybe if he were a boy, as well.

"So, how are things at Hardwick?" Sam asked during a commercial.

"The work?"

"No, Miss June. How is she doing?"

"It's hard to say. She still won't tell me what's wrong with her. I caught her using the elevator the other day. I think she knows that I saw. She naps now, too."

"How about Donald?"

"He's a nervous Nellie as always, but he seems to be holding up. The book keeps him occupied. He'll go to the ends of the earth to verify any small fact, no matter how obscure. I'm not sure what he'll do once she's gone."

"And you?"

"I don't know." It was hard to think about. "I guess I'm feeling a little foolish. About pretending this would never happen."

"It's not just you. I won't believe she's gone until I see it for myself. Not to sound insensitive, I mean."

"No, I understand."

"And the work?" Sam asked this gently, knowing it too could be a difficult subject. But Walt was forthcoming.

"It's a mixed bag. It's like an off and on switch—granted, off as much as on. It's tough."

She listened intently. As perceptive as he could be of others, Walt seldom offered insight into his own muddled being.

Sam had spent an entire marriage and beyond watching this big man, interpreting his movements and translating his dry humor as only she could. He appeared unflappable to the outside world—from day to day, year to year—a steady, content, sturdy guy, a comfort to most who knew him. He was a constant, despite being unreliable—a state that was most satisfactory to his appreciation of irony. Not just anyone could be a paradox. His goals had never been like those of others, nor was he driven by money or status. He did get down from time to time, but he almost never deemed a shift of mood worthy of comment, and would recover quickly enough to make it seem that things had not been amiss. Feeling blue was just feeling a little slower than usual, just one small part of life, not worth a mention. But Sam saw through his thick facade like no one else could. She had seen how his treasured aloofness had recently shifted, guessed that his failings didn't strike him as amusing as they usually did. It was subtle, but she saw it—he was fighting the pull of a tailspin. His hidden defenses—built so solidly as a child—had always shielded him, leaving the unpleasantries of adulthood for others. The defenses worked. They made sense. They had infuriated Sam as their marriage declined and then died, how they enabled him to not take life more seriously, to not *'act like a damned grownup'* as she had begged toward the end. But now maybe he had outgrown those defenses. Or, she hoped, he was choosing to move beyond them. The changes around him were real. Her baby *was* on its way. Her life with Arthur *did* illustrate what a normal version of their life could have been. And Miss June was dying. While Sam was unused to seeing Walt out of sorts, part of her secretly welcomed the sadness that had settled within him. It meant a chance for real change, that he might finally acknowledge that all was not well. She knew his turmoil was not something he could articulate. The battle he was aware of, the one he was fighting so hard, was for Miss June, and it took place in her parlor. But a much greater conflict was occurring within. Sam understood this. She had given much thought to her greatest love.

"As much as I know that I need to stick with it," he continued, "I'm still battling with … things. You know."

"I do know, big guy. I do. And I hate that she's asked you to do this. But I'm proud that you're trying. I really am."

"Well, I don't see that I have a choice."

"No, I don't think you do. And that's what makes you, you."

"No, when I don't finish it, that's what'll make me, me."

"You'll get it done, sweetheart," she said, the tiny degree of hope in her voice betraying what little conviction might also have been there.

He drifted off then to the sound of the game, unaware when he woke up later, alone and with the television off, that it had been Arthur who had removed his boots and covered him with a quilt.

* * *

Miss June's Imperial pulled into the cobblestone drive, its grille an expanse of chrome. Behind the wheel was Gwen, with Miss June's little head barely visible in the passenger seat. Walt tucked in his shirt, and then, touching his belly, reconsidered and pulled it back out. The two entered Hardwick through the back door, Miss June on Gwen's arm, an act of dependence that didn't pass Walt by. Once in the house, Miss June caught her breath, and then asked him if he'd just been standing there all morning waiting for her to return home.

"Oh, yes, Miss June. I'm just not myself without you to guide me through my day."

"What a coincidence," she said. "I'd been hoping you

wouldn't be yourself—but here you are, the same as always."

Apparently, she was fine.

"Now, if you two don't mind, I have business to attend to upstairs. Don't let my absence keep you from your work, young man."

"No, nor will I let your work interfere with my absence."

"Don't make sport of me," she warned.

"So, where were you two?" Walt asked as Gwen once they were alone.

"Oh, just out for some fun. Walnut Street, window shopping." She checked to make sure Miss June was gone. "I took her to a bar!"

"What?" Walt couldn't even imagine Miss June in the bar at the Waldorf Astoria.

"She needs to get out sometimes, too, you know."

"Really? She's always just had people come to her. It's much easier that way. Are you saying you just suggested it and she went?"

"Pretty much. We had some shopping to do first, and a stop at the bakery to buy you this," she said presenting him with a small white bag, "and then we stopped at Lou's for a drink."

"Well, I'll be."

"She'd needed a short rest. But, drum roll, please"—she made an accompanying drum roll sound—"Thursday I'm taking her to a hair salon."

For as long as Walt could remember, a plain woman named Norma showed up at Creighton every other Wednesday to do Miss June's hair, the same dull style each time.

"And she's going along with this? Are you sure she heard you right?"

"You bet. It's amazing what a little girl-talk can accomplish. She told me things you wouldn't believe."

"Do tell."

"Well, it wouldn't be girl-talk then, would it?"

She looked around the room, smiling at the transformation that was under way. "This is amazing."

Earlier in the day, the pendular darkness had shifted, and he had once again been able to work.

"Thanks. It's slow going."

"I'm sure it is, working alone."

"Well, Jimmy's gone, and unless I get a call that he's gotten married or needs money, I don't expect to hear from him for a while."

"How do you know he won't be returning?"

"Because he said he'd be right back."

"I see. Do you mind if I sit for a while? I don't feel like writing just now."

"Please. Pull up a toolbox and make yourself at home."

She did, and he got back to it, running a hand plane along a section of wainscot. She liked what the years had done to his face. On the radio, Gene Harris played the piano while ribbons of mahogany coiled onto the floor. Despite his thick arms, Walt had a delicate touch, and it almost made her tearful, though she wasn't sure why. Back in school, he'd had a mischievous quality, had enjoyed screwing with the administration. He was different now, this big man. Still one to crack a joke, but also quiet, nearly sad. No matter, he seemed at peace now as he leaned over the long panel and prepared to hoist it from the sawhorses.

"Hey, wait, let me help," she said, jumping up.

Uncharacteristically, he accepted. "Help would be great. I'm not as young as I used to be."

Together, they lifted the panel, with Walt leading the way across the room, trying to take as much of the weight as he could.

"Here, your end first," he said, leading Gwen into the corner where the panel would sit. The quarters were close, and she could smell the sawdust on his shirt as they knelt on the floor. "Now hold it still. Just like that."

He positioned his spirit level, an old one made of dark wood and brass, and watched as the bubble settled itself, agreeing that the piece was set right, close enough to level, but still at home against the crooked old floor. She saw his concentration, noted his authority. He started a few finish nails to pin the piece in place, and than handed the hammer to her to drive them in the rest of the way.

"No way. I don't want to mess this up," she protested, holding the hammer awkwardly.

"You won't. Here, like this."

He corrected her grip, and helped her swing it properly, starting from the elbow, adding finality from the wrist. It took time, and they worked closely until the piece was set. She felt as if she'd just been a part of something important.

"That's it?" she said quietly, afraid to break the moment.

Walt nodded in return. "That's it," he said softly. They lingered there, together, close.

"What are we doing here?" she whispered after a while.

"Building," he replied, in a whisper of his own.

Chapter 14

HE WAS CLEANING UP FOR THE DAY when he saw Miss June standing in the yard looking toward the house—at what, he wasn't sure. She wasn't one to spend time idly, and he was curious as to what she was examining. The damned shutters probably, though spring was still six weeks away. How many times had he taken those things down and put them back up? The same number of times he'd complained about it to the old woman, the two of them having their semi-annual argument over the value of the task. And now, Walt admitted that the day would come when he would perform the task for the last time. Worse, he considered that he might already have. She seemed smaller than ever, and less vocal, too, leaving him to his work, spending some time directing Donald and Gwen, but for the most part sitting in her study, writing letters and looking through photo albums. She walked toward the edge of the yard, looking at the gardens that Donald painstakingly tended. Was she walking with a limp? He turned back toward the room, looked at the mess he'd made, what he had gotten himself into. It was insanity, letting her think he would get this job done. The muse that was Gwen had lessened the task's immensity, but looking at it now, the room suddenly lengthened as if through the other end of a telescope, inducing a near syncope that threatened to expose him once and for all. He unhooked his tool belt and let it drop to the floor.

* * *

"Holy smokes, look what the cat dragged in," Gene said, wiping the bar.

"It's not been that long."

"A week, damn near." He drew Walt a draft.

"That's no record. Is it?"

"No, but for a while there you was gettin' as bad as Dumb and Shit over there," Gene said, indicating the usual pair of drunks at the end of the bar. "I thought maybe the old lady wasn't gonna let you leave until you're done with whatever the hell it is you've gotten yourself into. You eat?"

"Not yet."

Gene pulled a frozen lump of breaded something from the freezer and dropped it into the fryer. Walt was in the mood for a "Bull's-Eye Special"—a cheeseburger with a slab of ham on top—but Gene had already chosen for him. No matter. It all tasted pretty much the same anyhow.

Gene lowered his voice. "You keep your eyes out over there. When you're tearing them walls open, I mean. Word has it, she's got millions stashed away in that house. She acts like she don't got no money, but it's all there, cash, hid all around the place."

"If she had money, why would she keep it in the house? Why not just use a bank?"

"Nah, people from that generation, they don't trust no banks. Not after the crash. Shit, I don't trust 'em neither."

"Well, thanks for the tip, Gene, but I'm pretty sure that if Miss June had millions stuffed inside the walls, she'd let me know."

"I'd rather see you get it than that numb-nuts nephew of hers." Reggie was hated by pretty much everyone. "That bastard tried to buy my bar once. Did I ever tell you that? And it wasn't even for sale. He just came in here one day, all slick like, tryin' to talk me up, tellin' me what a good businessman I was. I asked him what the hell he wanted to go in the bar business for? 'Oh, I wouldn't do that,' he says, 'I want to tear the place down and build an office building.' 'Get the hell outta my bar,' I told him, 'before I shove this baseball bat up your skinny ass.'"

"That would be Reggie."

"Can you believe that shit? The way he came in here, smiling and acting like I was some kind of rube. I wouldn't sell him this place for a million bucks."

"Good for you."

"Then again, if that asshole was actually stupid enough to give me that much, I'd be outta here like a New York Jew."

Walt figured he meant "in a New York minute," but let it slide.

"Um, actually, the bar might be worth that much, Gene. Are you aware of that?"

"Get outta here. This place ain't worth no million bucks. Hell, I only paid twenty nine grand for it, liquor license and all. It was one-a them rent-to-own deals from old man Kasansky. He was pretty decent for a Polack, if you know what I mean. Did I ever tell you about the time when I was a kid—just out of the army—and old man Kasansky bailed me out for hittin' a cop?"

"Yeah, you did. But listen to me. This property is worth something. The university is buying up everything around here. I'm not saying they'd keep it as a bar, but they would pay a lot for it. Much more than Reggie ever would."

"Yeah, well, big brains or not, them college people ain't payin' no million dollars for a joint like this. Besides, I'd want it to stay a bar, you know? Someplace where a working man can get a drink for a decent price. You know how much some of these places charge for a drink these days? It's fuckin' crazy." To an older neighborhood woman a few seats down, he added, "Pardon my French."

"Well, just promise me this, okay? Don't do something crazy and sell this place one day without talking to me first."

"Yeah, sure, whatever. But I tell you," he lowered his voice, "once my mum's gone on, if somebody other than that Reggie come along with a big fat offer, I'd take it. I'd hope they'd keep it a bar, but no matter—if they give me enough so I can go fishing all day, I'm done."

"I understand. Just don't do anything rash."

"Shit. You known me, what, twenty years? When did I do anything rash?"

He had a point. He'd been standing right there behind the bar the whole time.

"Anyway, I seen your lady-friend the other day," Gene said.

"Sam?"

"No, the new one."

"Deena?"

"No, no. Cute, young, needs to gain a few pounds."

What the hell was he talking about?

"Said her name was Stef or something?"

"Gwen?"

"Yeah, that's it. 'Gwen,' she said."

She'd never said anything about going to Gene's. He looked

around the place, surveying its grunginess, feeling as if company had dropped by his apartment before he could clean up, not that that had ever bothered him before. And who had she been with?

"Anyway, she was in here with some friends. College-looking people. Two guys and another gal. Sat right over there. Got here around dinner time, looked like they were just warmin' up when I went upstairs. Nice kid."

Two guys and a gal? Was it a date? No, it couldn't have been. Just old friends from school. But why couldn't it have been a date? And even if it hadn't started as a date, it could have ended as one. Gene refilled Walt's glass, and he drained half of it directly.

"That was from Einstein over there."

Walt looked down the bar and saw Louis—he of the unsolved pretzel mystery—waving at him. Walt raised his glass and called out thanks. Louis seldom had money to buy a drink for himself, let alone for anyone else, and when he did either, it made people uneasy. Louis drunk was not a good thing. He was, for the most part, benign, but he was sensitive about how his intelligence was perceived, and adding alcohol to his system raised that sensitivity, causing him to misinterpret innocent comments from others as being insults, ironically proving said perceptions about his mental capacity to be true.

"Hey, Walt. Come sit with me."

Not wanting to be rude, Walt slipped down a few stools to within a couple of the younger man. "Thanks for the beer, Louis. What are we celebrating?"

"My probation's over today. I ain't in trouble no more."

"Well, congratulations." Walt wished he wasn't sitting there having this conversation. Did he have to share a drink over this? Couldn't he just send a card? Surely they made them for such occasions. Walt wasn't afraid of the oversized kid, as he was fairly certain that he could always outsmart him, and besides, Louis seemed to have respect for Walt, seeing him, as he did Gene, as an authority figure. But the circumstances surrounding Louis's arrest made Walt feel slightly ill, and he generally tried not to think about it. A couple of years before, Louis, while laboring for a concrete crew pouring a sidewalk, pushed a wheelbarrow full of wet cement off of a curb and into the path of a costly European sedan that was late for a meeting. The car hit the wheelbarrow, collapsing its fender and splashing concrete across its hood. The driver, upset, ignored Louis's apology and asked him if he was an idiot, a question that would be understood by most people to be rhetorical. Unfortunately for the driver, Louis, being of a more literal mind than most, didn't take to the question kindly, and before anyone could intervene, he did a curious thing. Rather than punch the man as one might expect, he grabbed big pinch-fulls of flesh from the driver's cheeks with his thumbs and index fingers, and pulled sideways as hard as he could. The man's mouth became a cartoonishly large oval, until finally an audible pop was heard, causing one of the concrete finishers to throw up on the spot. According to Louis's own testimony in court, pulling the man's face apart had been *"Like a potato chip bag—hard to get started, but real easy once you do."* Walt figured that Louis suffered from poor judgment more than anything, and didn't see how sending someone so impressionable to jail would do the world any good. Reluctantly, he'd agreed to appear at the hearing as a character witness, and Louis's sentence of nine months was commuted to two years of probation, contingent upon his staying employed for that same period of time. Because Louis didn't have a regular job, it somehow came down on Walt to keep him busy and out of trouble. With Louis's enthusiasm eclipsing Walt's own energies, Walt paid him to do any sort of simple task he could think up that required little supervision, including shoveling snow not only for Sam, but for all of her neighbors within a three-block radius. In the summer, he cut grass. Walt had him remove the overgrown brush in the empty lot two doors down from the Bull's-Eye, despite not knowing who owned the property. Any exhausting task he could think of, Louis attacked with frightening energy. Walt paid him minimum wage—money that he didn't have, and for which he took the occasional contribution from Gene. And as far as Louis knew, he was providing crucial services for Walt, whom he saw as being quite the entrepreneur. Louis was obedient, but spooked Walt nonetheless.

"Cheryl's happy, that's for sure," he said now. "She said she ain't gonna marry no convict."

Cheryl, a gum-chewing, Misty-smoking dynamo struck fear into Louis like no man ever could. She controlled all aspects of his life including his money, which she doled out so calculatedly that if he behaved just as he was supposed to, he could have exactly two beers on Friday afternoon. On behalf of Southwestern Pennsylvania, Walt was thankful for her existence.

"Again, congratulations," Walt said. "I'm glad everything's been cleared up." He slapped a stack of quarters on the bar. "Here, the pool table's on me."

"Thanks. You wanna shoot a few games?"

"I'd like to, but my dinner's just about ready. Gene's trying to poison me again."

"I love the food here," Louis said dreamily. "Them burgers is good."

"Take it easy, Louis."

Walt slid back down the bar to his usual spot.

"What, you don't wanna drink with that kid?" Gene asked.

"Very funny."

He ate his fried meal alone, the bar becoming end-of-the-week busy around him. Because he was minding his own business, the place seemed private. Bars could be like that, offering a peculiar anonymity made possible by an etiquette that held that because bar friends might feel chatty one day but not the next, and that no hard feelings should be taken if one prefers not to talk beyond saying hello. It was a comfortable atmosphere. Gwen must be aware that he spent a lot of time at Gene's, he thought. Everyone seemed to know his business these days, so it only figured that she did, too. He hoped she and her friends hadn't laughed at the novelty of the place, that they didn't consider their visit as "slumming it." He knew that Gwen didn't have that sort of meanness about her, but he also knew that much of the college crowd saw the place as being a goof, a shrine to kitsch and simple thinking. Snide judgment, fueled by alcohol, could be contagious.

As he pondered that, a tremendous thunderclap filled the room, a report louder than a starter's pistol. It shook the windows and scared most of the crowd nearly out of their seats, but Gene and Walt barely flinched, knowing that it was just Louis breaking the rack on his first free game. Unlike Deena, who also broke hard but could then run the table, Louis was terrible at pool, certain that a tremendous advantage was to be had by hitting every shot for all it was worth, firing each ball around the table as though from a cannon. *"Sorry,"* he would say as the balls left the worn green felt and scampered across the tables nearby. *"My fault."* Watching the big kid with the small head circle the table, Walt wondered if somewhere out there was the right job for him, something that would reward his fervor without taxing his intellect or jeopardizing the safety of others. Maybe janitorial work at an old folks home, where respect for his elders would keep his volatility in check. Someplace where Cheryl could pick him up after his shift, preventing him from trading his cow for magic beans on the way home.

Walt surveyed the many faces in the room: an assortment tonight; daytime drinkers having not yet gone home; college-aged kids; Clarence, the local scrap-man who traversed the East End with his shopping cart of tin cans and copper pipe; a tidy, older couple from the neighborhood who stopped in once a week, wearing the same threadbare suit and faded dress they had for years—bourbon neat for him, an old-fashioned for her. Talking to Gene was an old man who claimed to have played Negro League for the Homestead Grays, where he'd batted once against Satchel Paige. *That man could throw a strawberry through a locomotive.* Typically, this would be a lovely scene for Walt, a variety of souls offering their own rich tale. And though the people came and went, the bar was a constant—fixed and reliable, a pillar of life. But something big was changing and, incredibly, it was him.

* * *

The floorboards on the little porch groaned against his weight, and he looked at the door for a moment, at two wires where there had once been a button. He knocked. The loose glass rattled, making his knock louder than intended. He had no idea what to say, and even less idea of what her reaction would be to him showing up unannounced. This wasn't in the rules. He was looking at the yellow porch light when the door pulled open to frame Deena in a thin satin bathrobe, her long hair wet from the shower.

"Hi," he said.

"Hi."

Their first normal conversation, he thought.

"May I come in?"

She studied him with those black eyes.

"Sure."

As he entered, it occurred to him that she might not be alone. Thankfully, she was. He sometimes wondered if there were men other than himself, and, if so, who they were. A biker? A bartender? A minor league ball-player? The smell of the Harley was still in the room, although the bike itself was gone, ridden right out the front door and down the two steps, he supposed.

They stood. "I've never just stopped over like this," he said. "It feels different." She didn't blink. He looked at the knick-knacks on her mantel, the stack of magazines on her coffee table. *Good Housekeeping. Easy Rider.* "That doesn't mean I don't think about you though." At that, she broke eye contact. "Sometimes I wonder what would happen if I brought you flowers. I think maybe I should have." And with those words, *"should have,"* they both knew he was there to say goodbye, that their strange pairing was over.

She moved in close and put her index finger over his lips, her body firm beneath her cheap robe. She smelled clean, of grocery store soap, and she put her head against his chest, her hair wet and cool. On the mantel, three small candles were lit, and he could still smell the match—she'd lit them when he'd knocked. His hand found the small of her back and he pulled her in tight. They swayed almost imperceptibly, a slow dance to silence, just one final minute together ending with one light kiss and the awareness that they had just, for the first and only time, from their hearts, made love.

* * *

Having nearly finished the walls—a significant accomplishment on its own—Walt started in on the ceiling, the toughest part of the job. He wasn't completely done with the wainscoting, but his demons had begun conspiring to block his progress, so he decided to shift his efforts to up above in the hopes of faking them out. The scaffold that covered half the room was on rental. When he'd written the deposit check for it earlier that week, he'd had his usual concern about Miss June and her money, about what this work would end up costing. The millwork invoice alone had been nearly six figures. Before the project began, any house expenditure beyond a couple hundred dollars was frowned upon unless it was deemed absolutely necessary. But the bills for the parlor—from the electricians, the plasterer, the dumpster company—were paid by Miss June and her banker with no questions asked. Walt wondered if by reviewing the bills from the other tradesmen she saw that she'd been underpaying him all these years, not that he had ever felt miffed about it—taking money from Miss June had always been awkward for him. For the parlor, perhaps she'd arranged to sell some of the art from the house—she'd certainly been approached by auction houses over the years—as the money had to be coming from somewhere. But as he fastened his tool belt after lunch, it hit him. How obvious it should have been, how perfectly in keeping with her ability to see all of the chess pieces, to move them in ways that no one would anticipate—she was screwing Reggie. All of the project's cost, through some sort of loan arrangement with her banker, would ultimately come from the estate that Reggie would inherit. He was paying for it all. And for months, Walt had been worrying that this flood of expense was causing her stress when she was already weak, when in fact she was no doubt enjoying every minute of it. Of course she had manipulated the situation in her favor. What had he been thinking? Hell, maybe he'd buy himself a few tools and bill them to the job. He smiled at the old woman's resourcefulness, and at his failing to realize she would have crafted a clever plan.

"I'd offer a penny for your thoughts, but with a smile like that, I'm not sure I want to hear them," Gwen said from the doorway.

"Oh, my thoughts are pure, I assure you."

"I'll bet."

"How's the book going?"

"Pretty well, I think. I had a great morning at the library." Looking behind her to make sure Miss June wasn't near, she added, "Seeking my own sources. It's astounding how much money the Creightons once had. I had no idea. Oh, and I found the most amazing social records in the Pennsylvania Room archives. The people she knew! Families whose names are on street signs all over town. Listen to this," she said, plunking herself down on a drywall bucket and rummaging through her bookbag. "This is from *The Social Spyglass*, a wonderfully snooty societal record. It's high-end gossip, from what I can tell. These are entries from 1935."

A lovely blonde with fairness of complexion and slender stature is Mrs. Elmer McClintock, nee Miss Eleanor Roup. Mrs. McClintock, a sweet bud and bride of seven months now, is cozily established in a fine house on Craig Street. Her dowry was the sum of $100,000, made in glass.

"And—"

Mrs. Nathaniel A. Hurd, formerly Miss Mary Ann Beasley of Chicago, came to marriage independently wealthy in her own right, and is considered authoritative in all matters of refinement. Mrs. Hurd is of the brunette type and has charming dimples and is considered one of the loveliest girls in Pittsburgh.

"This is unbelievable," Walt said. "How did I never find this book?"

"Some don't fare so well."

Vera Glunt is a loyal friend and active bridesmaid for many gals. She is firmly domiciled in a great home with her sister on Aiken Avenue and has inherited some handsome jewels. She is known for her lovely teeth.

"On the other hand,"

Mrs. Anita Black is regarded highly for her fine home on Saint James Place. Her comfort is celebrated, and she charms in the role as hostess. She entered society a few seasons back, and is a recognized member of the cotillion set. It is thought she was worth $300,000 before entering marriage. Few are known for greater warmth.

"And now, this one," she warned.

Polite society welcomed Miss June Creighton at a parlor ball in her father's grand manse on Fifth Avenue. Sharp of mind, Miss Creighton is slender and holds herself with propriety beyond her age. It is rumored she will one day be the bride of Mr. Dwight Keating, formerly of Connecticut.

"Oh, my," he said.

"Indeed."

"I don't know what to say."

Neither did she. Finally, he changed the subject.

"Look at this," he said, pointing above his head. "You can see the pipes from the old gas lights. They were converted to electric, probably at the turn of the century."

"Cool. What comes next?"

"Next up is to chalk lines, to lay out the grid of the beams and panels. Then, I'll screw in the blocking and begin to assemble the finished work. You can see how the pieces fit together in the drawings. It's like a big puzzle."

"And how do you do this by yourself?"

"I'm used to it. Chalking the lines, for instance. I drive a nail in the ceiling on one side of the room, and hook my chalk line to it, walk across the planks, snap the line, walk back over, drive another nail, and so on. It's tedious, but it works."

"Would you mind if I helped?"

The question surprised him. "Mind? How could I?" As he heard his own words, he knew they could be taken to mean that he'd welcome Gwen's company or just the extra set of hands. He wondered which she'd heard. "But, uh, aren't you supposed to be writing?"

"Yeah, yeah. I can only take so much. I've been working non-stop seven days a week."

Except for trips to bars.

"Well, then, your offer is accepted. But, in return, you have to let me buy you dinner. Tonight. I know we've talked about it before, but things keep coming up."

He had been shy about asking her out, and he surprised himself now by insisting that it be tonight.

"Mr. Farnham, you have yourself a deal."

She caught on to the work quickly. Being smart doesn't necessarily translate to being handy, and academic types were the worst. But Gwen was good with her hands, and learned the process quickly. Like the best of helpers, she anticipated Walt's next move, was ready for him when he made it. He'd worked mostly alone over the years, using makeshift jigs to compensate, and he'd forgotten how nice it was to have someone hold the other end of a tape measure or snap the chalk-covered string after he'd pulled it taut. And she wasn't hard to look at, either.

"I must say, you are, without a doubt, the best helper I've ever had."

"That's me—Miss Competent."

"You are competent. All the way around."

"I was being facetious."

"But you are. You're good at everything you do."

"Ugh. I've spent so much energy trying to be successful. And for what?"

"The respect of your peers? To be published? And let's face it—money?"

"It's true, I have begun to get those things."

"Aren't they what you want?"

"We don't always want the smartest things, do we?"

"I'm confused. I can't see anything about your life that isn't going well. Except the whole divorce thing," he quickly added.

"Yes, that whole thing. Actually, that's one of the good things. This time away from Boston has cemented that for me."

"So what's the problem?"

She saw Walt's crappy truck through the window, thought about how he eked out a living.

"I shouldn't complain. I've got a lot to be thankful for."

"No, go on. Complain all you like. If I get sick of it, I'll tune you out. I do it well—I've worked with Jimmy for years.

"I don't know. People just assume things are easy for me."

Walt nodded, acknowledging that he was one of those people.

"And I suppose they are. Sort of. I can't feel casual about anything I do. It's my curse. I'm too driven to achieve. And I do. I visited my grandmother last summer, figuring it might be the last time we have together, and she was sewing a quilt by hand. She'd worked on it for a decade, and was only weeks away from being done. I asked if I could spend a little time working on it, just on one corner, to have a small amount of my work intertwined with hers. She was touched, and let me, but I went and stayed up all night and finished the damned thing, only to realize that I'd robbed her of the pleasure of finishing it herself. I had to undo most of what I'd done before she saw it."

"That's hardly a crime."

"No, it's not. But it's a tendency I have. I'm hard on myself. I have to achieve, or else —"

"Or else …"

"I don't know. It's just what I do. And because of it, because of how much I accomplish, people think my life is easy, which it's not, I assure you." She looked at him, and then away. "I get lonely."

"I believe you," he said. And he did, because he'd heard the change in her voice. But it never would have occurred to him, which proved her right. Gwen did seem perfect. Seeing her insecurities surface, he felt bad about misunderstanding her. The notion that someone like Gwen questioned herself made him feel less uncomfortable about his own recent introspection, his new tendency to ponder his own inner workings. Perhaps it was a good thing. But for now, he just wanted her to feel better.

"I'm sorry. I should be telling this to a therapist, not you," she said.

"Hey, I'm glad to hear I'm not the only one who's screwed up. And besides, we have something in common."

"What's that?"

"I, too, am an overachiever to which everything appears to come easily."

She burst out laughing and he joined in. It became the kind of laughter that escalates out of control. What he'd said wasn't all that funny, but the moment became about the laughter itself, not what had prompted it. They lay back on the hard planks, side by side, shoulders touching, trying to get the giggles to subside. It happened so quickly, they hadn't seen it coming, just as they hadn't seen Miss June peeking in from the doorway, pleased as punch.

Chapter 15

"HI, MOM," Walt said from Sam's back door.

"Well, if it isn't Mr. Nine-to-Five."

"That would be me."

"So it would seem. You're getting to be like Arthur."

"Well, let's not get nuts here. Where is the good doc, anyway?"

"At work. He called to say he'd be 'approximately twenty-three minutes late.'"

"I don't know how you stand the unpredictability of that fellow."

He poured some seltzer from the fridge—Sam subscribed to a local service that delivered it in vintage bottles each week—and sat down at the table. She noticed him trying to crack his neck, moved behind his chair, and began to massage his shoulders.

"God, you're tight."

"Tell me about it. I'm getting too old for this shit."

"What's the latest with Miss June?"

"I wish I knew. She still won't talk about what's wrong with her. She seems frail."

"I'm sorry."

For him, she meant. Her thumbs dug into his shoulders, and he let his head slump forward.

"Oh, for God's sake, you might as well get comfortable," she said, tugging on his shirt collar. "Come on."

She directed him into the living room, where he pulled off his shirt and lay face down on the rug. It took her a moment to get herself and her growing belly down on the floor to join him, and when she did, she straddled his behind. She pushed the heels of her hands into his lower back, hard, using her body weight to push forward, drawing from him a moan. She worked her way up his spine slowly, her hands familiar and confident. Sam loved to work Walt's muscles, and though she sighed loudly and acted begrudging about having to fix his back, in truth, she got as much from their sessions as he did. Walt knew that to be the case, but also knew better than to mention it, lest he screw up a good thing. When she massaged him, he felt the clearest connection to her, one that transcended circumstance, including that of the inconvenient sort, such as her being married to someone else. These backrubs felt so close to making love that he occasionally wondered if they were—if he and Sam were in fact cheating—but he relied on Sam's moral compass to know what was right. Thankfully, it was apparently okay. As she leaned forward to knead his neck and shoulders some more, he felt her new figure pressing warmly against him through her maternity blouse. He reached around and put his hand on her belly—her baby—feeling its firmness in his palm, pretty sure he could feel Sam's pulse. Satisfied that he was looser than when they'd started, she leaned forward, slowly dismounted, smacked his ass, and mussed his hair.

"Next!" she called as if to a waiting room.

He rolled slowly over onto his back and enjoyed a head rush. He pulled his heels toward his butt and rolled his hips from side to side, cracking his lower back while she struggled to get up.

"My God, I should have married you when I had the chance," he said.

"You did, remember?"

"Really? What happened?"

"You left me for a conga dancer named Conchita."

"Ah, yes. Conchita. She left me for a knife thrower from Bolivia, as I recall. Anyway, it was a bad move on my part. Leaving you, I mean. You make everything feel better."

"Eh. You men are easy," she said dismissively, dusting off her hands as if after a job well done. "Especially you. Your needs are simple."

While that had been true in the past, he wasn't so sure anymore. He looked at her towering over him.

"Can I ask you a question?" he asked.

"Shoot."

"If you were going out for dinner, where would you go?"

"On a date, you mean?"

"No, no. Well, maybe. I don't know. A place that would be okay either way. I'm so far out of the loop, I don't know what's around anymore."

Sam was suddenly very interested.

"So who is she? Anyone I know? Did you finally call Muriel Weber?"

"No, I didn't call Muriel Weber. It's nothing like that. Just an old friend. I need an all-purpose restaurant, one that's not overtly romantic."

"But one that could be if the evening takes a certain turn," she guessed correctly.

"Okay, Miss Busybody, something like that. But don't get your hopes up, okay? This is just dinner between old friends."

"Hmmm, mystery and intrigue abound. But, okay. What kind of food are you looking for"

"Just something good. Interesting maybe. Someplace that makes it seem like I haven't been …"

"Eating at Gene's for ten years?" she ventured.

"Precisely."

"All right. Well, there's Maiolo's on Highland. Forget Avon—it's overrated. There's a new sushi place in the Strip that's supposed to be good. No, Maiolo's is right. Go there.

"Thank you, sweetheart."

Standing above and facing him, she put her feet on top of his, like a child does when they want a grown-up to make them dance. He lifted his feet upward a little, pressing against hers—left, right, left, right—much like how couples squeeze each other's hands rhythmically when they walk down the street, secretly signaling *I love you*.

"Do you want to borrow my car?"

"My truck's running."

"I know it is, but it does have a certain, um, hillbilly quality you may not want to introduce to the evening."

"Ah, well, that cat's already out of the bag. It's okay. My truck comes with the package."

"Well, at least clean the inside, okay? Let's not scare her back to Boston."

He didn't acknowledge her guess. "I can't believe you would say that. The cab of my truck includes much of our history together. Wrappers from hamburgers we shared, your many beer cans, one of your shoes. It's like an archeological site from our marriage."

"Ruins, you mean."

"Ruins? It's a monument. A monument to you that I

painstakingly preserve."

"You're confusing me with Conchita."

"Ah, Conchita. How she could balance that fruit on her head, I'll never know. Now help me up."

Still standing on his feet, she grabbed his hands, and rocked rhythmically backward and forward as they both silently counted—*one, two, three*—before she leaned back suddenly with all of her weight, pulling hard, letting her increased mass and their mutually developed mastery of physics pull him up from the floor. They smiled at each other, recalling times long ago when her attempts to pull him up sometimes resulted in him pulling her back down for a continuation of the backrub that was more than what she'd bargained for.

"Hello, there," Arthur said from the doorway.

"Oh, hi, honey," Sam said. "We didn't hear you come in."

"I assumed not," Art said, not quite sure of what it was that he'd just witnessed, his pregnant wife hoisting her very large and half naked ex-husband from the floor with practiced aplomb.

"Don't worry, Artie," Walt said, not making him feel any better. "She's good as new."

* * *

Surprising himself, Walt did take a stab at cleaning out his truck before picking up Gwen, thinning out the food wrappers and coffee cups that covered the floor. The Chiclets had multiplied again. Perhaps an exorcism was in order. He had on a new shirt that he'd bought on the way home from Hardwick, stopping at a young, loud store, where he was clearly out of place. He felt somewhat embarrassed with himself, buying a shirt just for dinner, but most of his decent shirts had become work clothes, and he didn't want to screw this up.

Traversing the porch at Hardwick, he had an unusual impulse to ring the bell, although of course he'd never done so before. Instead, he entered quietly, and found Donald and Miss June ensconced in a corner of the music room, with Donald reading aloud. It took Walt a moment to recognize the passage as Proust.

"Aren't you kids sitting a little close?"

Donald slid quickly back over to his own side of the sofa, blushing like a teenager.

"Walter! What a nice surprise!" he said, his reddening face suggesting otherwise.

"Don't worry, Casanova. I'm not staying."

"I should hope not," Miss June said. "Your clumsy presence is the antithesis of the words Donald and I were just enjoying. But, that said, I must acknowledge that you look unusually presentable this evening, Walter."

He had been hoping she wouldn't comment on his attire, as he was already feeling as if he were getting his school picture taken later that day. He didn't need comments from the peanut gallery.

"Why, Miss June, you know I always try to look my best for you."

"I know you do, dear, and it's an effort that never fails to make your appearance that much more heartbreaking. Gwenneth tells me that you are rescuing her from the boredom of this house for the evening."

"A rescue, it is."

"Well, before you go, there is something for you on the piano."

His list.

"It can't wait until tomorrow?"

"No. While you're assuming that I've added new items to your list, I've not. On the contrary, so as to not discourage your unusually concentrated efforts in the parlor, I'm temporarily excusing you from your regular duties. Rather than your list, what you'll find on the piano is an envelope, inside of which you will find money for this evening's meal."

"You're paying for our dinner?"

"For Gwenneth. It's a reward for her hard work. For you, well, let's just say I'm hoping that some proper nourishment will help keep you on task. You're far from finished, you know. I can't have you keeling over before you're done, which is a distinct possibility given that you take so many of your meals in establishments of questionable repute."

"I'm speechless."

This was an uncharacteristically sweet gesture from his formidable old partner.

"Well, just leave us be, then. Donald reads so slowly, I'll be lucky to still be around by Chapter Three."

"Oh! Ha!" Donald responded.

"Psst," Gwen said from the door.

She seemed more beautiful than ever, to have somehow turned up the wick on her glow.

"Wow," he said. "Look at you."

"Me? Look at you. The girls are gonna throw rocks at all the other fellas."

"Well, then," he said, pleased at the compliment. "Our chariot awaits."

Following the suave owner through the hip restaurant, Walt felt conspicuous, like a farmer visiting the big city. And while their procession did turn heads, it was definitely not him who was the object of the room's interest.

* * *

At the same time that Gwen and Walt were being seated, and as Donald embarked on another cautious journey out of Hardwick's treacherous drive, Miss June rose from her seat, leaving her shawl behind. With her skeleton key, she unlocked the top left drawer of her writing desk, and from its farthest reaches retrieved her most prized possession. She moved to the middle of the room, the moonlight through the sash illuminating her photo album with a silver glow, almost making it seem that the images were not old. The photos were of her and Dwight. In one, he mugs for the camera in his bathing suit, flexing his muscles in jest. In another, he and his athletic friends form a human pyramid, one that Miss June could still see toppling moments after the shutter had clicked. And there, on an early spring morning, was Miss June herself. It was the most flattering photograph she had. In it, she looked alive and in love, feminine and free, unaware of the looming circumstances that would thrust her into a lifetime of constraint.

She turned the pages of the book slowly, as she always did on the rare occasions she allowed herself this trip. She saw herself with her parents, and her baby brother Thomas, all smiles and sweetness, not a hint of the tragedy he eventually would become. The grand parlor in its full glory, its woodwork intact, Miss June and Dwight in formal dress, being photographed before leaving for a ball. And on the next page, young Walter. He was not quite twelve, standing in the yard, his father at his side, hand on his shoulder. Tall and gangly, he looked proudly at the camera as he and his father stood beside a rickety arbor that they had just built for the roses, a project that Walt had completed largely by himself, using the hand tools he'd found in Miss June's garage. She recalled being unable to show him much praise, as if even at a young age, he should understand that accomplishments were not to be overly rewarded, that serious effort was to be expected. Although she had numerous photos of Walt—a couple from the university newspaper, one in a program from a history department event, a lecture that she had secretly attended—this photo of him as a boy was her favorite, though it sometimes brought remorse.

She had been so hard, incapable of allowing herself to act on what she saw—a sad boy being raised by a well-intended but removed man, a boy who desperately needed the simplest thing any child could want, love. This secret regret was the reason she rarely opened this heartbreaking book, and as she locked it back in its drawer, she again saw the danger of sentimental weakness.

* * *

"And that's the complete tale of my marriage," Gwen finished. "Any questions?"

"Yeah, what now?"

"In regard to what? Men?"

"Everything. Men, work, travel. You're young and talented. You can live anywhere you want, do anything."

"I'm not sure Harvard feels that way."

"Well, despite the great gig you've got up there, don't forget that you don't need to feel locked in."

"You're giving me career advice?"

"Who better to learn from?"

"Good point."

Their dessert arrived—one order of créme brulée with raspberries to be shared, but which Gwen ate herself, save one bite.

"God, this is good." She used the heel of her hand to wipe a little of the custard from the corner of her mouth, licking it clean in an unladylike fashion. "So, you're saying I should quit my job?"

"No, no, not at all. I just want…hmm, what do I want, other than my own dessert? I want you to do whatever it is that you know in your heart you should be doing. Since you're no longer married, I mean. If you're happy in Cambridge, fine, but if there's anything you've ever dreamed of doing, now's the time. Don't let inertia stop you."

"Inertia's never been my problem, but I get what you're saying. Or the spirit of it anyway."

"Wait, why am I giving you advice? You know what you're doing. Forget what I said. My advice is guaranteed to ruin your life. I just want things to be perfect for you, that's all."

"Argh! The 'P-word'! I can't take it. Screw perfection. Maybe I should strive for mediocrity. Relieve some pressure."

"Ah, in that case, I *can* give you career advice."

"Except I'd somehow manage to be perfectly mediocre. See? I can't win."

She excused herself to the ladies room, and Walt rolled his neck out of habit, finding that it didn't need to crack. Along with the massage, Sam had chosen the right restaurant, and he was grateful. It was good to be out. He'd fallen into the lazy habit of assuming that people who went to the restaurant of the moment were simply being trendy. And conversation with Gwen was easy and smart. When they were apart, Walt tended to build her up in his mind and, by extension, reduce himself in the process. But when they were together, he was comfortable, as if he'd never lost a step.

"Since we're on the topic of careers," she said settling back in, "what are you going to do with yourself? After Miss June's gone, I mean."

"I avoid thinking about it."

"I understand."

"I doubt that. Not even I understand what makes me do what I do." He sipped his coffee. "It's funny. I never used to even think about things like that—'what makes me do what I do.' Never."

"Never?"

"Never."

"But you do now?"

He sighed. "So it seems. But, shit, not thinking about such things has always been my specialty. It drives everyone nuts, but it's always worked fine."

"But not anymore."

"Not anymore." Christ, why was he saying all of this? "There's a real comfort in complacency, you know? But it seems I've become someone who thinks about life—the 'What the hell happened?' question, I suppose. I've lost my treasured contentment. Or something. I don't know." He undid a shirt button. "Is it warm in here?"

"A little. Should we go?"

"Let's take a walk."

He paid the check with Miss June's cash. He'd expected it to be a dated amount, woefully too little, but she had surprised him with more than enough in the envelope—dinner on Reggie, he thought, making it that much better. The cool night air felt good as they looked in the shop windows on Ellsworth Avenue, vintage clothing and modern art. Other pairs were walking slowly as well, and Walt wondered if he and Gwen looked like they did.

"I didn't mean to make you uncomfortable in there. Talking about yourself," she said.

"No, it's fine. For whatever reason, I'm okay talking about it with you. You have a curious effect on me, Miss Thompson. Not that I have any answers."

"Well, you know what?" she said taking his hand. "Maybe you aren't supposed to have answers. Soul searching isn't for everyone. Maybe for you, the answers are meant to come when you've got your tools in your hands."

"So, I don't need to figure out 'what the hell happened?' You're letting me off the hook?"

She took his arm and pulled herself close.

"Yes, actually, I am. 'I guess I just want you to do whatever it is that you know in your heart that you should be doing.' A very handsome man once told me that."

"Did he drive a piece-of-shit truck?"

"You know, he did?" she replied. "And it was wonderful."

* * *

As he pulled into Sam's driveway after dropping Gwen at Hardwick, he didn't notice the movement of Sam's bedroom curtain as she checked to see how long his evening had lasted, pleased that he wasn't home too early.

Chapter 16

SPRING THREATENED TO ARRIVE. Walt consulted his list—not Miss June's, but the one he'd made for himself. He'd started strong, but making a splash was never the problem. Still, he was halfway through the job, a state that just two months before would have seemed impossible. He hoisted himself up onto the scaffold and lay on his back, hand resting on his belly—the "bay window" Sam had been so fond of—and stared at the ceiling. He imagined the coffered ceiling he was to build, saw it in place. The blocking was done, which had been no small task. The vast surface was ready to accept the mahogany boards that would join to create hollow beams that would intersect to form squares, each nearly five feet across. Inside the squares would be veneer panels, held captive to the ceiling by period-style crown moulding. The veneer was "ribbon-cut," the material sliced from the log in such a way that would create a pattern that would glow and move in the light. The old plans showed exquisite proportion, with not one detail unnecessary, in the same way that a perfectly executed poem contains exactly the right number of words. Providing, of course, he could get it done.

The idea of being finished in a few months seemed as improbable as his levitating from the plank that pressed so firmly into the small of his back. On paper, it worked. The hours he would need for each portion, in theory, fit into the months he had allotted himself to finish. Miss June hadn't given a specific date, and he'd been afraid to ask. So he'd just broken each part of the job into smaller parts, and then divided those into steps that were smaller still, an unprece-dented attempt at organization. It was his best hope—to stay focused on the individual brushstrokes and let the larger canvas complete itself. The practical thing would be to hire some help. This was not a one-man job, not by a long shot. Other than Jimmy's early help and the few pleasant afternoons spent working with Gwen, he'd logged all of his days there alone. He knew a number of good trim carpenters who would drop whatever they were doing for the chance to work on Hardwick, but he just couldn't let strange hands touch the house.

Plus, there was the reason for the work. Miss June would see the parlor as it was when Dwight had proposed to her, so, for Walt, it needed to be by his hand that she would see it. He would forge ahead alone, perhaps recruiting Edward to help on the weekends if absolutely necessary. Although Edward was not a carpenter, he was tremendously reliable, if overly literal. He would do precisely what Walt asked of him, and never question the task. And Walt liked being with him—enjoyed pulling his leg, enjoyed the simplicity of their time together. But, still, he would call Edward only if necessary. In the way that each job felt different, with its own personality and meaning, this was the most different of them all, and Walt had to admit he was feeling something most impractical, that he wanted just the right *sort* of energy put into the work. The effort itself had to have the right feeling, as it would be captured within the room forever. This, though, he knew to be folly, as of course the parlor trim would last no longer than it would take for Reggie to tear it down, but in Walt's mind, the remaining length of time that Miss June would inhabit Hardwick would be forever, no matter how many days that might actually be. The room mustn't hold the haphazardness of Jimmy, the nervousness of Edward, or the dispassionate efforts of some unfamiliar carpenter Walt might hire. As grandiose a thought as it may have been, Walt knew in his heart, that he, and only he, was meant to restore the giant room. Despite the odds, he would go it alone.

"Goddammit, old woman."

* * *

When his father was otherwise occupied, he sometimes visited their bedroom. He looked at her things—the makeup on her dresser, the magazines by her side of the bed. *Confidential Confessions. Popular Romance.* Dust had begun to collect on them. In the closet were shoes and hat boxes, and he thought of how she got dressed up before they went shopping, looking fancier than the other moms, making him proud.

She'd been gone for months.

Always, he waited. At school or at home, his attention was toward the door, waiting for her perfume, the burst of energy. His father puttered, quiet and ritualistic.

"She'll come back, son."

"When?"

"She just will."

* * *

The intricate workings of Walt's inability to finish what he started often had him redirecting his energy to different, less pressing, projects — he would work on what he wasn't supposed to. This was a mild source of pride for him — he wasn't lazy, just fucked up. And so after considering the ceiling at Hardwick for an hour or so, he went to Sam's to fix the kitchen sink that had been leaking for years. It made perfect sense. Dewey, happy to have Walt home, agreed, and lay on the kitchen floor near his master's feet, which were in the middle of the room. The other end, the part above the shoulders, was inside the sink cabinet, which is how Sam found him when she came home from the grocery store. From the steadiness of his breathing, she knew he was asleep in there.

"What are we going to do with him?" she asked the dog.

Dewey groaned in reply, rested his snout over his left paw, and released an exaggerated sigh that made his cheeks flap during the exhale. *I don't know,* he seemed to say.

The sink was one of the many projects that Sam insisted be left for Walt to get around to, no matter when that might be. Arthur was as understanding as he could be about such things, and tried not to let the unfinished parts of the house bother him, despite disorder running strongly against his nature. It was important to Sam that Walt have his chance to get these things done according to his own baffling schedule, although the enticing alternative was clearly illustrated by the contractor who had finished the baby's room in a matter of weeks. Sam looked at the underside of Walt's belly peeking out from beneath his flannel shirt. She untied her apron and lay it across his midsection, grabbed her camera and took a shot for her collection. He was a terrifically deep sleeper, and she had numerous photos of him crashed out in odd places. As she pulled off his boots, an errant Chiclet fell out onto the floor.

Putting the groceries away, she heard a car outside, Miss

June's Imperial, with Gwen at the wheel. Sam stepped out to greet her, and the two women hugged.

"Sorry for dropping by unannounced. I hope I'm not interrupting anything."

"Don't be ridiculous. I'm glad for the company. It's been forever."

Gwen saw Walt stretched out on the floor, but given that Sam had simply stepped over him, she assumed he wasn't dead.

"Don't ask."

Gwen eyed the apron. "I wouldn't dream of it."

As Sam gathered coffee cups, milk, and the like, Gwen admired her hostess's belly.

"You look so good. You make me wish I were having one."

"Really? You want to have a baby?"

"Well, no. But you look great."

Sam poured, and Dewey padded over in case cookies might be involved, looking back and forth as if watching a slow tennis match with a great deal at stake.

"Again, I'm sorry for just showing up. I was looking for Walt."

"Well, there he is."

"So I see. I'm going stir crazy at Hardwick. I needed to get out."

"Well, shit, call me next time. I'm dying for company. I just waddle around here, listening to the faucet drip, which apparently isn't going to stop today." She reached into her pocket. "You want a cigarette?"

"No, thanks. I don't smoke."

Sam touched her belly. "Neither do I anymore. I was just hoping to watch you enjoy one."

"I could try."

"I'll live."

Pointing toward Walt, Gwen asked, "Is he okay, do you think?"

"He's fine. He can fall asleep anywhere. Drag him to a movie sometime. You'll see."

"It's funny you mention that. I've been asked to speak at the history department Spring Lecture Series. I was going to ask him to come, but maybe I shouldn't. He might start a chain reaction."

"Oh, go ahead and take him. It does him good to get out. This business at Miss June's is wearing on him, I think."

"I've wondered."

"That's why he's here right now. He's fixing my sink because he's afraid he'll lose momentum over there."

"He told you that?"

"No, but I understand how he works. He doesn't, but I do."

"Can you teach me?"

"It takes years, honey."

Gwen turned and brought her napkin to her face, and Sam saw that she had started to cry.

"Hey, what's wrong?"

"I'm sorry. I shouldn't be here. I just didn't know where else to go. I wasn't really looking for Walt, I was looking for you. You're the only woman I know here. My divorce became final today." She wiped her eyes and smiled uncertainly.

Dewey leaned toward Gwen and rested his chin on her lap.

"Oh, honey, I'm sorry."

"Don't be. It was an awful marriage. Terrible. I just … I wasn't expecting it to hit me like this, not after all this time."

Sam fetched a bottle of brandy and two glasses, a splash for her, a couple of inches for Gwen.

"Drink this. It'll make you feel better."

"The letter came from the state, and I was fine—happy, even—but then I got scared." She tried the brandy and winced.

"Jesus, this is strong." She picked up the cigarettes from the table. "Maybe I will try one of these things."

"No, don't. I used to get girls started in high school, and still feel guilty. Stick to the alcohol. It's more useful when it comes to men."

Under the sink, Walt drifted partially back into consciousness and looked at the pipes above him. Their simplicity was beautiful. They made sense. He'd done a lot of such contemplative staring over the years—at pipes, boards, wires. Physical things were easy to understand. As the fog cleared, he realized that Sam wasn't alone, that the voice he'd heard in his dream really was Gwen, and that, for some reason, she was here in the Friendship kitchen. He considered working his way out from inside the cabinet, but he was, oddly enough, pretty damned comfortable. Screw it. Rolling over to the fetal position, he drifted back to sleep. The girls watched until his breathing became steady again.

"Anyway," Gwen said, lowering her voice. "Don't misunderstand me. I don't need a man to take care of me. I could always take care of myself."

"But it would be nice to know that you've got someone to rely on. Someone who's not a fucking idiot."

Gwen laughed. "You do understand."

"I've got news for you, darling," Sam continued. "They're all idiots. Every last one."

"Oh, come on. That can't be true. Look at Arthur—from what Walt tells me, he's dear."

"Oh, he is. He's sweet and attentive and clueless. It's like this. You take a man—any man—and they're going to have attributes. Wonderful attributes. Some more than others. But whatever they have in one area, they lack in another. It's like something went wrong with natural selection or something. They're a little like apes—so close to being normal humans, but there's always some way in which they just aren't right."

"And the more wonderful they are in one way, the worse they are in another?"

"Exactly. You've got this figured out, too."

"So, then," Gwen asked. "What's a girl to do?"

"Marry one who's good in bed, of course."

Gwen laughed. Pouring more brandy, she added, "So, is that what you did?"

"Once upon a time," she replied, making Groucho Marx eye movements toward the man spilling out of the cabinet.

"Shh, he'll hear you!"

"No, he's still out."

"And Arthur?"

"He's fine. At my age, he's just what I want. Sweet and attentive. I'm very lucky. That said, he's not the most exciting man I've ever been with. I wished for reliable, and boy, did I get it."

"Well, not to sound jealous, but you're not making me feel any better about being single. 'Sweet and attentive' sounds pretty good right about now."

"He doesn't let me see him naked," Sam said.

"What?!"

They both laughed.

"I swear to God. He hangs his boxer shorts on the curtain rod when he showers and puts them on before getting out. It's like being married to a thirteen-year-old boy."

"I'm sorry for laughing, Sam, but that is really funny."

"I know. I'm tempted to sneak in on him sometimes, but I'm afraid he'll be traumatized."

"He could see my ex for therapy. He'd end up worse than ever."

"I drew the line when it came to sex. He tried to wear them then, too."

"No!"

"Yes. I told him there was no way I was having sex with a man wearing underwear unless he modeled for Calvin Klein. *'Who's Calvin Klein?'* he asked. So, see? They're all screwy. Great in some areas, not so much in others."

"So what do we do? For real?"

"I think you just try to find one who is compatible with whatever screwed up things you have going on yourself, you know? None of us is perfect. We just pair up as best we can."

Gwen's smile faded. "But don't you ever wish that it could be like in the movies? That men could be strong and brave and sensitive and…"

"And smart enough to know when you need them to be any of those things."

"Exactly."

"I'm sorry, but you're talking Cary Grant, honey. And he ain't around."

"It's a fantasy, I know," Gwen said. "But I wouldn't pick Cary Grant anyway. I like him, of course, I mean, what woman doesn't, but I never saw him as quite fitting the bill. He was too precious or something."

"I'm not the Cary Grant type either. Too skittish. Like if I squeezed him, he'd break. Humphrey Bogart," Sam said. "Now there was a man. Strong and no nonsense. And those hands. If I were Kate Hepburn in *The African Queen*, I'd have torn those coveralls off of him and had sex with him right there on the deck."

"Some women like a young Paul Newman," Gwen offered.

"Or an old Paul Newman," Sam added.

"Oh, yeah. He aged perfectly. I've never cared for Robert Redford though. Too pretty."

"Okay, then," Sam asked, "so who is your perfect man? The one who would fill all of your needs."

"This is like being at summer camp. I'm so glad you were

home. I've needed a girlfriend in Pittsburgh."

"Quit stalling," Sam said, stealing a sip from Gwen's glass. "Come on, 'fess up. Who's your dreamboat?"

"I don't have one."

"Bullshit. It's written all over your face. And hey, I gave you Bogey. I'll give you another—Robert Mitchum. Now there was a man."

Gwen looked out the window, at the sky, at the silver screen.

"Spencer Tracy."

"Ooh, good one," Sam agreed.

"I mean it. He seemed to have it all, you know? He was cute and funny, and he didn't take much guff, but you just knew he'd be there in the end."

"And what a face."

"Katharine Hepburn said he was like 'a baked potato—pure, and of the earth.' Dependable."

"*Pat and Mike.*"

"That's the one where he said he was just a bum who spoke 'left-handed English.' And that he and Hepburn were 'a plenty long shot.' She seemed to out-class him in those movies, but he always took the chance. He wasn't afraid."

"He was a keeper," Sam agreed.

"My favorite is *Woman of the Year*. She's a famous writer who knows world leaders and jets around, and he just wants to take her to a baseball game. That's all he wants. And he does. He's just so regular. And in the end, she stays with him, because it couldn't be any other way."

She worried the buttons on her sweater.

"Well, the ideal man doesn't exist, so don't beat yourself up for not finding him. We find who we're best suited for and appreciate them for who they are."

"I know that, Sam. I'm just feeling sorry for myself—it's been a rough day. But I have to believe Spencer Tracy exists.

I just do. He's out there, somewhere, plain and steady. My baked potato."

From inside the cabinet, Walt began to snore.

* * *

Edward's headlights cut through the dark driveway, illuminating the garage and capturing both Dewey and Walt peeing on the DORF's right rear tire. He cut the motor and got out.

"Something wrong with your plumbing, Walt?"

"No, Edward. Once it gets started, the pee comes out fine. But thanks for asking."

"Oh. I meant your toilet. 'Cause I always got my plumbing box in my truck."

"That's comforting to know. Actually, I was watching Dewey and got inspired. There's something about peeing outside, you know?" Actually, Edward didn't know. He was so modest that even when hunting alone, in the deepest of woods, he felt embarrassed while relieving himself, certain that at any moment a group of hikers would happen by and see his private parts. "But my toilet's fine," Walt continued. He shook off, stretched, groaned, and scratched his belly. He felt good.

"You ready for breakfast?" he asked his pocket-protected friend.

"You gonna put pants on first?"

Walt looked down. "Think I should?"

The Apache was its usual near-empty self.

"Good morning, Gus," Walt called out.

"Okay, boss," Gus said with a wave of his spatula, the only two English words the old Greek used.

Walt ordered the Apache omelet that had become his usual, and also a short stack, which seemed to make Lynda the waitress happy. Walt imagined her to be one of those women who like it when men eat.

"So, Edward. Tell me what's up."

"I don't know. We got more apartment units than ever. They're keeping me real busy. I was on a service call last night. Some lady's hot water heater went out."

That redundancy always got Walt—"hot water heater."

"Was it shot?"

"I thought it was just a thermocouple, but I replaced that and still couldn't get the sucker lit. Turned out to be the gas valve. Good thing I keep an extra in the truck, or else I'd have had to come back to the warehouse."

"A lady, huh? Did she give you coffee? A piece of pie, maybe?" Walt winked suggestively.

"She asked me if I wanted something to drink, but I didn't want nothing. I feel funny, you know, taking stuff from customers."

"Hell, I've based my career on how well a client might feed me."

"Well, it makes me feel funny. Plus, her being a girl and all. I mean, I ain't no ladies' man like you."

"Yeah, I'm a regular Errol Flynn. Speaking of ladies, how's your nurse friend?" Though they'd never met, Walt secretly hated the Donna woman, and he refused to utter her name for fear that, by doing so, she would gain permanence in Edward's life. The past few months had been an endless saga of rides given to, meals bought for, and complaints from the ungrateful pain in the ass with bad feet.

"Well, she ain't really a nurse, she's a nurse's aide. And we had kind of a fight, so I don't think I'll be seeing much of her no more."

Walt's relief was offset by the upset on his friend's face.

"What happened?"

"I don't know," he said, which was obviously untrue. "She got mad at me 'cause she said I don't show her no affection. She thinks I should be all romantic and that, and I just feel too goofy doing that stuff, you know? 'A real man wouldn't just bring me flowers,' she says. 'He'd carry me up to my bedroom. Why can't you be like the men in my shows?' She likes them soap operas, you know."

"Well, you've got to stick with what makes you comfortable. Or, don't do things that make you uncomfortable. Maybe that's more the point here."

"I done everything I could to make her happy. I mean, I bought her all kinds of stuff, and I painted her apartment, too. But I think she wants more..."

Walt knew the answer, but asked the question anyway. "Did you guys...sleep together?"

Edward's face reddened, and he began fiddling with his retractable keychain. "Nah. We messed around a little, you know? But I don't think you should go too far with a girl if you don't love 'em, you know? It just doesn't seem right."

"That's a rare and noble stance, Edward." Walt hoped his friend would stay a virgin until he met someone with whom he'd fallen in love, be they man or woman. He hated to think of the finality that would accompany the death of Edward's innocence.

Lynda arrived with their food, her gap-toothed grin bordering on the salacious. Edward waited until she left to continue.

"The thing is, I don't really want to mess around with her, you know? I just don't. And when I told her that maybe we should slow down a bit, she got mad and called me a homo. Just like the guys at work."

"Look, just because..." Walt sought his words carefully. "Just because you didn't want to sleep with her doesn't mean

there is anything wrong with you. I mean, in any way at all.
You shouldn't do anything you don't want to do. You're a smart
guy—you know that."

"Uh-huh."

"And, listen, everyone feels different about intimacy. I
think it's a mistake to get involved with someone you don't
have deep feelings for." Deena's El Camino roared through
his mind. "You need to stay true to yourself."

"I know that. And I don't care about Donna, not really.
She's mean. But other than her, if I think about, like, a dream
girl or something, I've just never met that girl, you know? The
one that makes me feel all lovey-dovey and stuff."

How sad Edward could make Walt feel. Like he'd failed him
as a friend. With his pressed khaki work clothes, his immaculate
truck, his continuous chatter—it was easy to not consider
his depth.

"I don't even know what that's supposed to feel like. To
meet someone and love them."

"It feels better than anything you've ever felt before. It's like
when you were a kid and you got new sneakers, and for that one
day, you could run faster than any kid in the neighborhood."

"Well, I've never felt like that about a girl." He fiddled with
the salt and pepper shakers, rearranging the condiments on the
table, building the little mixed-fruit jelly tubs into pyramids.
He did it for a solid minute, perseverating until Walt tapped
his wrist to make him stop.

"Does it bother you when the guys at work give you a
hard time? About women, I mean?"

"Ah, they're all right. They just mess with me, that's all.
They're my buddies."

"No, I don't think they are, Edward. It's okay to tease each
other about some things, but not everything, you know? Real
buddies don't do that. Because you're allowed to be any way

that you want to be. In your private life, I mean. Any way at all. Do you understand what I'm saying?"

Edward's rearranging of the condiments started again. He wouldn't look up.

"Those guys may be kidding around," Walt continued, "but in the end, you have to be true to yourself. That's the only way to be happy. When you're thinking about your life, about who you really are, forget that those guys even exist. They're nothing."

"What I don't get is how those guys are always goin' on about how much they like girls and that, but to hear 'em talk, they don't treat them so good. You know? If I had someone special, someone who liked me for me, and wasn't just lookin' for tires and stuff, I'd treat them nice, and not talk nasty about them at work."

"I know you wouldn't. You're a kind fellow. And you know what? Someday, and I know this in my heart, you'll meet the right person. Someone you can share things with. Someone you can love." He left gender out of it.

"Well, I don't think I'd recognize it if it happened. I've been alone all my life. I don't even know what it's supposed to feel like. To fall in love and all."

Walt sighed, wanting to tend carefully to his friend's poor confused heart. "Okay, listen. I'm no expert, but I suppose it's something like this. When you meet the right person, they're all you can think about. No matter what, you just want to be with them. When you're apart, you feel incredibly happy and terribly sad, and it's just written all over your face. And when you're together, things feel right in a way that you never knew could happen. The rest of the world just slips away a bit. It sounds crazy, but it's like a movie — everything beyond the two of you becomes softly focused, almost not real.

"What are we doing here?" she had asked.

"Anyway," he finished. "It's like that. You'll see."

"And you think I'll know when it happens?"

"Oh, you'll know. You'll feel like nothing in your life could be better, and at that moment, everything will be exactly perfect."

"So, it's kind of like hunting?"

Walt leaned back and drank in his friend.

"Yes, Edward. It's exactly like hunting."

Spring

The girl explored her father's library, tiptoeing its perimeter. Barely nine years old, she mounted the steep rolling ladder, waging battle with her fear of heights. Near the top, she met a vertiginous wave that clenched her grip and raced her pulse. She remained there, frozen, until one of the help happened by and guided her down safely.

"Thank you," she said. "I don't normally have difficulties."

"I know that, Miss June. Sometimes those heights just sneak up and take us by surprise. It could happen to anybody."

"There's no need for this to be public, of course."

"I don't even know what you talkin' about. Now you run along and play. Nice girl like you, bein' inside today. You alone too much."

On each day that followed, she returned to the library, grimly scaling the ladder to purge herself of shame. "Determination conquers emotion," she declared to herself.

Chapter 17

IN 1936, MISS JUNE'S FATHER, Julius Creighton, hosted the first annual May Day Circus on the great lawn at Hardwick, an event for the children of his employees. In creating more than a mere company picnic, he arranged with a regional carnival company to provide entertainment for the kids in the form of pony rides, jugglers, acrobats, knife throwers, and a great tent complete with a performance ring, its floor covered in hay, which qualified it in the eyes of the children as a full-fledged circus. That the first occurrence of the event took place on May Day — the international day of celebration for the labor movement — was by chance, but because Julius appreciated the efforts of his employees — and because they were unionized already — he decided to let them celebrate on his lawn, a gesture of goodwill. Julius's father, Clarence, would have sooner shut his company down than give the appearance of celebrating a workers' union — and his view would doubtless have been shared by his contemporaries — but the company was by this time Julius's to run, and for the years that Creighton Machinery lasted under his watch before succumbing to the almighty U. S. Steel, May Day was a day when the Creighton employees were invited to bring their families to the house that had been made possible through their—and in many cases their parents'—sweat.

Chartered buses bound for Hardwick would leave the parking lot of Creighton Machinery starting at ten. The guests would walk the grounds and marvel at the house, the men at the quality of its construction and the size—how much coal did it take to heat such a place?—while their wives speculated on how many rooms it had, and how on earth could you clean them all?

During those long celebrations, young Thomas would run through the yard and play with the visiting kids, sneaking sweets from the kitchen and later, as the skies darkened, cups of beer from the wooden kegs in the yard. His older sister would spend the day monitoring the situation, uneasy about the throng of strangers, about how these ruffians overtook the property. Was it possible they'd never been this far from the muddy banks of the Monongahela before? Why did her father need to humor these people? Her grandfather would not have—of that, she was certain. May Day was not, for her, a day to relax, and she spent as much of it as possible in her room, reading and trying to ignore the oom-pah-pah music that was popular with the crass ethnic crowd. Which is not to say that she hadn't first minded her manners as was expected, performing the requisite duties of junior hostess, greeting the guests as they arrived—using, of course, her full name, Miss June Bonwell Creighton—and making sure that they knew where the food and facilities could be found. But beyond those cordialities, she kept to herself, steering especially clear of the common young men who were bold enough to attempt to chat up the daughter of their employer. While reaching beyond one's station might be part of their American dream, young June Creighton made it clear that their reach would not trespass through the Hardwick gates.

But for everyone else, the event was a wondrous thing. As day gave way to dusk, colored lights hung on the wrought iron fence that marked the perimeter of the estate would glow, and the band that played polkas and circus music during the day would segue into standards for the rest of the evening—Glenn Milleresque arrangements, mostly—as the closely manicured side yard became a dance floor where the couples would hold each other close while their sleepy children watched from the sidelines, their parents gliding through the Pittsburgh night like movie stars.

The bedtime finale, what the children waited for all year, was the fireworks display set off from the grounds of a larger estate nearby, one whose land would later be donated to the city and become Mellon Park. Shooting stars exploded into streaming trails of color that fell slowly toward earth over Shadyside, their thunderous reports shaking both the stick-thin chests of the employees' children and the panes of glass of young June's bedroom as she looked down at the sated crowd below.

And so went the May Day Circus. Walt had seen photographs of its early incarnations among Miss June's collection, had always been intrigued by the dynamics of the affair. What a generous and unusual thing for her father to have done. And what had it felt like for those who'd attended? Walt liked to think that the guests appreciated the spirit in which the invitation was extended, that they were aware of the unusual largess of their employer. Of course there must have been those—especially as the day grew long and the beer flowed freely—for whom animosity became the theme of the day, those who saw only how the opulent surroundings made their small frame houses in Hazelwood and Braddock seem like tarpaper shacks in comparison. Examining the photos, Walt, so many years after the fact, hoped that those who might have felt beer-fueled anger over making their boss rich while toiling in hundred-degree heat didn't let their anger reach their children, for whom the day was largely designed. But mostly, he wondered what the day had felt like to Miss June. It was hard to imagine that, even then, in her youth, she would have let her hair down, literally or figuratively. He suspected that she became more fond of the May Day Circus when it ceased to be a circus at all, when it settled into the staid affair it would become under her stewardship. When Creighton Machinery became no more, when Julius Creighton had no employees to bring by chartered bus, the question of what would become of the May Day Circus had to be answered. Because of the amount of local press the event garnered, it seemed only natural that it would continue, and so it did, transformed by Miss June into an exclusive, private party for the well-heeled friends of the Creightons, and any consideration of the meaning of May Day was gone. It became a flowery affair of croquet and badminton, of tea cakes and lemonade. Activities for the rich families' children were still in place, although the circus motif was gone, all the better to make a clean break from the nature of the previous happenings. Now the main attractions for the kids were the pony rides—one of the few original activities that remained—plus sack races, organized games of Follow the Leader and Duck-Duck-Goose, and the periodic appearance of special guests—magicians, cowboys who did rope tricks, a trio of clowns who could juggle and play—all of whom were paid to keep the day magical.

And lest it appear that what had belonged to the workers was now simply another party of the rich, the public face of the gathering was that of a fundraiser for children's charities, and indeed it brought in quite a haul. Never mind that none of the children invited to attend had ever been in need. And Walt's guess was correct—Miss June was more comfortable with the annual May Children's Fundraiser than she had been with the sawdust and hay-covered May Day Circus. She comfortably navigated the more cultured social seas of her peers in a way that she never could the muddied waters of the commoners who had come each year to eat their food and gawk at the surroundings. She did at times consider, even as a teen, that she was perhaps unfair in the harshness of her judgment, and that the workers from her father's plant were largely an innocent bunch. But the coarseness of the men, the wildness of their children—how could that be excused? Were they not aware that their own behavior created limitations from which they could never escape? Did they see no need to improve their command of the English language, or at least their appearance? She decided that the men knew their place, that they were a happy enough lot, blessed by the absence of high aspirations. But the poor women. She saw how they admired the house, spoke in their most demure tones when they met the Creighton family. She wondered how they felt in their plain dresses, aware that both sides could feel the gulf between their circumstances. And while June Creighton felt no guilt over this disparity—breeding and gumption had, after all, made the circumstances what they were—she did feel for these women, whom she saw as having greater social awareness and, in some cases, aspirations than their simple men.

The May Children's Fundraiser continued on the grounds of Creighton for two decades beyond Julius's death in the 1950s, with blue-and-white striped tents and a temporary bandstand providing the backdrop for socializing, hobnobbing, and fundraising. The picnic motif continued as part of the event's tradition, with the wealthy women selecting their casual attire with the same attentiveness to which they'd choose a gown for a ball. As a child, Walt looked forward to the day each year as if it were Christmas, but by the age of ten, in similar yet reversed circumstances from Miss June's decades before, he began to feel out of place among the other children who came from backgrounds so different from his own. These were Reggie's peers, not his, and while the majority of them did not share Reggie's proclivity for being mean, neither did they seem to appreciate the magic of what was being presented to them—clowns! ponies! fireworks! They were more interested in seeking mischief than enjoying the excitement of the day. Of course, as with young Miss June's predicament, Walt's worsened in his teens, and as innocence was lost, so was the ability to see the display as anything but false. Eventually, with Miss June in her fifties, and perhaps not in a financial position to continue to personally support the cost of the gathering, the annual May Children's Fundraiser became just another evening ball held at the Pittsburgh Athletic Club, a stodgy affair to which, ironically, no children were invited. Sam and Walt got stuck attending as a married couple, with Sam barely able to make it through a half hour before dragging Walt out the door.

And while Walt would agree with Sam that the occasion was a bore, it remained more than that to him. Each year the evening brought a sweet sort of melancholy, one that had him recalling with delicious sadness the anticipation and wonder he'd felt about the outdoor party when he was a boy. But more—much more—he thought about young June Creighton, prim in her party dress, looking down from her bedroom window at the circus that was life, below.

* * *

On the first day of spring, Walt arrived early at Hardwick, ready for the long-anticipated day of setting wood panels in the ceiling. For this he would need help, would have loved to use Gwen, but needed the muscle of Jimmy, who had apparently not only survived his latest adventure, but had gained an improbable Banlon shirt, to boot.

"Christ on a crutch," Jimmy said consulting his watch. "What'd ya do, shit the bed?"

"Something like that." Walt had been waking uncharacteristically early for weeks, lying in bed, assembling the parlor in his mind, wondering about Sam's baby, and thinking about Gwen. The only thing it seemed he could do was to get to Hardwick early and start swinging his hammer—no morning paper with Sam in her kitchen, no lazy breakfasts at the Apache. And to show for it, the work had progressed. "I assume you're here to return my truck?"

In Sam's driveway that morning, he had found a mid-eighties Buick with a torn landau roof and fake wire hubcaps. The keys were in the ignition, so he took it to work. He found the DORF in Hardwick's drive.

"I need your jigsaw," Jimmy answered.

"Working for Irma?"

"Yeah. She makes projects up so I'll keep coming back."

Walt knew the reverse to be true, that Jimmy, with all of his energy, dreamed up things to do at his ex-wife's house just to keep himself busy. He was endlessly building shoddy retaining walls and unwanted shelves. None of the work was good, and Walt had been called in more than once to fix things after Jimmy had moved on. Irma's ex-husband's efforts caused her more grief than anything else, but they seemed to keep him out of trouble, so she figured it was best for all involved.

"So, you won't be around to help me today. Isn't that just like you."

"Sorry, pal. Maybe tomorrow."

He left with Walt's jigsaw and, thankfully, the Buick, which reeked of Vitalis.

Hardwick was quiet, and the morning's work went well. Miss June served tea—today there were M&Ms in a small silver bowl adorning the tray—but Gwen was at the library, a disappointment for Walt. She'd taken to writing in the parlor as he worked, sitting on the scaffold, computer on her lap. And she really had become a competent helper. More than once, Walt had arrived in the morning to find that she had straightened up the parlor the previous night, doing what she could to prepare for the next day. But most important, she was good for Miss June. Although Gwen was everything the old woman was not, the two had become closer as winter gave in to spring. They chatted about the Creightons, politics, books, and history. Gwen injected things into conversation with Miss June in a way that Walt never could. And they did go and get their hair done together, stopping afterward for lunch to show it off. Miss June had two new sweaters too, in colors she'd never worn before. Walt worried this might be too much activity for the grand dame, but Gwen assured him that they were in no hurry during their excursions, moving at a pace as slow as need be. Through it all, the parlor transformation had begun to take hold. Walt's progress was undeniable, and to those who didn't know him, the work would appear to be heading toward completion. And it was all for Miss June, performed against the sound of her ancient ticking clock, a steady but anxious race to fulfill her wish. The thought of her failing health was with Walt's every step, but privately, he was proud of what he had accomplished, proud to have had it unfold before Gwen, evidence of what he could be.

"Psst…" Gwen said, leaning in the doorway.

"Hey, there."

"Getting hungry?"

"I'm always hungry."

"Then get yourself down off that ladder—we have lunch plans."

* * *

She looked small behind the wheel of the Imperial—everyone did—but she steered it with aplomb, allowing it to roll around corners as if on a cloud. She'd put the convertible top down, and wore a silk scarf over her hair and dark sunglasses, as though in an Audrey Hepburn movie, or, if a lesser production, Doris Day. Between them on the seat was a picnic basket and a red-and-white checked blanket. He didn't ask where they were going, was happy enough to be heading anywhere.

Schenley Park's four hundred acres occupy the heart of the East End, donated to the city a century before by a family of much greater wealth than the Creightons. The WPA efforts of the 1940s widened its cinder-laden trails, adding to them the stone bridges that cross its creeks, and the secret steps that crookedly traverse its hillsides. Having followed one such path downward, Gwen and Walt found themselves at Panther Hollow lake, a man-made body not far from the railroad tracks that split the urban valley and led to God knows where. The park was weekday quiet, and they saw but one jogger as they lay on their blanket, picking from the basket of foods that Walt knew Sam must have identified as his favorites.

"A picnic in the middle of a workday. Are you trying to sabotage my efforts, my dear?"

"Indeed, sir, I am. Your progress makes my book seem like nothing but a pile of notes. Since I'll never catch up, I figure I'd better try to slow you down."

"I find that hard to believe. Donald tells me the first draft is almost done."

"It's true. He's been such a help."

"As have you, for me."

"Oh, come on."

"I'm serious. Both with the parlor, and …"

"Yes?"

"The truth? I find you to be an inspiration. In all areas."

"What the heck does that mean?"

"It's a compliment."

"Oh." She ran her hand along the blanket. "I'm not good with those, I'm afraid."

They lay back and listened to the breeze, to the faint sounds of traffic far away. The clouds were moving and they could feel the earth turn—if it were turning any faster, it seemed, they might pleasantly slide off. The sun was warm and, after a while, she spoke.

"When I was a little girl, my grandfather told me that if I were to put salt on a bird's tail, I could pet it. I tried and tried but could never get close enough. I wanted to so much. I would lie awake thinking about it. Why couldn't I do it? Why was it so hard?"

Walt rolled onto his side to face her, watched as she recalled.

"I remember one day in particular. I was about seven or eight. It was Easter and we were at my grandparents' house. It was warm and there were wrens in the grass. The grown-ups were watching from the window as I tried to sneak up on the birds in my little Easter dress, salt shaker in hand, quiet as I could be in my Mary Janes."

"That's darling," he said.

"I know. Everybody thought so. I was tip-toeing like always, getting oh so close before they would fly away. If I could only get closer, put the salt on its tail, I could pet one—I believed it was true. But that day, as the birds flew away, I looked up and saw the grown-ups laughing and I knew I'd been made a fool. I still feel that way sometimes."

She went quiet. He wanted more than anything to put salt on a bird's tail for her. On every bird in the park. He would bring them all to her and she could pet each one.

Instead, he kissed her as the clouds flew by, and the world turned fast and became irrelevant to them both.

Chapter 18

THAT THE NEXT DAY WAS A SATURDAY mattered little, as he'd been working on the parlor seven days a week. The previous day's picnic and its accompanying kisses still resonated as he drove toward Shadyside. Despite his focus at Hardwick, he made an unexpected left at Negley and Howe, stopping in front of a house he hadn't visited in a decade. Finding himself knocking, toolbox in hand, he felt as if he were in a play, one in which he didn't know his lines. Bill Stuart answered the door.

"Walt?" He looked at the toolbox, befuddled.

"Hi, Bill. Long time no see."

"Um, yeah, no kidding. *Wow.* Hey, I'm sorry, come in."

"Thanks."

Bounding down the stairs and making the bend to the living room came a teenage girl who Walt remembered as being a small child.

"Wow, it's really something to see you," Bill said. "Um, what brings you by?"

"Remember when I remodeled your kitchen? How I said I'd stop back to connect the range hood?"

"That? Yeah, I guess I do. It's okay. You know—we've kind of forgotten about it. It's, ah, been a long time."

"Well, I'm here to do it now."

* * *

Gwen asked Gene for change for the jukebox. Over the last few weeks, seeking breaks from Miss June, she had become both a semi-regular and the apple of Gene's eye. She took privileges no other Bull's-Eye denizen would dare, opening the blinds to let in the sun, washing the windows, and cleaning years of dust off the bottles that lined the back bar. She even manned the grill once as a lark, showing Gene that he didn't have to press the living shit out of a hamburger to get it to "cook right." This evening, a Friday, was magic hour at the 'Eye, and even Gene, who'd stayed a little late, was in a good mood. Although everyone was already drinking freely, he'd put both pretzels and Goldfish on the bar. Gwen fed the Rock-Ola Princess, a 45 dropped into place, and rollicking piano ensued. No one had ever danced at Gene's, but Gwen, who seemed intent on introducing new possibilities to the place, sauntered over to Jimmy and got him going to "Whole Lotta Shakin' Goin' On." Ice broken, the tables emptied, and soon the place was all swiveling hips and grooving elbows. Jimmy reached over and grabbed the arm of an older redhead and got her moving, while Gwen did the impossible, pulling Gene himself from behind the bar and getting him to dance, which—in a surprise to everyone—he did, like nobody's business.

Outside, Walt, sleepy and sore from his day, pulled into the lot longing for a quiet dinner. Instead, he walked into a Bull's-Eye episode of *The Twilight Zone*. Tables had been pushed aside, Little Richard screamed "Tutti Fruiti," sweat flowed, drinks were spilled, and Gene danced his ass off while Walt stood there, dumbfounded. Gwen smiled, waved, mouthed "Hi!" and then pinched her nose and plunged, doing the swim.

What the hell was happening?

* * *

Despite Miss June's medical condition—whatever the mysterious specifics—she hadn't completely discontinued her social calendar. Appearances were, for the most part, maintained. The previous afternoon, she had informed Walt that there would be visitors the next day, and that she expected both the parlor and him to be presentable for a brief tour.

"This may be a construction site, but we shan't have your slovenliness serve as reflection of us all," she had said.

"I suppose we shan't," he'd replied.

"And mind your behavior."

"Now, or tomorrow?"

She'd sighed. "I swear, how the most basic principles of deportment have passed you by is one of life's great mysteries. A clever primate would give you competition in matters of bearing."

Normally, her comments would have prompted a continued playful defense, but Walt had become uncertain as to just how much guff the old woman should be made to take, so he let it drop. Was it healthy to engage her in their usual banter? Did it help to keep her sharp, or was it unduly taxing to contend with him as he played the part of doofus? Because she was no longer secretive about her use of the house elevator, and because her afternoon naps—her *"constitutionals"*—had become much longer in recent weeks, he decided to go easier on her when she seemed tired or when the stakes were high, and for Miss June, there were few stakes higher than maintaining her dignity. Before leaving for the night, he straightened up his toolboxes and swept the floor.

Despite his large size, Walt had always been able to traverse a scaffold plank with grace. As he moved about, the thick southern-pine boards gave accordingly, and he imagined the flex of a gymnast's equipment—the elastic strength of the parallel bars that accommodated those strong little men who put themselves through their determined paces. The bounce in the planks provided a rhythm to his work, an optimism that registered with each step. He heard Miss June's visitors approaching—a blue-haired tour group, he was sure—and he considered greeting them with a spectacular dismount, a mid-air somersault with a twist, maybe a flying sit-spin, or perhaps even a double Lutz, although he was fairly certain he would need a ruffled shirt and a rose clenched in his teeth to truly pull off the latter. Instead, he hiked up his pants and brushed his chest free of cookie crumbs.

"Now I wasn't planning on showing this to anyone before the grand unveiling," Miss June was saying as the group approached, "but I simply can't resist letting you have just a little peek…"

The geriatric gaggle tottered in, and the gasp was collective. The parlor ceiling was spectacular. Walt's periods of inertia had apparently been outnumbered by bursts of success. He'd had an inkling of his progress upon arriving that morning, but chose not to think about it too hard and tempt fate. He'd simply strapped on his tool belt and decided to have another good day. The amazed group comprised Miss June's peers from local historical societies and book clubs, with perhaps a few stalwarts from the Victorian Society as well. Gwen brought up the rear, part tour guide, part shepherd.

"Young man," Miss June called up to Walt as if she didn't know his name, "would you please refrain from hammering?" Unable to resist the opportunity, Walt treated the elderly crowd to a little thrill, cupping his ear as if he hadn't heard, stepping toward the edge of the plank, and then pretending as if he might fall, windmilling his arms, leaning forward and then back and then forward again. The resulting "oohs," and "ahs," and "oh, my heavenses" from the crowd were synchronized with his every move, and rang through the room until he ended his act by pretending to regain his balance and wiping his brow in mock relief, the group finally comfortable that the large man up there in the clouds would be all right. Miss June rolled her eyes and wondered what she'd done to deserve this adult boy.

Minutes later, with the old woman and her flock having moved to the other side of the room, Gwen tugged on the hammer hanging from Walt's belt and said, "Hey, handsome. That was quite an act you put on up there."

"What act?"

"She's very proud of you, you know," Gwen said, her eyes indicating the same could be said of her.

"You're out of your mind."

"She is. Look at her going on about the place."

They watched Miss June holding court for her guests who were rapt as she waxed about the history of the house, her family, and the famous visitors who'd been in *"this very room."*

"She's proud of Hardwick," Walt said. "It and her bloodlines."

"And she's proud of you, as well she should be. I mean, come on, just look around."

Walt did, and had to acknowledge that the room looked good.

"Good? It's spectacular," she said.

"Don't get too excited—he's not done yet," Reggie said from the doorway.

"Reginald Creighton," Gwen said. "I know all about you."

"No, you don't," Walt said. "Trust me."

"Ah, don't listen to Walter P. Stick-In-the-Mud over there. He's no fun." He held out his hand for Gwen to shake, and then took hers in both of his. "I'm Reggie Creighton, as you already know. And you must be our resident historian. Gretchen, I presume?"

"Gwen. Gwen Thompson." She pulled her hand from Reggie's grasp and put it on Walt's arm. "Doesn't the room look marvelous? Walt does the most incredible work."

"It's incredible, all right," he said. "But then again, what's the point?"

"The point? What do you mean? It's your aunt's dream. To see the room in its original grandeur. What else is there to consider?"

"Only that…"

"Only that Reggie doesn't have the patience for restoration, that's all," Walt interrupted. "He's a developer. They prefer instant gratification."

"At least I finish what I start."

"Anyway," Walt said.

"Anyway," Reggie parroted, dismissing Walt and his concern for the old house.

"I'm going to see if Miss June needs help," Gwen said. "She seemed winded this morning." Turning to Reggie, she lied, "Nice to meet you."

"Of course."

The two men watched her cross the big room.

"Goddamn, Walt. She's kind of cute, you know? In a bookish sort of way, I mean, but still. Do you think maybe she'd…"

"No," Walt interrupted. "She wouldn't."

"Hey, check you out. Don't tell me the big man's ready to make a move on a woman after all these years."

"What are you doing here, anyway?" Walt asked. "Stop by to check Miss June's pulse?"

"If you must know, you prick, I did want to see how my favorite aunt is feeling these days."

"I'll bet."

"I did. Plus, you see that old guy she's talking to? Brown pants and suspenders? He owns an apartment building on Morewood I want to buy. I knew he'd be here this morning so I thought I'd bump into him. Outside of the usual business arena, you know?"

"Maybe you could push him down the stairs on the way out."

Reggie looked around at the parlor, seeming to notice for the first time the transformation that was occurring.

"Damn, lardass. You really are doing a nice job of it here. You're, what, three-quarters of the way done? Let's see, if I can figure this out right, that should put you at about time to lose focus and quit?"

"I have it at almost time to kick your ass."

"Tsk, tsk. Such hostility. And after I compliment you on what a nice job you're doing on my house. Christ, this is furniture quality." He ran his hand along a piece of trim. "The old lady wouldn't know the difference if you cheapened it up a bit. I mean, what's the point? This will all be destroyed six months after she's gone. Let me give you some advice: make it look halfway decent and get the hell out of here."

Despite how it sounded, Walt knew that Reggie wasn't rubbing it in his face. He was, in his own way, trying to do him a favor.

"Isn't this just like you," Reggie said, "You finally pull yourself together to accomplish something great, knowing the whole time it's all for naught. Doesn't that make you wonder about yourself? That you'd be willing to do something so futile?"

"Making Miss June happy is futile?"

"No, that's a nice thing. But you know what I mean. You're a grown man. And this is what you're doing at this point in your life. One last job for the old lady. What're you going to do once she's gone? When there's no one around to give you a to-do list? To reward you with milk and cookies?"

"I'm doing this because I care about her, Reggie. Not everything has to make sense. Not everything can be quantified. That's the difference between you and me."

"It certainly is." He rubbed his hand over one of the smooth panels on the wall. "This is the best work you'll ever do. And I'm sure you're making her happy."

"I'm doing what I can."

"I know you are. But I still think you're crazy."

"You're probably right."

After the room cleared, Walt stood alone in the middle of the parlor, which felt different now that others had seen it. He thought about those strange concepts in quantum mechanics where things can't be said to exist unless they are observed. Until now, the job felt almost imaginary. Now that the work had been witnessed, it hit him that there was a serious expectation he would get it all done.

"Hey," Gwen said, sidling up to his hip.

"Hey."

"Um, I was hoping to ask a favor?" She wrinkled her nose in apology, a gesture Walt remembered from so many years gone by. He could see her making this face as she turned in a paper, doubtful that it would be any good, which, of course, it would be, every time.

"Does it require heavy lifting? 'Cause I'm about to give out."

"It's nothing physical. Just mental."

"Mental? That's me."

She offered an oversized manila envelope.

"I was hoping you'd read the manuscript?"

"Me?"

"And that's not the whole of it, I'm afraid. I hate to ask, given all you've got going on, but I was hoping you'd give it an editorial pass? Not the whole thing, of course, but maybe just a chapter or two? I'm so close to it I can't tell how it reads anymore."

"I'd be honored to read it—to read anything you've written"—he remembered the mediocre poems of her youth— "but I'm hardly qualified to comment on your work. I've never written anything like this." He felt the heft of the pages, amazed at how many there were.

"You know what rings true. There's no one else I'd ask. Please just don't tell me it sucks."

"I can tell you sight unseen that it doesn't suck, but, sure, I'll be happy to give it a run through."

"Thank you."

She looked serious—this really did mean something to her.

"I owe you one," she said.

"One what?"

She gave him a light kiss.

"We'll see."

* * *

The manuscript was masterful. He read it at his small kitchen table beneath the bare bulb, Dewey's heavy head resting on his feet. Gwen was deft with her prose, telling the tale of the Creighton rise to wealth accurately—weaving in the requisite dates and diagramming of lineage—without being overbearing. For a potentially dense book, it was perfectly readable, and beyond that, holding it against what Walt knew of the family tale, it did ring true. The project, with its very existence the result of Miss June's vanity, stood from the beginning to not be particularly interesting to non-historians, but Walt could see how all sorts of people could be drawn in to the tale as Gwen let it unfold. She'd done research beyond the source material Miss June had given her and had worked in the less flattering aspects of the Creighton clan in a manner that stood a fair chance of withstanding Miss June's scrutiny. Perhaps. Surprisingly, Walt, blue pen in hand, felt comfortable noting suggestions as he read. His notes began modestly—correcting the odd bit of errant punctuation or the occasional repeated word—but soon ventured beyond suggestions of alternate phrasing to asking questions in the margins, noting additional avenues that could be explored, much as he had when he'd taught years before. The academic juices he'd begun to question had ever existed reappeared, and with them came a rush that surprised him. He continued on into the night, fascinated by Gwen's take on the family that spawned the woman who became, at once, the most manipulative, contrary, frustrating, judgmental, and important person in his life.

* * *

Grocery stores felt surreal to Walt, artificial, fluorescent, and overwhelming. Sam did most of the shopping when they were married, due to his tendency to "fuck it up." After the divorce, his food just seemed to appear, be it at Gene's, the Apache, Hardwick, or from Sam and Art's fridge. When he did shop, it was at small local markets rather than the larger supermarket, with its gleaming floors, mile-long aisles, and beeping registers. Watching the other shoppers confidently consult their lists and studiously compare brands, he had gathered that their missions were guided by some sort of planning, which happened not to be his forte. But now, Sam had sent him to the Giant Eagle with a list of his own, so there he was, wandering its byzantine floor-plan, no longer sure where the exit was, a stranger in an ordinary land. Had he followed the conventional shopper's path through the store, he would have found that the list Sam had penned was designed so that the items were ordered to roughly match the layout of the aisles—produce first, then canned goods, dry goods, meats, and then dairy. But Walt was not one to follow the obvious path. Nor did he have a pencil with him, and so as he did manage to happen upon the items on the list, he couldn't check them off, and had to reread the damned thing over and over to see what he still needed. And what the hell was "cumin"?

Putting the groceries on the counter, he called out, "Honey, I'm home!" but it was Art who burst in from the pantry to greet him. Curiously, it was he who wore Sam's frilly apron this time. With a peculiar gleam in his eye, he proceeded to talk up a blue streak about groceries and housekeeping, and Walt wondered if the good dentist had written himself a pre-scription for amphetamines.

"Walter! Thank you for going to the market for us. I've been trying to ensure that Sam gets her afternoon nap—that and to take the vitamins the obstetrician gave her—and I couldn't possibly make it to the store because of all the cleaning I need to do around here. This place is a mess!"

He gestured hopelessly at the kitchen, which was spotless.

"What's a man to do? I'd better get these vegetables put away before they melt!"

Walt found Sam lounging on the living room sofa with a candy bar and a novel.

"What the hell's gotten into him?" he asked.

"He's nesting."

"Isn't that what pregnant women do?"

"Apparently, he's doing it for me. That and everything else. I'm not allowed to lift a finger."

"Must be nice."

"He's driving me crazy." She pinched the bridge of her nose as if to kill a migraine. "Do you have a cigarette?"

"I don't smoke, remember? And neither do you anymore."

"I know, I know. I just love saying that: *'Do you have a cigarette?'*"

From the kitchen came a great crash—one that conjured images of Jerry Lewis playing a waiter in a fancy restaurant—followed by Arthur immediately calling out that he was "all right! I'm all right! Everything's fine!"

"God help me," said Sam.

"I never would have imagined him like this," Walt said. "I figured he'd prepare for the big day confidently, like the Boy Scout he is, and be done with it."

"Oh, he's prepared, all right. He's been making practice runs to the hospital all week. He's worried because I refuse to go with him. He even put a plastic slipcover over the car seat in case my water breaks en route."

"Practice runs? For what? He works across the street from the hospital. He parks in the same garage, for God's sake."

"Hey, I welcome the peace and quiet while he's gone. I don't know if I can take eight more weeks of this."

"Maybe I should take him out some night? Give you an evening off?"

"That would be marvelous."

But Walt quickly realized he had no idea what he would do with Arthur for a whole night. They both hated sports, Walt hated the symphony, and, given Art's current state, Walt doubted he could sit through a movie. Perhaps a blowgun and tranquilizer dart was in order.

"I'm vacuuming now!" came the call from upstairs where Arthur had managed to land, despite, Walt swore, having never gone up the stairs that were in plain sight. The vacuum droned above them, and he hoped the dining room ceiling would withstand the vibration.

Sam closed her eyes and let her book fall to her chest, and Walt absorbed her tough, beautiful face. Despite Arthur's behavior, she looked at peace. She was being taken care of.

* * *

He stood alone as the mid-morning sun streamed through the tall windows, causing dust to dance in its rays, bringing a pleasant feeling of near-vertigo. As his mind drifted, he realized that he hadn't seen Miss June all morning. She should have stopped in by now to comment on his lack of progress or the state of his shirttail. He let his tool belt drop to the floor and went looking.

"Have you seen her royal highness this morning?" he asked Gwen.

"No, not once. Her bedroom door was closed earlier. I assumed she was napping."

They exchanged worried looks.

Walt started toward the grand staircase.

"Do you want me to go up with you?" she asked.

"No, I'll go." Then, to both her and himself, he said, "I'm sure she's fine."

The floor began to tilt toward the bedroom as he made his way down the hall. Her door wasn't fully closed, nor was it open enough to see more than a sliver of light. Pausing, he heard nothing from inside beyond the tick of a radiator—she had had him keep the boiler on later in the season than ever before, complaining of a chill. He chose not to knock or call her name, knowing that the absence of a reply would never leave him. Sensing no movement, he pushed the door open quietly and saw her propped up in bed, arms crossed as if placed by a mortician. The floor now slanted uphill and he had to climb. He leaned close, detected her faint breath, and then allowed himself his own. He watched her. Gone, suddenly, was the familiar childhood guilt of trespassing in her room. He unfolded the blanket that lay near her feet and draped it carefully over her thin body, adding it to the others. He was as close to her as he'd ever been, even after a lifetime, and he acknowledged the event. For the first time, she seemed less than all-powerful. Next to her was one of her tablets from whence the lists emanated, and he realized she'd been composing one before falling asleep. Though a violation, he couldn't help but take a look. It had never occurred to him that she made lists for herself to complete, but that was exactly what this one was.

> *Review Gwenneth's work.*
> *Resign from Victorian board.*
> *Sign papers.*
> *Deed to Reginald.*
> *Confirm with Donald.*

And last, underlined twice—an emphasis he had not seen in a lifetime of Miss June's lists—was one more item.

> *Walter.*

"She's fine," he told Gwen.

She saw that he was shaken and gave him a long, anchor-like hug. While in her arms, he allowed himself to truly anticipate loss. And then, because it was what was done each morning at Hardwick, he went to the kitchen and put the kettle on to boil.

* * *

The Carnegie Lecture Hall wasn't quite full—this was a history lecture, after all—but still, there was a good-sized crowd. The event was part of an ongoing series that featured an author of a different sort each month, and in addition to the regular subscribers, academics from the local colleges and universities had turned out. The featured speaker was the hot historian of the moment, if there could be said to be such a thing. Walt picked the history professors out of the crowd easily—they shared the same rumpled clothes and slightly fuzzy affect as the English Lit professors, but without the sense of humor. Absent also was the visible degree of career resignation, as the historians had never dreamed of a life beyond campus to begin with. He wondered if he looked the same. Also present was the usual assortment of local amateur history buffs, oddballs who were more interested in history than those who held advanced degrees and got paid for it. These amateurs—cynics, romantics, and, worse, Civil War re-enactors—generally had some sort of axe to grind about how history was being taught, an axe that was coupled, always, with bad breath. They were to be avoided at all costs. Walt had accepted Gwen's invitation with reservations, as he was not looking forward to seeing his old colleagues. How things had changed since just last fall, back when life was normal and he didn't give a shit who he ran into so long as he didn't owe them anything. It was after he'd accepted that Gwen mentioned shyly that she'd been asked to be a speaker herself—opening for the main act, as it were—giving a reading from one of her more recent books. While Walt didn't welcome the extra attention that this would bring as they walked into the grand hall together, the reassurance of her grip on his arm for the most part countered the mild fraudulence he felt at being seen as her date. She sat him right up front, and then disappeared backstage.

The featured speaker, James Hunter, was everything a visiting scholar should be—smart, interesting, and at once both confident and self-deprecating. He read from his best-seller with humility, and the crowd ate it up. After the question-and-answer session came the book-signing portion of the evening—a portion that took entirely too long for Walt's taste. When it was finally over, the speakers, the organizers, and an assortment of hangers on moved to an indoor courtyard section of the building to drink wine and pick over cheese cubes and crackers. Walt had worked hard that day and had to fight to not scarf down too many. The hell with it. He filled his small plate again.

"Hi, Walt. What a surprise to see you here."

It was Stu Abramson, a moderately liked faculty member who, when given his periodic turn, took his responsibilities as Department Chair more seriously than were warranted. Way more seriously. Walt had been a splinter in Stu's ass for as long as they'd worked together, officiousness being one of Walt's least favorite traits, and Stu possessing it in spades. Not only did he think that everything should be done by the book, he thought that "the book" itself wasn't rigid enough. Stu and Arthur would see eye to eye on plenty of things, Walt thought, but at least Art had his earnest charm.

"Hey, Stu. How's it hanging?"

"I'm sorry?"

"How are you?"

"Oh, I'm fine, just fine. I haven't seen you in years." He eyed Walt's prominent belly.

"It's been a long time, it's true. So, are you Chair at the moment?" Walt asked, unable to think of anything else to say.

"No, it's not my turn," Stu sighed wistfully.

No one else wanted to be Department Chair. Ever.

"Well, it'll happen soon enough," Walt offered. Stu was no longer part of the dreaded establishment to him. He was just another middle-aged guy.

"He's brilliant, isn't he?" Stu said.

"Hunter? I don't know, I didn't read his book. Seems nice enough, though."

"He's bringing our profession a lot of attention."

"And that's a good thing?"

"Well, sure. I mean it has to be, right? He's causing a lot of people to feel the passion of history."

"I hadn't thought of it like that."

"Say, I hate to ask, but, speaking of history, do you still have my copy of *Archaeology of Contemporary Urban Identities*? It's been missing since, well, since you left."

"I have no idea, Stu. But if it's missing, I probably took it. Sorry."

"It's okay," Stu said, although Walt could see him sliding beads of debt across a mental abacus. "Anyway, I'm going to try to catch Hunter before he takes off. Good seeing you, Walt."

"You too, Stu." Hey, that rhymed, he thought as he was left alone.

The crowd waiting to speak with the charming out-of-towner was dense, yet Hunter appeared to give sincere attention to each. Gwen was at his side, looking like she belonged there.

"Holy shit, could this be the famous Walt Farnham?" came a voice from behind. "Renowned expert in southwestern Pennsylvania history? Nap-taker extraordinaire? The man who owes me both $35 and a soiled trench coat? The man who took his Intro to European History class bowling? Regularly?"

"I'm some of those things, it's true."

"The man who never gave a bad grade to a pretty girl?"

"They were all very smart."

"Jesus, Walt, it's good to see you."

Arnie Smith gave him a bear hug.

"Good to see you too, Smitty. It's always good to see someone else who hasn't lost weight."

"You're never in your office anymore. Things aren't the same."

"Come again?"

"Your office. You know, shitty room, big metal desk, a mountain of papers?"

"Arnie, I haven't taught in seven years. I don't have an office, remember?"

"Actually, you do. It's still there. Your buddies in facilities refuse to reclaim it. Officially, the room doesn't even exist anymore — they removed the room number. It's like those skyscrapers with no thirteenth floor. Apparently, you're still liked among the building's staff."

"Well, I'll be damned." What a weird bit of news this was. Walt's messy office was fixed in the department's mythology, having served as a hangout for confused underclassmen, a way-station for procrastinating colleagues, and a hideout for both duty-shirking janitors and Walt himself when he was in need of a nap. "I don't suppose it's been cleaned up, has it?"

"You don't fuck with a shrine."

Walt's lack of academic stress was the envy of many who struggled to publish.

Smith gestured toward Hunter. "So, what did you think of the genius?"

"Do I detect a note of jealousy?"

Smith exuded a nice mixture of reefer and scotch. "Of course you do. The motherfucker's managed to get rich doing this shit. And look at him, for God's sake. He dons corduroy and elbow patches, and the babes hang all over him." Hunter's hand was on Gwen's back as they laughed at something clever.

"Well, his fame and fortune will fade fast," Walt assured them both. "It's not like he wrote *History for Dummies.*"

"Or *Chicken Soup for the Historian's Soul.*" Smith shook his empty glass. "Come on, let's go meet the savior before he makes off with your date."

"What?"

"I saw you come in together," Smith said. "She's pretty damned hard to miss. Is it serious between you two?"

"No, I'm just tonight's arm candy."

Gwen saw Walt approaching and beamed. "There you are. You've got to meet James."

"So I hear." He extended his hand. "Hey. Walt Farnham. Good to meet you. That was a hell of a reading."

"The pleasure is mine. And thanks for the comment—I cringe at the sound of my own voice." Hunter had a good handshake, which he followed by handing Walt his card, prompting Walt to fish through his pockets and hand him, in return, a worn book of Bull's-Eye matches, the only thing he could produce that included a phone number he could sort of call his own. Above the number, the pack said *"Don't Call Us, We'll Call You."*

Whatever conversation Walt had interrupted picked up again, and the exchange of volleys was faster than he could keep up with. Unfamiliar books and authors were bandied about as if they were household names. Arnie Smith had detoured to the bar on the way over, leaving Walt alone and in a state not unlike that of being at the grocery store. He followed the conversation as best he could, not quite grasping it, but not particularly concerned, either, with the wordplay eventually becoming white noise. He nodded when it seemed to make sense to do so, and looked enough like one of the crowd. He heard Gwen say his name, saw her gesture to him and a couple of other folks, including Hunter, who nodded appreciatively, but Walt had no idea what she'd said. He smiled back like a foreigner. Smitty showed up, handed him a drink, and then started a conversation with the woman on his left, a lecherous gleam in his eye. The scene continued for a while, and plans were suddenly afoot to continue the party elsewhere, the beginnings of a big night in the air. The university provost—an assistant dean when Walt knew him—noticed Walt for the first time and made a big deal about how long it had been.

"I'm so glad to see you," the provost said. "You were on my mind just the other day!" Gwen looked pleased. "I'm converting a bedroom in my house into an office, and I need someone to build some shelves. Tell me you'll do it."

"You're a carpenter?" someone else asked. "Do you have a card? I can never find anyone good."

He was out of matches.

"Walt's the best artisan you'll ever know," Gwen said with protective pride, "but I'm afraid he won't be available for quite some time. He's busy with a historical restoration project, one that you'll all be reading about soon. It's going to be magnificent."

"I don't read," Arnie Smith said. Then, leering at his new romantic interest, he added, "But I do know how." Somehow he made it sound dirty.

"And I know how to call it a night," Walt said. Pulling Gwen gently aside, he said, "Listen, I know you want to go out with your friends, but would you mind if I passed? I have a long day tomorrow and don't have any business bar-hopping." He couldn't keep up with this crowd in any number of ways.

"No! I'm leaving with you. Just let me say goodnight."

"Gwen, please. It's all right. This is a big night for you. It's okay. Really. Your reading tonight was exceptional. You stole the show from what's-his-face."

"Hunter," she said. "And you're full of shit, but thank you for the wonderful lie." She made a point of giving him a very big kiss in front of everyone. "Then I'll see you in the morning," she said with a wink.

"Ha-cha-cha-cha-cha!" Smitty exclaimed.

The ride home was quiet, accompanied by a wave of melancholy. The DORF turned into the Bull's-Eye lot. Deena's El Camino was there. As he sat alone at the bar, she didn't look his way.

Chapter 19

WALT PLACED THE OILY PIECE OF CARDBOARD under his truck's leaky belly. The cardboard—a flattened old box that had once contained jars of pickles—was nearly soaked through and was due to be replaced. Before the baby, before the parlor, the state of whatever piece of cardboard Walt was using to protect the drive at Hardwick was his primary method of noting the passage of time. Finding a new, pristine box to collapse and use to replace the old saturated one always felt like a new beginning, like buying new shoes or getting a haircut.

"Well, look at what the cat dragged in," Miss June said from the side porch where she was sweeping the steps. She was holding herself with caution, moving with measure.

He consulted his bare wrist. "It's only eleven-seven, Miss June. I'm right on time."

"The sun's been up for two hours, young man. And now I suppose you're going to have tea and read the paper before easing into your workday."

"Well, if that's an offer…"

"I might just have to finish this project of yours myself. I'm not going to be around forever."

"You've been telling me that for thirty years now, Miss June."

"You've been listening? I find that hard to believe." She abandoned her sweeping and made her way slowly back up the steps. Walt discreetly held his hand a few inches behind her back in case she faltered.

There was dew that morning, and, under the sun, tiny jewels played across the great lawn. Donald took meticulous care of the grounds, spending hours each week weeding and fertilizing, piloting the little putt-putt riding mower with precision and concern. He did so in his gardening hat. The flower beds were nicely done, with not a thing out of place. He and Miss June had patterned them after plans found in Victorian landscape books, and had Walt build low flagstone walls to contain them. Jimmy'd insisted on helping with the walls, his sole qualification being that he was Italian, which in his mind made him an expert in all things masonry.

As if reading his mind, Miss June asked, "How is your musical friend?"

"Who?"

"The masher, I mean. The one who sings."

"Jimmy?"

"Yes. That's the one. He's been kind enough to spare us his presence of late." Miss June always commented on Jimmy's incessant singing and amorous ways, but Walt knew she liked having him around. Still, after all these years, she refused to acknowledge that she remembered his name.

"Jimmy is Jimmy."

"That he is."

"I can call him if you want. I'm sure he'd be right over."

"Oh, please." She turned to face him. "I'm hesitant to confess it, but I do somewhat admire your willingness to see the better attributes of so many different sorts of people, even if to do so isn't warranted."

"If there was a compliment in there somewhere, thank you."

They moved to the wicker sofa on the veranda and surveyed the grounds. In the grass, wrens chased after bits of food and one another.

After a minute of silence, she asked, "Walter, have you reconsidered rejoining the academic world?"

"Oh, please. We settled this long ago." He couldn't believe she was bringing it up.

"I know that in your mind we did, but I, seeing a larger canvas than you seem willing to consider, don't think that it's too late."

"'Too late would be an applicable phrase if I wanted to go back. But I don't. You can bring this up all you like, but my answer won't change."

But as he said this, he felt an unexpected twinge, a quick wonder of what his prospects could be. He fended it off.

"All I know is that, despite your usual lackluster performance and penchant for shooting yourself in the foot, you've got quite the clever mind and could do an institution of higher learning a fair amount of good. I remember well the enthusiasm with which you once spoke about teaching. The opportunity to mold young minds, the chance to lead them toward eclipsing your own accomplishments."

"Eclipsing my own ... Jesus, where do you come up with this stuff?"

"It's as simple as day, Walter. For whatever reason, you possess a natural ability to teach and inspire, and I think it a—pardon the expression—a damned shame that you don't use it. Being a handyman is all well and good, but you could do so much more."

"It's served you well, hasn't it?"

"Don't be disrespectful. I think you should contact the chancellor—or perhaps it would be better that I do it for you—and tell him that you're ready to come back and pursue your right place as a serious scholar. Certainly you could just write whatever paper it is you're supposed to write, get your degree, and be done with it."

"That ship has sailed. There was a time when I belonged in that world. No more. I've found my place."

"Oh, have you? Have you really?"

"Yes, I have. Well, not exactly," he admitted, "but I'm getting close. Look, I agree that I've been in a rut. But things are shifting."

"Ah, shifting, you say. Well, disregard my concern then. Shifting, things are."

"I can't explain it."

"Listen to the unrest in your voice, Walter. I think it to be a good thing. And I'm not suggesting that returning to school is your only option. I'm simply putting forth that you shouldn't settle. Remember, despite my long telling you that you should above all strive to reach your potential, what's truly important in life is finding your proper place, no matter where it might be." She looked to the garden paths where she and Dwight once strolled. "And no matter who it might be with."

Donald's Buick tooted and backed out of the drive in only one try, a rare occurrence that Walt noted from the porch. He'd arrived in a yellow cardigan sweater and white slip-on canvas shoes to take the elderly object of his affection on Saturday morning errands. Walt imagined Donald fretting each day over the proper wardrobe choice before embarking on his voyage to Hardwick just ten blocks from his efficiency apartment. Gwen had yet to make an appearance that morning, as the activities after the lecture had turned into a late night. Walt was tempted to stand outside her bedroom door and fire up his circular saw just to let her know how late she'd been out, but didn't have the heart. As he smiled at that thought, she appeared in the screen door, clutching herself in her thick terry robe, hungover and beautiful.

"Coffee," she managed.

"Did we drink too much last night?"

"We didn't think so at the time."

Walt thought about Jimmy's vile hangover cures, wished he knew how to make one for her.

"You go lie down and I'll see what I can conjure up."

"What time is it? I'm supposed to meet Donald at the library later."

"Don't worry about it. He's happily occupied at the moment."

Gwen made her way back up to her room, while Walt went to the kitchen to make what he did know how to prepare—tea and toast. He arranged it on one of Miss June's silver trays, accompanied by the morning paper, a glass of orange juice, some strawberries, and, with apologies to Donald, a bunch of tulips from the garden. Worried that this wasn't enough to make Gwen feel better, he filled a dish with the British jelly beans Miss June thought she kept hidden from him in the back of the Hoosier.

Gwen was curled up in a ball when he put the tray on the bed next to her. Propping her pillows for her as she pulled herself up, he kissed her forehead and smelled Dove soap and toothpaste that almost masked the lingering scent of cigarettes and remorse. She smiled at his kiss and drained the orange juice quickly.

"You smell like a liquor store."

"Don't talk so loud." She was feeling better, but continued the act. It was nice to be cared for.

"Sorry. Did you have fun?"

"I did. I'd be lying if I said it wasn't fun."

"Lying is okay sometimes."

"You think so? I don't."

He took a piece of her toast.

"Well, not always," he said, "just so as to not hurt someone's feelings."

He fed her a bite.

"Would it hurt your feelings if I asked you to lower your voice again?"

"Not at all. I won't do it, but it won't hurt my feelings."

"In that case, shut up."

"Shut up? I bring you breakfast in bed and you tell me to shut up?"

"Let me finish." She pulled him in by the shirt. "Shut up and kiss me."

She tasted like juice and toast and her skin was warm and there was nothing else he wanted. Her robe fell away easily and had Miss June been home, she would have soon heard sounds coming from Gwen's room that hadn't been made in Hardwick in decades, if ever at all.

The strawberry left his hand as if from a launch pad. Against the backdrop galaxy of infinite white ceiling, it turned over and over in its path, a space capsule spinning perfectly out of control. After reaching its apogee, and having made a small arc just shy of the plaster above, it began its uncontrolled descent back to earth, where it was expertly received by her mouth and devoured directly. She was very good at this. Walt had thrown five in a row, and Gwen had caught every one except for the mis-launch that hit his own forehead. That one, she collected and fed to him. He wasn't surprised that she could catch the strawberries so easily. She was the kind of person who was good at all sorts of stupid tricks. She could juggle, place stacks of quarters on her elbow before flinging her arm down quickly and catching them all in her hand, crush a ping-pong serve, throw a boomerang, and produce the most piercing whistle imaginable by forming her thumb and pinky into a circle and blowing like hell. Usually he found such people annoying, but Gwen was an obvious exception. Her strawberry catching was unparalleled, and he thought maybe they could take their act on the road. Instead, she caught the next one in her hand, gently traced it around his lips, and then placed it in his mouth before turning onto her side and drawing herself in close, her arm across his bear-like chest. The linens on the bed were fresh, like those in a cottage by a lake, sun-dried sheets best enjoyed during the day, and certainly not alone.

"Well," she said. "Do you think I should put that in the book? Hardwick does figure in it prominently."

"I'd have to think it was a historic occurrence. For Hardwick, I mean."

"For me too, actually," she said. "It's been a long time."

"I'm honored."

"And you?"

"And me?"

"Has it been long for you?"

He pretended to consider this for too long. "Define long … She pinched his belly.

"That's a rather personal question, don't you think?" he asked.

It was a joke, but when she didn't reply he guessed that she realized she might not want to hear his real answer.

"Hey, I was kidding," he said. "It's been a long time for me, too." He thought back to the last time he'd been with Deena, which had probably not been as long ago as Gwen had meant, but, given the nature of that particular relationship, maybe it didn't count anyway.

She pulled in closer and they were quiet for a while, watching the curtains blow in the breeze. Walt wondered if they'd blown harder when they were having sex, like curtains did in lieu of love scenes in old movies. That cinematic trick now made perfect sense to him, as for the first time he understood its inherent beauty. Cars on Fifth Avenue made their noises and the curtains blew and a bee flirted with coming inside. Elsewhere, children played in playgrounds, landscapers cut grass, Miss June was over-accompanied by Donald, and Sam felt the kick of her baby. Sam would be delighted by today's development, Walt thought.

On cue, Gwen asked, "Was Sam your last love?"

"Yes." After a pause, he said, "And I'd sometimes wondered if that's what she would remain."

"Ah, but don't you men say that you get three great loves in your life?"

This sounded oddly familiar.

"Where did you hear that?"

"Jimmy told me. He was pretty convincing, but I think I heard it in a movie once."

"He claims to know a lot of things, that Jimmy."

"But wait! That's no good. If Sam was your first great love, that makes me Number Two. You have one more to go!"

He thought and then gestured around the room. "No, we're safe. This house is Number Two. You're Number Three."

"You're close," she said, and kissed him on the side of his chest. "Your other great love owns this house. And Number Three thinks it's sweet."

* * *

"I've found it!" Donald said with a snap, returning to the study table, an open volume in his hands. The Pennsylvania Room at the main branch of the Carnegie Library in Oakland was exactly as such a room should be, with tall ceilings and exposed radiators, chest-high marble panels adorning the walls, and the staid smell of recorded history. It was a room whose regular inhabitants had little tolerance for nonsense, and the Dewey Decimal System was not to be mocked. He rejoined Gwen at their long table and showed her what he'd found.

"Look, it's right here on page two hundred fifty-seven, an account of the wedding of Vera Gainnes Creighton's parents, showing a clear connection of her side of the family to a royal burgh in Scotland, one where, if I'm reading this right, her grandfather served as provost. Ha!" He was clearly pleased that he'd found reason to further bolster the Creighton family's standing.

" 'Ha,' indeed," she said. "You are truly a wonder, Donald. I don't know what I'd do without you."

"Oh, go on," he blushed.

"I mean it. You've really got a knack for finding things, and just when I'm sure I'm at a dead end."

For months she'd been sending Donald off on quests for obscure information, whether it was really needed or not. The quests brought him such joy, she couldn't help herself. And she made a point of telling Miss June what an invaluable help he'd been and how she couldn't have made such progress without him. She smiled at what Walt had said just that morning: *"Lying is okay."*

Donald, gesturing toward the table, suddenly looked distressed. "Oh, um, ha-ha. We're not supposed to have beverages in here."

She glanced at the iced coffee next to her purse. "Oh. I guess you're right. Well, I'll be finished soon. No harm done."

"Yes, um, but you see, the books here are very old, and the tables are too, and I'd be remiss if I didn't point out how that could spell disaster! Not to imply that you're clumsy, though! On the contrary, I've seen you successfully handle beverages on numerous occasions since your stay at Hardwick began, but it just makes me a little nervous to, you know, be a party to the breaking of rules. Ahem." He looked around nervously for the library gestapo.

"Duly noted. And as soon as I'm finished, I'll throw my cup in the trash—I promise—and I won't do it again. Now, you were telling me about the Scottish wedding of Vera Creighton's parents? The Gainneses?"

"Oh, yes, I have it all right here…" After a moment's deft page turning, aided by the caramel-colored rubber thumb and finger protectors he had donned prior to making the attempt, Donald once again found his place in the large volume and began to read.

"Berwick-upon-Tweed, a district that includes the holy islands, was claimed for England in 1482 by Edward the IV, when… I'm sorry, but do you think we might be able to just put the drink on the floor by your chair? So as to not be so visible, I mean."

"It's not a Molotov cocktail, silly. It's coffee. I won't spill it, I promise."

Donald emitted a sound of genuine distress.

"It's just that I'm known here at this branch, and I'd hate to imagine the circumstances that might arise if…"

"Okay, okay! You win! I'll get rid of it!" She found the whole thing quite funny, and didn't want to hurt his feelings by smiling, but the relief on his face as she removed the cup from the table showed that the situation, for him, went beyond simple embarrassment: he *needed* to have the cup moved. At the other end of the spectrum, she could picture Walt sitting there eating a pizza without a napkin in sight.

As Gwen dumped her coffee into the ladies' room sink, she looked in the mirror above the worn marble counter. She smiled at the sight of herself—the morning with Walt had left her glowing. She decided it was obvious to all that not only was she in love, but that she'd had sex—great sex—just hours before. Further, she didn't care who knew. She thought of her ex-husband. What a turn things had taken. She hadn't come to Pittsburgh expecting this to happen, not with anyone, and certainly not with Walt Farnham. He seemed so settled in his ways, and what with Jimmy, Dewey, Sam, and Miss June, there didn't seem to be room for anyone else. But if she wasn't mistaken, he seemed to be trying for her. Trying what, she wasn't sure, but she suspected his efforts in the parlor had given rise to his efforts in the bedroom.

"Well, then, where was I?" Donald said when she returned. He looked greatly relieved.

"Um, perhaps you could just give me your notes on those pages."

"Ha! Fair enough." She watched as he made notations in his precise little longhand, deciding in the process that he was becoming one of her favorite people. Not someone with whom she'd ever be truly close, but whom she'd always be glad was out there somewhere.

"What do you think about Walt?" she suddenly asked.

"Walter? Oh, he's quite the kidder, he is. Pulls my leg quite a bit, you know. But a kind soul nonetheless."

"I agree."

"He's always been around, you know. At Hardwick, I mean. For all of the years I've been friends with Miss June, he's been around. Pops up at the darnedest times, he does."

"At times when you wish you and Miss June had a little more privacy?" she teased, dragging her toe along his calf. Had her coffee still been on the table, Donald himself would have spilled it.

"No! My goodness. Miss June and I share the most pleasant of friendships—when she's feeling amenable, that is—and Walter's whereabouts have no bearing on our decorous social behavior, truly, and further…"

"Donald, it's okay to like to spend time alone with her. It's fine. I like to spend time alone with Walt these days. It's okay. Really."

"Well, of course it is, I just didn't want you to get the wrong impression."

"You're quite the worry-wart, aren't you."

"I just don't like to leave much open to misinterpretation."

"Perhaps you should turn over a new leaf."

"Walter has suggested that from time to time."

"He knows of what he speaks."

"He leaves plenty to chance, I'll grant you that. Practices what he preaches."

"I like you, Donald."

"Well, goodness. I like you too, Gwenneth." He blushed. "And you like Walter—that's good to know. For all of his quirks, he's taken great care of Miss June over the years, and for that I'm appreciative. It's not an easy task, I can assure you."

"I'm sure it's not."

"He's quite reliable for her, in his own unreliable way."

"That's a nice way to put it."

"She's in good hands."

In good hands. She let that sink in. Donald went back to writing his notes, and Gwen resisted the urge to tease his calf some more. She thumbed through a large pattern book of Victorian-era architectural details. Floor plans and elevations were shown for all sorts of houses, from Gothic Revival to Italianate, from Second Empire to Queen Anne. The book had scale templates depicting the patterns of the elaborate moldings and porch brackets that adorned the facades, and even reproductions of newspaper advertisements for building products from the time—beautifully illustrated layouts describing the wonders of cast iron "ventilators," gas chandeliers, wall sconces, and hand-crafted shutters of the variety that nearly killed Walt twice each year. He was born in the wrong century, she decided. Turning the page revealed a grand Queen Anne that featured a roof line similar to Hardwick's.

"Well, that gem looks familiar," Donald offered, pulling her from her daydream.

"I think Walt would have liked living back then," she said. "Building a house like this one from scratch."

"He's done a masterful job on the parlor."

"It's breathtaking, isn't it," she agreed with pride.

"Oh, yes. Especially all things considered."

She didn't want to spoil her thoughts by addressing Walt's difficulties.

"I know he has trouble getting things done. But he's been doing so well with this. It means a lot to him." And to me, she thought.

"And it's all the more remarkable given the eventuality of the circumstances," Donald noted.

"The eventuality?"

"The fate of the house, of course."

"I don't understand."

"Certainly Miss June's told you."

"Told me what?"

"Oh. Well. Perhaps it's not my place to say anything. I'd better leave well enough alone." He attempted to retreat into his notes.

"Donald!"

"It just that, well, as much as we all love Hardwick, it won't be with us for long. At least not in its current state."

"What are you talking about?"

"Miss June is leaving it to her nephew."

"Reggie Creighton? The developer?!"

"It's family protocol. He's the last remaining male. I thought you would have known this."

She felt a rush of sickness and wondered if she'd have to run back to the ladies' room.

"It's the way things must be," he said not with resignation, but in full support of Miss June's propriety.

* * *

She barged in.

"When were you going to tell me?"

Walt lay in his bed above Sam's garage, the place its usual mess. Gwen had never been up here, and having her burst through the door had the strange effect of not startling him but, rather, causing him to zone out into a peculiar calm, his usual reaction to stressful situations.

"I don't know. I figured you'd find out when you would," he said, wishing he had a better response.

"What the hell does that mean?"

"I'm not sure. Just that things always happen the way they're going to happen." He felt himself backsliding into his role of helpless passenger. She felt it, too, a shift of sorts, and she figured she'd caused it by surprising him as she had. Still, she was upset. Dewey wagged his tail and offered her his tennis ball, an offer that was seldom turned down, but this time was rejected.

"Tell me what this is all about," she said, falling into bed next to him.

The request was fair, but he wasn't sure how to sort it out. The answer could be a simple reporting of what she apparently already knew, that the house had to stay in the family, or it could be a long tale that broached the difficult territory of how he felt about it all, which, it occurred to him as he lay there pondering the situation, included facing that the loss of the house represented the removal of his own foundation. Rather than choose, he didn't answer.

"Fuck," she said softly, letting him off the hook.

They lay there quietly, and Walt began to feel that rather than making him tell the tale, she was simply absorbing how he felt about it all, gaining insight into the decades of emotions that were tied up between him and that house. He was glad for this transference of understanding—it was freeing.

"I know the parlor means a lot to you," he said, finally. "I really do."

"It's about us," she said.

"I didn't mean for it to turn out like this. I wanted to tell you. You just seemed so happy with the way things were going. And, frankly, it's been a while since I've made anyone happy. Truly happy."

They woke a few hours later, spooning and in need of a blanket. It had gotten dark, and the lights from Sam's house played upon the bed. Gwen pushed her back into Walt's belly, and they lay still in the quiet that follows an unexpected nap. Whatever upset had been caused by Walt not sharing Miss June's plans had faded as they slept, and they both knew all was forgiven. This suited Walt especially well because, like most men, he preferred not to talk about it. Silent communication was good, as was his hand on Gwen's hip as he pulled her closer.

"I don't want you to talk to Miss June about the house," he said. "I've been through it with her a million times. I don't want to upset her. Not now."

"I know you don't." She rubbed her foot against his ankle. "She's lucky to have you. You're quite reliable for her—in your own unreliable way."

"I'm what?"

"Nothing."

They drifted for a short while until Walt's hand ventured from her hip to places that freed his mind from the gated confines of Hardwick.

The two of them showed up later at Sam's with takeout Vietnamese, causing Arthur a bit of consternation. He was an enthusiastic and polite host, but he didn't like surprises, especially now that the baby was only eight weeks away. After their nap, they'd called Sam on the way to Tram's on Penn Avenue, asking if she and Art were hungry. Walt knew that Sam always was—the call was made at Gwen's insistence.

"We can just drop in on them," he'd said. "I do it all the time."

"I'm sure you do," she replied. "What's their number?"

She had handed her cell phone to Walt to dial, but he couldn't manipulate its buttons with his thick fingers, squinting his eyes as if they'd suddenly gone bad. After a moment's fumbling, he handed the confounded thing back to her with exaggerated disdain, holding it between his thumb and index finger like a dead mouse.

Now, the two couples sat at the dining room table, the aroma of exotic sauces causing the familiar stir in his loins. He added Vietnamese food to his list of olfactory aphrodisiacs, filing it between tire stores and gasoline. The couples ate and chatted. It was the first time Walt had brought another woman home—that was the exact phrase that went through his mind: *brought another woman home*—and Sam seemed pleased with the surprise. After dinner, they played Pictionary, the teams being Sam and Walt versus Art and Gwen. Walt's undecipherable scribbles were easily deciphered by Sam, who knew him too well for the game to be fair, while Art was so serious about his engineer-like attempts at drawing that, even after Gwen had correctly guessed what he had sketched, he continued to work on the illustration to get all the details right.

"She guessed it, Arthur!" Sam exclaimed. "Move on!"

"I heard her, but ducks have feet, you know!" he complained as the others laughed at him.

"She already said it was a duck!"

"But it's not finished yet!"

"You tell her, Artie!" Walt cried.

Walt was at a disadvantage, though, when Sam was drawing, as making art was not among her talents. Gwen drew quickly and well, and because Sam was good at guessing, had the teams been boys against the girls, the boys would have been slaughtered. When the game was over, the boys were sent off to do the dishes while the girls relaxed.

"Well," Arthur said. "Gwenneth is lovely. Simply lovely."

"And you're wondering what she's doing with me," he joked.

"I was implying no such thing. I simply think she's a very pleasant young lady, and that you make a very nice couple."

" 'A very nice couple'? Jesus, Art."

When the men returned to the living room, Sam was explaining to Gwen what it felt like to be pregnant.

"Yeah, it's heavy. Heavy as hell. But sometimes I forget it's there. I'm always spilling food on myself and bumping into things."

She was pretty damned big, Walt thought with affection. Sam yawned.

"And we should be going," Gwen said.

"Hmmm?" Walt was still lost in Sam's new physique.

"Gwen was saying it was time for you to be going," Sam said, consulting her watch. "The question is, to where?"

Walt, not all that quick on the uptake, looked around the room for a clue as to what that meant. Arthur had begun his ritual tidying of things that weren't messy, and hadn't been listening.

"To sleep?" Sam helped Walt out.

"Oh," he said. Apparently the women had been talking when he and Art were in the kitchen, pondering how Gwen might spend the night at Walt's, given that she was supposed to sleep at Hardwick. Miss June, he realized.

"I could call her," Sam said. "Tell her you're over here and are spending the night."

"Well, that's silly. I can call and tell her that myself," Gwen said.

"I don't suppose it would be much help if I called her," Walt contributed and was duly ignored.

It was Gwen who called Miss June to inform her of her whereabouts, telling her that she was at Sam and Arthur's house, with Walt, that they were playing Hearts, and that it had gotten late. Would she feel unsafe if she were to spend the night in Sam's guest room?

"Dear girl, I understand the kind intent of your inquiry, but rest assured, I've slept alone in this house for most of my life and don't intend to begin having problems now."

"Of course not. I just wanted to make sure you were feeling all right."

"Thank you. Your call is appreciated, but I feel fine. Might I note one thing, however…"

"Yes?"

"If a tale of this nature is to be feasible, it would be wise to not include within it the premise of Walter playing cards. He hasn't the concentration for it."

Dewey, reluctant to give up his usual spot next to Walt, managed to perch himself on the edge of the bed next to Gwen. Before she fell asleep—and before Dewey would gradually insinuate himself across most of the mattress—she watched the tree branches produce their nightly play on the bedroom wall, Walt's heavy arm making her feel safer than she had in years.

* * *

By morning's light, she could only laugh at his apartment. While it wasn't an absolute mess, it was utilitarian at best, following as it did the man-and-his-dog/literary/construction school of interior design. Along with the impressive collection of books that graced the cinder-block and wood-plank shelves, there were various tools strewn about, and a few massive bags of dog food in the kitchen. There was so much dog food, in fact, that she wondered if Walt had taken to eating the stuff himself. She had gotten up with the idea of making breakfast, but no one could have come up with something based on the ingredients at hand. Instead, she woke him with a jump onto the bed, and he took her to the Apache, where Lynda distinctly did not give Walt the horny smile, but did give Gwen the cold shoulder. Walt left a big tip, and then it was off to Hardwick.

"Listen, sweetheart, I'm tellin' you," Jimmy was telling Miss June in the kitchen where he was sautéing onions, "what this house needs is a fountain. A great big one, right out front.

A woman holding a fish. One that spits water."

"The woman or the fish?" Walt asked from the kitchen door, certain that in Jimmy's vision, said concrete woman was topless. "How about a statue of Louis Prima, too? I bet you know a place to get one cheap."

"Actually, I do." Turning his attention to Gwen, he said, "I can get anything you want, hon, and you don't even have to pay. Him on the other hand," he said with a wink, "*Maledizion*—through the nose!"

"No matter the cost," Miss June announced, "the only statue destined for erection on this property will be of me, posed in eternal wait for my parlor to be finished."

"That's our cue, Jimmy," Walt said. "Why don't you give me a hand for a while."

"Sorry, but I'm cookin' with my girlfriend."

"I suspect I can survive a short while without you."

"But can I survive without you, sweetheart?" he said to Miss June, moving toward her, arms outstretched, as if to do the unthinkable and give her a hug.

"Keep your distance, you rake. You go and help Walter before his moment of enthusiasm for work passes. I'll tend to these onions. I do know a bit about cooking, believe it or not."

"Just don't let 'em get brown. That's the kiss of death to a good sauce: brown onions. That and adding sugar—whoever first thought to do something as dumb as that should be shot."

"What are you cooking for anyway?" Walt asked. "It's not even ten in the morning. Hell, it's not even your house."

"Every place should have sauce cooking. This house ain't seen good food since the last time I cooked here. No offense meant, sweetheart," he added for Miss June's benefit.

"None comprehended. I assure you, we aspire to different culinary ends."

"You got that right, toots."

"Come on, Jimmy, let's go. As much as I hate to say it, I do need your help," Walt said.

"Anything for you, my boy. I peeked in there earlier—it looks like a hundred bucks."

"While I am skeptical of your aptitude for landscape architecture, Mr. DeLuca," Miss June noted, "your accounting is spot on."

In the kitchen, Gwen thought that despite her maintaining her usual repartee, Miss June looked winded, and wondered if it was from clearing Jimmy's mess or from the effort it took to contend with his wordplay. She moved slowly about, not displaying any particular ailment, but with a deliberateness that Gwen guessed might be more apparent to Donald and Walt. Gwen considered offering to help, but having gotten to know the old woman as she had, knew better. Besides, she reasoned that keeping up some level of activity was good for her. Like the others, she was at a loss over what to do.

"That Italian man is nothing if not exhausting," Miss June said as she wiped the counter, and then, as if he might pop back in, gave the onions a quick stir before shutting off the flame. "Come with me to the garden, dear. I want a bit of fresh air."

"Jimmy is a live-wire," Gwen replied.

"Perhaps he might share his energy elsewhere."

"Oh, come on now, you like having him around, don't you?"

"Only in that his jocundity does seem to light a spark under our young Mr. Farnham's hindquarters. Beyond that, he's a pest."

The spring garden had begun to take hold, Donald's perennials providing color among the ground cover. With their backs to Fifth Avenue, it wasn't hard to imagine Victorian couples in casual attire playing croquet while servants tended to matters, unnoticed. The two were silent as they strolled the garden paths until Gwen broke the peace.

"Donald told me about Reggie inheriting the house."

Miss June leaned forward slightly and pinched off a rose that didn't meet her satisfaction.

"And?"

"Frankly, I was taken aback."

The older woman resumed her slow pace. "Taken aback, you say."

"I love this house. So many of us do. But for it to go to *Reggie*." Gwen's mouth worked around the name as if fielding a bad olive.

"You are not the first to tell me this, dear, although I suppose you may be among the last. My plans for my own house seem to draw strong reactions from those who've grown attached to it."

"And is Walt correct that there's no point in trying to talk you out of it?"

"Unquestionably. If he's learned anything over the years, it's that I am resolute in my decisions. I made my arrangements long ago, and further discussion needn't take place. Not that it has ever been anyone's business but mine. Mine and my grandfather's." She looked toward the house, as if Clarence Creighton were present, nodding in approval of his granddaughter's devotion.

"Well, I wish you would consider the feelings of the rest of us."

"Gwenneth, your intentions are good. So were those of Walter, of Donald, of the Western Pennsylvania Historic Commission, the Landmarks Foundation, half of the architects and scholars in the area, and the many others who've had no compunction about prodding into this aspect of my private affairs. There seems to be more concern about the fate of my house than over my own demise."

"But you're leaving it to Reggie, anyway. To do with it what he wants."

"He is a Creighton. It's what my grandfather wanted. That fact alone should end all discussion."

"But he'll ruin it! You're clinging to a technicality." Gwen was getting angry, but felt no "compunction" about it at all. "You care about 'family protocol,' or whatever is driving this, more than you care about what the house means to those you're leaving behind." Her dander had come up, and she wasn't afraid to hold the older woman accountable, to "call her on her shit," as Sam might say. "You're taking the easy way out, and that's something I never thought you'd do." She saw the mansard roof beyond the weeping willow on the western lawn, and sighed. "You're not really thinking about this at all. You're choosing not to."

Miss June regarded the younger woman with a self-assuredness that Gwen knew she herself would never possess.

"Young lady, know this—while not all that I do makes apparent sense to those around me, all of my bidding is carefully considered."

In the fixed set of Miss June's eyes, Gwen saw not the immediacy of the matter at hand, but a certainty that spanned decades. There was no arguing with that.

From the parlor, Jimmy noticed the two women outside in the garden.

"Son of a bitch—my onions!" He stormed down the hall to tend to what was important. It was just as well for Walt, who looked around the vast room and saw the scale of what he had accomplished. For the first time, he believed in his gut that he could pull this thing off. To get absolutely every last detail done. And looking out the window at the two women, he had two other thoughts—that by completing the room, he might just show something to Gwen, and also, watching his longtime companion bend over so gingerly just to pluck a rose, he had to find out definitively what was wrong with Miss June.

Chapter 20

FROM THE PHONE AT GENE'S, Walt had tried a number of times to get ahold of Dr. Hudson to pry loose the facts. He knew doctors weren't supposed to share patient information, but these were not usual circumstances, and Miss June was not the usual patient. But because he had no useful callback number to give the receptionist, his efforts had done no good, a rare occasion in which he had to concede that his aversion to telephones sometimes made it difficult to navigate beyond the insulated world he inhabited. Finally, he made an appointment for himself as a way to get in, citing a few urgent-sounding, although seemingly unrelated symptoms to get an appointment quickly. When the list grew sufficiently, the appointment was made by the irritated voice on the other end, if only to get him off the phone. The practice was in the East Wing of Shadyside Hospital, about a mile from Hardwick on land that had once been part of a much larger estate. Now there was a Wendy's nearby. Wings of the hospital were named for family

members of clans that were once familiar with the Creightons, the ancestors of whom remained, if flickering, within
Miss June's social galaxy. These were the families that still
invited Miss June to polo parties, graduation events, silent art
auctions and other benefits, as well as to birthday parties for
their grandchildren. Along with having been well-schooled in
decorum, they possessed curiosity, if not reverence, for those
alive when their families' fortunes were made.

It had been a few years since he'd been to Dr. Hudson's
office, a welcome break after a decade of miserable trips made
in the company of Miss June. Walt was certain the disastrous
visits for her annual checkup were clearly her fault, with her
complaints about his driving and how business was conducted
"these days" being excessively sharp, and bordering on downright mean. From her viewpoint, Walt's public exhibition of
immaturity was an unbearable spectacle in the context of a
hospital, and so their mutual decision that Reverend Nate
would accompany Miss June to future medical excursions
was a relief to them both.

Turning left past Information, where a woman gave him
complicated directions he pretended to understand, Walt
paused by the donor wall and read familiar names. The Oncol-
ogy Lab had been contributed by a family with whom Miss
June had stayed in contact over the years despite all of the
older family members having since died off. Walt wondered if
Miss June was held in the same regard by them as they were
by her. Was she the honorable matriarch of Fifth Avenue, or
merely a watermark of the past? Despite her forceful nature
and storied reputation, it would make sense that her fallen fortune would have affected her status. Regardless, these families
meant the world to her. Her stories were filled with them, of
their accomplishments, their contributions to the community,
and the ways in which their parents and grandparents had

been interwoven with the Creightons. Their presence served as more than a social context for Miss June — they were living ties to her life of decades ago, to her father and the antique world to which she'd clung for decades. And, above all, they were a connection to noble young Dwight.

Wandering around, Walt finally happened across the correct office suite, signed in, and took his seat in the waiting room among the elderly. Anything but a germaphobe, he sorted through the cough-covered magazines, finding that the selection was intended for aficionados of golf, southern life, vegetarian living, and gossip. He perused a worn copy of a women's magazine whose cover promised instruction on not only how to get that great summer body, but also eleven sexual secrets that would drive him wild. Walt was disappointed to find that the sexual secrets article was not only hard to find, but also scant and vague, and had clearly been written for the benefit of the magazine's readers rather than for their men. The gist of the plan was to prepare an elegant dinner and then, once in bed, to move slowly and seductively in order to entice him "to the point of unbridled desire," then to follow the experience with plenty of cuddling. Having missed breakfast, Walt did find the dinner idea enticing, and was thinking about it when his name was called by the receptionist. No, he didn't have health insurance, and yes, he really did intend to pay for his visit with his own money, actual cash, right on the spot. He was led down an unpleasant hallway to exam room number three, where his weight and blood pressure were scrutinized by a woman named Patty, who promised that the doctor would be with him soon. Walt couldn't remember the last time he'd seen a doctor, false pretenses or not. Other than his usual carpenter's aches and pains — most of which were fixed by the hands of Sam — he'd had no need. Colds and flu were simply waited out, and the occasional flesh wound was handled on the job with band-aids, rags, or duct tape. The worst mishap he'd suffered was a few years back when Jimmy accidentally fastened two of Walt's fingers together with a pneumatic nail gun, an event that, later, at the bar, found Jimmy's telling of the story including the suggestion that Walt's fingers never should have been in the way when Jimmy'd pulled the trigger, and Jesus H. Christ, you'd never believe how fast a man that big could move when he wanted to.

After an eternity spent playing with the tongue depressors, the door opened and Dr. Hudson walked in, no older than Walt, but a true grown-up by comparison.

"Walt Farnham. It's been some time. How are you?"

"Fine, actually."

"I'll be the judge of that."

He consulted a file folder that held a single sheet of paper, which Walt assumed to be the list of symptoms he'd given over the phone.

The doctor adjusted his glasses. "Let's see. Dizziness, with right elbow pain. Occasional frequency with urination during the day, accompanied by a burning sensation... in the ears?" He looked up at the improbable presentation that sat on the exam table before him. "Periodic tightening of the scalp accompanied by excessive saliva production?"

"It's a bitch, doc."

He shined a light into Walt's eyes and felt around his throat. Grasping at straws, he asked, "Have you been working with any strange chemicals? Anything out of the ordinary?"

"Strange chemicals? Never. Strange people? Constantly."

"Well, let's take a look at you." He pulled his stethoscope from his neck. "Take off your shirt, please."

"Listen, doc, that won't be necessary..."

"We've all gained a few pounds—don't worry about it. But, if you really want, you can leave it on." He pressed his stethoscope to Walt's back. "Okay, deep breath in"—for some reason, Walt did as he was told—"and out." They repeated the process a few times until Walt felt dizzy for real, although his elbow remained fine. "Your lungs are clear."

"As they should be. Listen, Doc, I need to tell you the truth. I made my appointment under false pretenses."

Dr. Hudson looked at the paper again. "You made all this up?"

"Yep."

"Thank God." He removed his glasses. "There's no way I could have helped you." He leaned back against the small writing surface by the door. "Okay, then. Talk to me. What's going on?"

"I'm here about someone else."

"I see. And is this the part where you tell me that you've 'got this friend'? One who has a problem of a personal nature?"

"I'm here about Miss June."

"Miss June?" His alarm was instant. "Has something happened?"

"You tell me."

"I'm confused. Why exactly are you here?"

"I want you to tell me everything there is to know about Miss June's health. Everything."

"I can't discuss one patient with another—you know that. Not that I'm sure you're actually a patient at this point."

"Look, I see her deteriorating before my eyes. She's moving slowly, she's taking naps now. She's not the same."

"She's an old woman—what do you expect?"

"Can we cut the crap? I already know. She made the announcement, months ago. But she won't tell me any details. None. For all I know, she should be in bed, and there I am letting her make my lunch."

"Walt, I can see you're upset. And I know you care about

Miss June a great deal. But I'm telling you, I can't talk about her health. It's simply against the rules."

"Oh, and she plays by the rules? That's bullshit and you know it. I'm the closest thing to family she's got. I want to know what's going on, and I want to know now." He was getting pissed, and if the exchange had been taking place at Gene's, heads would have turned.

"I understand that, but even if I were to break confidentiality—which I'm telling you, I won't—there wouldn't be much to discuss."

"Not much to discuss? She's dying, for God sakes."

The doctor looked up. "Dying? Miss June?" He laughed. "Who told you that?" He dropped the bogus chart into the trash. "Walter, *you* should be so healthy."

* * *

When pushed past its inadequate limits, the DORF—with its worn engine and loose steering—rode like the fastest machine on earth. Rounding the corner from Morewood to Fifth at thirty miles an hour, its tires squealed and its body rolled like in an old cop show. The passenger door popped open as it was wont to do, as did, coincidentally, the glove compartment, leaving a quarter-circle spray of Chiclets in the intersection before the door closed itself once the turn was complete. Walt and his crooked truck blew through the light at Aiken without a glance and barreled into the drive, screeching to a halt in the porte-cochére. Despite not caring about being seen as a fool, he was enraged at having been played for one.

"Where are you?" he bellowed into the house.

The kitchen was empty, as was the pantry and dining room. He circuited the first floor, his anger fueled by reserves that had been dormant for a lifetime. His voice boomed as he made his way through the cavernous manse, both preceding and trailing him in its echo. Pushing his way back out through the side door, he called again, "Miss June!"

There she sat in a wicker chair on the side porch, calmly perusing the *New York Times Book Review*.

"For goodness sakes, Walter, we're not in a gymnasium. Your voice does carry, you know."

"How could you do this?" He kicked the small wicker table off the porch and into the yard. It traveled much farther than he would have thought. She remained calm.

"Long before middle age should come the loss of petulance, dear. Now, tell me—what is all this ruckus about? And do so in a genial manner, if you don't mind."

"You told me you were dying!"

"Excuse me?"

He was incredulous. "Are you denying it? You said it! You said it to all of us, to me, to Donald, to Gwen. We were all there."

"Are you, per chance, referring to the day we first discussed your restoring the parlor?"

"Don't be coy! And don't treat me like I'm stupid. Of course that's what I'm talking about. You sat right there on the sofa and said you were dying. And now I find it's not true."

"You wish I were dying?"

"No! But you said you were. You looked me right in the eye and said you'd be dead soon."

"I beg your pardon? If I'm not mistaken…"

He was beyond belief. She was sitting there before him, having spun her web, now spinning history, but in a very immediate way, not through her usual means of wearing him down with slight changes in details until he eventually came to accept her version of the truth.

"…what I said was that I 'wouldn't be around much longer.'

There's a difference, you know. Word choice is paramount, Walter—you really should pay attention when spoken to. The English language is a marvelous instrument when played correctly. But even the greatest composer relies upon on an attentive audience."

"God, you're infuriating!"

"I had quite simply reiterated something I had been telling you for years, which is that it was important for me to have my affairs in order before my eventual demise. Pardon me if that end doesn't come soon enough to suit your schedule."

He tried not to follow her misdirection. "You told us you were dying."

"I said no such thing."

"Okay, excuse the technicality. You implied that you were dying."

"We're all dying, Walter," she said dismissively. "Why would I 'imply' such a thing?"

"To get me to build your damned parlor! To get me to jump through another hoop. Me, and everyone else."

"I've never engaged trickery to enlist your help before. Why on earth would I begin now? And besides, I am paying you for your work, and quite handsomely, or so I've intended. But if this is a matter of money…"

"That's not it and you know it. You tricked me. You made me think you were dying so you could get what you want. Because that's what you do. It's what you've always done. You're the grand manipulator. You …you …you sit here in never-never land, stuck in 1936, not daring to venture out into the real world with its real people and its real problems, moving the people in your life around like chess pieces, strategizing your next move in whatever bizarre game it is that you play. And you know what?" he asked, advancing from the angry to the hurtful, "you're the only one playing your damned game.

You might get others to participate—fools like me—but all of us, we also have real lives. Our world doesn't end at your gate."

"Well. I have never been spoken to in this tone, and I don't intend to accept it now. You've had your say, but I'll warn you to mind your manners. It's as if I've never done one thing for you, Walter. As if I've been but a thorn in your side."

"Look, it's one thing to boss people around because you're old and because you can. Or even to take advantage of my good nature to some degree. But this kind of manipulation, it's just sick. And just so you could get your damned room ready for a fucking party with an imaginary guest list." He started down the porch steps, and then turned to face her one last time. "You used me. Used me so you could pretend that the last sixty years never happened."

And as she watched him drive away, his trail of blue smoke slow to fade, she knew he thought he'd never return.

* * *

"It's me…"

Gwen's words carried up the garage stairs with the melodic rhythm of a *"Honey, I'm home."* Hearing them, he knew his falling out with Miss June was going to come between them. The parlor had provided a context for the pair—literally, a platform from which he could perform—and without it he was back to being his regular self. Who had he been trying to kid?

She kissed his forehead and then sat across from him at the old Formica table.

"She told me what happened."

"Recounting my insolence and betrayal, no doubt."

"It wasn't quite like that. At least not the betrayal part."

"I don't want to hear about it. I'm done with her," he said, the words sitting just fine.

"I still can't believe it all. This must be some kind of mis-understanding," she began.

"No. She lied to us, plain and simple. You heard her as clearly as I did. We were killing ourselves for her, you with the book, me with the house, and she was toying with us all along."

"Well, I'm happy I'm writing this book."

"You don't feel manipulated?"

"Of course I do, but I don't have your long history with her. Maybe I feel like this was all part of life's plan, to get me here to write this book, to get me away from Boston, from the ashes of my marriage, to … this."

He missed the subtle emphasis of her last word.

"Well, I'm plenty upset. And you know what? I'm pissed the most because I didn't see it coming. After all these years, she got me again."

"But the parlor … it's beautiful."

"So what? It'll be destroyed after she really does die, assuming she ever will. Frankly, I don't care anymore."

"Hey, come on. You care. I know you do."

"Don't tell me how I feel, Gwen. And don't defend her to me. She's a condescending, self-aggrandizing snob, and she's not interested in anything but her reputation."

"And she loves you very much."

"Oh, give me a break."

"Don't you see? The parlor wasn't about her. It was about you. You've done the best work of your life, and she made it happen."

"It was folly."

"You feel humiliated. Believe me, I get it. And for that, I'm angry with her, too."

"Well, you're not acting like it. You sound like one of her defenders."

"No, not at all. I think it was a rotten thing for her to do.

But there's more to all of this, and I'm hoping you can see it.

He looked at his bookshelves, at the many colored spines.

"She was presenting you with an opportunity, something you could grab. A chance to let your passions stir. To fully be you."

"You're giving her credit for kindness that's beyond her."

"That's where you're wrong. She was showing you love."

"Love?"

"In the only way she can."

"By putting me through this."

"By getting you out of the rut you'd been in. She wants you to do real things. To be fulfilled."

"Oh, like she's done for all of these years?"

"No, but that's it exactly. She wants more for you than she's given herself."

He chewed on that for a moment.

"Maybe. But I'm giving her nothing more. I'm through."

* * *

Disappearing proved reliable as ever. It wasn't so much an active hiding as a passive checking out. Just don't show up in the usual places. If you continue not to answer it, the door eventually stops being knocked upon. And because Miss June's parlor trick had occupied his time for as long as it had, he had no other work lined up and felt no pressing need to deliver on anything old that he owed anyone. Her deceit had moved him beyond guilt. But much like at the 'Eye, his time spent above Sam's garage began to seem strange. If it weren't for Sam and Art's daily newspaper, which he read at their kitchen table each morning over a bowl of Arthur's cereal, he wouldn't have known what day it was. And while Sam was never one to hold anything back, especially venom toward

Miss June, she was noticeably quiet about the situation, which suggested to him that her silence had more to do with him than with the old woman. She could have easily bugged him to finish some things around her own house. The baby's room was complete, but the Friendship house wasn't lacking Walt's unfinished handiwork. The dining room ceiling remained a cracked map of procrastination. But Sam wasn't pressing him, and Walt wondered if she hadn't finally given up. Then again, she could just be focused on the impending arrival of the baby—she was now enormous. Regardless, time was passing, marked only by evidence of the paper boy, Dewey's daily needs, Sam's biweekly book club, and his own avoidance of Gwen. Along with disappearing from Hardwick, he'd avoided the phone messages she'd left at Sam's. They'd come often at first—recorded by Sam on the dry-erase board on the refrigerator—along with a couple of notes in Gwen's handwriting left in his door when he'd pretended to be asleep. But eventually, her attempts ended. He took to sweeping Sam's floors and doing her dishes, simple acts that had purpose. He even wore her frilly apron once, trying unsuccessfully to get a laugh. Checking himself out in the hallway mirror, he concluded that he didn't look too bad. Her smile held only pity.

Edward's truck pulled into the drive for the third time in as many Thursdays, arriving, with hope, for their weekly breakfast. Dewey nudged Walt and whined that his friend was there, but Walt already knew. And while it was unlike him to ignore poor Edward, he just didn't have it in him to explain what had been going on. "Next week," he again told his dog, but that morning was the last time the truck showed up. The sad part was Edward probably thought that he'd done something wrong and that Walt was "sore" at him or, worse, that he wasn't important to him anymore. Although Walt wasn't ready to face him, he wished he somehow could let him know that it wasn't true, *"Honest injun"* and all.

* * *

Certain sounds are unmistakable, specific noises that locate a time or place like nothing else — the complaint of a squeaky stair tread in your childhood home, the bedroom footsteps of your spouse. Walt heard the exhaust note of the Imperial in the drive as he lay in bed on a sunny afternoon. He had just polished off a *People* magazine that he'd stolen from Sam, one of her vices he made fun of and for which she didn't apologize. Walt cringed at the car's sound, knowing it was Jimmy who, having stolen the car, had come now to steal him from the doldrums in which he was willfully entrenched. But from the rap of thin knuckles on the glass of the door, he knew it wasn't Jimmy who'd pulled up in the great car, and having avoided her for over a month, he felt he owed it to Gwen to answer her knock. And though other men might have dreaded the moment, Walt had disappointed enough people over the years that he was well-practiced at facing them after the fact. He opened the door.

"Walter," said Miss June.

He said nothing.

"I'd ask to come in but I'd rather not see where you live." She'd been to the Friendship property once, years before at Walt's insistence, to an anniversary party Sam and Walt had thrown for themselves. Now, under circumstances that couldn't be more different, Walt looked beyond her at the house. The exterior trim would need to be painted in a few years, he thought. He remembered the last time it had been done, he and Sam up on ladders, him working at his own steady pace, her working fast and hard and bitching the whole time. He'd thought they'd never need to paint that trim again, that it would last them forever.

"I'm not usually in the practice of hunting down my creditors," she said, "but I don't cotton to outstanding debt." Stealing his attention back from the house, he looked down at her but said nothing. "Here you are," she said, producing an envelope.

"I don't want your money."

"Poppycock. Everyone wants money, even you. You're just not good at acquiring it."

He didn't move. She turned toward the street.

"I remember this area when it was grand," she said. "Before its decline." Walt was a champion of the neighborhood, but wasn't going to get goaded into an argument. "It was once full of doctors, you know."

"Yes, you've told me that. Doctors and 'the dutiful corporals of the captains of industry.' Thank you for stopping by. Now, I have things to do."

"No doubt." He could tell from her tone that she was trying to be civil. This was Miss June at her kindest. "You know, Walter, that in your absence, the parlor has not finished itself. It would be most lovely if you were to come back and finish what you started. I was examining your work this morning, and you're oh so close to completion."

"I'd say that I can't believe you have the nerve to ask me to come back, but of course you do."

"Well, the way I see it, you did promise to complete the job, and while that particular promise extended the traditional boundaries of your commitment, I foolishly believed that you'd meant it."

"But you tricked me!" he said, hating how it made him sound like a teenager.

"Am I to blame if you misunderstood one conversation

we had months ago? For someone who once taught at a university level, your communication skills are middling at best."

"And now you're insulting me?"

"I wouldn't bother traveling here to insult you. Anyone can do that, and from closer proximity. I'm here to ask you back to finish my parlor."

"I can't believe this."

"Now, in your mind, I imagine, such a request would comprise my asking you for a favor, whereas I see it as a warranted attempt to get you to fulfill a commitment to which you've apparently chosen to pay no heed. But, in defiance of logic and in the name of civility, I'm willing to go against my usual grain and pose the question as if asking a favor of you. So, Walter—will you please come and finish my parlor?"

Well-practiced in reading between her lines, he understood that buried in the question was, if not an apology, a proposition that they return their relationship to what it had been. Her driving over here in her big car—coming to him rather than demanding that he come to her—was an extension of an olive branch larger than he thought her capable of hefting. To anyone else, her words would have sounded insensitive at best, but he knew better than that. Her manner had kept Sam from ever warming up to her, even though they had more similarities than Sam would admit. Walt had defended his allegiance to Miss June during their marriage, explaining to Sam that the impossible woman's words needed to be run through a filter to be translated into what she really meant, into words she was unable to actually say. *"She speaks pretty fucking clearly to me,"* Sam had said. Still, he had stood by Miss June, sympathetic to her peculiar brand of emotional isolation. Now, though, he'd been humiliated, and with the humiliation had come shame—how could he have been so stupid?

"No, Miss June. I won't be back."

And very simply, he shut the door.

Shortly after, horizontal again and visually tracing the angled lines of his own ceiling, he heard the door at the bottom of the stairs open, knew it was Sam. Dewey did, too, and bounded down to greet her.

"Hey," she called up.

"Hey," he called back down.

"So, what did she want?"

"Obedience."

"She said that?"

"No."

"Hmm. Well, unless you come down here, we're going to have this whole conversation like this, 'cause I'm sure as hell not lugging this baby up there."

"This works for me."

"Okay, then. What exactly did she say?"

"That she wants me to come back and finish the parlor. To act as if nothing happened."

"I see," she said. He waited for more, but none came. Finally, she added, "Well?"

"Well, what?"

"Are you going to do it?"

"Are you serious?"

"It's not like you didn't know she was manipulative."

"You're saying I should go back?"

"Well, you're not exactly knocking 'em dead up there."

"Christ, Sam, I figured if anyone would understand, it would be you."

"Of course I understand. I wanted you out of that house years ago. But as shitty as this all was, I hate seeing you here doing nothing." He fingered the *People* magazine. Exchanging a look with Dewey, she added, "You can't stay up there forever."

He supposed she had a point.

* * *

Opening Gene's front door on a hot morning always brought a dependable blast of refrigerated air, stale beer, daytime television, and half-assed regret. Today, it also offered the uniform of the potato chip man as he backed his dolly out into the heat. "Thanks, Walt," he said as the door was held for him.

"No problem, Mike."

It had been six weeks since he'd been to the 'Eye. Showing up today was his response to Sam noting that he couldn't stay holed up in the garage forever. As nonjudgmental and neutral as Gene's was—an alcoholic Switzerland of sorts—Walt felt momentarily awkward as his eyes fought to adjust to the dark, and he knew the regulars were looking in the back bar mirror to see who'd come in. Gossip flew fast around Gene's, and he wasn't looking forward to discussing the events at Hardwick at the bar, to hearing what version of the story had developed over time. He needn't have worried, though, as no one even acknowledged his arrival. Apparently, the length of his absence had eclipsed their attention span. Gene, ever the mystery, gave him one of his distant nods and placed a small draft in front of him. Walt really wanted coffee, but because he wanted to enjoy his reentry in peace, he flipped a twenty onto the bar, nodded once for Gene to set up the other, older, fellas, and commenced to watching television as if the parlor escapade had never happened. Grabbing the glass, he saw that his fingers were dirty. He hadn't driven his truck in a few weeks, and he'd had to jump the battery from Sam's car. The soap dispenser in the men's room was an ancient metal can with a chrome lever at the bottom, which, when lifted, deposited a shake of gritty powder into your palm, soap abrasive enough to stop a train in its tracks. Walt wondered where Gene got supplies for his antiquated equipment. Probably the same place where he bought the pomade for his hair and the off-brand condiments he had at the grill—the Devil-Pict olives, the Goody Good mayonnaise, and the Hardi-Hen pickled eggs that sat purple and heavy by the register. Walt never saw any of that stuff being delivered—Gene just lugged it up from the basement as if it had been there for years, crappy provisions stockpiled long ago in case the Russians dropped the big one. Having abraded his hands sufficiently, he noted in the mirror that he looked like shit, wiped his hands on his pants, and left for more forgiving pastures. From his vantage point by the bowling machine, he could see the whole bar: a few motley heads—two watching TV, and the other counting change, hopeful for another drink—and Gene, stubby pencil behind his ear, studying the newspaper. *Other people just pass time, too.* Armed with that comforting thought, he sat down to find a bowl of soup beside his untouched twenty, letting him know his cosmic tab was still open. The soup was thick, bland, and reassuring.

"Hey, Walt," Gene called from down and across the bar, his brow creased in thought. "What's a four-letter word for 'Current status'?"

"Back."

* * *

Weeks since she shook Walt loose from the garage, and still no baby. The city had gotten hot, and Sam no longer waddled outside. She looked increasingly uncomfortable each morning when he stopped in the house to eat breakfast and steal the newspaper, which had long been read by the time he moseyed over. He'd begun taking Sam and Art's paper to the 'Eye, as

Gene was possessive with his own copy. "Hey, piss-ant," he'd say to whomever made the mistake of leaning over the bar to grab it. "I'm still workin' on the Jumble in there." No pretzels for them. This morning, Jimmy was the culprit.

"Cool your jets, Susie," Jimmy replied. "I gotta see if I hit the number."

"You didn't."

"How do you know?"

"Because I'm not an idiot."

"One-a these days I'll hit that sucker. Then you know what I'll do? I'll buy this place and put some decent toilet paper in the men's room. Where do you buy that stuff, the hardware store? It tears me up."

"You have a sensitive bottom," Walt speculated.

"As a matter of fact, I do. Sensitive but firm. Irma says I got the ass of a matador."

"She says that about me, too," Walt said.

"Yeah, an AMC Matador," was offered from down the bar.

"A Pacer," someone else said. "Remember them? Ugly car if there ever was one."

"They don't make no good cars no more," Gene said wistfully.

"You got that right."

"Amen."

"Fuckin'-A."

"Watch your French," Gene said. "What's the ugliest car you ever drove?"

"Walt's truck," Jimmy answered.

"That don't count."

"Geez, I don't know then. That's like asking what's the ugliest girl you ever had sex with. You can't answer that."

The exact logic of that remark slipped past Walt, but he trusted that it made sense.

" '53 DeSoto," Jimmy said.

" '65 Rambler wagon. Puke green."

" '74 Cordoba."

"Cordobas ain't ugly," Gene stated as fact.

Walt was thinking that he liked all of those cars. They had personality. It was new cars that he found ugly or, more specifically and worse, nondescript and ubiquitous. They all looked the same—from the cheapest Chevy to the priciest Mercedes, he never knew what was what. He pictured the Imperial.

"Who's the ugliest girl you ever had sex with?" came from someone.

"Your wife," was shot back.

"In a car, I mean," clarified the question's originator.

"Still your wife. Your car, too."

"I've never been with an ugly lady," Jimmy said, meaning it. "They were all beautiful, every one of 'em."

The conversation then lost whatever steam it had, and the television began to win the day. Soap operas had a powerful effect on the men at the bar, and soon they were sucked in, offering the occasional comment to the players, as if their advice could be heard through the smoke and glass.

"No, honey, don't listen to him," Gene said to the screen. "He loves your sister, not you. Stupid broad."

"No, the sister ain't real, remember?" Jimmy clarified. "This girl got hit on the head with amnesia and thinks she's two people now. The guy in the shirt thinks he loves the sister, but he don't know it's the same one 'cause she wears a wig. He's just using this one."

"She got hit on the head?"

"Yeah, and it's a shame, 'cause she's beautiful," Jimmy answered.

"She looks like Meryl Streak," Gene noted.

"Fuckin'-A."

"Watch your French."

"No, you've got it wrong," Walt said. "She faked amnesia so that she could pretend to have a sister, so she could extort money from Alan Winston, the rich guy with the ascot. This guy, Christian, who is indeed a sleazebag, is lying to her just as Gene said, but he doesn't know that the woman he's lying to is a fake. Got it?"

"Sounds complicated," came a voice from the door.

"Gwen."

"Walt."

They looked at each other, motionless for a moment, as the others pivoted on their stools and tried to ascertain if the pair might provide drama more interesting than the tale on TV.

"I'm sorry," he finally said. "Can I get you something?"

"If you want to."

The barflies turned back to the soap.

"Of course," he said. They moved to a booth. Christ, she looked good.

"So."

"So."

Breaking the pause was Gene, who, pinky extended, brought Gwen what looked like a Shirley Temple, although Walt had never seen such a thing at the bar before. "We miss you around here, honey. Don't forget about us now."

She thanked him, and he left them to their awkwardness.

"I got your notes," he said. "I'm sorry. I just didn't know what to say. I've not been at my best."

"I won't pretend I wasn't hurt."

"I don't expect you to. This thing with Miss June. I can't go back to Hardwick. Not after everything."

"But you could've seen me. If you'd wanted to, I mean."

"I did want to. This is just…what I do."

She sipped her fizzy concoction. "So, you're really not going back? Not ever?"

"No. I'm really not."

"Things were almost complete."

Walt wasn't sure she was talking about the parlor. Either way. "It's as close as I ever get," he said.

"I wish you'd finish it. Just so I'd know it was done."

"Part of me wants to."

She perked up. "Well then do it! You can, Walt. You can just finish."

"I can't forgive her. I know I sound stubborn, but it's hard to explain. It's about more than the big lie that she told. This is about a lifetime."

"But you've always known she was capable of this. To a degree, right?"

"To a degree," he admitted.

"So what's the difference? Whether or not you like Miss June right now, you do love her. I know you do. And she loves you, too."

"She's incapable of love."

"You're wrong. She's incapable of opening her heart. Or at least she was. Since you've been gone, she's been different. Softer. Sadder, too. Resigned to things."

He wanted to ask, but was reluctant to get sucked in.

"Regardless of her," she said, "you should do it for yourself."

"Please don't ask me to do this," he said. "I don't want to disappoint you again."

She was silent. He was fucking things up, just as he had with Sam. He knew it and couldn't stop.

"So the parlor will be unfinished when she does eventually die," Gwen finally said.

"She could get someone else to do it."

"It wouldn't be the same."

"I can't go back. There's too much history."

This provided an unfortunate segue to what she had come to tell him if the conversation had gone as it did.

"Well, then. Speaking of history, I'm going back to Boston. Sooner than I'd planned. I'll finish the book from there."

A game show began, all colored lights and brassy theme song.

"When?"

"There's a flight in the morning. I guess I'm going to take it. I'll work from there, send the galleys to Miss June for review. I suppose there's really no reason I need to work from here anymore." She looked away. "No reason to stay." The last was suggestive of a question, one that lingered between them, his for the taking.

"I'll miss you," he said, before adding weakly, "miss us."

"I already do," she said.

"I'm sorry."

"I shouldn't have assumed so much." She got up, flushed, holding back tears. "I feel foolish."

"About me."

"About salt on a bird's tail."

Chapter 21

ACCORDING TO JIMMY, what Walt needed to do was accompany him on a quest to find the girls he'd met the night before at the track. He knew Walt wouldn't go, but it had always been Jimmy's job to keep him off-balance and prevent his rut from getting too deep, and women were the preferred weapons in his arsenal. Despite garnishing the proposition with a couple of shots, Walt wouldn't bite, so Jimmy gave up and moved his attention to the other fellas at the bar. For the thousandth time, Walt read a small plaque that hung near the register:

I'm not a slow bartender,
I'm not a fast bartender.
I'm a half-fast bartender.

"Hey, do me a favor here," Gene interrupted. "I gotta settle things with the beer guy. You mind takin' Ma her supper?"

For all of Gene's bravado, his devotion to his mother was true and complete. And because his feelings of maternal respect extended beyond his own family, should an unschooled visitor to the bar make a disrespectful comment about anyone's mother, even in jest, Gene would retrieve the baseball bat from its home under the bar and both demand and receive a quick retraction. None of the regulars made mother jokes. Anything else, though, was fair game.

Walt took the tray—grilled cheese, soup, fruit cocktail, and chocolate milk—and headed up the narrow stairs.

"Hello…" Walt called as he finished his ascent, not wanting to startle her.

She looked up from the TV, a big walnut console model from which Michael Landon kindly smirked. The volume was too loud, and so Walt turned it down. "I know you," she said. "You're that one that I like."

"I brought you your supper, Mrs. Greb."

"Well, you sit right down and eat, then."

"No, this is your supper."

"But aren't you going to eat it?"

"No, ma'am, this is for you."

"Well, if you say so," she said politely, and started to get up from her chair.

"No, no, you can just stay there. I'll bring you your tray." She smiled the apologetic smile of the elderly, not certain if she was doing something wrong. "Do you remember me? I'm Gene's friend, Walt. I come upstairs and watch TV with you sometimes." In fact, he hadn't for a while, and felt bad for saying that he had.

"Gene is my son," she said proudly.

"That's right. And he's my friend, too. I used to come up here in the afternoons and watch television with you. Do you remember that?"

"I suppose that I do," she said, ever the sport.

"Do you mind if I sit with you now?"

"That would be nice if you don't have to be at work."

"You know, oddly enough, I don't?"

They watched *Little House on the Prairie* while she ate. She chewed methodically, as if to a very slow metronome. After it seemed she'd had enough, Walt took the tray. She looked at him with awakening. "You're the teacher, aren't you," she said. "At the college."

Given that some years before she would have been right, he said simply, "Yes, that's me."

"Gene brags about how smart you are."

"Well, I think that your Gene is smarter than me, running his own business and all."

"My husband is a foreman at the mill."

"He used to be Mrs. Greb, a long time ago."

She looked at the tray.

"Was that his supper I ate?"

"No, ma'am, that was yours. Mr. Greb passed on."

She smiled again. "I know that. I don't know why I say these things. I'm silly as a loon."

"Well, it's been a long day," he said, for lack of anything better, and, in fact, it felt true.

"My mind plays tricks sometimes."

"Mine, too," he said. "Constantly."

"Can I show you my pictures?" she asked as always, and then launched herself from her chair, surprisingly spry. She beckoned him to the framed photographs that graced the top of the Zenith. There were the usual old studio portraits of the same depression-era faces that witness the goings on in modest living rooms across America. There was a high school graduation photo of Gene's sister, who'd left town shortly after the picture was taken, and one of a young Gene in uniform. Walt didn't know what rank a cook held in the army—perhaps it was simply that, "Cook"—but he wore the uniform well, like he took shit from no one, regardless of rank. Walt's favorite image was a 1970s color snapshot of Gene on a motorcycle wearing an open-faced helmet and cut-offs, his bee-hived mom perched on the back, sidesaddle—a gag shot for sure, but the spark in her eye suggested that she might not have minded a quick spin around the block. Gene's father was dead by then, thus the impulsive moment. In another, taken the same day, Gene and his mum stood on the sidewalk in front of the bar, his arm around her stiffly, eyes hidden by mirrored sunglasses. She smiled, he didn't. On the wall above the big set, framed by its rabbit ears, was a particularly gruesome plaster Jesus, complete with blood, thorns, and agony. To the right of that, a more serene and vibrantly colorful airbrushed portrait of Him was suggestive of roadside Mexico. There were more photos along the wall, and Walt listened as Mrs. Greb explained each one, not missing a detail, as far as he knew. After the last photo, her monologue trailed off, and she stared at Walt, fixing him with a pleasant and undivided look that was either vacant or spookily all-knowing—he had no idea which. It was a curious moment that could have gone on forever, yet it wasn't uncomfortable. Her confusion spared him the feeling of judgment.

Holding her gaze, she said, "You're one of the ones from my collection."

"You're one of my favorite people too, Mrs. Greb."

"You're the teacher. Gene brags about how smart you are."

"He's always been a good friend to me. You must be very proud of him."

"His father works a lot, you know. Nights, at the mill. He's there now."

"He used to, Mrs. Greb. He's been gone for quite a few years now."

She looked at the trinkets on a shelf near the photos. Cheap porcelain figurines of sprites and fawns, plaques that pronounced love for family.

"He's buried in Lawrenceville," she said.

"Gene tells me he was a hard-working man." Gene had also told him that he was a brutal man—drunk, mean, and unrelenting. But in true Gene fashion, he had simply reported this as fact, not as indictment, speaking instead with reverence for the ferocity with which the man had treated his only son. About how his father could beat him like no other.

"Eugene is going to get married someday."

"Sure he will," Walt lied.

"He needs to find the right girl."

"I think you're his girl, Mrs. Greb."

She smiled her pleasant smile.

Looking at the remains of her sandwich, seeing how it had been cut neatly into triangles, he added, "He loves you very much."

"Gene is my son," she offered, as if for the first time.

Walt called Sam from the bar phone but got Arthur instead.

"Art? What're you doing home so early?"

"It's seven-forty, Walter, not early at all."

Walt confirmed this fact by looking at the dusty TV. *Wheel of Fortune.*

"Listen, Art, can you let Dewey out? He hasn't peed all day. I hope."

"Sam brought him over earlier. He's asleep in our kitchen as we speak."

"Oh, good."

His dog, he realized, lived a life of his own.

"Say, Walter. Are you okay?"

"Sure, why do you ask?"

"No reason. You just sound a little funny. Drunk, maybe?"

"I was wondering the same about you, Arty. Maybe it's a bad connection."

"Hmm, maybe you're right. I have half a mind to have the phone line checked."

Arthur had served that one up so well that Walt could've hit it out of the park, but he just didn't have it in him.

"Well, thanks for taking care of Dewey."

"No problem. And, um, Walter? Take care?"

Picturing his dog curled up happily under the table where his pregnant ex-wife and her current husband had just shared dinner, he decided that the prospect of watching Gene wipe down the bar to head upstairs to be with his mother was more than he could take. He left the 'Eye for the solace of the DORF, hoping to fade into whatever anonymity such a conspicuous vehicle could provide. The overcast day coupled with his mood to render the surroundings in black and white, and his seasoned truck meandered accordingly. Stop lights came and went. Miss June's appearance at his door. The comfort of the bar. The care with which Gene arranged his mum's supper on the tray. And most important, Gwen's disappointment. As streetlights came on, he rolled slowly through the Hill District, past the faded deco marquis of the old New Granada Theater.

At a bus stop by a soup kitchen was a beautiful little boy and his grandmother. He was a small black child, no more than four years old. Tied to the boy's wrist was a red balloon, perhaps the last brilliant object in the world. The balloon held the boy's hand aloft, and with that hand, the boy privately smiled and waved to Walt, waving the sweet wave that only small children make, palm facing the wrong way, little hand opening and closing, clasp-like. Walt waved back and smiled sadly.

Though he thought he'd been driving aimlessly, apparently he did have a destination, as his truck turned into the parking lot of the building where he'd once taught. Since learning that he still had an office, he'd caught himself occasionally fingering the old key on his ring. Given the hour, the chances of running into former colleagues were slim. The building was a large gray horizontal bunker, the product of a late-sixties school of design apparently endorsed by the concrete industry. He entered from the back, slipping in as he used to slip out. The hallways smelled the same—an unfortunate mix of musty tenure and carpet adhesive—and the lighting still cast a sickly green glow on all who passed by. Ascending the stairwell—no one trusted the elevators—he paused on a landing and through the window saw Flagstaff Hill, the sloped expanse of lawn where on a snowy day he once took his Early American Thought class out to play, stopping first in the cafeteria to steal trays for use as sleds.

The key to his office still turned, exposing the academic ruins of Pompei, an unapologetic mess that had hosted countless hours of comfortable loafing, and he settled into the old green leather chair to try for a couple more. His feet found their regular place on the corner of the gunboat-gray metal desk, and the chair remembered his tipping point exactly. The water-stained Rorschach splotches on the ceiling tiles still offered their vaginal mysteries, and he considered them for a while, curious as to whether the passage of time might provide new insight into their meaning. Apparently not. His in-box offered a package of petrified Cherry Nibs, each one having turned to hard red plastic, and he worked a few steadily with his jaw, eventually softening them to the point of near edibility. He could imagine Dr. Art's expression if only he knew.

Panning the room, he considered the possessions he'd once chosen to surround himself with. The leather football helmet. The rubber chicken. Albert Einstein sticking his tongue out. The Polish coffee mug with the handle on the inside. The bottle of Maker's Mark. The french horn he didn't know how to play.

The bow and arrows, the Oliver Hardy shoe horn. He panned back a few items and landed again on the whiskey. How the hell had he left that behind? Breaking the seal, he splashed an inch into the Polish mug and, tilting back in his chair again, toasted the inviting marks on the ceiling. The whiskey burned and he closed his eyes, certain that the longer he sat in his old chair, the drunker he'd be, regardless of whether or not he drank another drop. Which, of course, he did. He and Sam used to have lunch in his office, hers being the scene of too much work for his taste, and the cafeteria an enticement to his students to join them. Walt was a celebrity. He and Sam would sit on the stolen sofa and play footsie while she complained about administrative idiots. He remembered her admonishing him once when she found a roach in his desk drawer, and then sneaking off with him to smoke it in the parking lot. Now, he reached by habit and grabbed a few student papers from the stack on the floor, final papers he'd graded and had intended to return. The first was bad enough to warrant a shot straight from the bottle, an act that was satisfying and detective-novel cheap. The next was better, written by a young man who would have reminded Walt of himself, had he had his shit as together at that age. After that was a memorandum from the administration reminding faculty that attendance at fraternity parties, while technically not against regulations, was frowned upon by those who were paid to worry about such things. Beneath more of the same was a manila envelope, the contents of which Walt knew immediately.

Of Sweet Departures
by Gwenneth Thompson

He read the poem, and then another. They weren't as graceful as she'd meant them to be, but reading them now, more than before, he could feel their want. Sharing them had been no small thing for her, as she was shy not only about her talents, but also about exposing herself. He thought about her marrying the wrong man. He wished himself back to the Student Commons, thanking her for her poems, and telling her to choose her love carefully, to protect her heart with all of her might—not so that it would remain closed, but so that it could fully open when love at its truest arrived.

"...*I have to believe Spencer Tracy exists.*"

Walt turned toward the big telephone on his desk, an obsolete two-pounder that matched the green chair. He marveled at its clear plastic buttons that lit up with conversation. Consulting the matches from his shirt pocket, he punched a button and hoped, rewarded when its amber glow registered the report of his drunk finger.

"Bull's-Eye!" the voice said.

"Jimmy?" Walt said.

"Jimmy's not here."

"Jimmy?"

"Who wants him?"

"It's me, Walt."

"Walt's not here."

"I know that. I'm Walt."

"Then what're you calling me for?"

"Jimmy, don't hang up." He did that sometimes.

"Where you calling from?" Jimmy asked.

He looked around. "Nineteen ninety-three. Listen, Jimmy, I need a favor."

Bar noise filled the background.

"Shoot."

"Are you still unopposed to procuring things by nefarious means?"

"By what?"

"Nefarious means."

"Come again?"

"Felonious methods?"

"Speak English, why don't you."

"I need help stealing some shit."

"A caper? Count me in."

An hour passed before Jimmy—who was always up for a caper—parked his most recently borrowed car across two parking spaces and whistled his way through the halls until he found Walt's office.

"Nice joint," he said. "Who was your decorator, a garbage man?"

The rooms they needed to burgle were opposite one another in a fourth-floor hall of the Library Sciences Building, a building that fell under Sam's command when she headed the department. Walt attempted to be silent as he walked, an effort made pointless when Jimmy began to sing loudly, his take on an old Van Morrison tune.

"You-ou are, my one-eyed girl. Do you remember when, I used to sing?"

"Jimmy, keep it down, will you?"

"Sha-la, la, la, la, la, la, la, la, la, la, dee-dah ..." Jimmy replied.

"Okay, here we are," Walt said, stopping outside of the room whose door said, simply, *CELLULOID*. "I need to get in there."

"No problem. I'll crawl out on the ledge from the bathroom and jimmy the window from outside."

Not even entertaining the visual that would accompany that particular mistake, Walt looked straight up and said, "I was thinking of a more direct approach."

Hoisting Jimmy up through the suspended ceiling was easy. Though no spring chicken, he was both light and nimble as hell. From Walt's shoulders, he slid a ceiling tile aside and disappeared into the dark space above the hallway's tired, beige panels. A flashlight would have been a good thing, but had Walt brought one, its batteries would no doubt have been dead. He considered tossing up his book of Bull's-Eye matches, but in Jimmy's hands they would not have been a good addition to the mix. Fortunately, enough light leaked upward from the ghoulish fluorescents that, once his eyes adjusted, Jimmy was able to see. From his station below, Walt heard his enthusiastic friend making his way across the ceiling above, forging good progress in exactly the wrong direction.

"What are you doing? Be careful up there," Walt said in a loud stage whisper. He was drunk enough to have started this escapade, but sober enough to not want to get caught.

"Don't worry about me, baby, I'm like a cat," came a muffled voice in reply.

On cue, the cat's left foot broke through a ceiling tile about thirty feet down the hall, nowhere near the room he was supposed to be dropping into.

"What are you doing down there? Come on, Jimmy!"

A fair amount of bumping and clomping could be heard from above, first off to the left, then off to the right, and then, curiously enough, from behind Walt. What had been a fairly simple plan now seemed likely to end with Jimmy getting lost in the bowels of Library Sciences forever. Walt scooted down the hall, picked up the pieces of broken tile from where Jimmy's foot had come through, and deposited them in a trash can nearby. It was unlikely anyone would pass through this part of the building at this time of night, but if they did, hopefully the remaining dust on the carpet wouldn't prompt them to look up.

"And stop whistling, for God's sake," he called up.

Just then, a door opened behind Walt, and Jimmy welcomed him into the Celluoid Room as if he were hosting a cocktail party.

"The girls' dorms aren't in this building, are they?" he asked.

"Never mind that," Walt said, beginning to wonder what he had set into motion. "I need to get into this other room, too, the one across the hall. Up you go."

Again, Jimmy disappeared upward and could be heard scampering about. Again came the sound of whistling, but this time it was neither melodic nor originating from above. It was the deliberate, time-passing whistle of someone making their rounds. Quickly, Walt slipped into the Celluloid Room and pulled the door shut just before the security guard rounded the corner and entered the hall. Not willing to risk the click of the lock, he left the door open a crack and turned off the lights. He doubted that Jimmy, with his lack of peripheral awareness, knew that the guard was there, but by chance, at that moment, he wasn't singing. Walt listened as the standard issue footsteps worked their way toward his hiding place, heard them mosey past, and then heard them stop. Through the crack, he saw the guard pause and sense that something was, if not downright fishy, then at least slightly out of place. He lifted his cap and scratched his head in thought as if miming the part of a security guard in a bad play, and Walt had to bite his lip to keep from laughing. The rent-a-cop lingered for a moment, looked back down the hall from where he'd come, seemed to consider the situation to the greatest degree possible, and then, in another theatrical motion, shrugged before resuming his rounds. Walt exhaled. The guard almost reached the stairwell, but stopped at an unmistakable bit of clumsiness from above. Suddenly, he looked up at the spot where minutes ago Jimmy had been boosted through. Walt, cringing, did the same, only to see that the panel had just been put back into place, the slightest amount of fine dust falling from its locale. Thank you, Jimmy. The rent-a-cop shrugged again and moments later was gone.

Hitting the light, Walt turned to see the familiar heavy shelving, a couple of gray desks, and, thankfully, on a heavy oak table, the small drawers that contained that most enigmatic yet pleasing collection of clues, the Dewey Decimal System. All of the library's collections had been transferred to computer years before, but the card system hadn't been eliminated, which was a good thing, as Walt hadn't the slightest idea how to operate a computer. Besides, given what he was here to search for, the old-fashioned cards were more fitting. After a minute of flipping through, he found the card he sought, and a short while after that, emerged from the room with a pizza-shaped box in hand. In the meantime, Jimmy had managed to open the room across the hall, in which he'd found a number of wheeled carts, and was making a game of racing one of them up and down the hallway.

"What are you, ten years old?" Walt asked, aware as he said it, that not only was the answer "yes," but that it was one of the things he loved most about Jimmy. "And where are your pants?"

"They got caught on something up there so I took 'em off," Jimmy replied. "Nice legs, no?"

They were nice legs, Walt had to admit, nicer than his own, which were many years younger. Jimmy's briefs were brilliantly white, and contrasted nicely with the tired brown carpet. Peering in the open door of the second room, Walt saw big racks of electronic equipment—stacks of cables, laptop computers, sound mixing boards, and various gizmos that he couldn't possibly have identified.

"What is all that shit?" Jimmy asked.

"Hey!" came the answer from down the hall. The security guard was back, this time with a cohort, an honest-to-God campus policeman, and from what Walt remembered, those fellows meant business—they carried not only flashlights and thermoses, but also batons and guns. The earlier pantomimed head scratching must've been an act.

"Hi, officers," Walt began with a smile that might have successfully suggested that there was a perfect explanation for all of this, had it not been for Jimmy's lack of pants. And as proud of his friend's legs as Walt may have been, the cop, he knew, was not likely to care.

"Freeze!" the cop said as if on television.

"Oh, wait, no, listen. Really, there's no need for all of this," Walt said. "I can explain just fine, you see, I used to work…"

But before Walt—who, with his calm affect of an unmade bed, was pretty good at diffusing situations—could even begin, Jimmy, who was halfway between him and the cops, suddenly took matters into his own hands, making a quick running start with his push cart, riding it toward Walt before leaping—this time truly like a cat—onto the big man's chest and scampering up and over his shoulders, and back through the ceiling, taking with him all possibility of escaping the episode with a bullshit story. The three men left in the hallway looked at the hole in the ceiling, then at each other, not sure what to do. Walt recalled all of those movies where the bad guy shoots at the ceiling indiscriminately, hoping to prevent the hero's escape, but there were no sudden movements, no chase, just a quiet moment of collective head scratching, this time genuine. Above them, Jimmy scrambled around, running, it seemed, both to and fro, his feet accidentally finding their way through the occasional tile as the dumbfounded spectators below tracked his erratic path.

"Jimmy, what the hell are you doing?" Walt yelled, a question that elicited a distant Curly Stooge sound in response.

Finally, the real cop decided that some action was required. Unfortunately, the first thing he did was to radio for back-up, and Walt knew that this would soon result in a blazing spectacle of flashing lights outside. "Jimmy!" he repeated.

The second thing the cop did was to start jumping up and smacking the ceiling tiles with his baton, trying to trip Jimmy each time he heard him approach. The spry old Italian continued his nonsensical activities up above, running along the thin ceiling grid, which was beginning to buckle under his weight, leaving Walt to hope he didn't catch his underwear on something, too.

"What the hell are you doing up there?" Walt called through the square hole.

"The question is, suckers, what're you doing down there?"

The security guard joined the tile-smacking efforts of the real cop, using a broom he'd found at the end of the corridor. The hallway was now a complete mess, with at least half of the ceiling tiles having been either stepped on from above by Jimmy or poked at from below by the law. One of the light fixtures now hung dangerously low.

The campus cop was getting pissed. "You, up in the ceiling, you're under arrest. Come down here immediately!" he yelled.

A few feet behind him, Jimmy's head popped down through a hole, like an upside-down gopher. "Why don't you come up here and get me, flat-foot?"

Apparently, that did it, as the real cop then had the fake cop try to boost him up through the hole to begin pursuit. Above, Jimmy was laughing and whooping it up. The cop, who was neither as small nor as nimble as Jimmy, struggled to hoist himself up, and as he did, Jimmy called out the most peculiar thing: "Look out now, boy, Deena's coming!"

Walt, transfixed by what was happening, became calm as the smaller guard tried to help the bigger cop through the hole. It was like watching a movie. *Deena's coming…* Walt hadn't thought about Deena for quite some time. In the months since his fallout with Miss June, Deena hadn't been by the bar once. He hoped that wherever she was, she was happy. No, "happy" didn't sound right. *Satisfied,* maybe. *Sated?* She certainly was a woman who took what she wanted, and he had assumed that after their arrangement had ended, she'd moved onto other things. Still, he had to wonder what exactly she'd been up to, and he had the sincere hope that she'd found someone who met at least her carnal, if not emotional needs, assuming she had any.

"For Christ's sake, I said, *Deena's coming!*" Jimmy repeated, this time with urgency, as the cop had made his way through the opening.

Snapping out of his reverie, Walt got the message. *Get the hell out of here.* The cops occupied, he ducked into the door to his left, pushed past the high-tech gear, and made his way back to the rear corner where the older equipment sat. Hoping it was the right thing, he grabbed a heavy, rectangular case, one with gray houndstooth vinyl covering and worn brass corners. Hurrying down the hall, away from the action, he made good his escape. If anyone had been born to create a diversion, it was Jimmy DeLuca.

Tossing the ill-gotten booty into the back of the DORF, he left the parking lot in a slow, thick, oily cloud of exhaust as the predicted battalion of overly enthusiastic police-issue Chryslers screeched into the parking lot, sliding sideways and generating enough noise to prompt the ghosts of a thousand librarians to deliver their universal, disapproving command of "Shsssh!"

* * *

In the relative quiet of his truck, as distance placed itself between him and the craziness that was Jimmy, distraction slipped away and he regained the purpose that had prompted the night's strange events. Judging by the sky, he guessed it to be near midnight. His head was clearing and he felt pleasantly sober, both full and certain, and he revisited the ache brought on earlier by the beautiful boy with the red balloon.

Stopping at Sam's garage, he collected a few things — a long extension cord, a pair of sawhorses, and a square of plywood. He wished he could collect Dewey as well — he suddenly missed his dog very much — but he was at Sam's, sleeping, no doubt, heavy against her, just as he himself had once done. Good for you, Dewey, he thought — I don't blame you one bit.

Hardwick's generous back yard, with its well-tended paths and sparkling greenhouse, garnered mixed feelings. It was where his father had tended to Miss June's plants, taking his lunch break there on hot days when he was too sweaty and dirty to be in the house. His father followed the rules of class separation without question, a fact that young Walt had observed and filed away. His entrance was through the back and, even then, used only if he was specifically needed inside. The greenhouse had been a place of magic for Walt, a place to play and imagine, and when the late afternoon sunlight hit the wavy panes, small jewels would project upon everything inside, moving slowly and mixing with the fertile warmth to create enchantment. And it was those powers of enchantment that he was counting on now, feeling that things had, in some odd way, come full-circle, and hoping that tonight, in return for his own years spent maintaining the graceful glass structure, he would, with any luck, be paid back in spades. The blanket of clouds from earlier in the day had blown eastward, and the sky was black and adorned with stars. A bright quarter-moon provided the light under which he set about his task, setting things up quietly—unhinging the big speaker from the hound-stooth box, threading the reel just so—his big heart beating solid reports of hope. Closing his eyes, he pressed the switch.

Two floors above, covers pulled tight, Gwen slept as cool night air blew gently through the open window. As it did, her dreamscape shifted, ushering in a different soundtrack, one with a changed tone and different voices. Familiar voices. She dreamed lightly for a while, not of things specific, but rather hovering in the hazy twilight between worlds. She opened her eyes but the dream voices remained. As if in a spell, she went to the window, and looked in wonder as the earnest face of Spencer Tracy soared thirty feet high, projected against the crystal panels of the greenhouse, filling the night with warm dependability. Each pane was a magical piece of a mosaic comprising what she wanted most in the world. She wrapped herself in a blanket and watched the movie on her knees, chin and arms resting on the sill.

"Are you always too busy?" he asked.

"What did you have in mind?" replied Katharine Hepburn.

"I'd like to take you to a baseball game."

And, in the shadows near the whirring old projector, she saw another giant of a man, equally valiant and sweet and strong, standing in the grass and watching as well. He was a hero of a different sort, one who fought battles of his own. One who had come back, in the nick of time, to win his very own damsel.

That night Walt had dreams too, dreams he couldn't remember. He'd left Hardwick before the film was over, deciding to just let it run its course. She would probably take the flight. What would be would be. Meeting the early sun, he went downstairs to retrieve Dewey from Sam's. Sitting on the tailgate of his truck was Gwen, looking like she would have waited there forever.

The Heart
of June

They sat at their usual table at Stouffer's, the woman and the subdued boy. It was his thirteenth birthday, his first since his father's funeral. Around them, elderly clientele picked at their turkey devonshires and under-tipped the waitresses. He broke the silence with the question he'd been afraid to ask.

"Is my mother coming back?"

She put down her fork and looked him straight in the eye.

"No," she said. "Your mother is never coming back."

Chapter 22

"CREIGHTON PROPERTIES."

"Reggie, please." He was using Sam's kitchen phone while Gwen made coffee, Sam cooked, and Arthur paced.

"Just tell him to pick up or I'll kill him," Walt said, though not unkindly. After reuniting with Gwen that morning, he felt more certain than he had in months.

"Walter," Reggie said a moment later. "Long time no speak."

"How did you know it was me?"

"The death threat was a clue."

"Again, how did you know it was me?"

"Oh, how I do miss your slashing wit. And now that you've interrupted me, what can I do you for? Do I owe you money?"

"Probably, but that's not why I'm calling. I need to borrow Edward for a couple hours."

"Who?"

"Edward."

A pause. "My handyman?"

"He's your Maintenance Specialist."

Gwen squeezed his hand.

"Oh, right. His title. You know, I should give him a promotion. Make him the Duke of Plungers or something."

"You should give him a raise, is what you should give him. Anyway, I'm taking him for a couple of days and I'm telling you first so he doesn't worry about getting fired. And don't give him a hard time about it. He's nervous enough already. And don't dock his pay."

"So, you're venturing outside of that bar, huh? I heard you'd pretty much moved into the place. What, did you get a big job or something? Find some new, unsuspecting customer?"

"No, no new jobs. Just tying up loose ends on an old one."

"Whatever. Just don't keep him too long. That little squirt works his ass off from what I hear. It's a crime how little I pay him. I should be ashamed of myself."

Before Walt could answer, Reggie'd hung up, getting back to his putting or preening or whatever it was that he did all day. Sam—unlit cigarette behind her ear at the ready for the moment the baby was born—put a plate of pancakes on the table. Walt added maple syrup to his list of arousing smells, filing it mentally between Magic Markers and beach balls. The baby was a week overdue. Arthur, who had begun his own maternity leave, was banned from cooking, as his anxiety over the pregnancy had turned him into a klutz. Chastened, he had taken to hovering at the perimeter of whatever room Sam inhabited, looking intently for any sign that labor may have begun. Gwen protested Sam's efforts, saying that she and Walt should be cooking for her, but Sam said that if she sat down she might not be able to get back up, adding, apropos of nothing, that she wouldn't be in this goddamned mess if it weren't for men. Arthur looked guilty. Walt ate another pancake.

"You sure this is your baby, Art?" he asked through a

mouthful. " 'Cause if it was, it would have been born right on time."

"Ha!" Arthur laughed too loudly, following it with an uncertain glance toward Sam, not doubting her faithfulness, but instead, fretting at the idea that the child might not prove punctual.

Parked on Devonshire Street sat Edward's truck—mud-flaps pristine, bug deflector gleaming. It was in front of a security building with countless door buzzers. Walt pushed a dozen of the buttons at once, and when various voices talked at him through the tinny speaker, he said, "It's me," and the door clicked to let him in. He wandered the halls until he found Edward's plumbing kit outside of an apartment door. He leaned his head into the flat and saw that it was vacant.

"Plumbing inspector," he called out.

"Oh! Gosh! Hi! I'm just fixing a faucet—no problems here!" came the panicked voice from the other room. Edward was terrified of authority, and there was none higher than an inspector. Quickly rounding the bend from the kitchen, he saw his old friend smiling, and closed his eyes as if he'd just dodged a bullet.

"Jeepers, Walt, you scared the daylights out of me."

"Sorry. I couldn't resist."

"I thought it was really an inspector. Those guys are sneaky."

"So I hear. But I'm sure whatever work you're doing would more than pass any inspection."

They looked at each other for a moment. The creases in Edward's uniform pants were as sharp as ever.

"Um, what're you doin' here, Walt?" he asked. "Is everything all right?"

"No, actually, it's not. You stopped coming around to pick me up for breakfast."

"But you wouldn't come down no more."

"Is that any reason to give up?"

"Well, if you put it that way, I guess not."

"Damn right. So, next Thursday, I'll expect to hear your truck in my drive."

"I'll be there." Edward smiled and Walt smiled back.

"I'm sorry I wasn't around. I didn't mean to leave you hanging."

"Heck, I ain't sore at you. I figured you was busy or something."

"You can't be too busy for a friend. Don't you agree?"

"Yeah, I guess I do."

"Good, because I need your help with a few things over at Sam's. Whatever Reggie pays you, I'll double it."

"Heck, you don't need to pay me nothin'. Is Saturday okay?"

"Nope, it's got to be today." Anticipating Edward's reaction, he added, "Don't worry about your stupid boss—I already cleared it with him."

"Mr. Creighton? And he was okay with it?"

Edward looked distraught.

"Don't worry. You're not in trouble."

"Well, okay then. If you're sure," he said, clearly uncertain.

"I'm sure. And what's with the 'Mr. Creighton'? What did we agree his name was?"

"Shithead," Edward said, grinning.

"Right. Why? Because he is one. So, having re-established that, pack up your tools. We'll get some lunch, and then get you busy."

"Okay then."

"But there is one catch."

"What's that?"

"I'm buying."

They went to the Apache, where Edward put too much sugar in his coffee, and the greasy food had its usual weight. Gus had waved his spatula when they came in, offering the usual *"Okay, Boss."* Lynda watched Walt eat his gyro from across the room, making him feel dirtier with each bite. Edward, oblivious, was talkative in the way that only people with peculiar social skills can be, delivering a rambling monologue with no end in sight.

"So then I tell him, I ain't payin' fifty bucks for a scope that shoots left. Now, I could try adjusting it, but there's no guarantee. And so then he says that his dog has gout."

This was what Walt needed—a steadily moving train of words that required little response from its recipient. Edward was channeling, and Walt nodded occasionally, knowing the story would plow forward regardless of his participation. In fairness, he didn't tune Edward out intentionally, but rather the cadence of the delivery was so unchanging, and the content morphed so seamlessly from one unrelated subject to another, that comprehension of the tale was impossible anyway. There was a hypnotic quality to its inanity.

"…and then the other lady, the one from the day before, she said she charged her dentures at Sears, but even so, they still slipped something awful. So I says to her…"

Walt thought of Hardwick. He'd pushed the parlor from his mind during his lost time at Gene's, but now that Gwen was staying, he wondered what, if anything, was going on there. One unpleasant possibility was that it had been completed in his absence. He imagined his tools having been moved to the basement, put there by a crew of anonymous carpenters who would then blow through the rest of the job quickly and without feeling. The prospect was unlikely but torturous, and he tried not to give it reign.

"Hey," he interrupted. "Whatever happened to that nurse?

The crabby one."

"Oh, her. You were right. She wasn't no good. I don't hang out with people like that no more, you know? I'm doing things different now."

Good for you, Edward, he thought. Good for you.

After lunch they went to Sam's, where Walt had to assure Edward once more that Shithead really did say he could take some days off. He gave him a tour of the house, showing him some of the things he'd been meaning to get to for years—leaky faucets, a jammed garbage disposer, a silent doorbell, and other things that he had to work at to remember but that Sam could have recited off the top of her head. Edward said he figured he could have the whole list done in about six hours' time. "Seriously?" Walt asked, taken aback. "Hey, why don't you take your time on this one. Make it last a couple of days, or you'll make me look worse than I already do." Edward looked proud, which was, of course, the real reason Walt had brought him here. Getting his old chores done was merely a bonus. They made their way to the living room, where Gwen sat on the big sofa, looking remarkably glamorous, although she was only knitting. She and Walt had no specific plans for the rest of the day, but both knew they'd spend it together, smitten like teenagers.

"So, you're the talented Edward I've heard so much about," she said.

"Me?"

"Unless Walt knows another."

"No, there's just the one of him," Walt said.

"That's right," Edward agreed, red-faced. Clearly, he did not do well in the presence of beautiful women.

"I hear you've come to bail Walt out of trouble."

"Well, he's helped me out plenty of times," Edward replied, although standing there, Walt couldn't think of one.

"Yeah, maybe this'll make us even," he suggested. "Anyway, listen. Gwen and I are taking off for the day. Sam's asleep upstairs, and I suggest you don't wake her. If you see a nervous dentist fumbling around, that's Dr. Art. He likes to be called 'Arty.'"

"He does not," Gwen corrected.

"Anyway, if you see Arthur, just smile and ignore him. He's odd, but harmless."

"Got it. Don't wake up the pregnant lady, and ignore the dentist."

Walt sized him up. "Was that a joke Edward? There's hope for you yet."

Standing, Gwen hooked arms with Edward and spoke toward Walt. "And competition for you, wiseguy."

It seemed like a free day, made fresh from the night before. They got into the DORF and began a lazy trip around town, with no particular place to go. Dewey had begun the trek riding in the truck's bed but after a few blocks, lonesome and jealous, whined and pawed at the back window until they stopped to let him join them up front. "He prefers the window seat," Walt apologized. "It would be easier for us all if you just gave it to him—trust me on this one." This suited Gwen just fine, and she nestled in between her two bulky fellas.

"You're very sweet," Gwen said as they pulled away again.

"Are you talking to me or the dog?"

"I could have meant him, but this time I meant you."

"Thanks. But listen, last night, that was …"

"No," she interrupted, "I'm not talking about last night. I don't think I have words for that. I meant for whatever you did just now. For Edward. I don't know what it was, but I know you did a good thing."

"I'm fond of him," he admitted. "I just wish I could help

him be more comfortable."

"I think it's nice how much you care. You're a good friend."

They approached another Creighton Properties apartment building, a generic box with a rental sign permanently fixed to its dull facade.

"I'm just glad I don't live in that place," Walt said.

"It is awful," she agreed. "It looks like a prison."

Cobwebs lifted. *"A prison,"* Walt thought, feeling fog dissipate. "Oh, shit," he said.

"What?"

"I need to call Sam."

* * *

The university police station was nicer than Walt expected, better than most of the academic buildings on campus, in fact.

"May I help you, ma'am?" the desk sergeant asked Sam, ignoring Walt.

"Do you have a white-haired Italian here? This tall, never shuts up?"

At that, a burst of laughter came from beyond a closed door behind the desk, and all three of them turned toward it.

"Never mind," said Sam. "I'll find him myself."

"Wait, you can't go back there," the cop said as she lumbered past him with the impatient authority of the well-overdue. A man had done this to her, the cop was a man, and therefore the cop would do well to keep to himself. She shot him a glance that made him recoil.

"Save it," she said.

Walt shrugged at him as they opened the door and followed the laughter down the hall and around the corner to where they saw Jimmy in a jail cell, telling a story through the bars to four young cops.

"So I'm tellin' you, boys, you gotta date a nurse. You listen to me now!"

"Give it up, DeLuca. We're bailing you out," Sam announced.

"Hey! Sammy, my love. Christ you look good. Big as a house and still sexy as hell. Isn't she sexy, boys?"

An embarrassed bit of foot shuffling and polite acknowledgment was offered by the cops, which Sam waved off. "Spare me the bullshit."

"Walt," Jimmy said. "You come to spring me, too. That's my boy. I didn't fink on you, you know. I didn't say shit. Nada." He mimed zipping his lips.

Just as Walt had forgotten about leaving Jimmy in the ceiling, it hadn't occurred to him that the cops might be looking for him, too, especially since he was the one who had actually stolen something. He looked around for the officer from the night before, but he wasn't there.

"I know you didn't fink on me, Jimmy. I had no doubt. Sorry you got locked up."

"Eh, it's nothin'."

As Sam dialed the nearby wall-phone, one of the cops opened his mouth as if to say something, but thought the better of it.

"The chancellor," she said into the handset. "Tell him it's Sam." The cops looked at Walt as if to ask if they were in trouble, and if so, might he be an ally. All he could offer was a helpless gesture indicating that they were all in the same boat. "Bill," she said after a moment.

To the cops, she said, "Do you mind?" Frozen, they stood there, useless. "I'd like to sit down?"

They couldn't move fast enough to produce a chair. "Thank you," she mouthed.

"Me too, Bill. Yeah, I know. Yes. Still. Well, that's sweet. But listen, I need a favor." Again, to the cops, she said, "Do you mind?" and made a whisking motion.

The men in blue took the hint and moved obediently and en masse down the long hallway, stopping short of rounding the bend when she snapped her fingers and they stopped. Walt tried to join them, but with another finger snap she froze him in his tracks, too. Jimmy laid back on the cot in his cell and hummed, apparently happy enough.

Sam spoke with her longtime would-be paramour for a while, repeating Walt's version of the night before, although she did add a number of words he hadn't used, "idiots," "morons," and "sophomoric escapades" being among them. Sam said finally that she would be greatly appreciative if he could make this problem go away. Further, she would personally pay for any damages that the idiot in the ceiling had caused. "It's hard to explain," she said looking at Walt, "but it was in the name of love."

"Okay, Bill. You too," she said before putting her palm over the mouthpiece, the words bringing a slight reflex of jealousy from Walt.

She motioned for the admonished cops to come back, which they did, moving together in a timid shuffle. When they arrived, she handed the phone to the closest one, his ensuing conversation eliciting from him quite a few "yes, sirs" before he hung up. He looked at Sam with wonder, then unlocked the cell door. Walt wasn't surprised in the least. Business settled, he held Sam's arm as she waddled up the hall. Stopping, he looked back at Jimmy who was still in his cell.

"Um, Jimmy, come on."

"Nah, that's all right. You two go. I'll catch up."

"You're staying? In jail?"

"I was in the middle of a story. These boys'll bring me back. Hey, Sammy—I owe you one. Go have that baby so I can pay up."

At the end of the hall, Walt felt something foreign in his pocket, a piece of celluloid from the night before. He held it up to the light, two frames of redemption. He turned back to thank his friend, but the little man had already launched back into his story, animatedly entertaining the troops. Once again, the indefatigable Jimmy DeLuca.

In the lobby, Sam suddenly paused and then looked at the desk sergeant. "Shit. I think I need your phone."

"Do you want to exchange more pleasantries with Chancellor Bill?" Walt asked.

"No, dumbass—it's the baby. I'm having contractions."

* * *

She called Arthur and told him to meet her at the hospital. No, she didn't want a ride from him. No, she didn't need a ride from the cops either. Walt would take her. "Just meet me there," she said, interrupting his protestations, and hanging up on him. "Christ on a crutch."

Walt drove slowly at her request. A smooth, even trip on a big bench seat was what she wanted.

"Take Fifth Avenue," she said.

"Fifth is no good this time of day," he replied.

"Surely you're not going to meander through the park."

"When in doubt, meander."

"You're fucking kidding me. Fifth heads straight there."

"I know, but they're tearing it up to replace gas lines or something. Trust me." She looked skyward for help as he made the turn off of Fifth that led to the narrow back road that sloped treacherously down a steep hillside below the back of the Carnegie Museum and into Schenley Park. They were soon surrounded by a surprisingly dense show of nature.

"This is not good," she said.

"Don't worry, you'll be fine. Five minutes ago, you were spitting nails and scaring cops. Don't fail me now. I'll have you there in ten minutes, I promise." It would be closer to twenty, he knew, but he figured that if the baby was as stubborn as its mother, and since it had already decided to be late, it would come out in its own sweet time. As they bumped over the railroad tracks, the DORF's worn suspension bounced them heavily in their seats as around their feet tools clanked, coffee cups rolled, and Chiclet wrappers crinkled.

"Oh, your truck is a mess."

"Now you notice?"

"No, I mean it's *really* a mess. My water broke."

"I'm guessing that's not good?"

His plan had been to follow alongside the railroad tracks, and then cut up the service road that let out behind the park maintenance facility, a plan that worked perfectly until they got there to find the gate locked.

"Jesus Christ, Walter, how about a tour of the whole god-damned city?"

Walt, despite being a veteran ex-husband, was about to deliver a smart-ass answer to her rhetorical question, but thought the better of it when she suddenly produced four quick, forced breaths.

"Um, you are going to make it, right?" he hated to ask as he turned around and headed back down the hill.

"Yes!"

"Good."

"No!" she corrected.

"What?" He was starting to space out.

"Pull over!"

While Sam didn't quite share Walt's aversion to modern technology, she did share his dislike of cellular phones, and, consequently, the two of them might as well have been on the moon.

"Oh, Christ, this baby's coming, Walt. Do something."

Do something. He jumped out of the truck and considered his options. Taking a walk wasn't one of them—he was fairly certain of that. He wished that Gene were there with his apron and smelly bar rag, always in command. Gene would know what to do.

"Arhggh!" Sam said, noting the urgency of the matter. She scooted sideways and lay back on the seat, and then began to speak loudly in tongues, which Walt hadn't known could include profanity.

Walt had long defended the unkempt state of his truck by pointing out that its collection of miscellaneous stuff had came in handy on many occasions, but it seemed that this was not going to be one of them. He didn't know what was needed to deliver a baby, but was pretty sure that a pipe wrench, a broken tennis racquet, two tape measures, seven parking tickets, a rubber Halloween mask, and a pair of Jimmy's white tasseled loafers weren't it. There was a bedspread though, the same one that he and Sam had used on their bed a dozen years before. It was old and torn and by now barely suitable for even a spur-of-the-moment picnic, but Walt kept it under the seat under the auspices of "emergency use." Really, though, it had been kept for sentimental reasons. In an unimaginable pairing of the two, he spread it across the seat and tucked it under Sam as best he could.

"This baby is coming out *now!*" she said, pointing at him psychotically as if he had asserted otherwise. He believed her.

Adjusting the blanket as if to stall for time, he asked, "How could this have happened so fast?"

"Fast? I've been pregnant for nine months, if you haven't noticed." She was red-faced and breathing hard, sweat beading on her upper lip.

"That's not what I meant," he said, but then realized that once again Sam was right. Despite his big initial reaction to the baby, it hadn't seemed truly real until now.

"Little help, please?" she managed through clenched teeth as the next wave of pain approached.

"What? Oh, sure! Yeah. Okay. Here goes," he said, leaning into the truck cab and staring into the dark, active, changing void between her legs.

She was writhing now, emitting primal sounds that gave the surrounding woods a jungle-like effect and sending, Walt was sure, all nearby animals fleeing to the next county.

"Uh, Sam?" he interrupted.

"What?!"

"What exactly am I supposed to do?"

"How should I know? You're the carpenter!"

He wasn't sure what that meant, but knew better than to ask. He thought back to all the old movies and sitcoms he'd seen, the ones where people had babies in taxicabs. He decided to draw from that useless bag of tricks.

"Breathe!" he commanded arbitrarily.

"Fuck you!" she replied.

"Okay!" he said for some reason.

And so they continued, developing an impromptu cycle, with Walt imploring her to "Breathe!" and Sam relaying the subsequent sentiment of "Fuck you!" which was, in return, followed by "Okay!" and then another command to "Breathe!" If only because of its rhythm, it was surprisingly effective.

A hundred yards above them, on the rim of their urban valley, modern life went on, unaware. A few remaining late-spring students walked across campus. Buses rumbled. Street sweepers swept. Jimmy entertained the cops, and Arthur paced the hospital where his pregnant wife had not arrived. And a few miles away on Fifth Avenue, Miss June strolled through her garden, plotting, as always. Sam, her dress up to her neck, was breathing and grunting and sweating and doing what she needed to do, while Walt, looking to further establish some sort of command, put his hands around her ankles and squeezed hard, making sure she knew she wasn't alone. When he dared to look, he saw the baby's head appear, a beautiful, frightening, impossible eclipse. The well-worn old couple continued chanting their sweaty, frantic, cyclical mantra—"breathe, fuck you, okay"—until Sam, in the most amazing physical feat Walt had ever witnessed, suddenly sat straight up, looked him in the eye, and screamed, "Now!" at which point she pushed for all she was worth, sending the latest slippery little addition to the planet safely into his ready, calloused hands.

At the hospital, Arthur was beside himself.

Sam collapsed backward, her hair wet and matted against the vinyl seat.

"What the hell just happened?" she cried.

"You had a baby, Sam. A baby."

"Really?"

"Yes." In his hands, Walt saw the wonderful, glistening, little figure moving—subtly at first, and then defiantly with clenched fists and a yell—Sam's child for sure. He watched as the sheen on the perfect little face suddenly presented a perfect, clear circle on its forehead, which he realized was the drop of his own tear from above. Wrapping the baby in his flannel over-shirt, he placed the crying bundle on Samantha's chest.

"Sam," he said. "You have a little girl."

"Oh my God. She's beautiful."

Walt leaned forward, reached across the cab, caressed Sam's matted hair, and blew cool air on her forehead. He looked at the tiny creature.

"Baby Chiclet," he said.

The emergency room doors slid open smoothly, although Walt thought they should have burst open like they do on TV. The DORF was right outside, and although the emergency was over and they'd driven slowly, he had parked one wheel up on the curb for effect. Arthur appeared instantly, bolting through the door to see his wife. Walt stayed back as Arthur hugged his family, kissing Sam until she made him stop. As the attendants fussed with blankets and prepared to move mother and child to a gurney, Walt simply walked away, hands in pockets, leaving the new trio to complete their day. The hospital could move his truck out of the emergency lane — the keys were in the ignition, not that they were needed to start it anyway. A block from the hospital, he passed an Indian grocery store, one that also sold 220-volt appliances. Someone asked him for spare change, and he gave them what he had. Judging by the sun, he figured that if he walked straight down Fifth, he might just make it in time for his afternoon snack.

* * *

"I suppose you think I'm going to feed you," she said from her spot at the kitchen sink.

"It hadn't crossed my mind, but since you've offered."

"How it must feel to be unencumbered by the restraint of social graces."

"Pretty good, I think."

And so things returned to normal.

Chapter 23

AFTER FINISHING HIS SNACK — crustless rye beneath slices of Emmenthaler and a dish of strawberries—Walt, passing by the music room, was surprised to see a list on the piano. He found Miss June at her writing desk, sealing a letter with a small sponge from a cut crystal dish, as it was far too crass an act to lick an envelope.

"I have a list," he said, brandishing the evidence.

"And I am its author," she replied, not looking up.

"Imagine that."

"Quite."

"I don't understand."

She looked up and peered above her little reading glasses. "It's quite simple, really. I record the tasks that I wish for you to perform, and then you attempt to complete them. Of course, in practice it proves more taxing, but that is the crux of it. Surely you haven't forgotten your role in my epistolary endeavors."

"No, I mean that I don't understand why there is a new

list. I thought you'd forgone it until the parlor was done."

"And so I had."

He went queasy. "Did you hire someone to finish my work?"

"Don't be daft."

Relief, then confusion.

"I still don't get it."

She put down her pen and addressed him directly.

"Apparently," she said, "you're unaware of the progress you've made."

"Come again?"

"The parlor. You're nearly finished."

She was right. What he'd remembered as a typical mess was in fact a nearly complete restoration. Usually, revisiting old business presented evidence of failure, a test of his ability to gloss over what he had left undone. But this time his absence had had an opposite effect. All that remained to be completed was the running trim at the long south wall—the tall base-board, the sculpted chair-rail, and a last bit of the cornice trim that he'd been working on before the falling out. Even his tools were not in the disarray that he'd remembered. Taking it all in, he realized that if he were to resume his previous pace, he could be done in a of couple days. Done.

He strapped on his tool belt and got back to work.

Later, he looked up to see Gwen in the doorway, quietly grinning as she watched him work. For all of his befuddlement in other areas of life, he was in command in this world.

"You know, so often I work," he said, "wishing that a beautiful woman would stop by and leer at me, and now it's finally happened."

"I wasn't leering," she objected. "You just happened to be where I was looking."

"I see." He came over and kissed her. "I think you were spying. Sent by the owner, perhaps?"

"I don't think she'd resort to using spies."

"Hmm."

"But forget that—I just got back from the hospital. The baby is beautiful. She's perfect."

"How's Sam?"

"Fine. She doesn't even look tired."

"And Arthur?"

"He had to be sedated."

"I'm glad they're well."

"Thanks to you."

"Well, Sam might not agree about that. I'm not sure she appreciated my little detour on the way to the hospital."

"All she said was, 'It figured.'"

"Should I steer clear for a while?"

"I think you're safe."

"Good," he said, pulling her close, letting his hands roam. "Maybe I'll call it a day. We could go to my place."

"Mmmm, I don't think so." She pried his hands away. "You need to keep your head clear."

"Clear?"

"Like a boxer. In training. I don't want to be a distraction while you're finishing up."

"I see."

"And besides, I don't want to jinx things."

"Jinx?"

"I want things to be just the way they were when you were doing so well in here."

"Doing well?"

"Kicking ass, if you will. And if I recall, we weren't having sex during most of it."

"And sex might jeopardize my progress."

She winked. "Call me superstitious. I just think things should be the same as they were until you're done."

"This sounds like sexual blackmail," he said, grabbing her belt buckle. "And you're being a tease."

"Who, me?" She pressed her leg between his.

"Yes, you."

"I don't know what you are implying." She pushed away, feigning decorum. "You'll have to finish things here before we can explore the matter further. But we will, I promise."

Nursing mild discomfort and a pained grin, he got back to work.

* * *

Sam sighed deeply. The baby breathed, too, quick, shallow, little breaths, followed by a big yawn and a tight-fisted shudder. Sam pressed her hand gently against her daughter's back, in wonder at her movement. She looked over at the next bed, where Arthur lay sleeping as if it were he who had given birth. What was it that made us what we were? She and Walt hadn't spoken much about it after the fence-building day last fall in her garden, but she'd already envisioned his place in the baby's life. She looked forward to seeing him with her, to see what this tiny creature might bring out in the big man.

* * *

The sky had long gone black. The watch that he didn't own would have told him that it was 4:30 in the morning, his fourteenth consecutive hour, though he was neither hungry nor tired. The work had begun to flow and he simply continued, neither dictating nor interrupting the process. He and the house were in harmony, and there was no need to be anywhere else. The stack of trim sat along one wall, and all day and night he had pulled from the pile, cut every piece just right, so that nothing else could have rested in its place, and set each nail with care, securing Miss June's vision and so much more. He chose not to think about his actions, didn't allow thoughts of their significance. Instead, he thought about Sam and about Gwen, about Baby Chiclet, and about the bar. About Mrs. Greb and her collection. About his own collection. He turned to see that he was down to the last piece, all that the pile had left to offer. He walked the room, checking to see what else might be missing, but a close inspection showed that this was really it. Returning to the last piece of moulding, he picked it up, sighted its length, considered its bow.

As he measured and marked, the room shifted slightly, taking a turn, as if affected by the weight of years-long culmination. He worked the board from one end to the other, guiding it into place as he went. The movement of the room increased, and he likened it to the sway of the Imperial when he gave it the gas. As he approached the middle of the piece, he thought of himself and Sam buying the Friendship house, and of how she'd laughed when he said he could "fix it up in a jiffy." He thought of Jimmy's grin and Edward's creased pants, of how Dr. Art's virtues would make him the father he himself wouldn't be. Approaching the end, toward the final joint that he'd coped, he felt the presence of Miss June, reflected on the dozens of years the two of them had been together. How she'd been hard and unrelenting and always, always there. There was a place for one last nail. He decided against turning to look at the room to recognize the moment. He chose not to register what he was about to accomplish, nor to entertain thoughts about exorcising demons. Instead, as he took the nail from his mouth, he thought about Gwen. Her bad poems and wrinkled up nose, Spencer Tracy and the hope in her eyes.

He drove the nail home.

* * *

The best parties are never over-planned. This one, thrown
together in a few hours, quickly benefited from a groundswell
of excitement, good will, and, frankly, wonder at Walt having
finished the job at Hardwick. Gwen had dropped Walt at the
hospital in the late afternoon to visit Sam and pick up his
truck, and he'd agreed to meet her at the 'Eye at 7:00 for what
he thought would be a quick drink and then early bed. In the
meantime, Gwen and Jimmy made phone calls and met there
early to decorate, so by the time Walt sauntered in at 8:00 and
a cheer went up, the place was packed. All of Walt's favorite
people were there, sans Sam and Chiclet, whose real name
turned out to be Lucy. Old friends from the university were
there—a night janitor, former colleagues, and the chancellor
himself, who'd driven past the bar a thousand times and would
never have thought to stop in. Jimmy'd rounded up a good
number of tradespeople—electricians, plumbers, and roofers
who were familiar with Walt's habits. A few neighbors from
Friendship made appearances as well, as did, inexplicably,
Walt's mailman. Another man might have been embarrassed
that such a crowd would gather to celebrate what for most
people was a typical occurrence—fulfilling a commitment
as promised—but the party suited Walt just fine. These were
the people from his various worlds all in one place for once,
and he felt privileged to be among them.

"What da'ya think, my boy?" Jimmy asked Walt, gesturing
toward Sam's close-cropped old library coworkers, obvious
lesbians, every one. "You think any of those ladies might like
to have a go with old Jimmy DeLuca?" The question had not
been made in jest.

"How could they resist, Jimmy," Walt replied. "Just be persistent."

The door opened and more people spilled in, including one for whom Walt could make the case of being the real man of the hour, Dr. Art, there in a real live tavern. Walt made his way through the crowd and gave him an affectionate slug on the shoulder.

"Artie, I'm so glad to see you. Congratulations, buddy."

"Thank you, Walter, but I'm here to congratulate you on a job, well…" he paused, "*done*."

"Was that a joke Art?"

"I think it was, Walter."

"Well, it was a good one."

"Why, thank you. And to think that Sam wasn't even here to hear it. I'll have to remember to tell her about it later."

"Why wait? She and the baby are at the end of the bar."

Panic struck Arthur's face as he scanned the room for his wife and daughter, only to look back and find Walt smiling.

"Come here, you knucklehead." Walt laughed and gave Sam's husband a bear hug that was long overdue.

The jukebox played fast songs—*Splish Splash*, *Sea Cruise*, *Great Balls of Fire*—before settling into the old Ray Bryant R&B chestnut *The Madison Time*, with the drunken crowd attempting to follow the record's spoken-word dance instruction.

"When I say 'Hit it,' go two up and two back, double cross, and freeze…"

Walt rubbed elbows and hugged and laughed. Arthur settled into a game of pool with Deena, the two making a stranger pair than Jimmy and the librarians. Gwen dragged Walt to the middle of the room, where he displayed his clumsy style of dancing, a rare occurrence. What the hell, he'd decided. Besides, he couldn't look much funnier than Gene, who was once again tearing up the floor, partner not required.

"Now this time, when I say 'Hit it,' I want the big strong Jackie Gleason, and then back to The Madison … 'Hit it!' And awaaay, we go!"

"Speech, speech!" a cry came out when the jukebox was between songs.

"All right, if you insist," Jimmy said standing on a chair.

"Come on, Walt, say something," came another shout. Others, including Edward, joined in, and there was much laughter as Walt was put on the spot.

"You know, I did start to prepare a speech, but would you believe I didn't finish it?" he smiled.

"Oh, no, not again!"

Various catcalls and groans were offered in agreement.

"Okay, okay. I, ah, shit … I'm not sure what to say. Hell, if I knew you'd have thrown me a party, I would have finished something years ago. But I do want to thank everyone here. All of you. For sticking with me through this ordeal and the many others that preceded it. And listen, I know that not one of you had any doubt whatsoever that I'd pull this off … ." He had to pause until the laughter—including his own—died down, and then continued. "But I can say, in all seriousness, that I've never had doubts about any of you, or had any moment over the years when I didn't know how lucky I am to have you as friends."

"You still ain't gettin' outta payin' your tab," Gene yelled.

"Fair enough! Just let me quit rambling here and get back to having some fun."

And at that, the front door opened and light from the street lamp shown through, commanding the attention of the room. A large, dark arm held the door from outside, and a moment later, for the first time, into the bar at her own regal pace walked Miss June Creighton herself, followed by her chauffeur and escort for the evening, the somewhat Reverend

Nate Cornsweet. A low buzz swept through the place as she made her way into the room. Gwen started toward her but Walt instinctively held her back, the better to let the old woman have whatever moment she'd come here to have. Even though he now knew she wasn't sick, it still struck him that it took Miss June a while to make her way across the floor, plus it was strange to see her anywhere other than at Hardwick. Arriving at the center of the room, she took in the crowd and its relative silence.

"Well, I didn't come here to kill a party." She looked around. "What does it take for an old woman to get a drink around here?"

The tension broke and Walt and Gwen went to her.

"I don't imagine you expected me to darken this particular door," she opined.

"Miss June, I can't think of anyone I'd rather see here tonight."

"Don't be ridiculous—I'm sure there are others. But, my reason for coming to your little soirée, other than to publicly acknowledge my thanks—which, I might add, is not required under the rules of etiquette, seeing as I am paying you for your work—is to give you the final payment for your efforts, lest you cry poor in my presence and attempt to make an old woman feel bad."

"Don't listen to her, Walt—she came here to dance with me," Jimmy interrupted.

"I most certainly did not, you delusional wolf. You'll not count me among your peccadilloes. But thank you, regardless, for your unwelcome offer."

"We'll dance later," Jimmy assured her.

"As I was saying," Miss June continued, "here is your payment. Please let me know if the amount is disagreeable." She handed him an envelope.

"Miss June, I'm not sure I can take this. This," he said, gesturing around him, "is payment enough."

"Don't be mentally irregular, Walter. Of course you should take payment. You've honored your commitment. Believe me— this is money I am more than pleased to spend."

Reggie. Walt had forgotten again that his money was ultimately funding the work.

"Then accept it, I will," he said pocketing the check. "And I believe you wanted a drink?"

"Good Lord, no. Not that the coarseness of this gin mill isn't enticing, but I think I'll leave before that music machine restarts and the rumpus begins. Enjoy your evening, Walter." She looked around. "Enjoy the enthusiasm of your friends."

"See you, Dummy," Nate Cornsweet added. "Nice job over to the house."

The departure of Miss June brought not only the return of the music and the pouring of drinks, but also the arrival of Reggie, whose cologne cut a path through which he traversed the crowded room. The dancing had resumed, too, and Walt and Gwen were shoved toward the pool table, where Dr. Art was still hanging out with Deena, her sleeveless black tee-shirt and muscular arms quite the contrast to his version of casual attire.

"Well, what do we have here?" Reggie asked Walt. "My 'maintenance engineer' tells me you finished the parlor. I had to come down myself to see if it was for real."

From across the worn felt, Deena shot him a scowl.

"Apparently it is," Walt said looking around at the party. "The last few days are a blur, but from what I hear, I got it done."

"How about that. After all of these years, old Walter Farnham finally comes through. I can't believe it. Congratulations, buddy."

"Yeah, will wonders never cease," Walt added. Gwen held his arm tighter. "Have a drink, Reggie. The bar is open."

"I was thinking," Reggie said, "maybe since you know the house so well, you can help with the demolition once we get going. Given your new work habits, I'll bet you could tear the place apart in no time."

"Such a nice offer. I'm sure you pay well, too."

"We'll start with the parlor."

"Come on, Walt, let's dance," Gwen said, ready to pull him away.

"Hell," Reggie continued. "If you play your cards right, maybe I could keep you on as the handyman. Fix my toilets and whatnot."

The punch came faster than Walt could have imagined. Faster than a thought, harder and more accurate than any verbal jab he could have delivered. In the years to come, it would become like Mazeroski's home run that ended the 1960 World Series, in that more people would claim to have seen it than could possibly have been there. Little Richard screamed from the jukebox as Reggie's head spun and his health-club body hit the floor, out cold before he landed. Deena towered above him, fist still clenched tight.

"Asshole," she said.

Chapter 24

WALT WASN'T EXPECTING REVEREND NATE to be driving the bus himself, but indeed, it was him behind the wheel of the battered yellow Blue Bird when it pulled to the curb, discharging a few dozen kids from the Hill.

"They're all yours, and there's more comin'," he called before pulling away for another trip.

Under the late morning sky, Donald's annuals were taking hold in the raised beds, and the little man himself was on hand to fret—though not unkindly—over the possibility that a pack of excited boys might leap the low stone walls and tread on his posies. The two donkeys had already eaten more than their fair share. Hay covered much of the grass, the bandstand was in place, a giant blue-and-white striped tent had been erected, and rows of tables offered plenty of food.

The May Day circus was on.

He had laid it out as close to what he could remember from his youth, making sure there were chairs for the older folks, and also that the kids had room to run free. Jimmy was, for once, of genuine help, with the atmosphere of a circus proving exactly suited to his traits. The older man directed the rental company workers while they set up the chairs, showed the caterers how to man their grills, told the clowns to give it their all—"Pratfalls, fellas, we want pratfalls"—and, microphone in hand, led the children in a few frantic and comical rounds of "Simon Says." He made Walt and Gwen step up onto the bandstand to play the game, at which they failed miserably, much to the delight of the kids. When the game was over, and after he'd given Donald a few pointers on gardening—"You gotta piss in the dirt if you wanna grow tomatoes"—Jimmy reminded Sam that the old lady's house had a hell of a lot of bedrooms and if she wanted to slip upstairs to make a little springtime whoopee, he'd make sure that Arthur and Walt were otherwise occupied while they went about their business.

"You couldn't handle me, DeLuca," Sam said, then gave him a full kiss on the lips, prompting him to clutch his chest and feign a heart attack.

Dr. Art had stationed himself next to the immense bowls of candy that Walt had arranged, handing out free toothbrushes and delivering brushing lectures to the kids. The donkeys, the ponies, and the small train—fresh from an Easter stint at the Monroeville Mall—circuited the grounds of Hardwick, the rule being that the children could go as many times as they liked, so long as they got back in line and waited their turn. These were kids who needed a circus, Walt knew. He spied Reverend Nate across the lawn, and the two men nodded to one another. Two screw-ups who'd done something right.

The adults sat at the tables as the day progressed—most seemed to be grandparents—talking and laughing and observing the chaos. As day fell to twilight, Edward threw the switch to the colored lights he'd strung along the wrought iron fence, and the circus music gave way to softer songs, signaling the adults to take over the lawn just as the Creighton factory workers had done decades before, swaying in pairs beneath the dark spring sky while their tired kids—faces painted, bellies full—lay on the grass taking in the spectacle.

Gwen pressed her face to Walt's chest as they rocked slowly on the grass dance floor, her slight body nestled against his. She said something soft that he couldn't quite hear, and when he asked, she shook her head slightly, so as to not break the moment. He suspected it was "I love you," something they'd not yet said. He wasn't a good dancer but could have continued this one forever, or so he was thinking when Jimmy tried to cut in.

"Sorry, Jimmy. Not now."

"No, it's okay," Gwen said. "I promised him a dance. He can finish this one, but the last one's for you."

As Walt made his way from the dancers, he heard Jimmy say, "But I thought I could get the last dance with him."

Leaning against the fence, watching what he'd created, he thought of the happiness the circus had brought him as a boy, and also of the sadness the memory triggered as an adult. How the event seemed to spotlight his innocence, how he lived the year waiting for that day, waiting for what the rich kids took for granted. Sam had once said that she wished she could go back in time and tell that little boy that everything would be all right, that he was loved. But now he'd done something better, something real. He considered slipping away through the gate to preserve the memory of this new circus just as it was at that very moment, with the music and the children, the silhouette of the tent, and Gwen's eyes-closed smile as Jimmy DeLuca twirled her across the lawn.

Just then, Sam sidled up and laced her fingers through his, leaning her head on his shoulder.

"You spent all of your money on this, didn't you?" she said. "The money from the parlor."

"Of course I did," he replied. "Every penny."

June Creighton looked down upon the scene from her bedroom window as she had nearly seventy years before, watching the dancers lost in their moments. Absent was her disdain.

* * *

"Someone's knocking," Gwen said.

The two were tucked together tightly and had, until that moment, been asleep in his worn bed.

"They'll go away," he mumbled.

The knocking persisted.

"I don't think so."

Hung over from cotton candy, he donned a pair of boxers and tried not to fall down the narrow steps.

"She's been calling for you all morning," Sam said at the door. "Sorry to wake you, but she's not going to let up."

He scratched. "What time is it?"

"Not quite nine."

"Did she say what she wanted?"

"No. I don't think anything's wrong, though. Just errands or chores."

"Jesus."

"Yeah."

He kissed Gwen back to sleep and drove to Hardwick. On the truck seat beside him was a jumbo candy circus peanut of the dense, orange, near-styrofoam variety. He had no idea how it got there, and its presence made his stomach turn. Two blocks later, he ate it anyway.

"I suppose you've left the mess on the grounds for me to clean up?"

She was standing at the butcher block in the kitchen. Like most of her questions, this one was rhetorical, as it would clearly take a crew of workers to dismantle and collect the remains of the circus.

"If you're offering, sure—knock yourself out," he said. "Did you wake me up just to ask that?"

"No. We need to discuss my plans. But first, I suggest you examine the inside of your mouth, which is of a rather unnatural hue this morning."

He looked at his orange mouth in the distorted reflection of a chrome pot lid. The peanut had left it tasting like shit. "It must be going around," he said, working his fuzzy tongue, "because yours is orange too." He held up the lid hoping to make her look.

"Tea," she commanded, pointing to the array she'd assembled. He poured.

"Okay, I'll bite," he said. "Your plans."

"My travel plans, to be precise."

The teapot moved slightly and he spilled a few drops into his saucer.

"Travel?"

"Yes, travel."

"I don't get it."

"Surely, you've heard of it. It means to move one's self beyond a usual distance? To embark upon a planned journey? There are many varieties—aeroplane, sailing ship, automobile."

"So I hear. And this impromptu tea party is your way of telling me you're going someplace?"

"Impromptu, nothing—I, and the rest of the city, have been awake for hours."

"Okay, okay—'uncle.' Can you please just tell me what's

going on? You're making my head hurt."

"All right, but pay attention this time. I'll use simple words, so you might understand." She looked him in the eye and spoke slowly, as if he were a dog. "I am going on a trip. For pleasure. I am making my arrangements. You are a factor in the arrangements. Therefore, I have summoned you."

He noticed the travel magazines near the tea service. They were not there by chance. The orange flavoring was now wreaking havoc in earnest, so he drank his tea, which was not quite cool enough for comfort.

"Miss June, are you asking me to go on a trip with you?" Incredibly, it didn't sound like that bad of an idea.

"Don't be absurd. The prospect of dragging you across Europe would exhaust me before I could depart."

He rubbed his temples.

"But I should thank you for inspiring my trip. At half my age, constraining yourself to the streets of Pittsburgh, you've proven quite the example of what I should avoid."

The conversation began to feel like an odd sort of travel in itself, travel during which she engineered a silver-wheeled train of articulation, while he struggled to pilot a half-witted donkey through fog. Miss June had left southwestern Pennsylvania rarely since Walt was a boy, and then only for short trips — Philadelphia and New York for societal affairs, Chautauqua for lectures, and the like. But it had been a decade since she had been more than a morning's drive from Hardwick as best he could remember. Now, she was talking Europe.

"But you're not going alone."

"No. While it would be grand to escape the burden of the interruption of others, I do think that some company will prove helpful, if only for toting luggage. Therefore, I've requested Donald's accompaniment."

"Sounds like quite the warm invitation you extended."

"Oh, please. I was more than kind about it. I'm nothing if not well-mannered. I phoned him early this morning. He was quite taken with the idea, as you might imagine."

"I'd rather not." No doubt, Donald's bags were already packed.

"So, my reason for waking you before noon was to ask if you might stay here at Hardwick next month in my absence. The house has never been empty, you know. For well over a century, it has always had a heartbeat." She watched as he played with his teacup. "I trust you have no pressing business that will pull you out of town? You're not taking your little carnival on the road? No repeat performances?"

"No, there was just the one. But won't Gwen still be here?"

"It's funny you should mention that—as of this morning, her whereabouts are a mystery." Her look was one of feigned disapproval—she knew damned well where Gwen was. "But yes, I do anticipate that she will still be here, working on her galleys. Even so, you know this house so well—I'd hate to think of anything going wrong in my absence without the proper response at the ready."

"And you have no problem with my sleeping here with Gwen?"

"Of course not. There are plenty of bedrooms here—I'm sure you will find one that is of sufficient distance from hers." This time she tended to her teacup rather than make another attempt at disapprobation, with Walt knowing she didn't want to risk a smile.

"Yes," he said. "It'll be a wonder if we even bump into one another."

"So to speak," she replied.

"Miss June!" he said as she did smile. "Why, I never!"

She busied herself about the kitchen while he flipped through the magazines, noting the paper-clipped articles about

Bourbonne-les-Bains and *Provence*. Along with the magazines was an old encyclopedia, volume O-P, a bookmark separating "paresis" from "Paris." It had taken awhile, but now he understood.

"This is about Dwight," he said.

"Of course it is," she said, surprising him with frank admission. "There were many things we were going to see, us two. Places he wanted to share."

"But you've never gone before."

She put down her dishtowel.

"Yes, Walter, that is true. I've not gone before. But seeing as we are about to drop this subject, might I suggest that we conclude our chat by agreeing that people can, in fact, change their stripes?"

Given the recent events in his own life, he had to suppose that this might be true.

* * *

"I used to date the mud-flap girl," Jimmy said.

"The what?"

"The mud-flap girl. The broad they used to model for the mud flaps. You see her on all the trucks. Chrome? Stacked?"

"I didn't know she was real," Edward said.

"Believe me, there was nothing fake about that girl."

Walt winked at Edward. The three of them were at Hardwick raking up hay, which was all that remained of the circus.

"She used to sit there kind of sideways for me, just like how they made her famous. What do you call that?"

"Bullshit?" Walt ventured.

"No, when you just see someone from the side?"

"Her silhouette?" Edward guessed.

"Yeah, that's what it was. The silhouette. Anyway, we had

a beautiful thing, me and her. At least until those damned mud flaps came out."

"What happened?" Edward asked, fairly certain that this was, as Walt suggested, bullshit, but curious either way.

"She got so famous, she couldn't even leave the house no more. It was ridiculous. All 'cause of her shape."

Edward grinned.

"That girl had the guns of Navarone," Jimmy concluded.

"You're something else, you know that, Jimmy?" Walt said.

"Volare … "

In the library, Gwen waited while Miss June reviewed the manuscript. Outside, the men were laughing and taunting each other with rakes and donkey manure. She perused the old books, wondering how many of them Miss June had read. All of them, she decided, if only out of determination. The library, with its oak shelves and leather reading chairs, was largely unchanged from when Clarence Creighton had walked its floors, selecting weighty volumes before repairing to his study.

"You don't have to do this," Gwen interrupted.

"Of course, I do," Miss June returned. "While I have no doubt about your competence, I am certainly going to assess your work and will likely make comments before it goes to print."

"That's not what I meant. You don't need to leave Hardwick to Reggie. It doesn't have to be destroyed."

She didn't look up from the page. "I've spent my lifetime in certainty, young lady. To suggest that I've not fully considered the fate of my home would be to not grant me my due."

"I don't doubt you've considered it. I just think you're wrong."

"Do tell."

"You are leaving your house to a man who cares nothing

about it or its history. You're married for some reason to an ancient—and dare I say asinine—family protocol."

"So, you know my innermost secrets."

"This one I do. Yes."

"Are you through?"

"I don't know." Gwen's words had come in a torrent and she wasn't sure where she stood.

"Well, let's mutually decide that you are, so that I may respond. First, while I do appreciate your concern, I do not appreciate the assumption that I do not act out of will. I can assure you that my choices are never made lightly, and they certainly are not born from blind obedience. Every decision I make is my own. The fate of Hardwick has been decided by me, after careful consideration, and of my own volition."

With that, she shut the manuscript.

"Your writings are fine. Please continue with the draft as you see fit."

Crossing the room, she stopped at the door.

"You'll do well not to question my determination again."

* * *

The Bull's-Eye phone rang as Walt and Gwen were in the midst of a Saturday afternoon game of Gin. She was cleaning his clock as usual.

"Hey card shark, it's for you," Gene called.

"Me?" Gwen asked.

"No, him."

"Who is it?" Walt asked.

"The asshole."

Walt hefted the old Bakelite handset. On the TV behind Gene, the Pirates were losing again.

"Walt," Reggie said, sounding strange. "It's Miss June."

* * *

They left the DORF in a physicians-only spot. 'Information' sent them to the cardiac floor, where Reggie stood in the waiting area, his fading shiner pale green in the hospital light.

"They called me," Reggie said. "I guess I'm listed as next of kin."

"What do you know?" Walt asked.

"Nothing. Just that she collapsed in the garden. The mailman found her. I haven't seen the doctor yet, and the nurses don't know anything."

Gwen squeezed Walt's hand as Dr. Hudson came out of the cardiac unit and made his way to them.

"Walter," he acknowledged.

"How is she?"

"Miss June had a myocardial infarction—a heart attack. From what we can see, she's suffered silent heart attacks before. Those damaged the muscle, setting her up for this. It's a wonder she hadn't complained. Regardless, her heartbeat is irregular, but I've stabilized things with medication. She doesn't remember falling, but she's alert and seems to understand the diagnosis."

"Heart problems?" Walt wanted to know. "This hasn't shown up in the past?"

"It doesn't always. In the years that I've known her, she's been in fine condition—her pulse steady, her lungs clear. She's never allowed a significant examination. She makes a yearly appointment, arrives right on time, and then won't let me touch her beyond checking her vitals and looking into her eyes. Heck, she interviews *me*—asks about my family, where my siblings went to college, and so forth. She's even told me I didn't look so healthy. But she is old, so we shouldn't see this as a total surprise."

Walt wasn't ready to buy that.

"Is there surgery?" Gwen asked.

"It's difficult at her age. A pacemaker could prove to be an option, but further tests are needed. I mentioned this to her, but she refused it out of hand."

"Refused it?"

"Actually, she said I should go back to medical school. But, frankly, she's probably right to refuse. Given her age and the degree of damage, a pacemaker may not be the best option."

"What are her odds?" Reggie wanted to know.

"She's not a race horse. But, in short, they're not good. I'm sorry."

"Can we see her?" Walt asked.

"Soon. The nurses are tending to a few things. They'll call you in when she's settled."

The alcohol and floor wax smell of the hospital was making Gwen sick, and she excused herself to the waiting area around the corner. A box of thin hospital tissues sat on the table in front of her, a sad offering to families in grief. Walt and Reggie leaned against the wall. They attempted small talk but it went nowhere and so they let it drop. Finally, the door swung open.

"Creighton?" the nurse asked.

"That's us."

"Are you family?"

Reggie put his hand on Walt's shoulder and gave it a genuine squeeze.

"He is."

The curtained alcove was mercifully dark, the glow from the machines the only light. She looked tiny and cold.

"Hey, old girl," Walt said.

"Walter." Her voice, while not a whisper, was not strong.

He sat in the lone chair and covered her hand with his,

disregarding her aversion to touch.

"You gave us quite a scare."

"I've disturbed Donald's garden, I'm afraid."

"I've done worse."

"I feel silly, causing all of this fuss." She gestured at the room around her. "You'd think I was the president."

"Thank goodness you're not—the country would learn they're behind on their chores."

"I'm sure that they are."

She smiled and closed her eyes. They were quiet for a moment.

"You know I'll take care of you, right?"

"Don't get soft on me now, Walter."

"I don't want you to worry."

"I seldom do. I've taken care of all that matters."

The machines whirred and blinked and brought no comfort to Walt, offering only evidence of her frailty.

"Knock-knock," Doctor Hudson said as he entered and drew the curtain behind him.

"Okay, Miss June," he said. "You'll be in this room tonight, and tomorrow we should be able to move you to a regular room down the hall, still on the cardiac floor. My guess is that you'll be here for a week or so total."

"A private room," Walt clarified.

"All of the cardiac rooms are private," the doctor said. "If the week goes well, which I think it should, I'll recommend that you be transferred to a skilled nursing facility for further care. There's one in particular I think you would like."

"I will do no such thing," Miss June said, sitting up with surprising strength, as if to get out of bed.

"Whoa, there," the doctor said. "You can't move like that."

"I'll move myself right out of this hospital if I so choose. But I will not, under any circumstances, go to a nursing home."

"We can discuss it more next week. For now, let's just rest and get over the excitement of the day."

Walt cringed. Obviously, Hudson didn't know his patient as well as he thought he did.

"You, sir, can rest all you like," she said. "I, on the other hand, will use these next few days—three at the most—to regain my bearings and restore my resources, and will then return to my home and continue on as always."

The lights and jagged line graphs on the monitoring machines jumped in response to her dander.

"Return home? I'm sorry, but as your doctor, I must firmly say no. You're not ready to go home."

"Mind your manners, William. If your father were alive, he would swat your behind and tell you to heed my wishes."

"You knew my father?"

"Of course, I did. Do you think you were selected as my doctor by chance? Now go run your tests and whatnot. You have three days to do so. After that, I will return to Hardwick. Feel free to stop by for tea. Now, good day."

Three days later, a private ambulance pulled into the drive, delivering her home.

Chapter 25

AT NIGHT, HE SAT IN A CHAIR outside of her room. Her bedside seemed to tempt the end, so instead, he sat in the hall. Home care nurses visited on schedule, monitoring the I.V. and administering medicine. They showed Walt and Gwen how to record her vital signs, how to change her position to prevent bed sores. Walt declared that it be done only when she was asleep, as she would be mortified at the indignity.

Gwen read to Miss June, awake or not, often portions of her manuscript, but also from the *Pittsburgh Social Register* from the 1940s, reciting aloud the gossipy reports that included the family names she knew were important to her, sticking to stories of cotillions and returns from travel, avoiding wedding announcements and rumors of romance. Donald was kept occupied with errands. Reggie steered respectfully clear, for which Walt was grateful.

Walt's hope that she would rebound once she was back in the confines of her castle was met with the reality of her illness. She slept much of the time, and did not improve as the days went by. While moving home hadn't necessarily made her worse, it wasn't making her better either. Nor, apparently, was Miss June going to will herself well. Gumption could only take one so far.

"How long?" he asked Dr. Hudson.

"It's hard to tell. Months, weeks. She could rebound a little, decide that she's going to last a while longer, but you should be prepared."

He swept the porch for her, as she had always done on Wednesdays.

On her bureau were photographs of her parents framed in pewter. Walt studied her mother's face, searching for resemblance, finding little. In another, young Thomas leaned against a Stutz Bearcat. Walt took the chair beside the bed, daubed her lips with cool water. He unfolded a paper from his shirt pocket—her own, personal list of things to be done. He had found it on her writing desk, drafted, he supposed, the morning of her collapse.

"I took care of this for you," he told her sleeping figure. "I had to, with you being so unreliable and all."

She became blurry, and he fought it.

"'Stop blubbering,' you would say." He exhaled and continued. "Anyway, I took care of everything I could figure out. I mailed the letters on the table, and picked up the items from the market. I'm not sure what you meant by 'Zippers,' so I had to skip that. I crossed everything off, just like you always do." A bus rumbled down Fifth. "We're getting low on cookies. You're supposed to keep up with these things."

Her breathing was barely visible.

"I noticed the gutters need cleaning. I'll get to them this

week. The screen door out back is sticking again, too. Humidity, I guess. Summer came fast this year."

He put the list on the night stand.

"I need you to get better, you know. Like you say, I'm not good without direction."

He smoothed her covers, adjusted the fold.

"But I'm trying, Miss June. I really am trying."

* * *

The sound of the mower rattled the kitchen windows. Stepping out onto the side porch, he saw it was Jimmy, wrestling with the old machine in his chinos and crisp shirt, whistling as he worked. Jimmy pretended not to see Walt approach, and then turned quickly as if to mow him down, laughing as his big friend jumped. He let the motor buck and die.

"So, you're a landscaper now?"

"I figured I'd cheer the old lady up. All broads like it when you cut their grass."

"It's a nice gesture, but I don't think she knows you're here. She sleeps all the time now."

"That lady? Believe me, she knows."

He's probably right, Walt thought. He went to get a rake.

* * *

Baby Chiclet sat on the butcher block in her bouncy seat. Gwen, hoping to lighten the mood, had invited Sam and Arthur over for an evening of pizza and Scrabble in Miss June's kitchen. She had opened the windows to clear the heaviness of inevitability, and indeed, there was a welcome lightness to the incoming air.

"Snatch her up," Sam whispered in Walt's ear, gesturing

toward Gwen who was making a salad. He stepped on her foot in return.

The two couples ate and drank and played in an unspoken effort to give Walt a break from his worry.

"Arthur," Sam said. "Are you going to make a word before the baby is in pre-school?"

"Almost there …" he promised. "Can't rush these things …"

Gwen's foot rubbed Walt's leg under the table.

"There!" Arthur said. "B-U-C-C-A-L. Ha! *Buccal.* Let's see, 3, 4, 6, 1, plus 1, is 15, plus a double letter score on the second 'C' makes 18. *Buccal.* Eighteen points, please."

The others looked at the board and then at each other before bursting out laughing.

"What the fuck does *buccal* mean?" Sam asked.

"Buccal!" Art said, incredulous. "As in tooth surface? Hello …"

"This isn't a dental game, Arthur," Sam said. "You already played *tartar* and *frenum.*" She hit him over the head with the lid from the box.

"My frenum feels buccal," Walt noted.

"Well, these are the words I know," Art complained. To Sam, he said, "I suppose it was better when you added *shit* to *dog*?"

"Don't listen to your parents, Lucy," Gwen said. "They really do love each other."

As if to prove it, Sam gave Arthur a kiss.

The visiting nurse interrupted from the backstairs. "She's not doing well. I've called Doctor Hudson—he's on his way."

She struggled to breathe, turning her head back and forth as if to avert an onslaught.

Gwen touched a washcloth to her face.

"Walter," Miss June croaked.

"I'm here. We all are."

Walt had never heard a death rattle before, had not had occasion to know they really existed, but knew he was hearing one now.

"Shhh," he said. "It's all right."

She writhed in pain. He'd never seen her out of control before.

Dr. Hudson arrived, and after listening to her lungs, motioned for them to follow him out to the hall.

"This is it. She doesn't have long."

"What should we do?" Sam asked.

"Say your goodbyes."

Walt couldn't let this happen, not yet. "Isn't there anything else, another drug or something? Because, listen, if there's any way that we could …"

He thought he had made peace with knowing she would soon be gone, had even privately wished her a quick departure so she wouldn't suffer. But now he found himself grasping for ways to somehow change the circumstances, to will them to be different. To get the doctor to say that it wasn't really time, that more could be done. He didn't want her back to discuss regrets, or appreciation. He didn't want to discuss their past or assign meaning to it. He simply wanted to bicker with her some more. To listen to her gripe about his laziness, to hear about how the floor boards in the back hall still squeak, about how they'd better enjoy the side porch now, because if he doesn't get a coat of paint on it by next spring, it'll rot away into nothing. He wanted her to make him more tea. He wanted his other half.

"All I'm saying, Doc, is that if …"

"Walter," Arthur interrupted. "It's time." He gave his friend a hug. "It's time."

"Let's go in," Sam said to Gwen and Art, leaving Walt and

Dr. Hudson alone in the hall.

"How does this work?" Walt asked. "What about the pain?"

"I'll connect a morphine pump to make her as comfortable as I can."

"I want her to be comfortable. God knows she's stoic, but there's no need for this to drag out."

"You press a button to administer a dose. It'll help. I know she's in pain, but legally, I can only authorize one dose every twenty minutes. It's the best I can do. Any more would hasten things."

He looked at Walt, hard.

"I'll trust you to decide when each twenty minutes is up."

Donald had arrived and was at her side. She turned his way as he held her hand. She smiled weakly as he spoke to her but was too worn to reply and, Walt would later swear, attempted a throat-slashing gesture with her finger as Donald went on too long. She faded out again as he clutched his handkerchief and said goodbye, and Gwen ushered him out, comforting him as he sobbed. She came back in and stood next to Walt, leaning close.

"Thank goodness for him she can't talk," Walt said. "She would have lectured him on composure."

"Only to hide that she was touched."

"I don't know. After all these years, I still don't know."

* * *

Ten minutes passed, and he pressed the button. The morphine eased her fitfulness, and as she settled, she spoke the occasional fragment, though nothing made sense. Her eyes opened, but it wasn't clear whether she saw them at her side.

"Should I leave you two alone?" Gwen asked.

"I think so. Yes."

"I'll be outside if you need me."

"Thank you." He gave her a hug, buried his face in her hair. "For everything."

"I'll be in your chair."

* * *

And so they were alone.

The rattle returned.

He pressed the button.

He saw her hairbrush on the night stand, remembered the moment he'd witnessed the previous fall—her solitary figure seated at her dressing table, brushing her hair and humming to herself.

"Dwight," she managed.

"Yes, Dwight. You loved him."

She tried to speak, couldn't.

"It's all right. Shh."

She became agitated, struggled to speak.

He pressed the button.

"Day."

"Shh, just rest."

"Galaxy."

"Oh, of course. I can tell it." And so he did, hushed and dreamlike. "He was strong and noble. A magnificent swimmer, you always told me. Like no other."

He pressed the button.

"And on the day he died, the galaxy lost a star."

She settled. He held her hand. He wondered if she was holding his in return. She opened her eyes and found him.

"Walter…" she managed and then began to fail.

"Shh," he said as she went quiet. "It's okay. I know."

He sat with her for some time after she became still, moved her hands onto her chest like he knew she would have wanted. Straightened her pillow, arranged her covers. He cradled her head forward and released her hair from its bun, helped it fall across her shoulders. The brush was heavy in his hand, its bristles soft against his thick palm. Gently, and with all of his heart, he brushed her hair, tracing careful lines in smooth and steady strokes.

Epilogue

"I DON'T BELIEVE THIS TASK should take you so long," she called up the ladder from the yard below.

"Maybe you should try it sometime. I'm sure it's quite simple from down there."

"Honestly, they're only shutters. And it's not like you haven't done this before."

"It's true, I've been made to do this many times, although why I continue to comply is beyond me."

"It would seem that many things are beyond you. These shutters are just one example."

* * *

The reading of the will, performed in the office of her banker—actually, an attorney, as Walt had long assumed—included the reading of a handwritten letter from the grand dame herself. Present, at her request, were Reggie, Donald, Gwen, Sam, and Walt. The attorney read aloud.

To those I have left behind:

Because you are hearing these words, you know I have departed your world. A lifelong atheist, I know with certainty that this is the end. However, on the small chance that I am incorrect in this matter, you should assume that I will be watching you forever. Act accordingly.

I am not an overly affectionate woman. That said, I hope my demeanor has not been misinterpreted as a lack of concern for any of you. I hold you dear, in various and unique ways, and I am pleased to have spent my life in your company. The specific details of what follows have been carefully recorded in advance of my passing. Goodness knows I am not one to leave a mess.

I've long made it clear that adherence to familial tradition and propriety are the foundation of my being. Reginald, as the last remaining Creighton, my house is meant to belong to you. However, a true Creighton, such as myself, while respectful of their predecessors, is also strong in opinion and apt to consider all factors in matters of significance. My grandfather's intent was good, and I respect the spirit in which it was put forth. But a century has passed since his declaration was made. He could not have imagined the parties now involved. This fact charges me with the task of reinterpreting family protocol, distilling the meaning of his wishes to a finer point, one that assures that Hardwick will remain in the possession of one within whom its charms have become ingrained. Therefore, with no further explanation, Hardwick will belong to Walter Farnham. Walter, I believe you understand.

Now, Reginald, I understand that this development is a thwart to your plans. Sadly, you possess a remarkable

*entrepreneurial bent, but lack accompanying civic respon-
sibility. To borrow parlance from Walter, you behave like
a "shit." Still, because you are my kin, you will inherit a
sizable parcel of land, one that none of you knows I hold.
To you, I leave the original site of Creighton Industries,
forty-eight acres of urban riverfront property. The industrial buildings that remain will never again come to life,
will never again put food on the table of an earnest worker.
I take no exception if you wish to tear the buildings down
and develop what you will. That said, various governing
bodies may have a say in the matter, as it seems that
the industrial practices of the times gave no consideration
to the environmental concerns of today. If I understand
correctly, the soil is poisoned. The cost to make it suitable
for inhabitation is greater than the land's worth. I believe
the phrase 'White Elephant' might appropriately be used.
While I confess to appreciating the poetic justice inherent
in this situation, I do wish you well in the endeavor.*

*Donald. To you I leave certain books from my library. You
know the volumes; I need not list them here. Also, please
take any plants from the garden that you desire; they are
your children. Should you want other keepsakes, please
discuss them with Walter—I can't imagine him taking
exception. Now, listen carefully: Your companionship has
been cherished. But this chapter has closed. Visit me in the
cemetery if you like, but you must move on. As one last
favor to me, please pursue a rich life, one that might even
include an appropriate paramour if you so desire, one who
can share your affection without reservation. You are a fine
man, and deserve no less.*

*Samantha, to you I leave my respect and admiration.
Although we did not always express great camaraderie,*

I believe we shared many of the same concerns and exasperations in managing our uncommon friend. You and I were too similar to be close. If not for our personalities' tendency to collide, we might have found ourselves the best of friends. Given our combined strength, however, Walter is probably relieved that we didn't. Again, my admiration.

Gwenneth, I am grateful for the passion with which you have embraced your role as my family's chronicler. To you, I leave permission to write our history as you see fit, not merely as I might wish for it to read. I can only rely on my confidence that when all is recorded, our name will remain in good stead. If not, then so it is that we deserve. You have treated me sweetly in these last months, more so than I usually allow. You have a certain way about you, and it appears I am not the only one who knows it. If I can be so forward as to assume you will be spending more time with a certain person, please know that I am most pleased at the prospect, as I could not find you more dear. It's as if I had arranged this myself …

And finally, Walter. Our years together render any attempt to sum things up here pointless. We've always been clear with one another, so you know where we stand. Please keep me with you as you move forward through life. Retain your focus. When you falter, hear my voice. Should that not suffice, feel my foot on your behind. For decades I have told you that there is nothing more tragic than not realizing one's potential. Now, though, I will tell you something different: That it is far worse to be misunderstood. I understood you, Walter. Moreover, you understood me. That is something I had felt only once before. Thank you.

* * *

"Honestly, they're only shutters," she said. "And it's not like you haven't done this before."

"It's true, I've been made to do this many times before, although why I continue to comply is beyond me."

"It would seem that many things are beyond you. These shutters are just one example."

"And I thought my last customer was tough."

He came down from the ladder and took Gwen into his arms.

"You think you get to take a break?" she teased.

"Did I mention that this is pointless?"

"Repeatedly."

"I can't believe you keep making me do it."

"It's tradition."

"The ladder makes my feet hurt."

"Wherever she is, she's smiling. She knows you're taking care of things."

"If you're so hellbent on making her happy, why don't you climb up there and hang a few?"

"You'd send a pregnant woman up a ladder?"

"You're damn right I would."

He pressed his belly against hers, which, while also round, was much firmer in comparison.

* * *

Although the collective wisdom at Gene's usually runs thin, on occasion the barflies are right: Miss June had been loaded. The amount of money she left Walter was staggering, although it wasn't buried inside Hardwick's walls—her banker had been minding it all along. The regular meetings the two held had been to manage the family portfolio, and also to handle—and keep private—her considerable philanthropic efforts. The discovery of her wealth left Walt to look back carefully through his life with her, searching for clues that the Creighton fortune had been there all along. More accurately, he looked for specific things she might have said to indicate that it *wasn't* there. Of course, he found none. If Miss June were alive to field his questions, she could have correctly answered that she had never stated that she had little money, and would have pointed out to Walter that he had simply never asked, which was a very good thing, as to ask such a question would be quite rude. Her diversionary tactics aside, however, certainly she had implied that money was scarce. The question was why. The obvious answer was simple adherence to frugality, that she saw no reason why money that had been around for so long needed to be spent, and if it didn't need to be spent, then there was no reason to discuss it. But concealing her fortune didn't make sense in that it suggested failure on the part of the Creightons, that, once mighty, they had fallen. Other great families had withstood shifting economic tides, yet theirs, it would appear, had not. The dissonance that would result from the idea of Creighton failure being public knowledge would outweigh any value that such a front could offer. What could be worth the humiliation?

In memory, he could smell the grass mixed with gasoline and exhaust, feel the sweat on his young chest as he struggled to push the mower. He felt the sting in his hands as he scraped the side porch floor boards while the boys from school spent their Saturday afternoons roaming the streets of Squirrel Hill, sneaking into a matinee at the Guild, looking for minor trouble. She had concealed her wealth solely for him. Gwen was right — she'd raised him the way she knew how. Money would have complicated things, made it harder to teach him what she thought he needed to know. She made his effort necessary. And with time, the insular world she'd created kept him closer still, which allowed her to do what she felt was necessary — to continue to manipulate his life as a man, especially when he'd lost another strong woman through divorce, and his nature could have let him falter. The gall she had—the certainty that she knew best. The lack of faith in him to succeed on his own.

He pondered their situation further, the pattern they had settled into in the later years. Her premise of needing to keep a close eye on him had shifted into her dependence on him, a slow swing of a heavy pendulum she would never acknowledge existed. And yet, despite her keeping him close for her own needs, she had put forth her greatest talents of deception for his benefit, manipulating him and the other players in his life in ways no one else would dare, using her last year to try to fix him once and for all. And although the final results may not have been precisely what she would have chosen, in principle, she may well have succeeded. His life had consistency now.

Much of this musing about Miss June took place at Gene's. This was one aspect of his new-found wealth that was most certainly not in her plans. Once Mrs. Greb found her place in Lawrenceville beside her husband, Walt bought the bar, paying Gene more than he had ever dreamed about during his decades of wiping down the tired Formica. Walt received a postcard from Gene months later, a generic beach shot with a caption that read simply "Florida." The bar was pretty much the same. The sign outside would always read "The Bull's-Eye," although the neon had been fixed, its animated arrow once again having life. Everyone still called it "Gene's," which was how Walt had answered the phone when Gene himself had last called. Walt's concern that his old friend might not adjust to things down there was relieved during the course of the call, which Gene had to cut short, as his new fishing buddies were outside "honking the horn like their ass was on fire." One noticeable change to the 'Eye, beyond the rejuvenated neon, was an improvement in the food, thanks to the new cook who worked the weekday lunch shift, simmering soup and cutting fresh ingredients for the healthy items that now shared the menu with the usual crap, which Walt insisted on keeping. Sam enjoyed the work, enjoyed getting out of the house now that her daughter was in preschool. It helped keep her sane, following four years at home with only Chiclet and Jimmy to talk to, the latter having taken it upon himself to move into Walt's old place, the same day he helped Walt move out. Arthur remained unclear as to how that had happened. Sam's role as cook armed her with sharp implements with which to fend off Jimmy's advances, and also afforded Walt ample opportunity to drive her crazy, but such had always been the spice in their life. She made it a point to remind Walt that she could now keep a closer eye on him, but in truth, since marrying Gwen, he was happier than she could have hoped, and he finally no longer needed much tending. Her secret worry that Gwen might not be able to withstand his oddities were allayed during a visit to Hardwick, when Sam saw her slide the oily piece of cardboard under the DORF after a trip to the grocery store.

Gwen's decision to leave Cambridge for good had been surprisingly easy. Failure had always been difficult for her to stomach, and she expected to feel that abandoning the position she'd worked so hard to attain was akin to quitting. In the end, though, she simply left. She liked Pittsburgh. It had the man she loved. The Creighton history took her three more years to complete, as once the pressure from Miss June to work quickly was gone, she was able to be more thorough, giving the book an entirety it could not have had otherwise. The result was beautiful—hand-bound at great expense. Gwen balked on behalf of Miss June, but Walt would be damned if he didn't get to spoil his old counterpart just once. He and Gwen flew to Camberwell in London to meet with a bookbinder to decide how the volume would be put together. Watching the man work in his small shop—pressing paper with his slim bonefolder, sewing together signatures in the traditional style—Walt wondered if he had missed his own true calling. As a result of their trip, exquisite production volumes would grace the shelves of university libraries, historical societies, and other concerned organizations, and a limited number of handmade full calf-leather volumes would be given to a select few, the chief of whom was Donald, whose copy featured a gold-lettered inscription from Gwen. As for the content, Miss June, if she truly wanted accuracy, would have been pleased, although Gwen's suffering over how to handle her own conjecture about the woman's personal life caused her a fair amount of worry. "Just be honest. Write the hell out of the thing," Walt had advised. "She wanted it that way, don't you see? If not, she wouldn't have died before you were done—believe me. She's allowing you to tell the truth." He's right, she'd decided. And it wasn't as if Miss June's life was scandalous. On the contrary. But there was sadness and lack of fulfillment to be implied, and Gwen did so with simplicity and grace. Walt approved of the result and, given his place in the picture, his was the final blessing she'd needed. The book done, she took a position at the university, teaching in the same building in which she'd first met Walt. Given tenure upon hire, she was politely grateful, but relatively indifferent about the matter—Walt's influence, no doubt.

"No, honey, no," Jimmy cried. "You don't put that much water in the sauce. Wait, is that sugar?! What the hell are you doing over there?" He made as if to come around the bar.

"Keep your hands away, DeLuca, or I'll cut your goddamned thumbs off."

Walt looked up from the morning paper, content with business as usual.

* * *

The Imperial rolled smoothly through the gates of Home-wood Cemetery, Walt at the wheel, Gwen by his side. He drove the winding paths, past the pond, beyond the Chinese section, through the shadow of the smooth stone pyramid. The ceme-tery was home to Pittsburgh dignitaries—senators, judges, jazz pioneers, and hard, gray men who had given rise to the steel industry. Walt cut the ignition and the car went silent. Summer wafted through the open windows. It had been five years.

"It still seems surreal," he said.

"I know it does, honey. It's supposed to."

He made his way to the plot while Gwen stayed behind. The cemetery was like Pittsburgh itself, alternating hills and valleys, and the Creightons were buried at the crest of their own mound. It took effort to make the ascent, and Miss June would have admonished him for being out of shape. Six headstones were arranged before a granite mausoleum—a substantial structure with heavy bronze doors and stained glass win-dows. Clarence Creighton had wanted an impressive building marking his tomb, although it was to be purely ornamental, as he believed that people should be buried in the earth, not kept in marble drawers. Miss June's stone was lighter in color than those of her family, but with time that would change. The grass was well cared for, and the flowers that Donald had transplanted from Hardwick were in full bloom. In the corner of the plot was a granite bench. He sat down.

"Hey, old girl."

From the lofty setting, he took in the view—mostly trees and distant rooftops, but also, far to the east, a wooded valley and the George Westinghouse Bridge. She would have liked that. He sat for some time. Despite the ancestral presence that had informed the air at Hardwick, he'd always thought it was just the two of them. She, the grand dame, and he, her clumsy, poetic complement. Now he wondered if she was finally among those with whom she naturally belonged. He thought about what must have been her utter bewilderment over how to raise a half-grown boy. For the first time, he understood the magnitude of her decision to do so. He spoke aloud to her grave.

"We were something, weren't we?"

By the time he reached the foot of the hill, his right hamstring was sore from the climb. He really was out of shape. That, or getting old. Gwen waited with a stolen flower as he approached. Together, they headed back to the Imperial.

"Well," he said. "That would be that."

ACKNOWLEDGMENTS

My warmest thanks to:

My wife, Kate, and our children, Lily, Evan, and Sydney, for their love and support, and for tolerating my strange behavior during the writing of this book. Many thanks also to Kate for her book design—I can't picture it any other way.

Stewart O'Nan, for his belief in this tale, and for writing so many great books through the years.

Liz Atkins, Penny Berlin, Rob Maiolo, Lisa Dennis, John Martine, Carole Honeychurch, Nikole Lopretto, Leah Patgorski, and Cy Williams, for support, commiseration, and feedback. You know who did what.

Sandi Lifson, for warmth, generosity, and a long-standing spot on her couch. I'll be back.

Earl Cohen, my ninth-grade English teacher who taught like hell because he cared.

Vincent DiLucente and Ann Whitmire, for reminding me of what might have been, and that leaps of faith lead to what might be.

Jeffrey Condran and Robert Peluso, true gentlemen and publishers extraordinaire, for ushering this story into the world. It could not have been in steadier hands.

Geoff Radkoff, for the word "DORF," and so much more.

Carol Pickerine, for enduring faith, proofreading prowess, and putting salt on a bird's tail.

And finally, to Vivienne Radkoff, the best storyteller I know, she, who never fails to believe.